TRE

Carla Vermaat

TREGUNNA

Carla Vermaat

Published in Great Britain in 2015 by
Carmichael Publishers, Cornwall

A CIP catalogue record for this book
is available from the British Library

ISBN 978-0-9933339-0-3

Typeset in Meridien by Varwig Design
Cover Image © Carla Vermaat – Design by Varwig Design

Printed and bound in Great Britain by TJ International, Cornwall

Carmichael Publishers
www.carmichael-publishers.co.uk

For Dave – who would have been proud

PROLOGUE

A narrow lane leads down to Hawker's Cove, a small coastal settlement on the estuary mouth of the river. Halfway, the farmhouse stands alone on the hillside, its old weathered walls dark and hostile in the gathering dusk of a gloomy afternoon. A buzzard stills above the gorse, yellow flowers bright against the darkening sky. Rooted in a pile of granite rocks is a single hawthorn tree, its branches bare, bent and shaped by westerly winds.

The temperature has fallen to just above freezing and a sharp wind blows cold from the northeast, sending in dark clouds that have gathered above the ocean. In the distance, the lighthouse at Trevose Head flashes its warning lights at regular intervals.

There is a chill in the air, a cold and disturbing quietness. Inside the farmhouse, the kitchen has turned into an obscene pantomime, dialogues silenced forever.

When it happens, the man is sitting at the table, his fat torso squeezed into a grubby, once white vest, lips curled in a cruel twist whilst moaning to the woman, as usual, about nothing in particular. She stands at the sink, ignoring him, her thoughts miles away, hands quietly dumping plates in soapy water, head hanging low between her shoulders, defeated by the latest outburst of a voice she once loved. Every so often she looks out of the window as though seeking comfort from the view towards the fishing village of Padstow.

The first blow of the axe hits him by surprise. Blood

splashes over the table as the sharp blade digs deep into his left arm. Eyes wide open in disbelief he tries to cry out but no sound comes. The second hit is aimed at his face, but it sinks into the thick flesh of his thigh, narrowly missing his hipbone. With a sudden jolt of panic he tries to stand up, but his attempt to lift his big pudding of a body comes too late. As he gives two small coughs, he falls awkwardly aside, stretching out his right arm to avoid a third blow. It all happens so fast and so silently. Almost immediately the nerve ends stop communicating with his brain. He doesn't feel the pain, he doesn't even feel the cold numbness creep into his soul. As his dying eyes stare into oblivion, he fails to understand what might have caused the anger of the attack.

Floorboards creak and muffled music drifts from upstairs. A sound, a movement behind her, pulls the woman out of her secretive thoughts. She wipes her hands on her apron and a faint smile lifts the tiredness from her face. As she turns, her expression puzzled for the briefest of moments, she freezes with horror. And with the realisation of what is about to happen, she feels the pang of immense regret. In the instant before the axe swings for the third time and hits her in the waist, she lets out a scream like the collective howl of a pack of wolves. Landing sideways on a chair, another blow cuts through her belly, opening her intestines like the unexpected eruption of a sleeping volcano. Unlike the man's, her death is slow and painful.

The stillness is disturbed by footsteps, a voice humming with hope and expectation, growing louder as the girl descends the narrow staircase. As she becomes aware of the unusual quietness, a hesitation enters her movements, and her small voice dies with the knowledge that something is amiss.

A variety of smells meet her just before she enters the kitchen: stewed beef and onions, the sweet aroma of home cooking. Or perhaps it is something else, something she can't fathom.

She lets out a horrified shriek as her eyes rest on the

man's bloodied body lying lifeless on the floor. His arm is still reaching out as though in hope that he can turn the tide. His eyes, hollow in their emptiness, are staring at her, his soul already gone.

The girl carefully steps aside, away from the curved puddle of drying blood. As the silence of death screams through her head, she kneels down beside the woman's body, whispering her plea for the last time, 'Mummy?'

PART ONE

MAY,

AND EARLIER, APRIL

1

MAY

They say you'll always remember your first dead body. For me it's true. Every so often, even now, the slow motion images of his death on that dark and rainy night pop up in my head.

In his mid-twenties, tall and lean, his strawberry blond hair highlighted by the headlights of passing cars, he was lying on the bonnet of a taxi, his head thrown backwards and his arms and legs spread out as though he was about to embrace the world. Blue jeans, a dazzling white shirt unbuttoned at the top splattered with blood, black shoes polished to a perfect shine, a thick silver chain around his neck, he looked as if he was on his way to a blind date. He would never meet her.

His eyelids fluttered and an odd smile crossed his face. Words were formed in the pockets of his brain, but were left unspoken as reality dawned on him that he might never be able to get up and walk away.

One second before, he was full of life and looking to the future, crossing the street with optimism and cheer in his limbs, a happy smile on his face. He would have made it, if it were not for the dull blue van whose driver was chatting and laughing on a mobile phone. Brakes screeched. The side mirror crashed into his head, and ripped off his ear. In an effort to regain his balance, his body teetered and he put out his arms to balance himself. Another car. More squeals of brakes, tyres desperately trying to find grip on the wet tarmac. There was no escape for him. His body was scooped up and he landed on the bonnet of the taxi, head first, almost crashing through the windscreen. The taxi driver had been sat facing backwards, negotiating a fee with his passenger. He was lucky enough not to see it coming. His passenger had seen it all though.

In her early fifties, with swollen ankles and grey roots shining through dyed blonde hair, she was now sat on the edge of the pavement with her head between her knees, traces of vomit on her skirt. Although she must have emptied her stomach in the gutter, she was still suffering from contractions that periodically made her gasp for air. The horror was etched on her face as she kept on staring at the young man.

His right ear was ripped off, so was half the side of his face. His lower jaw was badly smashed up. What was left of his teeth glistered in a mixture of blood and saliva that emerged from one corner of his mouth. His blood mixed with the soft rain and ran down the bonnet beneath him, forming pink streams, dripping in a puddle on the tarmac. His heart was still trying to keep him alive. But it was a losing battle. It was only a matter of time before he was to become the first dead body in my career.

For an instant, he stared straight into my face, as though about to tell me his last thoughts, his fears for the unknown, the unexpected twist in his life. One of his legs shuddered, the expression in his eyes already fading.

There was nothing we could do. I was pulled into an unexpected companionship with the taxi driver as we stood and watched and waited, silenced and stunned. Someone tapped the taxi driver's poor passenger on her shoulder, murmuring words of comfort. Passing traffic had begun to slow, white faces stared from behind weather-beaten windows. A murder of crows quickly gathered on the pavement; excitement in their expressions as they feasted their eyes on the widening pool of blood.

A distant siren grew louder. The dripping of blood eased

as the ambulance appeared. Blue lights flashed and bounced off the walls of surrounding buildings. Two men in green uniforms hurried towards us, focusing on the body, carrying equipment that they wouldn't need.

There is still the sound of liquid dripping. Is it blood? A sudden wave of panic takes my breath away. I can't remember where I am. Or who I am. I can't feel my legs. My hands fumble with the unfamiliar cotton across my chest. My mouth has gone dry and my tongue and throat feel like sandpaper.

I'm floating on a turbulent sea of mixed memories and a dawning presence. The ambulance siren has finally been silenced. Another shard of memory - I can see the trained crew in green attending to the young man, I can hear his blood dripping in a puddle and for a brief moment I feel relief because maybe somehow they will be able to bring him back to life.

'Mr Tregunna? Can you hear me?' Footsteps stop beside me. My body is aching badly now. Someone is putting a band around my arm. Stirring in protest, I open my eyes. A black woman with large earrings dangling beside her fleshy cheeks comes into focus. Gently she squeezes my fingers. I can smell red peppers, onions and a touch of garlic on her breath. She tightens the band. I try to scream, but it's like I'm stuck in one of those nightmares when you want to shout for help but no sound comes out.

'Hello Mr Tregunna! Good to see you're awake.' Her lips part in a smile revealing two wide rows of gleaming white teeth. I remember now. I am in a hospital room. A colourless tube connects my left arm to a stand with bleeping and flashing monitors. Vaguely I remember the green room with bright white lights, trying hard not to shake in the freezing cold. I close my eyes and take a deep breath, trying to ignore panic rising at the same speed as the adrenaline in my blood. I grip the edge of a pale blue blanket and reach underneath, sliding my fingers down to my belly, hesitating as they reach the bandage.

It is there. They slid a razor sharp knife into my flesh, cutting out a growth that shouldn't have been there in the first place. They stitched the wound, then moved upwards, another cut, this one for... something I still can't fathom. They've shown me pictures of what to expect, what this terrifying dubious sort of lifeline would be like...

I don't want to think about it, nor about its implications.

'How are you feeling, Mr Tregunna?'

My voice scratches like a nail on a school board. It rasps that I am good. A lie. I can't feel my legs, my hips, my bottom or anything else that's supposed to be down there. I must be paralysed from my waist. A wheelchair springs to mind, followed by the alarming thought that I might have lost the ability to walk or drive, or make love.

'Would you like some water?'

I want to say that I would die for a cold pint, but the words seem inappropriate. I keep quiet, and try to nod. She understands. She picks up a plastic bottle that is sitting on the bedside cupboard and puts a straw between my lips. The water is tepid. She pulls away the straw before I can take a second sip.

'Later. You'd better have some rest now.'

The words are accompanied by a big smile and before I can say anything, or object, she disappears through pale blue curtains that have rusty brown spots splattered on them. Many months ago one of the patients must have left bloodstains from some terrible injury, marking their territory.

Trying not to think of my legs, I feel myself drift into unconsciousness, forming a new dream. Or perhaps it is a memory floating through my brain. This time it's not the young man dying on the taxi, but a woman who is already dead. Jane Croft.

The last thing I am aware of is the sound of quick footsteps. Soles squeaking on the polished lino. An irritated mutter, 'Oh, can anyone fix that tap?' Then the dripping stops.

2

APRIL

It is amazing how fast news travels among reporters keen to acquire the ultimate story. With their sixth sense for breaking news they always seem to know where the action is. In this day and age of mobile access around the world, they often arrive at crime scenes before the police do.

It is my first murder case. I drive to the scene, a sense of inadequacy and suppressed excitement in my mind. As I park my car in front of the police tape, I nod at an officer wearing a fluorescent jacket over his uniform. Hands folded in front of him in an arrogant pose, he is concentrating on his job, trying to keep the press and prying members of the public away.

'Morning sir.' His voice is as vacant as his expression.

'Good morning, Giffey.'

Glancing past me, a tiny smile breaks through.

'Here we go,' he mumbles between his teeth, his voice laden with a mixture of relief and cynicism. The reporters have spotted me. They come running towards me like a flock of hungry seagulls preparing for a fight over the same slice of food.

'Sir? Inspector? A word please?'

It is early days. Any attempt to get a statement at this stage is pointless. Since the message came through, all I know is that a woman's body has been found and that her death is to be treated as suspicious. They may well know even more than me.

'Detective Inspector?'

Tall and skinny with spiky brown hair Frank Devon from *The Echo* has spotted me. Grabbing a small recorder from the pocket of his jacket, his long legs propel him in my direction faster than those of his colleagues and rivals.

'Not now, Devon,' I say, turning away.

'Come on, Tregunna. What can you tell us about the Car Park Murder?' His colleague Kimberley Naylor from *The Cornish Gazette* emerges from his long shadow. Smiling sweetly with a cute pair of dimples in her cheeks, she thrusts a mobile phone in my face. Tall and sexy, full breasts and curved hips, all proportions seem slightly overdone, but she looks like she is probably popular with men. She's dressed in jeans and a yellow T-shirt, arms bare in the warm April sunshine. I know she is a reporter with a vivid imagination and I suspect the term 'Car Park Murder' is hers and I've no doubt that it will be used in headlines on other newspapers.

'The Car Park Murder?' I ask, frowning.

Without acknowledging my question, she opens her mouth, but as her next question forms in her head, she is pushed aside by an older and more experienced reporter.

'Give us something, Mr Tregunna.'

Gerald Hill is the proverbial nail in any policeman's coffin. We've met a couple of times and the best I can say is that we share a mutual dislike towards one another. He must once have been an old-fashioned Fleet Street reporter fighting for scoops with like-minded colleagues. Having been deported, it seems, to the far southwest, all that is left of his ambitions is a mixture of frustration and anger.

'There will be a press conference later today,' I say, trying to fob him off.

'Oh, come on, Tregunna, our deadlines!' Kim Naylor's clear voice speaks for all of them.

For the briefest of moments our eyes meet. 'I'm sorry, Kim. I know as little as you lot.'

I duck under the police tape which is attached to a

streetlamp at one end and to a concrete pillar at the other. Behind this, shopping trolleys are parked. The no-go area covers about eighty per cent of the supermarket car park. With a bit of bad luck most of the car park will remain closed off today. Bad news for the manager who has no doubt been stocking up for the busy Easter weekend.

'Tregunna?' Frank Devon won't let me go. There's something in his voice that makes me slow my steps. As far as I can like a reporter professionally, I don't mind him. Unsurprisingly, he knows it well enough to take advantage of it.

I shake my head. 'I'm sorry, Devon. Not now.'

From the corner of my eyes I see another car arrive, parking next to mine. Devon mutters something obscene, letting me know that I am clearly a disappointment to him. He too has recognised DCI Jason Guthrie. For a second he seems unsure whether to take off towards my superior, now standing alongside his colleagues, or try one more go at me. Deciding to take his chance with me, he stands still, gazing at me expectantly, a crooked smile across his face. His voice low and with a hint of secretive excitement, he says slowly, 'They say the body's a woman. Stabbed.'

Against my better judgement I nod, acknowledging his persistence to drag information out of me. I feel inadequate and unprofessional. But the damage is done: I have just confirmed his scoop.

He grins, pointing two fingers to his temple. 'Thank you, sir. I expect you have no identity yet? Anything?'

'No.'

'All right. Cheers.' He turns to join his colleagues who are trying to get information out of Guthrie. The DCI loves being in the spotlight. I secretly believe he finds it the most attractive part of his job. In that respect he has nothing to fear from me. I am not one to get great pleasure out of having my face appear in the papers or on TV.

Painted a bright blue, a metal barred fence borders the

car park. On the other side are less than two meters of rocky ground, ending abruptly into an almost vertical drop to the beach below, or, when the tide is in, the sea. For a moment I stand still and look at the stunning view. Steep cliffs rise up from a sun-drenched golden beach and the sea is a magnificent blue under a cloudless sky where seagulls float in a gentle breeze. Clusters of surfers are riding perfect waves and, nestled in the curve of the bay, fishing vessels dance gently in Newquay Harbour, with the iconic hotel on top of the hill, dominating the town.

'Mornin', sir.' Small and rather plump, with dark short-cropped hair, a round face and a mouth like a rose bud, DC Jennette Penrose is waiting for me at the end of the car park. I nod in agreement.

Perched between the fence and the edge of the cliff a square canvas tent is erected to protect the victim from weather conditions and prying eyes. Two unidentifiable figures dressed in white suits are kneeling beside the body, which is partially wrapped in black plastic. They are arguing and pointing. A couple of other officials are examining the surrounding area, taking photographs and working with pairs of tweezers to scrutinize every piece of soil and debris, carefully placing anything of interest in plastic evidence bags.

'What do we know so far, Jennette?' I ask.

She looks at me blankly. 'Nothing much, sir. A woman. About fifty years old. No identification.'

One of the two people in the tent suddenly becomes familiar when he stands up and stretches his back. It's David Jamieson, the pathologist, carrying out a cursory examination of the corpse before it's moved for an autopsy. In his early sixties, his narrow face is almost as pale as those of the bodies he examines. Smoothing his blue latex gloves across his palms, he nods briefly. 'Andy.'

'Morning David.'

There is sympathy in his eyes. 'Your first murder, hey?'

'I guess.'

While I wait, rather than ask what he can tell me at this early stage of what will officially become a murder inquiry, I look at the person he's with. Kneeling on the ground is Andrea Burke, a forensic scientist, with dyed ruby red hair and red clothes shining through her white suit. As she turns briefly, a ray of sunlight is reflected in her red-rimmed glasses.

'What do we have, David?'

The pathologist looks down thoughtfully, as if unsure whether the body is indeed that of a dead woman. Before he can reply, Andrea turns her head and answers with an ironic smile: 'We have a body. Sir.'

The single last word comes out as an afterthought, almost as an insult. I try to ignore her. We haven't been on the same wavelength from the moment we met. Other people may, but most times I fail to understand her sense of humour, or predict the mood she is in.

Jamieson smiles, shakes his head and opens his lips as if he is about to whistle. 'A white female. Late forties or early fifties. Grey hair, dyed dark blonde. Blue-grey eyes. Fully dressed. A lavender skirt and white blouse, a string of pearls and a golden ring with a small amethyst. No wedding ring.'

'Cause of death?' I venture.

He chuckles teasingly. 'You know I can't confirm that until I've carried out the full post mortem examination, Andy.'

I try to suppress my impatience. 'Yes, but what's your assumption so far?'

He hesitates. 'There are stab wounds in her neck. A lot of blood on her clothes.'

'Any ID?'

'Not yet.'

Andrea Burke is rubbing her gloved hands together to warm them as though she's been sorting through the contents of a freezer. 'No handbag. She's not wearing a coat.' Her voice is serious and professional, devoid of any mockery.

'I'm afraid that's all we can say at this moment, Andy.' Jamieson stretches his back again, hands on his hips.

It's not enough. 'Time of death?' I demand.

Although I know the question is almost impossible for him to answer, I ask it anyway. I can't wait for the full post mortem report. Any snippet of information will help kick off the investigation. This is my first murder case and I want to get started with something to build on. I can't afford to blow this because precious time is being wasted.

At least Jamieson understands. 'Difficult to say, in these circumstances, the body being in a plastic bag, in the sun.' He pauses for effect. 'My wild guess is not longer than 24 hours.'

Andrea purses her red lips, using her body language to let him know that in her opinion he's gone too far.

I look around. I find it hard to imagine that the body hadn't been reported earlier.

'Someone must have noticed...'

Reading my thoughts, he interrupts, 'She definitely wasn't killed here, Andy.'

'Which leads us to the assumption that a lot of forensic evidence is irrelevant,' Andrea adds curtly.

Jamieson shrugs as if apologising for her hostility. 'We'll do our best, Andy, but you'll have to wait for the official reports.' As he turns, he starts peeling his gloves from his hands, a smile in his eyes. 'The good news is that the killer didn't tip her over the edge. Which means vital evidence may not be lost in the sea.'

3

APRIL

Most of the car park remains closed for the rest of the day, the police tape fluttering in the sea breeze. Obviously the supermarket manager is all but happy with the situation. Usually the Easter Bank Holiday weekend is wet and cold, but it has been exceptionally warm and if the weather holds a few more days it will be one of the warmest on record. The investigation is in full operation. A SOCO team is still examining the sealed off area. Photographs and videos are entered into computers, and all sorts of possible pieces of evidence are bagged and labelled and sent off for painstaking examination. Witnesses are being questioned; statements added into the computer system that is programmed to filter and sort until, ideally, one name pops up. I wish it were that simple.

Lauren Gardiner and her two sons are on top of my list of people that I wish to interview personally. They are waiting at the police station in one of the interview rooms, having already given an initial statement.

In her late twenties, Mrs Gardiner is tall and slender. Ginger curls cascade down her shoulders and brush them with her every movement. She's nervous and fidgety and clutches an orange beach bag on her lap. Her pale blue eyes are restless and every so often she chews her bottom lip. Dressed for a day on the beach, she's wearing a long cotton skirt and a matching blouse so thin that I can see the top of her bikini underneath. Her sons, identical ten-year-old twins, sit on either side of her, their boogie boards by their feet. When I enter the interview room, she reaches out for their hands, seeking reassurance herself rather than offering it.

'Sorry to have kept you waiting, Mrs Gardiner.' My smile is not returned.

'I just want to go home.' Her bottom lip trembles. She's close to tears.

Penrose has such a huge lack of self-confidence about her own appearance that she instantly despises any other woman who is more attractive than her, which is any woman under the age of forty who can make a man smile. Lauren Gardiner's quiet, natural beauty turns Jennette Penrose's face into a mask of defiance and instantly clouds her opinion.

I sit opposite Mrs Gardiner and her sons and Penrose takes the seat beside me. With a body language that speaks volumes, I sense that she has already made up her mind. Whatever Lauren Gardiner says, she's a suspect at the very least, if not guilty. The boys are quiet, clearly overawed by everything that has happened. They sit in silence, eyes wide open, gazing around as though absorbing every detail. Other than their pale blue eyes, there's little resemblance to their mother. Hair black and straight, their skin has a touch of Mediterranean genes.

I smile reassuringly. 'This won't take long, Mrs Gardiner.'

Her blouse is open at the top, revealing the smooth skin of her neck, reddened by the sun and freckles as far as I can see. I try and concentrate.

Opening a brand new green manila folder I find in it little else than a printed and signed statement and a couple of sheets with some hastily scribbled notes, some of which have questions marks on them.

'Is everything all right, Mrs Gardiner?'

Looking up suddenly, I catch her stare at one of her sons, whose face looks red. With a deep frown she rests her fingertips on his forehead, checking his temperature as well as to reassure him that she too wants to go home.

Penrose stirs, taking in a sharp breath. I know she is very keen to get on with the job. Mrs Gardiner has already given a statement. Clearly Penrose can't see the point in interviewing her and the boys again. Perhaps she has a point, but creating a relaxing atmosphere for witnesses is just the way I like to work. 'Can I get you anything, Mrs Gardiner? Tea, coffee?'

I can see thoughts drifting across her face like shadows of clouds. Surprise, hesitation, a near acceptance, until she remembers that she wants to go home, leave the horror of the day here at the police station. The boy on her left side stirs. Shyly, clutching his mother's hand, he casts me a hopeful look and whispers, 'I'm hungry, Mum.'

His brother is not so shy. 'You promised we'd go to MacDonald's, Mum!' His thin voice holds a blunt accusation.

Embarrassed, her eyes avoid mine. 'We've had some tea already, thank you, inspector.'

'I'd like a Coke.'

'Joe! Please!'

'Me too. I'm thirsty, Mum!'

'No, please.' Blushing, the mother wants to please everybody at the same time. 'I'm sorry if my sons seem a bit… rude,' she says to me.

Waving away the apology I gesture at Penrose to find some drinks for the boys. It is the least I can do. Instead of spending a day on the beach, riding their surfboards, they are now trapped in a web of bureaucracy only because they happened to come across a corpse and reported it.

Two minutes later Joe and Stuart Gardiner seem happy with a can of Coke and a Mars Bar each. It releases the tension slightly, which I am grateful for.

'I can assure you, Mrs Gardiner, this won't take long. But I'd like you and your sons to answer some more questions.'

'We've told everything we know, inspector.' There is a sharp edge in her voice.

'I'm sorry, there's a few more things we need to know,' I say apologetically.

Glancing at the windowless, bare grey walls, she straightens her back and is suddenly angry. 'Inspector, do we have to sit in this awful room? As if we're suspects?'

'Of course you're not suspects,' I say softly. 'And you're right, this is hardly the atmosphere for the three of you, especially on a glorious sunny day like this.'

She's slightly taken aback. 'I'm sorry. I didn't mean... It's just that...' she finishes the sentence with a gesture of her hands.

'Mrs Gardiner, I understand. It is indeed a beautiful day and I'm sure the three of you want to spend it on the beach rather than here.'

Drumming her fingertips on the edge of the table, Penrose has clearly had enough. She knows me well enough to let me go on, but she cannot control her need to express her impatience and annoyance. She's ambitious – but has a lot to learn. 'Mrs Gardiner, this is a serious case,' she says, a little too harshly for my liking.

'Yes of course.' Lauren hesitates, her tension easing with my encouraging smile. 'Do you know... who she is... was?'

'At this moment, we have no ID yet, which makes it very difficult for the investigation.'

'And if we had, we wouldn't tell you at this point,' Penrose adds nastily. To avoid further delay, she presses the red button on a recorder. 'We will record this conversation now, madam.' Her voice has a tone that try as I might, she most certainly won't accept any further interruptions.

I look at the notes in front of me. 'What time did you arrive at the car park, Mrs Gardiner?'

'I can't remember exactly. Somewhere around eight.'

'Do you go there very often?' Penrose's voice is curt and to the point, with an undertone that smacks of an accusation, which makes Lauren Gardiner frown uncertainly.

'Sometimes. Not regularly.'

'Did you see anything that struck you as odd?' I ask.

'No. It was early, quiet. I can't remember seeing anything

unusual.' She pauses, then adds with a hint of annoyance, 'I would have told you instantly if I had noticed something.'

'Hmm. So the body... was already there?'

'It must have been, yes.' Her eyes show a mixture of concern and alertness as she glances at her sons and realises they are too young to have seen so much. They are wearing bermuda shorts and T-shirts over their wetsuits. Joe, in a green T-shirt, is sprawled on a chair, his feet dangling just above the floor. One hand is in his pocket, I can see his fingers fidgeting in an annoyed manner. There's something provoking about him, which is reflected in his eyes.

I stare at his identical brother. 'Was the body already there, Stuart?'

'Yes, sir.' His voice is soft and timid, the horror of the memory etched inside his head.

'There was a man,' Joe interrupts suddenly. 'A man with a dog.'

The mother blushes as though caught telling a terrible lie. 'Oh yes, I remember now! I'm sorry inspector, I forgot all about him! He came out of the supermarket after me. His dog was waiting outside.' She stops and frowns. 'But I'm sure that he came nowhere near the... the fence.'

Penrose stirs beside me. We are both aware that neither Lauren, nor the boys, mentioned a man with a dog in their first statement.

'Did you know the man?' I ask casually.

'No.' Shaking her head, a beam from one of the ceiling lights catches her hair, highlighting her flowing locks. For some reason I have difficulty in concentrating on the case. All I can do is wonder what it would feel like to bury my face in those long ginger curls.

'Can you describe him, Mrs Gardiner?' Penrose asks impatiently.

Lauren stares blankly at her, the feeling of antipathy is mutual. 'Sixties? Seventies? His hair was white. And he was tall. That's all, I'm afraid.'

'Not to worry,' I reassure her. 'If he's a regular customer of the supermarket, we'll find him. What can you tell us about his dog?'

The boy in the green shirt replies. 'Black and white. A spaniel.'

'Well done, you're Joe, am I right?' Intercepting Penrose's surprised look, I'm aware that she hasn't connected Joe with his green T-shirt and Stuart's with the blue.

'Did you notice anything else, Joe?' The boy inclines his head to look at his brother. Something unspoken is discussed between them. I sense there's something they're not telling me.

'No, sir.' A shake of a dark head.

'What about you, Stuart?'

'No, sir.' An identical shake. 'Nothing.'

'Was there anything else at the other side of the fence, Joe?'

'Like what?'

'I don't know. Maybe there was something else on the ground. Like possessions. A handbag. A purse. Money.'

It wouldn't be the first time that a trespasser has taken something vital away from a crime scene, either deliberately or by accident. Something valuable to grab is always tempting. People might feel that stealing from a dead person is somehow not illegal. A ten-year old boy could easily have thought that.

The mother makes a gesture with both hands. Her face wears an expression that reminds me of a lioness desperately defending her cubs. Wary. On alert. Ready to defend no matter what.

'Are you suggesting my sons have stolen something, inspector?' With a fierce expression on her face she is even more beautiful. Desirable.

'I'm not suggesting anything, Mrs Gardiner.'

'We haven't stolen anything, sir.' Stuart's voice is loud and clear. Joe says nothing. Eyes downcast, he is attempting to look bored.

'Maybe there was a coin, or even a folded bank note. I

can understand it if you thought that there was no connection with the victim. But we can't be sure and that's why forensics will have to examine everything.'

'There was nothing beside... it,' Stuart replies in a firm voice.

'OK. I understand that you were wandering around the car park while your mother was in the supermarket.'

'We just wanted to look at the beach.'

'And at the surf,' Joe adds defensively, 'it looked good.'

Stuart clears his throat. 'At first we didn't even see what... it was.'

'Right.' I lean forward to make them understand that this is serious. 'Which one of you climbed over the fence?'

'That was me, sir.'

'What made you do that, Joe?'

He examines his thumbnail. 'I don't know.'

'OK. Now look, Joe, this is important. You climbed over the fence and kneeled down. Did you touch anything? Did you open the plastic to see what was in it?'

Shifting on his chair, his face pales suddenly and his eyes widen as he relives the full horror of his discovery. 'I think so, sir.'

'Was the plastic open?'

'A bit, yes.' Moving his bottom to the back of the chair, he swings his legs rapidly.

'Inspector.' His mother looks concerned, torn between an instinctive worry about her sons and her willingness to help the inquiry.

Joe sits up straight and gives me a look that is suddenly almost that of an adult. 'I just lifted a piece of the plastic and the wind caught it and then I saw... it.' Tears blink in his eyes and his mother opens her mouth to warn me not to push him too far. I hesitate. She's right. It is time for them to go home, or to the beach.

Penrose thinks otherwise. 'Did you have any idea what was in it?'

'Of course not!'

'We were… just curious.' Joe's voice is low and his eyes flicker towards his mother.

'And you, Stuart, were you curious too?' Penrose presses on.

'I never touched it! Never! I didn't even climb over the fence.'

I gesture at Penrose. There is no need to press them any further. They were just unlucky to be in the wrong place at the wrong time.

'We will need your fingerprints. If you aren't telling the truth now, we will find out!' I try to joke. They aren't amused. The mother casts me a pitiful glance.

'I didn't touch nothing!' Joe insists, pointing at Penrose accusingly with his index finger.

Still feeling that there's something they aren't telling me, I try one more time. 'And you're sure you didn't touch anything else other than the plastic, Joe?'

He moves restlessly. 'No! I already told you! Soon as I saw it… the blood I mean, I stood back. I didn't want to touch… anything.' He rubs his hands together like they could be contaminated.

'Listen inspector, my boys will have to come to terms with this… dreadful thing. I mean, they're only ten years old and you are dealing with us as if we're criminals. We've done nothing wrong. We've got nothing to do with it.'

After this emotional plea, I pick up my pen, roll it between my fingers, and meet the raw fury in her eyes. 'You are right, Mrs Gardiner, it must be hard on you.'

I feel ashamed somehow. I almost forgot that the boys are nothing more than kids. Instead I have treated them as adults, as possible witnesses, perhaps even as suspects.

I don't know much about children. My marriage ended before we ever considered having any. At that point Lucie and I agreed that it was good that we hadn't but suddenly it strikes me that I may have missed out on something important.

Avoiding those unsettling pale blue eyes, I stand up, gathering my papers from the table. 'Jennette will help you with the fingerprints, Mrs Gardiner. After that, you're free to go.'

'Thank you, inspector.'

'Please don't hesitate to call if any of you remember anything else. Anything at all that might help us with the investigation. Just give us a ring, please Mrs Gardiner.'

I find a simple white card in my pocket and she takes it between thumb and forefinger, unsure whether to accept it or drop it on the table. Clearly she wants to erase everything that happened today from her memory. Keeping my card will prove that it wasn't just a nightmare.

She nods obediently, but her face wears an expression that she has no intention whatsoever of calling us. With the prospect of escaping from the inquiry room and going to the beach, eventually, the boys seem more relaxed now, smiling and grinning at one another. As I look at them they seem okay, but deep inside the shock of the discovery is lurking, waiting to break out. Lauren Gardiner will need all her love and energy to deal with that, to help them when that time comes, to be there to comfort them.

4

MAY

Pain keeps me awake. Brightly coloured spots dance in front of my eyes. White, then red, green, yellow and white again, flashing like alarm lights on a switchboard. A full moon peeps through the curtains. Whoever measured them has made a mistake because whichever way you pull them, they don't cover the window entirely.

I lie on my back and stare at the ceiling. A bent paperclip is wedged in the corner holding the remains of silver tinsel. A leakage, a burst pipe on the floor above has left a circle of yellowed stains. Right above my head is a black spot. A dead fly. Do flies still stick upside down on to a ceiling when they're dead? It must be alive, asleep, dozed off by the mixture of tranquilizers and painkillers in the atmosphere.

Turning onto my other side, I quickly remember that this side is even more uncomfortable. I consider asking for a sleeping pill. I was offered one earlier, but I stupidly, stubbornly, refused. A pill will help me to sleep, but will also bring back memories and confusing images that won't leave me alone when I wake up. Whole conversations, word for word, scene for scene, play through my brain like a video on YouTube. Faces flash. Lauren. Marie. Stella. Jane. Amazingly, it is mostly women who nag me in my dreams and beyond. The sad thing is that I know exactly why.

My first case, my first murder inquiry as a Senior

Investigation Officer and it was taken off my hands before I achieved anything substantial. I had almost four weeks to solve a murder, and I failed. The killer is still walking free, looking over his shoulder less times as the days go by.

For the first time in my working career I am on sick leave. The word alone makes me sick. I have three keyholes in my belly, the stitches self-soluble. It's hard to believe that the red scratch-like wounds have presented the surgeon a good look inside my body. While he was peering into his keyhole camera, negotiating a different route for the contents of my bowels, a shortcut so to speak, his colleague cut something else out of my body, something malignant that was growing inside me. I don't want to think about it. I want to sleep. Forget. I need a pill.

Footsteps, voices, and laughter tell me it is visiting hour. Parents and children, husbands and wives, friends and colleagues pass by my door without pausing, without even spying at my name on the wall beside it. Lifting my head a few inches I try to listen, but there's nothing familiar in the footsteps or the voices. I turn my head towards the window. I don't want to get caught looking longingly at the doorway. I can do without someone else's pity. I have loads of that myself.

Without being pathetic I can't think of anyone who would call me a friend, let alone visit me in hospital. There's hardly anybody who knows I'm here in the first place. Not even my parents... DCI Guthrie knows of course, Jennette Penrose, and Marie...

A nurse has appeared. Did I ring the bell? I can't remember. My voice is thick and hoarse, my mouth dry. I can barely make her understand that I want that sleeping pill after all. She smiles and three moments later she returns with a little plastic beaker and something liquid. Listening to her footsteps as she disappears in a hurry to answer someone else's call, I swallow a bitter substance that will do the trick. I close my eyes and allow myself to drift away into what comes dangerously close to self-pity, so close that it almost makes me want to cry. I try not to panic: don't think about your body. Think about something else, about your work. Or sleep. Images of the present mix easily with recent history and suddenly I am in a horrible nightmare.

The killing has attracted much publicity. DCI Guthrie thrives on the attention and he has already scheduled a meeting with the press. Clutching a bunch of papers, he gives the impression that he is on top of everything. I feel inadequate and awkwardly exposed without any paper support. Like equal pals we sit behind clusters of microphones, but every question is quickly answered by him. My contribution is more or less limited to opening my mouth and moistening my lips. I feel like a goldfish trying to plea for a larger bowl.

The one time I do actually say something is when we are asked for a description of the victim's features and clothes. As Guthrie seems to have lost the sheet with the information, I suddenly become involved in his act, albeit very short-lived.

Kim Naylor is on the front row, holding a mobile phone for her own private recording. In her other hand is a yellow pen which she clicks with the frantic speed of someone who thinks she could be spending her time more efficiently. Already having dismissed me as a person of interest, her scrutinizing eyes are constantly fixed on Guthrie as though she wants to put words in his mouth. Words that should remain secured in his mind for the sake of the inquiry. Leaning against the wall, Gerald Hill has the bored attitude of someone who has been sent by his superior, but fails to see any benefit in his presence. Every so often he looks at me with pity and sadness.

The room is crowded with reporters, but gradually more people appear, crowding in the doorway, pushing. Voices whisper, getting louder. I can no longer hear what Guthrie is saying. It must be something important because the tension in the room is growing. Then all of the sudden it is dead quiet. At that very moment someone farts. Embarrassingly loud. In the middle of the crowd a woman rises from her seat. I recognise

Andrea Burke, but as I stare at her wondering what she is doing amidst a crowd of reporters, her hair looses its ruby red shine and becomes a dull grey. Her red dress has disappeared as well and she is now wearing a lavender skirt and a white blouse. She looks like the woman we found on the cliff edge. Correction, she IS that woman, dead eyes smiling at me. Once more I hear a fart and I can see tears dropping on her blouse, turning red as they fall. Everyone in the room is now staring at her, even Guthrie, his mouth still open, unspoken words on his lips. Another fart, less loud this time but it lasts longer.

Looking around her nervously, she clears her throat. 'I have a stoma,' she announces with a clear voice. 'And I fart because I can't control it.' Next to me Guthrie stirs. I guess he is annoyed because the full attention of the crowd is drawn away from him. Gerald Hill is no longer leaning against the wall. Popping up next to Kim Naylor, he says loud and clear, 'I have a stoma and I fart because I cannot control it.' Someone applauds and all of the sudden other people rise and repeat the announcement until they are all standing and staring at me. Waiting.

'Tregunna?' Guthrie hisses through his teeth.

I nod, get up and speak the words, 'I have a stoma and I fart...'

A phone rings in the distance and I am relieved when the dream, the nightmare, disappears into nothing. To my horror the images won't. I know I'll have to deal with the changes in my body and its enormous impact on my future, but right now I can't. I know I will have to at some point, but not yet. I'd rather sink back into memories of the past couple of weeks, to drown in the first investigation of my career. I think of Jane Croft's body lying on the edge of a cliff, unable to see the beautiful views around her, to hear the cry of the gulls, to listen to the waves crashing onto the rocks below. At first it was just a woman's body without a name, without an identity. Until I gradually got to know her, until she came to life with all the secrets of her past.

5

APRIL

There's a wall of glass windows between me and the post mortem room, but I can still smell the odd mixture of death and anti-sceptics. High windows with frosted glass have plastic blinds pulled closed and the bright tube lights on the ceiling are reflected in the tiled floor. It is one of the most hostile places I can think of, with stainless steel and plastics in white and green. An artist once explained to me about the artistic value of complementary colours. The three primary colours, red, yellow and blue, tend to look deeper and brighter when used next to their respective opposite colours, green, purple and orange. I can see the logic from the butcher's point of view when they use green linings of fake lettuce between displays of red meats, but I fail to see the reason for me thinking this now.

The woman's corpse lying on the stainless steel autopsy table is clean and ready for the examination. A shiny white plastic band is tucked around her ankle. Her hair is combed back from her face and spread out like a 19th Century ladies fan. Samples from her blood, fingernails and hair have already been despatched to the lab and X-ray photos are stored in the computer.

Putting on thin rubber gloves that match his green uniform Ray Campbell speaks through an intercom system, apologising for Jamieson's absence without telling the reason.

Clean-shaven, his skin wears evidence from an early morning blunt razor knife. Perhaps he knows too much about cutting into flesh to trust himself with sharpened knives.

'You look tired, Andy.' From behind metal-framed glasses his eyes are piercing through mine as if he wants to read my thoughts. Briefly looking at the corpse he asks casually: 'Lost some weight recently?'

I hesitate. 'I have, actually.'

He picks up a tool from a tray table and scrutinises it as though he wonders where it came from. 'I wasn't aware you were dieting.'

'I'm not trying some fancy new diet if that's what you mean.'

He looks at me, frowning. 'You know what they say about unexplained weight loss, Andy?'

He is what I think comes close to being a friend. We have occasionally met for a drink before he met his wife and his lifestyle changed gradually. Every so often they invite me to their house parties. He doesn't bother when I decline most of them.

'Can we start the post mortem please, Ray? I'm sure you'll understand the circumstances...'

'Just friendly advice, Andy.'

'Okay.' I step back and find a plastic chair. His reference to my health makes me aware of how hard and cold the seat is. He doesn't appear to notice when I have to shift to find a comfortable position. I know I ought to see a doctor, but the first hurdle still seems too high.

His face tight with concentration, Ray pulls a plastic apron from a metal dispenser on the wall and taps a voice recorder, which is attached to his chest pocket. As if on cue, an assistant appears with a camera and Ray starts the procedure, speaking dates and details in his recorder. I briefly observe the assistant. I think that I would rather photograph families with loud and annoying children than shoot close-ups of human body parts.

Watching the actions from behind the window I listen

to the metallic sound of Ray's loudspeaker voice while he comments on his findings that will later be typed into the computer by his secretary. Meanwhile I pick out the most relevant information and tap quick notes into my mobile.

Albeit not officially identified yet, the woman has now been named. According to a library card found in a little bag strapped under her blouse, Jane Croft has just about lived up to her fifty-sixth birthday. Her home address is in Trispen, a village near Truro. In the little bag there was also a five pound note and two tenners, a handful of coins, a key ring with two keys and a coin for supermarket trolleys. Her only daughter, Stella, is on her way from Falmouth to fulfil the sad task of officially identifying the body.

The way her body was left on the cliff edge is nagging me. It doesn't make sense. I presume that it must have been the initial intention of the killers to tip her body over the edge. They must have known that at some point the body would surface again and wash ashore on a nearby beach, most likely after a few weeks. Why didn't that happen? Why take all the trouble of bringing the body to the coast to dispose of it and then just leave it, almost carelessly? Either they weren't familiar with the area and they didn't know about the beach below, or they were somehow disturbed in the action and panicked. I shake my head. It just doesn't add up.

'I'll email you my report ASAP.' I am barely aware that Ray has finished the examination. Pulling off his gloves, he chucks them in a white plastic bag held by a stand with just a lid.

'Like I said, Andy, she died of stab wounds in her neck. Of course I can't tell you the actual time, because I don't know where she was held and under what circumstances. But she must have been dead for give or take 10 to 30 hours. I'd say with a thin, sharp knife. Forensics are already on to that. With a bit of luck we can let you know which type of knife it was and where it was bought.' He stops to wink. We both know how unlikely it is to find the killer through that specific line of investigation. It's not like in the old days when everyone bought their tools in the local hardware shop. Nevertheless, we have to investigate it painstakingly, although to me it seems like a time consuming waste of effort.

I get up, stretching my legs and shoulders and, as I enter the post mortem room, I try not to look at Jane Croft's body. However, apart from the strong lines of the Y-shaped incision, and the wounds in her neck, her body looks barely damaged, I find it difficult to see her like that. Disrespectful, perhaps.

Ray smiles. 'Take good care of yourself, Andy.'

'Hmm.' Avoiding his piercing eyes, I think of something he mentioned earlier and ask, 'What do you think, Ray, could she have been killed by a woman?'

Picking up an unused tool from the tray, he taps the end against his front teeth in a rhythm only heard by himself.

'It is possible. She must have been taken by surprise as there are no signs of a fight, so yes, it may have been a woman as well as a man.'

He is silent for a few moments and I wait, well aware that his brooding expression suggests he is not entirely sure. Scratching the top of his head with the back of the tool, he resumes thoughtfully, 'The body weighed about seventy-five kilos. It must have been a strong woman, though, fit and trained, to carry a dead body.' He pauses, taking off his green cap to rub his forehead. As a result his blond hair is charged with static electricity and thin yellowish blond hairs wave uncontrollably around his skull. 'However, I can't rule a woman out for that reason entirely. You know what determination can do, Andy. In certain circumstances, a human being is quite capable of doing the impossible.'

'Two women?'

'That seems more likely. But one fit strong man could have done it on his own.'

'Thanks Ray.' I turn away, suddenly strangely hesitant to leave the room. I'd like to invite him for a pint. Perhaps deep down I want to talk to him, tell him about my physical suspicions and listen to his assurances that everything is all right. But the prospect that he might share my worries and tell me so honestly, makes me wary.

He drops his tool and it clatters on top of the used ones on a metal tray. With a wide smile, he indicates that he's actually read my previous thoughts. 'How about a drink, Andy? Are you doing anything this Bank Holiday weekend?'

I nod. 'Work.' It sounds like a bad excuse.

6

MAY

Beads of perspiration gather on my forehead. Everywhere. I am feeling hot, feverish. Sweat soaks into the sheets. It began with a sore, stiff neck, gradually getting worse until a sharp pain cuts through my body, taking my breath away. I feel like I'm dying. In fact I hope I am and that the agony will soon be over. The surgeon had explained what he was going to do, which was to cut in my belly and bottom, yet, bizarrely, the pain hits my right breast and shoulder. I've been given a couple of tablets, and a little plastic cup with a morphine drink. It is not enough. Like a drug addict, I need more, much more.

Squeezing my eyes shut, my fingers find the bell and I press the button as though I'm drowning and suddenly find a buoy to cling to.

A dimmed light shines through the curtains that half hide my bed. I fail to work out whether it is the sun or a hospital light. Bedclothes rustle and a male voice mumbles something that sounds like a curse. Footsteps are running, coming closer. The door opens wider and a beam of light silhouettes a figure. Two figures. More. People enter the room, but none of them seem to be interested in me. It's as if I am already dead and everyone is waiting for a nurse to take my body to Ray to carry out another post mortem. No doubt he will find out what caused this terrible pain in my shoulder.

You don't feel anything when you're dead, they say, so I must still be alive. Only just. I hear whispers. Are they talking about me or about the poor fellow in the other bed? I remember he was brought in earlier. With him came a stand on a trolley, hooks with plastic bags containing clear fluids, trailing down tubes that disappear in his arm. There's a similar stand next to me. A tube junction is attached on the back of my hand with white hospital tape. On my pulse is a plastic band with my name and date of birth printed on it. I can read it when I lift my hand. The familiar information is comforting somehow.

'How are you feeling, Mr Tregunna?' A hand opens the curtain. It is the black nurse with the golden earrings. This time she doesn't smile, her face has a serious, concentrating expression. She is followed by the surgeon. He looks relaxed as if he is about to go to a barbecue with his family and friends. Or play golf with his colleagues.

'Mr Tregunna, how are you?' I fail to understand how he can ask a question like that when he has put me in so much agony. I'm still contemplating a reply that covers everything, including my murderous feelings towards him, when the nurse jumps in. 'It is the gas, sir.'

Her voice is muffled, possibly in an attempt not to wake the man in the other bed.

'It is the gas.' The nurse repeats her words or perhaps they just echo in my head. Gas. I feel like laughing out loud. I am in a hospital room, not in some bad comedy show. How on earth can they talk about gas? They don't mean laughing gas?

Unless there's a gas leak somewhere. Frozen in a sudden jolt of panic, I consider the options. Perhaps the pair of them have appeared to evacuate me. I can't walk because I can't feel my legs. No, this needs a correction. I couldn't feel them before, but now there is an itchy tingling in my toes. I can almost cry out loud with relief, but the pain in my shoulder is predominating.

'Please,' I say, tears springing in my eyes. 'Can I have

something for the pain? Morphine?'

The surgeon examines my face as if trying to remember who I am and what he did to me.

'He's already had his painkillers, sir.' The nurse checks the file that is clipped at the foot end of my bed. They are on either side of my bed, talking about me as if I am vegetating between them. The surgeon is tall and broad shouldered and his skin wears an unhealthy tan that was probably obtained in a beauty salon or during a recent skiing holiday. Looking down at me, his lips part and I can see pink gums along teeth bleached unnaturally white.

'We'll see what we can do for you, Mr Tregunna.'

'Please.' My pride gone, I am begging. I feel like a junkie with someone holding drugs but refusing to hand them over. If my body would allow it, I could easily kill him with my bare hands. No exception for the nurse.

'Yes. We know. It is the gas. ' He nods, making it sound as though he is instructing a mechanic about some failure with his car. 'I'm sorry, Mr Tregunna. In short, during the operation we filled your belly with carbon dioxide gas to expand it. This makes it easier for us to see the area and work. Now it has gathered in one place in your body and it has to escape. Unfortunately it is a slow and painful process.'

I don't understand much of his explanation. I don't care either. I just want him to give me something that will knock me unconscious for as long as it takes the gas to disappear.

'Have some sleep, Mr Tregunna, and be patient.' For a moment he rests his hand on my arm and there is something that resembles empathy in his eyes. 'You'll feel much better tomorrow.'

Nodding at the nurse, he turns and disappears behind the curtains. I can hear the soles of his shoes sucking on the lino as he leaves the room.

'Doctor Cole is getting you something.' The earrings swing and jump as the nurse nods in an attempt to sound reassuring. I find it difficult to believe her.

'I'll be back soon, Mr Tregunna.' She finds a gap between the curtains and disappears to my neighbour. 'Mr Wood. How are you feeling?' Softly she talks to my invisible companion. I don't think he understands anymore of it than I do. He curses and groans, explaining to deaf ears that he wants to get out of bed and use the toilet.

I close my eyes and try to do as I am told, but I'm finding it impossible to relax. I don't know whether to laugh or to cry. It feels like I want to do both at the same time. I know it seems daft, stupid, but I'm thinking that if I'd known about this horrendous pain I would have left the malignant tumour in me to grow. After all, it has never caused me any pain, just some discomfort.

Cold fingers of yet another nurse lift my arm. A syringe with some pale fluid is emptied in the tube that disappears on the back of my hand. Almost an instant later I feel myself drifting off. Without warning, through a cloud of white mist, I see Lauren appearing at the surface of my dreams, a soft smile on her face. Then, with some unfathomable trick of the mind, I find myself sitting on a bench in the zoo. Surrounded by lions and elephants, flamingos and sinister looking crocodiles, I listen to the shrieks of animals hidden in trees and to Jane Croft's daughter's soft sobs, feeling awkward in my inability to comfort her. Then suddenly we're in an obscured room and we walk hand in hand through a tunnel of glass, blue water beside and above us and sharks with crazy eyes circling, waiting for Doctor Cole.

7

APRIL

I meet Stella Croft at the entrance hall of the police station. She is in her early thirties; blonde hair is pulled back in a loose ponytail, a thick fringe covers her eyebrows. Her face is blotched red from crying. She has just identified her mother. She tells me that she came alone. Glancing at her distracted stare, I wonder if she's in the right state of mind for the drive back to Falmouth, where she lives with her partner.

'Miss Croft, I'm so sorry.'

Tears well up from her eyes and gather on her pointed chin, before dropping barely noticed down onto her pink polo shirt.

'I'm really sorry,' I repeat. Normally I can deal with crying people, but somehow this silent despair hits my nerves.

'I just can't stop.' She forces a smile but it looks pitiful. She's like a dog being tied to a tree, sensing that she's going to be left there by someone who she has always been a loyal pet to. Not understanding.

'Can you answer some questions, Miss Croft?'

'I expect there will be many.' She is fidgety and uneasy, looking up every so often when police officers and visitors enter the entrance hall.

'Would you like to go somewhere else, Miss Croft?' I don't want to expose her to the cold and impersonal interview rooms.

'Like where?' From her gaze I sense that something with a sea view may not be a good idea.

Without thinking I say the first thing that pops up in my mind. 'We can go to the Zoo.'

'Newquay Zoo?' Surprise stops the flood of tears for a moment. 'Isn't it almost closing time?'

I check the time on my phone. It is ten to five. 'You're right. I didn't realise… Well, I'm sure we'll find something that offers some privacy.'

She sniffs and looks around; hands tightened around a cotton handbag with pink and red flowers sewed on it. For some reason I assume that her mother made it for her.

'Anywhere. I… I'd rather not see where she was found. Not yet, anyway.'

'I understand.'

'Some people don't understand.' She hesitates, a distant look appearing in her eyes. 'Nowadays people… even strangers… lay flowers… '

'There are some.' I don't tell her that there are dozens of cards and bunches of flowers attached to the fence. Or that people stop and stare out over the ocean, trying to imagine what happened to the woman they didn't even know, yet they feel sympathy. Or, as Guthrie stated cynically, people like to say to their friends that they went to the place where that poor woman was found. It's as if it has become a tourist attraction.

She nods. 'The Zoo will be all right, though I'm not particularly interested in seeing animals right now.'

My car is parked in front of the police station. She adjusts the seatbelt thoroughly, then stares through the window. Not seeing. She was sensible enough to bring a couple of packets of paper handkerchiefs. Clutching one in nervous fingers, she has difficulty opening it. I have already seen used ones disappearing in her handbag and the pockets of her jacket.

Starting the car, I say casually, 'Tell me about your mother. What kind of person was she? Open and trusting, or careful and reserved?'

The fact that she's no longer facing me and that my attention is merely on the traffic helps her relax. Most of her tears seem to have dried out, but I can sense that they are just below the surface. 'I suppose I have always been a disappointment to her,' she blurts out.

'Why?'

'Mum was the type for pink dresses, for roses and lace. Dresses and skirts, curls and braids with flowery clips.' She smiles sadly, for a moment stuck in a fond memory, forgetting the reality.

'Everything pink? My mother would probably have been the same with a daughter.' I feel a pang of guilt all of a sudden. Stella Croft will never be able to see her mother again, whereas I can still visit both my parents. Perhaps I should go and see them at the Easter weekend.

'Pink and lavender.' She shivers, blows her nose. 'Mum never liked bright colours.'

I remember her mother's clothes. The white blouse, half covered with blood, and lavender skirt are now bagged in an evidence box, or already being examined by Andrea Burke.

Stella continues. 'I've never been a girlish daughter. I climbed in trees and played football with the boys. My mother bought me dolls, but I'd rather have a football or a cricket bat. I was never invited to girls' birthday parties, which bothered Mum more than me.' She pauses, lost in childhood memories that don't seem to be so awful in retrospect.

I'm not particularly in a hurry, but it annoys me suddenly when the brightly painted road train pulls out in front of us on a roundabout, with tourists of all ages enjoying an open-air ride through Newquay. Her thoughts miles away, I doubt that she noticed that we have slowed to a walking pace.

'I never had a boyfriend,' she continues, 'I wasn't interested in boys at all, yet it never occurred to me that I liked girls more in that way. I was sixteen when I met Karen, one of the social workers that came to our house every so often. I fell in love with her.'

'How did your mother feel about that?'

'She didn't know. Well, not in the beginning. She didn't notice that I always made sure I'd be at home when Karen came round.'

'Was she your first lover?'

'Oh no! Nothing like that! She was a lesbian, of that I was certain, but… well, nothing ever happened between us. It was just that… knowing her made it obvious to me why I'd always felt so… different. It explained a lot. Soon after that, I met a girl and we became… close friends. Mum was so happy that I'd finally found a best friend. Until she saw us kissing when we were supposed to be doing homework up in my room. She cried for days.' She laughs bitterly. 'I shattered her dreams. It must have been such a disappointment to her.'

The road train also seems to have the zoo as its destination. The traffic is too busy to overtake and I grit my teeth. 'What about your father?'

'He was a waste of space.' Her face darkens. 'Mum worked in a post office. My father always claimed he couldn't work because of his back. He didn't have a job, he just stayed around the house. Like a househusband I guess.' She frowns, then adds, her voice with an edge of steel, 'I've never understood why they got together in the first place. They divorced when I left home.'

'We'll need to talk to him too.'

'I haven't seen him for… years. He moved to Bristol, but I have no idea if he's still living there.'

'It would be helpful if you have his last known address,' I say softly.

Diving into her handbag, she finds a diary with a cotton white cover printed with stylish black flowers. Definitely not a gift from her mother. 'As I said, I'm not sure if he's still living there. It has been about five years since we last spoke.' She writes the address on the back of a supermarket receipt.

'There's a café over there.' I point towards a café just outside the entrance of Newquay Zoo. The road train has stopped. A few passengers get out to photograph Trenance railway viaduct towering above us, but it is probably too late for a visit to the zoo.

'That's fine. The police station was so depressing.'

We are the only customers in the café and she chooses a table at the window, her back to a counter with the remainder of the day's supply of mouth-watering cakes.

I order two cappuccinos and a large piece of homemade chocolate cake for her. She starts as though she hasn't eaten for days. I guess it is the chocolate or the sugar that she needs. She's quiet, seeming to have moved all horrible thoughts about her mother to the back of her mind. She knows she will have to deal with them later.

I hesitate to pull her back to reality. 'Did your mother have enemies?'

She chuckles nervously, distracted by the ridicule of the question. From the way she portrayed her mother, I think I gained an insight into her mother's personality and I can understand her reaction. Yet it is a question I have to ask.

'Enemies?' She cuts a slice of her cake with the side of her spoon. 'My mother was a softie. She always seemed old, old-fashioned, if you know what I mean. I guess most children say that about their parents, but I think it's true. Mum was old fashioned in many ways. In the way she dressed: she would never wear jeans and she hardly ever wore trousers. But she was also old in her opinions, the decoration of our house, everything basically. Although she had a job, she would have loved just being a mother and a housewife. She had no other ambitions than to make us happy.' She pauses and I can see tears gathering behind her eyelids. 'I can't see why anyone would want to harm her.'

A young couple, almost teenagers still, come in, struggling with an obstinate toddler insisting it wants to be carried. A smaller child in a buggy starts crying in solidarity with its sibling.

'Why did your parents divorce?'

She looks down at her hands. 'As I said, he was a waste of space.'

'Was he violent? Or abusive? Did he ever hit her?'

'I don't know. If he did, I never noticed. But then again, Mum would never have told me. Or anyone else.' She finishes her cake, licking the spoon thoughtfully as though hoping to find some more chocolate crumbs.

'Did she meet anyone else?'

'O no! I'm sure she didn't! She was a catholic, you know. Legally she was divorced, but I think in her heart she felt like she was still married to my father.' She stops, stirring her spoon around the dregs of her cappuccino froth, thoughtfully licking traces of cocoa powder.

Suddenly she looks up, eyes piercing into mine. 'You haven't told me how she died, inspector.'

I've been wondering about that, but now I understand that she wasn't ready. 'She was stabbed.'

'Stabbed? You mean, like someone stuck a knife…?'

I can't make it easy for her. 'Yes.'

She gasps. 'I thought… Wasn't it a robbery?'

'We don't believe it was,' I reply carefully. 'We found her money in some sort of a small bag hidden under her clothes.'

'She was terrified of being mugged.' A faint smile of sadness falls across her face.

'Your mother seems to have been a quiet, gentle and introverted person, I say gently, it doesn't make sense that she died… in the way she did.'

'No.' Absentmindedly she adjusts her bra strap on her shoulder. Then she shakes her head and her eyes gaze hard into mine. A thought is hovering on her lips. 'Her face looked … kind of the same.'

Luckily the loud young family decide on ice cream for the kids and leave the café in peace. 'I know.' I nod.

I am quiet for a while to let her settle. The horror of her visit to the mortuary has caught her by surprise, probably transporting her back to the reality that she will never be able to speak with her mother anymore. Everything that she may still have wished to say will forever remain unsaid.

'We weren't that close, Mum and I. She only accepted the fact that I'm a lesbian because I am… was her daughter. She never came to our house, however. She said she just couldn't meet Tracy, my partner. It was like what she couldn't see with her own eyes, wasn't there.' Her mouth twitches cynically as she continues, 'Tracy has a job in a supermarket. She works evenings on Tuesdays and Thursdays. I used to meet Mum every week on Thursday. After work I'd go to Mum's, we'd have a meal and chat. Sometimes I take… took her out. I'd go home at about nine.'

'When you last saw her, was that last Thursday?'

A week ago. 'Yes. I was… I was supposed to see her again… this Thursday.' She sniffs, blows her nose again. Another used paper tissue lands in her bag.

'She didn't mention anything about meeting someone?'

'Not that I can remember.' She pauses and her thoughts drift away. 'I guess I'll have to make arrangements for the funeral, sort out her house.'

'Not just yet, I'm afraid. The house has been sealed off at the moment. As we've now established her identity, we can send forensic specialists in.'

She is quiet for a moment, then says thoughtfully, 'She had a diary in her handbag. She used to scribble everything down, because she was afraid she would forget an appointment or a meeting.'

'We haven't found her handbag,' I say. 'It would help if you can tell us what your mother's handbag looks like.'

She shows a watery smile. 'You know what they say about women and handbags, inspector? Even Mum had several. She didn't like black, and she thought a white bag would get dirty. Hers were either dark blue or beige, to go with most of her clothes. I'll have to see what's in her house to know which one is missing.

I make a quick note. 'You'll be contacted by a family liaison officer.'

'I don't need that. I don't...'

'It's procedure.'

'Oh.' She sniffs. I can see her reluctance.

'You'll find it useful to have a contact with the police. That way we will keep you informed of the progress of the investigation.'

In truth, appointing a family liaison officer usually works to the benefit of police as well. They sometimes develop a close emotional attachment with the relatives and can thus discover valuable inside information that wouldn't have surfaced otherwise. After all, a large percentage of murders are committed by family and friends.

'Oh. OK.' She nods vaguely, tears coming back. I can see them gleam in her eyes. Perhaps it would be wise to call her partner.

She reads my thoughts. 'I think I'd better call Tracy. I don't think I'm in a fit state to drive.' Offering a weak smile, she admits, 'I didn't believe it, you see, when the police told me. I thought it was one big stupid mistake. Stolen identity, something like that. Not for a moment did I believe that my mother... that I would never see her again.'

8

APRIL

The heat of the day still clings to the air. A huge red ball is sinking in the sea beyond the headland. Long stretched snippets of cloud drift towards the horizon, blocking the orange sunlight for a while, casting dark shadows on the calm water in the bay. After one of the hottest days of the year, Newquay town centre is filling with teenagers who have spent the day on beaches and surfboards. Now they are ready to celebrate for any reason they can find to have a drink. Soon enough, police and medical carers will be busy trying to protect the girls from drinking so much that tomorrow they won't remember anything. Or keeping young men away from cliff edges, which they fail to see as dangerous. As always, the authorities are fighting an uneven battle.

Although I have questioned her this morning, Lauren Gardiner and her twins keep popping up in my mind. Something is nagging me, but I cannot think why. I have to see her again. Not to classify her as a suspect, but for my own satisfaction and understanding.

She is wearing a loose cotton skirt that swirls around her calves. A lime-green sleeveless top accentuates her skin that has caught the glow of the sun. Her red curls are damp, she smells of apple and lemon shampoo.

Raising an equally reddish blonde eyebrow she studies

me closely. Then, without a word, she nods quietly and steps back, opening the door wider to let me in. The door closes behind me as though I am caught in her web.

Muffled voices come rushing down the staircase. Music, a pop song I don't recognise. Lauren glances up the stairs, hesitating.

I read her mind. 'I'll have to talk to your boys again later. Not now.'

The expression on her face is still vacant, but her shoulders betray her relief. She hesitates in the doorway to her living room. 'Shall I put the kettle on?'

'Why not?'

'OK, give me a sec. Sit down please.' With a hint of nervous relief she vanishes into the kitchen.

I lower myself on to a two-seat couch facing a TV screen that shows a man with a broad smile, hosting a game show. While I wait for the ever-comforting tea, red boxes numbered one to twenty-two are being randomly opened, revealing amounts of money that are either disappointing or exciting. Every so often the contestant gets an offer from 'the banker' and has to answer only one question: deal or no deal. Predictably, today's lucky contestant can't cope with her nerves. Having greedily accepted, she declines thousands of pounds more than she settled with. Her happiness dissolves in regret and self-hate before the audience cheers her up. Although declaring bravely that she's happy with her money, she can't hide her disappointment.

She should have gone all the way, I think. As so many other viewers who are not actually facing the challenges, I think I know better. I guess it's different when you're on the game show yourself. The chance to win a quarter of a million pounds often reveals traces of character that no one can foresee. The programme is more a mind game, a test for personalities.

I gaze round the room. Two windows with pale green net curtains look out over a narrow garden that ends with a wall criss-crossed with ivy and gnarled, twisted, wisteria. Dark cobblestones are overgrown with mosses and lichen. Two surfboards rest on a shadowed wall. Terracotta pots with pink and white flowers are lined up at one side, probably the side that catches most of the sun. Above the shoulder-high surrounding walls are rooftops with chimneys and poles with telephone lines. The grey slates glean like copper in the evening sunlight.

In the living room the furniture is an odd mixture of old-fashioned oak and more modern, white stained beech. The wallpaper is painted a warm yellow. I suspect the oddly scattered, colourful abstract prints are there to hide holes in the walls. On the floor is a burgundy carpet with flowers in every available shade of green and brown. A white painted bookcase holds a collection of modern crime novels and chick-lits, with half-finished Lego buildings on the bottom shelves. The room has a warm atmosphere that makes me want to stretch my legs and doze off comfortably.

Lauren returns with two mugs on a blue tray that has pictures of lighthouses and seagulls scattered on it. Steam swirls in front of her face, blurring her soft eyes. She glances at me expectantly. Perhaps she is wondering why I'm here, suspecting that it may not totally be for professional reasons. This may well be right.

She pours tea and milk, and opens a pack of custard creams. Without a word she lowers herself on to a brown leather poof. I hesitate. Looking young and vulnerable, there is something about her that makes me want to protect her from the evil bits of life. 'I'm ready for the questions,' she says, crossing her legs, absentmindedly scratching an ankle.

She isn't aware that unconsciously she repeats words that seem to involve a major part of the TV programme with the red boxes that goes on behind her back.

'Please tell me what happened, Mrs Gardiner.'

'I've told you everything already.'

'No, you answered our questions. Now I'd like to hear

your story. In your own words.'

Her eyes flutter and with one hand she gestures toward the ceiling. 'Maybe you'd better talk to my boys.'

'Not just yet.'

I have always been fixed on details. In my opinion they're more important than straightforward facts. Having her telling me in her own words what happened will provide me with many. Hopefully at least one will prove to be significant.

Brushing a stray strand of hair from her forehead, Lauren cups her mug and stares in it as though reading invisible tealeaves. Her voice starts off soft and husky, but grows more and more upset as her story evolves.

Lauren liked to think the prolonged period of heat was the main cause of her tiredness. Yet deep down she knew her lack of energy was due to an on-going mixture of grief, hard work and a responsibility she could barely handle.

That Tuesday morning she woke with a start, eyes hurrying towards the alarm clock on the bedside table. Then she realised she'd taken the day off because of the school holidays. Pushing her face in the pillow, she tried not to listen to the sounds that reached her from the bathroom. The partition wall of plasterboard, not even insulated, was hardly a barrier for the thin young voices arguing about subjects she didn't want to hear. A door slammed, four bare feet ran down the stairs. And up again. She scratched her face; there were two insect bites on her left temple. Turning to lay on her back, she pulled the bedclothes up to her chin and fixed her eyes on the door handle.

'Let's go to mum!'

'No! She's still asleep!'

'We'll wake her up!'

They were identical twins but she knew them so well that she could easily tell from their thin voices who was Joe and who was Stuart. Listening to their arguments she presumed it was Stuart who was objecting to waking her up. Of the two,

Joe was the more impatient one, the most eager to live his life and inspect his boundaries to find the weakest points. And cross them. Stuart was slightly more hesitant and sensitive.

Her bedroom door sprung open, bumping back as it hit the doorstop. With a naughty grin Joe immediately walked in.

'Mum! Wake up!'

She groaned. 'Oh boys, why can I never have a lie in?'

'Lie in?' That was Joe, disbelief in his voice. 'Why? We want to go out!'

'It's only ten past seven!'

'We've been awake for hours!' She'd gathered that already.

Stuart reckoned it was time to start arguing with more sensitivity and persuasion. 'It will be really hot today, Mum.'

'Yeah, it said on TV this morning.'

'Can we go to the beach now? Please?'

For their tenth birthday their father had bought them surfboards and wetsuits. Since then, they seemed to have become addicted to surfing.

Lauren sighed. 'We'll go to the beach later. I promise. But I really do need to vacuum the house. Punch's got fleas, haven't you noticed? If we don't get rid of them now, our home will be invaded by those horrible little creatures!'

'We can help you when we come back,' Stuart argued, instantly being poked in his ribs by his brother. 'Oh shush, Joe! Mum, we'll help you.'

'Yes Mum, we promise!'

Their blue eyes were so full of plea that Lauren knew that she was beaten. 'OK. But we won't leave without breakfast. No Joe! Don't try me, otherwise we won't go at all! How do you think champion surfers start the day? Not without breakfast, I'm sure!'

Half an hour later she already felt exhausted. There was no bread in the bread bin and the cereal box had dropped in the sink, soaking up water before she could even attempt to rescue some of the flakes.

'We'll have to buy some food before we go to the beach,' she insisted, wiping her forehead with her fingertips.

The boys knew better than to object. Persuading their mum to go to the shop nearest the beach, the three of them took off to a supermarket that had recently opened its doors. Situated on the edge of a cliff, its car park offered a perfect view of the coast. As Lauren hurried along the aisles filling her trolley carelessly, for once the boys, dressed in their wetsuits and beach towels on their shoulders, waited outside. Surfboards under their arms, they headed towards the fence at the far end to look down at Tolcarne Beach where surfers were already riding the waves.

As Lauren appeared from the supermarket, her eyes had to adjust to the bright sunlight. Looking around for her sons, she couldn't help smiling with love and pride as she watched them wandering along the fence to get a better view at the beach below. For a moment she stood, wondering how to attract their attention. The plastic shopping bags were cutting into her fingers. Her eyes fixed on the boys, as though trying to let them know telepathically that she had finished shopping and was waiting for them.

They stopped, leaning on the fence. Something on the small strip of uneven rocky ground between the fence and the edge of the cliff seemed to have attracted their attention. Lauren stood frozen, too horrified to move or even scream, watching her son, probably Joe, climbing over the fence. She opened her mouth, but there was nothing but a whisper. 'No. Please. No.'

From the corner of her eye she noticed a man appearing between the automatic doors behind her. In his seventies, dressed in jeans and a greyish jacket smudged with paint, he halted to tuck a folded newspaper under his arm. His cheeks were red and blotched with tiny blue veins. Long white hairs waved around his head like a halo. As he remained within reach of the electronic eye, the sliding doors kept opening and closing in a comic rhythm. Hovering uncertainly in front of the doorway, he looked lost and his eyes seemed to be locked in a world of confused memories, as though he'd forgotten what he was doing there. For a fleeting moment he gazed at Lauren, but as soon as their eyes met he looked away with a hint of embarrassment. The leash of a black and white dog was hooked on a ring next to the doorway. With a shrug he bent over and unhooked it.

As the images flicked rapidly through her head Lauren decided he wasn't the person to ask for help. Yet she must have made a sound, because he looked up and smiled briefly as if wondering whether they'd met before.

The dog came forward, sniffed at her feet. At the end of the car park, seagulls shrieked.

'Come on, Rover, leave the lady alone.'

'It's all right.' She didn't know why she'd said that. Maybe she hoped that when she looked at her sons again she would find that Joe hadn't climbed over the fence at all, that it had only been a strange trick of light.

The old man studied her, uncertain. She could hear Joe yell something. Or was it Stuart? She was so nervous she couldn't even tell. Fear stopped her from thinking sensibly. Somehow she found herself stuck between the old man and his dog. He held the leash firmly as though to prevent her from escaping the circle she was trapped in. A seagull flew low overhead, dropping something on the man's shoulder. Unconsciously he wiped it off with his hand, not realising what dripped from his fingers. Despite herself, Lauren felt a nervous giggle forcing itself upwards from deep down her throat.

'Mum!' An echo of two voices with a mixture of fear and anxiety in them.

The old man didn't move. 'R'them your kids?' He sounded almost accusing as if he was prejudicially criticising her abilities as a mother.

Lauren drew in her breath sharply, hearing it whistle through her teeth. She gave a quick nod, wanting to escape, but she couldn't move.

'I have a son. But at the end of the day, dogs are more loyal.' The statement was delivered with a bitter accusation that made her sense a world of grief and pain. It wasn't the right moment to encourage him to release whatever was on his mind.

'Mum!' Something in the tone made her more frightened suddenly. She hadn't imagined that Joe had climbed over fence. He was kneeling down at the edge of the cliff, clutching at a black package that lay stretched out in the young heather plants. Stuart had dropped the surfboards on the pavement. He was jumping up and down as though he was on a bouncy castle, waving at her with both his arms.

Instinctively she knew something was very wrong. Her mind became full with different scenarios, each one worse than the other. The only comforting bit was that she could still see and hear both her sons, neither had fallen over the edge, neither seemed to be hurt nor injured.

'Mum! Come here! Help!'

She dropped her bags. The old man's dog began to explore its contents that half spilled out on the tarmac. Packed sandwiches. Bananas. Bags of crisps. She couldn't care less. Lauren started to run.

It couldn't have been more than a hundred yards, but it seemed endless. It was as if someone kept pulling the end of the car park away from her. Her heart was in her throat and there were white spots circling before her eyes. As she came closer, she noticed that her sons' faces were deathly pale, eyes dark and huge. Stuart threw himself in her arms and started to sob, but she half ignored him, and fixed her eyes on Joe who was still on the wrong side of the fence. What the hell did he think he was he doing so close to the edge? Didn't he realise that if he came too close the rocky soil could crumble away under his feet?

She clasped her hands tightly round the top bar of the fence and she was very close to an angry outburst, but seeing the expression on his face she held in her words and took a couple of deep breathes. When she spoke, her voice was almost under control.

'Joe, what's happened?'

'We f-found… this.' His face was a pale greenish grey. On his chin was a trace of vomit. Wiping his nose with the back of his hand, he sniffed in an attempt to act as though he was in control of the world. But his eyes were flicking nervously from side to side, avoiding hers. Suddenly Lauren got the sinking feeling that nothing would ever be the same.

'Joe? What's wrong? Are you sick?'

Her voice betrayed something of her relief. She opened her mouth to summon him to climb back over the fence, but the boy thought otherwise. Silently he shook his head, then stood up and stepped sideward, nervously fumbling with his hands. Wanting to put them in his pockets, he seemed to have forgotten he was wearing his wetsuit.

'Joe?'

He didn't look up. Shaking his head as though someone else was pulling the strings that made his head and limbs move, he pointed at the package at his feet.

'Joe, please come on this side. If the rock crumbles you'll fall down.'

'No. Mum, look!'

Somehow she couldn't look at the package. Perhaps because instinctively she knew what it was.

'Joe, I'm scared, darling. Come on this side. Please.'

'No, Mum. I… I can't.' His voice dissolved into a whisper of despair.

Swinging her leg over the cold iron fence, she felt Stuart's hand on her arm, helping her like he had previously helped his brother. Joe was crying now. He wouldn't meet her eyes as she carefully pushed him towards the fence. This time he moved obediently and she was now able to pull her attention away from him.

Nylon yellow rope was tied around a long black package. On the side was an opening as though it had been torn open by bramble thorns. Through the opening she could see a white hand. Unmoving. Her stomach turned as realisation dawned on her. Bile was burning in her throat. Closing her eyes for a moment, she breathed deeply through her nose, cupping both her hands over her mouth. Shaking her head in shock, not wanting to believe her eyes, she fought to stay focused and do whatever was best for her sons. They were more in need than the body inside the package.

'Mummy.' Stuart's voice seemed to have become that of a toddler. Reaching out for her, his thin white fingers trembled in mid air.

'Mum, it's a body.' Joe whispered, glancing over his shoulder as if worried someone might have overheard. His eyes, unnaturally wide, flicked back and forth between Lauren and the package as though waiting for the reassurance that this was all a nightmare. Briefly she wondered whether she should try to hide the horrible truth from her sons, but at the same time she couldn't see any point in denying it. They were not stupid, they already knew.

Wishing she didn't have to, but knowing she had no other option, she knelt down. She licked her lips. Tiny beads of perspiration gathered under her nose. Her hands were shaking as she took a slip of the black plastic between her fingertips. It wasn't her imagination. Pale human flesh, a white hand, an arm. A body, dressed in a smart lavender skirt and a white silk blouse. Smudged with blood. She could not see the woman's face and she thought that maybe it was for the better.

Rising to her feet again, she wiped her hands on her hips. Joe had climbed back over the fence and her sons stood quietly, arms over one another's shoulders. From their restless eyes she understood that they were reluctant to watch, yet fascinated like willing a Pandora's box to open.

A dog barked in the distance. A car drove by, leaving behind strings of stamping music. The air ventilation system of the supermarket hummed. Seagulls and crows circled, as if waiting for them to leave so that they could explore the contents of the package.

Lauren looked around. Normally people would come to the car park, get a trolley and enter the supermarket, coming back out with their items in cardboard boxes and plastic bags. Now, for some reason, everyone seemed to stay away like it had become a contaminated area.

'Mummy? Is she dead?' Stuart asked timidly.

'Course she is, stupid! Why else would she be lying there?'

There was harshness in Joe's voice, as though his childhood had come to a sudden halt.

With the realisation of what they had found, Lauren felt herself sinking through the first stages of shock. All she could hear was the quick beating of her heart, and all she could feel was cold sweat leaking through her pores. She was afraid she would faint and with a surge of phobic panic she knew she couldn't let that happen. Her sons were shocked already and she didn't dare to imagine the effect on them if something terrifying happened to her as well. Suddenly she felt desperately alone and lonely.

The old man with the dog should still be around. He could help her handle this horrible discovery. She turned towards the entrance of the car park and couldn't believe her eyes. At least half a dozen cars were parked on the car park. All empty. Why wasn't anyone coming to help her? What on earth could she do? Walk away and act as if nothing had happened? Leave the body to be found by some other unlucky shopper? Another child?

'I think we ought to call the police.' Her brave smile failed to be reassuring. She remembered she'd left her phone at home; without signal it wasn't of any use on the beach anyway.

Half turning his head away from her, Joe rubbed the back of his hand fiercely across his face. His eyes were two huge pools of misery. Stuart was sobbing, a soft pitiful howling sound. Lauren swallowed. She knew she had to move, find help, but she felt more like sinking to her knees and crying.

*

There is a long pause when Lauren stops. She clutches a ball of tissue paper to her heart. I see tears welling up in her eyes. She blinks and they fall. We sit in silence for a while. Then she leans forward to pick up her mug. Staring in it. I feel as though her horror is reaching out for me, touching me with icy fingertips. She drinks her tea, unaware that it went cold a while ago. I almost want to suggest making us fresh tea, but somehow I know Lauren will want to do it herself. I don't want to interrupt her train of thoughts. In her mind she's still at the supermarket car park and with the horrific memory so fresh still, she may get second thoughts about my interviewing her sons again. Glancing sideward at her profile, I sense she is shocked about how much more she told me compared to what she said earlier. She's probably wondering what will happen, now that she's revealed that she too had touched the plastic, even the body. I decide that it may be time to leave her alone for a short while.

'Can I use your toilet?'

My words hang in the air like a cobweb clinging to fragile branches. I can almost scrape the surprise from her face. Standing up I straighten and try to ignore the dull feeling in my bottom.

'Of course you can,' Lauren says with a hint of embarrassment. 'The bathroom is upstairs.'

She is neat and tidy but apparently she has too little time. The carpet on the stairs is spotless, with little piles of neatly folded and ironed laundry on the bottom steps. A jumble of coloured clothes. T-shirts and rolled up pairs of socks. Blues and army greens for the boys, yellow, pinks and purples for her. The lacy edge of a pink vest pops out. Strings of a bright blue bikini droop from under a lemon yellow blouse. Trying not to imagine her in that bikini I step past the little piles. My mother had piles of laundry on the sides of the steps. She used to say that I should never go upstairs empty-handed. It seems wrong to just step over Laurens little piles.

The music and muffled voices grow louder. For a moment

I stop at the top of the landing, feeling seduced by wanting to talk to the boys. I'd better not do that without supervision from their mother.

As soon as I open the bathroom door, I can understand Lauren's embarrassment. She said earlier that they'd left in haste, her sons not allowing her time to tidy up. A pair of pink and white striped knickers with white lace on the edges lies carelessly on the floor. Damp towels hang over the sink with an open tube of toothpaste on the edge, its top hasn't made it through the drain. There's a faint ring of dried soap halfway down the bathtub.

The toilet seat is up. I lower it, pull down my trousers and sit. Relax. False alarm. It happens quite frequently lately.

Suddenly I feel embarrassed about using Lauren Gardiner's bathroom. I'm an intruder in her life. I reach out for toilet paper. It has orange and blue stars printed on it. A couple of sheets folded, I wipe, hoping in vain they remain clean. Red spots appear amongst the stars. Perhaps the death of Jane Croft has changed my perception of life and death, sickness and health. I don't know. All I know is that I can't deny it any longer.

9

APRIL

I like the early hours when the police station has not yet woken to its normal daily routines. With my second coffee in my hand, I stare at the two photos of Jane Croft, as though I am forcing her to tell me who took her life. The photo taken when life and soul were no longer with her is in sharp contrast with the one her daughter gave me: that one is of a happy woman, dressed in pale pink, laughing carelessly at the camera. Happy. Old-fashioned. Innocent.

The phone interrupts my thoughts. It is the desk officer, sounding rather tired at the end of his night shift, telling me that a man called Peter Prescott is insisting on seeing me. He is waiting in one of the interview rooms.

I sigh, annoyed by the interruption of the morning's peace and quiet. 'Offer him some coffee and tell him we'll be with him shortly.'

'He's already had two coffees,' the desk officer says in a monotone voice. 'I'll ask if he wants more.'

'Thank you.'

In criminal cases like this there are always people who claim that they're the murderer the police are looking for. Annoyingly, they waste a lot of police time, pathetic in their miserable plea for attention. I suspect this Prescott is such a person. He is probably someone the police have dealt with in the past; a drunk abandoned by his family, a squatter who thinks a couple of nights in a police cell is as good as a holiday abroad. Or he is just a loner, a nutcase seeking attention. Penrose will have to talk to Prescott as soon as she arrives. Her impatience will put him off wasting our time.

The day has barely started and I feel tired already. I want to go home. I need the bathroom, the privacy of my own home. There's that dull ache in my bottom again, which I can't ignore anymore. And there are other signs now too, alarming enough to seriously consider seeing my GP.

I look at the phone, digging deep in my memory for my GP's phone number. With a sinking feeling I dial, my fingers are trembling and it is a relief to be connected to a tape recording. *The surgery is open daily from eight till four, please call the following number on Saturday or Sunday. In case of a life-threatening situation call...* Looking at my watch, I realise that it's only just after seven. I'll have to find the courage again later. Meanwhile, focusing on my job will isolate my suspicions regarding what may be wrong inside my body. I sigh, dismissing the idea of waiting for Penrose and letting her deal with our early visitor.

Peter Prescott is not at all what I expected. In his mid thirties, he has one of those totally open faces, pink and rather puffy. His thinning blond hair is combed across his balding skull and he is wearing thick, gold-rimmed glasses that make his blue eyes bigger as if he is constantly amazed. The watch on his wrist is worth more that I earn in a year, which convinces me that he isn't the squatter I expected. Unless he has retrieved it from someone else's wrist.

Introducing myself, I shake his firm hand. 'Sorry to have kept you waiting, Mr Prescott.'

He gives me a calculating look. 'I was just making up my mind whether to go home.'

Silently I wish he had. 'Would you like a drink, Mr Prescott? Tea? Coffee?'

His mouth twists to one side; it takes me a moment to realise he's smiling. 'I've already had a few, but...why not?'

Somehow the atmosphere between us has changed. As though we are old schoolmates meeting one another years after graduation, we explore the coffee machine. I have normal white coffee, no sugar, and he presses the button for a latte, adding extra sugar. Then we fill white plastic cups with water from the cooler and re-enter the interview room with our cups in both hands.

He lowers himself onto a seat. Perhaps it is only me who finds mine highly uncomfortable.

'I understand that you believe you can tell us something about the body we found yesterday, Mr Prescott,' I say carefully.

'Well, I might, but I hope not.' He struggles, uneasy suddenly, replacing his faint smile quickly with a look of concern. 'They said on the radio that the woman has not yet been identified.'

I hesitate, strangely reluctant to tell him the truth. 'It is early days.'

He leans forward, suddenly looking very serious. 'I think I may be able to help you, inspector.'

'You haven't come forward to tell me that you've killed her, Mr Prescott?'

It is too early for a joke, even for a miserable one. His colour fades to a translucent white and anger flashes in his baby blue eyes. 'Good Lord, no! How can you even think that?' He looks genuinely shocked and I feel like apologising as though I have insulted a prude spinster.

'I didn't mean it like that, Mr Prescott, I'm sorry.'

He nods an acceptance and clears his throat. 'Inspector, I'm sorry if I haven't made myself clear. I think I know her. Or rather, I hope not.' He is silent for a few moments, then blurts out, 'I'm afraid it may be my wife.'

I don't know why I leave him in anguish. Yet there's something that holds me back from letting him know at this point. Perhaps I'm being cruel, or just curious. His wife is missing. It's very likely that she has left him and has moved in with her lover. Yet, it is not that, that seems to worry him.

Except for anger and uncertainty, I can't decipher genuine grief in his eyes. For some reason he is convinced that his wife is dead. As if he knows.

I sit back and stretch my legs, uncertain. 'Do you mind if I record our conversation, Mr Prescott?'

He seems surprised, shifting on his seat with a sudden reluctance. He reaches for his back pocket, looking for something, his mobile phone, perhaps. Anything.

'It saves me from making notes as we speak.' I explain gently.

'Ah.' He nods, only half-convinced. 'Of course.'

I press a button to record the conversation, mention names, the date, the time.

I believe it is highly unlikely that Jane Croft has married someone without telling her daughter, however, I am fully aware that stranger things happen in life.

'What is your wife's name, Mr Prescott?'

'Trish. Short for Patricia.'

'Can you describe her for me?'

'She's thirty-four years old, brown eyes, about five foot four, slim.'

'Black, brown or white?'

His brows rise in surprise. 'What? Oh, I see. She's white. Dark hair. Well, she dyes it. I don't know the actual colour, to be honest. She's been dyeing it ever since we met.'

Looking in his face, I keep my voice calm and soothing, conveying a wealth of sympathy and understanding. 'What do you think happened to your wife, Mr Prescott?'

'I don't know, but... well, when I came home last night, she wasn't there...' He inclines his head and lowers his voice, looking down at his trembling hands. 'And when I heard that a woman's body was found, I thought...'

I lean back, noticing that my coffee has gone cold. A thin layer of milk floats on its surface. 'When did you last see her?'

'Monday morning. Breakfast time, before I went to work. Every so often I have to go up country for a few days. I had several appointments in the area around Bristol.'

'And when did you last have contact with her?'

'We spoke briefly on the phone on Monday, at about six.'

'And she seemed all right?'

He shakes his head, thoughtful. 'Yes, well… in hindsight, I can't really say. But at the time, I had no reason to think otherwise.'

'She didn't say anything about going somewhere? Visiting a relative? Her parents perhaps?'

'Her parents are dead.'

I glance at my watch. Twenty past seven. I need to prepare myself for the briefing at eight but for some reason I don't want to cut him off. I am curious. I want to know what exactly made him come to the police station at this time of day. 'I will need a recent photo of your wife, Mr Prescott.'

His face suddenly turns pale, almost ashen. 'Does that mean…?'

'Oh no, Mr Prescott, please don't misunderstand me.' I offer a reassuring smile. 'To tell you the truth, from the description you just gave me, I can confirm that the body we found is not that of your wife.'

'But I understood that you didn't know who the woman is?'

'The identity has not yet been confirmed.' I don't tell him that it is only a matter of time before the details and identity of the body will be released. 'Anyway, your wife is missing and we'll have to do our utmost to find her, won't we? Well now, shall we start at the beginning?'

Peter Prescott could not sleep. His eyes were aching and he was strongly anticipating a migraine. These headaches had come up more frequently recently. That Tuesday night it seemed even worse. Restlessly he pushed the bedclothes aside, but without cover the tiny drops of sweat iced on his naked body. Every now and then he gazed at the empty space beside him, part of him relieved that his wife wasn't there, the other part wishing she were.

Looking at the pattern on the ceiling of the bedroom he asked himself what had gone wrong. A sequence of small events, the meaning of which he hadn't noticed until it was too late. He couldn't recall when the downward spiral started, or at what point he would have been able to stop the process, turn the tide. Perhaps it was the day he ran away from the hospital. His grief had been so enormous and selfish that he wasn't able to stand by her in the hours of need. He couldn't deal with it himself, let alone with hers. So he ran out of the hospital and jumped in his car. His eyes peered into the dark winter night without seeing, his cold hands trembling and shaking so fiercely that it was difficult to put the key in the ignition. He drove for hours and afterwards he couldn't recall where he had been. When a first pale glow of sunlight appeared on the horizon, he stopped at a lay-by. And cried.

When eventually his tears dried, he returned to the hospital to find her calm and self-restrained, but she seemed to have become a shadow of what she had once been, with eyes big and hollow, devoid of any emotion. He knew then that in that night something had changed her. It wasn't just the loss of their son, it was much deeper than that, beyond the essentiality of life. A couple of days later they stood at the tiny grave, joined in their loss, but not joined in their feelings and emotions. He would never forget the force of her rejection when all he wanted was to hold her hand. Denying his touch, she stepped away from him, from the bond of their marriage.

The morning he prepared for his business trip to Bristol, Monday, she sat at the kitchen table, an untouched plate with buttered toast in front of her, hands folded around a glass with orange juice as if she was afraid it would be taken away from her.

'Will you be all right then?' he asked, swiftly going through his briefcase, checking if all necessary files were there.

'Of course.' The surprise in her voice made way for sarcasm, cynicism even.

'I'll try to be back as soon as poss.'

'Sure.'

He was slightly taken aback by this new attitude of hers. As if she knew… 'These meetings are important for me, Trish,' he said in a shallow attempt to explain why these visits were necessary. They both knew they weren't, not really; he could easily have asked someone else.

'I know. Don't worry about me. I'll be fine.'

Somehow he was not convinced. There was something in her eyes, like the fragility of a micron layer of ice on water that almost made him change his mind about the business trip. Then he quickly dismissed the idea as absurd.

'I'll try to be back by Wednesday, lunch time-ish. And of course I'll be off on Good Friday. Perhaps we can do something? Together?' The last word came out with enough hesitation to make them both aware how fragile their relationship had become.

A few very quiet moments later she said stoically, 'Be careful on the road.'

Thinking back to that moment, he realised that he'd stopped asking her about her life, how she spent her days. She had no job to go to. Once a week, he wasn't even sure on which day, a Polish woman came to help her clean the house. She had no hobbies other than going to a fitness club, which she seemed to do frequently. Occasionally, she ran in a nearby park, but he didn't know for certain if she did that on a regular basis. In fact, he didn't know much about her current life at all.

Realising suddenly that he had let her down in many ways, he felt a pang of guilt and regret. If she'd been lying next to him at that moment, he would have woken her, forced her to start talking, listening.

As promised, he had called her in the evening. They'd spoken briefly, exchanging polite questions and replies with no meaning. He'd called again on Tuesday but she hadn't answered. Not at home or on her mobile. He'd left messages, spoken lies that he'd truly tried to come home earlier, but that he wouldn't be able to. At that moment, he had been relieved that she hadn't answered. Easy. No room for guilt. Yet, it must have been about nine, he'd changed his mind, left his drink unfinished, ordered a double espresso and got into his car for the long journey home.

He came home just after midnight, but she wasn't there. No reply on her mobile to any of his messages. He tried to remember whether she had mentioned going somewhere. Perhaps she'd gone to the cinema with a friend, a pub afterwards. He had waited until tiredness kicked in, then he went to bed. Alone. Worried. Angry.

Hours later he woke with a start. Blinking, squinting at the red digits on the alarm clock on the bedside table, he found the bed next to him still empty. It took a while before he realised what had woken him. As he stumbled out of bed, his muscles stiff, he staggered to the chair where he had left his clothes. The tones of a silly love song on his mobile filled the room, grating his ear. With shaking hands he quickly reached for his trousers. A bunch of keys dropped on the floor, a sound as loud as if someone had fired a shot at him. He found his mobile, but fear stunned him and he hesitated.

Trish? For a moment he stood motionless, unable to press the button and make the connection. Fearing what she might tell him, he felt reluctant to do anything. As the last notes of the ringtone echoed against the walls, silence crawled into the bedroom. The display lit up and went blank. The skin of his naked body grew cold. He stared at the display with a mixture of hope and reluctance. Had it been Trish? Heart pounding in his throat he pressed the button to redial. The world around him was shaking as though he was in the centre of an earthquake. Yet he knew it was just his brain playing tricks on him. His guilt.

His call was answered by a mumbling voice. Thin and muffled. 'Huh...?'

'Trish? Darling, where are you?'

'Huh?'

Although it was impossible to recognise the voice, he was

certain it wasn't his wife's. 'Hello? Who is this?'

A ripple of muffled laughter, a giggle. Then a whisper, 'Who's that?'

Was that a different voice? Perhaps, but it was definitely not Trish's.

'I don't know, some nutcase... No! Don't!'

Anger replaced Peter's worries. Blinking at the blank display, it took him some time to realise that the line was dead. His knees trembled and he sat down on the edge of the bed, knowing instinctively that something terrible had happened.

10

APRIL

At twenty-six, DS Ollie Reed's round face still wears scars of acne. When upset or excited, they turn red and stick out against his otherwise pale skin. It may make him vulnerable, but he doesn't seem to care. Perhaps he's grown used to the bullying.

He is a serious, thorough policeman with his heart in the right place. Tenacious, keen on details and punctuality, yet I foresee he won't reach much higher on the career ladder. Despite all his efforts, he lacks imagination and flexibility. I may have to review my opinion, though, because he appears to have found an important witness.

Accompanied by his older and more experienced partner DS Tom Barnes, Ollie dutifully carried out door-to-door interviews. When they moved further away from the designated area, Barnes expressed his doubts and subsequently dismissed Ollie's suggestion to proceed on to the next street. There was a short exchange of opinions and Barnes went off for an appointment with a dentist, whilst Ollie proceeded with the inquiries on his own. This is when he struck gold in finding Mrs Megan Taylor.

I quickly read Ollie's notes from his first visit to Mrs Megan Taylor, written in neat and tidy handwriting. As I whistle through my teeth, he is standing in my office, waiting for my verdict, unsure what to do with his hands. I can sense his excitement in the way he breathes. Shallow and quick.

'Good work, Ollie.'

His face reddens. 'A gut feeling, sir.' He offers a shy but triumphant smile.

As I rise from behind my desk there is a brief sharp pain somewhere deep down in my belly, which I choose to ignore. It's not important, the investigation is. For now.

As if someone has a telepathic gift to sense my feelings, my mobile vibrates on my desk. It is the receptionist at the GP. 'Mr Tregunna?'

I look at Ollie. He seems totally oblivious to my sudden anxiety.

'Speaking.'

'Mr Tregunna, you called for an appointment with Doctor Warren, but there has been a mix up. I'm afraid we'll have to cancel. But could you come tomorrow at 10:40 instead?'

'That's fine,' I say, not meaning it. A sudden fear tightens my throat. I wish now that I hadn't called the surgery in the first place.

'Thanks Mr Tregunna,' the receptionist says cheerfully, and she hangs up before I can say anything more, leaving me feeling frustrated.

I put my mobile in my pocket, nerves making my heart pound, yet trying hard to act normal. 'Well, Ollie, it's time to have another chat with Mrs Taylor, don't you think?'

'Sir.'

I open my mouth to call Penrose, then change my mind. 'Come with me, Ollie?' After all, he found the witness.

Edgcumbe Avenue is almost around the corner from the police station. Although the forecast for the Easter Bank Holiday weekend has been adjusted to lower temperatures, more clouds and even the threat of some showers, Newquay is crowded with tourists. Despite the chilly breeze from the sea they are wearing bermuda shorts, short-sleeved shirts and flip-flops.

Treventon Court is a granite building with black and white

frames. The front garden is layered with tarmac to provide for a small parking area for the residents. Two storeys high it has a wide entrance door, which leads into a small square hall. On the wall opposite to the staircase are four letterboxes. From Ollie's detailed statements I know that Mrs Ivy Hancock lives on the ground floor. She's in her late eighties, slow and deaf, with a huge modern TV screen and three little white poodles to keep her company. Although she complained to Ollie that she hardly ever slept, she hadn't seen or heard anything out of the ordinary, admitting rather crossly that she had missed the excitement surrounding the discovery of the body.

The apartment next door is that of Edward and Dora Wheeler, both retired teachers. While Ed Wheeler was rather absentminded his wife insisted on offering Ollie a dark Earl Grey and scones with strawberry jam and clotted cream. As a result Ollie found himself sitting on their couch, sipping tea and feeling unable to resist Mrs Wheeler's offering of more scones. They were very sorry but they couldn't be helpful. They always slept so deeply that a burglar could steal the false teeth from their mouths. When Ollie finally left, he felt awkward and regretful having wasted too much police time. But the Earl Grey tea reminded him fondly of his childhood and the scones had been mouth-watering.

A midwife from one of the apartments on the first floor seems to be on holiday. According to the Wheelers, she's on a luxury cruise in the Mediterranean Sea, presumably to find herself a Greek tycoon.

Mrs Megan Taylor is the fourth tenant. She's in her late seventies, five feet tall and she has a faint smile that never seems to leave her face. Her hair is white, her wrinkled face thickly powdered. Thin cracked lips have a bright pink glossy shine, and behind her rimless glasses I notice a bluish shadow on her eyelids. As I introduce myself, holding up my warrant card to let her study it, she nods and interrupts me impatiently.

'Yes, inspector, I know who you are and I know why you're here. Do come in, please. Can I offer you tea?'

Her way is rather abrupt, as though she's in a constant hurry. Stepping back to let us in, she looks past me as if expecting there to be half a dozen colleagues following us.

'Nice to see you again, officer.' She smiles at Ollie as though he is one of her long lost grandchildren.

'Likewise, Mrs Taylor.' Obediently Ollie acts like one.

She gestures us towards a rather dark living room with burgundy walls and heavy oak furniture that occupies most of the room. The top of a buffet is scattered with framed pictures of girls at different ages. Her granddaughters.

'As I told this young officer, I was out. I spent the night with my son in Truro. He and his wife went to a wedding party and I looked after their children.'

Wriggling her hands, effected by arthritis, she takes a seat and stands again almost immediately as though remembering something significant. 'I'll put the kettle on. Please sit down.' She gestures towards a pale green sofa and two matching armchairs that look as if nobody has sat in them since last Christmas. We sit obediently, Ollie on the couch and I choose one of the armchairs. Casting a quick glance out of the window, I notice that it merely overlooks the street and that there are no hidden views of the supermarket or its car park, not even the tiniest glimpse of the ocean beyond. I half sympathise with Barnes who instantly dismissed the residents of Edgcumbe Avenue as possible witnesses on the principle that they live too far from the car park.

As if she's been expecting us, Mrs Taylor is back in an instant, carrying a tray loaded with cups, saucers and matching plates, paper napkins printed with yellow and blue irises and a big plate of home made buttered scones, which she places on the coffee table.

'Help yourselves please.' One moment later she returns with a teapot in the shape of an elephant, striped blue and white with pink eyes. Following my gaze, she smiles softly. 'A present from my granddaughter. I have three grandchildren. All girls. My son is my only child.' A life in a nutshell.

'I'm sorry, inspector. You must think I ramble from one end to the other.' She lowers herself gracefully on to the other armchair, lacing her crooked fingers, then she frowns and adds, 'Are you not using a notebook?'

'I don't use one.'

As if on cue, Ollie produces a small black notebook from his chest pocket. As soon as he has found a pen, she declares, 'I have already told Ollie about that night, Mr Tregunna. I presume you're here to hear it again?'

Clearly she likes a dramatic touch. I don't know anything about her personal life, but I'm sure she'll take advantage of her audience. Preparing for a long visit, I shift in my seat, aware of a vague ache and discomfort.

'That is exactly why we've come back, Mrs Taylor. Will you please tell us again what you told me earlier?' Ollie smiles at me apologetically, as if feeling personally responsible for Mrs Taylor's rather incoherent outbreaks of words.

Lifting her head, she stares at the ceiling for inspiration. 'It was yesterday, about nine in the morning, when my son came to pick me up. He's always in a hurry, as most young people are nowadays, I guess. He stopped on the road and waited until I came down. That's probably why I didn't notice there was something going on near the supermarket.' She stops abruptly and frowns as if recalling something half forgotten. 'We had a late lunch, then my son and his wife left and I stayed the night with my grandchildren.' She pauses, as though expecting some other player in the drama to put in the next line. The room is dusty and warm, lacking a constant flow of fresh air. It seems like my mind begins to slow down and my eyelids feel heavy. I find it difficult to concentrate.

Once more she jumps to a different subject. It's as if an invisible person is playing with a remote control, flicking though the channels of Mrs Taylor's mind.

'As you are as old as I am, you don't need much sleep. Usually I wake up at about three, half past. I get up and watch TV or I stay in my bed and read for a bit.' She pauses, a sad memory floating across her face. 'It's not so long ago that I had a dog, Blackie, although she wasn't all black. She had quite a lot of brown and white, actually. Anyway, when she was getting older, I had to take her out for a wee more frequently, even at night sometimes We used to go to the area which is now the supermarket car park.'

She stops to stare out of the window and for a moment she seems to be somewhere far away in fond memories. I clear my throat.

'Yes inspector, I am getting to the point. I just want to make sure you understand why I did what I did.'

'Take your time.' I'm glad that Ollie manages to look patient. It would have been so different with Jennette Penrose.

'Blackie's been dead for a few months now, but when I wake up and I can't sleep, I sometimes get dressed and go out. Like I used to do with Blackie.'

'As you did early Tuesday morning,' I encourage.

'Well, yes.' She frowns, uncertain. 'Eh, do you think it's weird?'

I offer a reassuring smile. 'I guess it's part of the mourning process.'

'Well, yes, that may be so. Nobody seems to find it strange if you walk in the streets at night with a dog, but if you haven't got one, people think you're getting a bit funny.'

'People in similar circumstances will understand.'

'Do you think so, inspector? Anyway, that night I woke up and I went for a walk. It had been hot and murky all day and it didn't feel as if there was a breath of fresh air.'

I want to keep her on a straight track now. 'Do you remember what time it was?'

'It was ten past four when I left my home.' This is exactly the time in Ollie's notes. 'A bit further up towards the town centre were some youngsters yelling and shouting. I'm not particularly worried, but I don't like it when people are drunk. I wasn't sure whether to wait until they passed, but thankfully they went the other way.' She lifts her hand as though she expects me to interfere. 'Like I said, the youngsters went the other way and I decided to go to the car park at the supermarket. Sometimes I just cross the street and sit on a bench and look out over the sea. It's amazing how light it can be at night.' She stops for effect. 'That's when I heard a car approaching. He was driving fast. I could hear its tyres screech. It came from Berry Road. I was just about to cross the street and I remember thinking that it would be better to wait. I don't think the driver saw me. I was expecting him to pass, but he drove straight on to the car park of the supermarket. At first I thought he was drunk because he hit the waste bin at the entrance. There is a lamppost with one of those cameras. It's there because they fine people who leave their car there longer that they're allowed, you see.' I make a mental note to follow this up. No doubt the men from SOCO have already covered this, but still I wish to be sure. With a bit of luck, we will find useful images from the supermarket's camera. Ollie, apparently following my train of thoughts, shakes his head to steamroll my fresh expectations. 'We've checked it already, sir. The supermarket owns the car park and parking is limited to ninety minutes for their customers. The camera only operates in the daytime, when the supermarket is open.'

'Hmm.'

'I thought he would crash into the lamppost too.' Mrs Taylor continues. 'He didn't. He must have missed it by an inch and then he drove to the end of the car park.'

I think I have missed something too. 'Mrs Taylor, did you just say that this car actually hit a waste bin?'

She nods, swirling the tea in her cup and looking into it as if seeking inspiration. 'Yes, he did. That's why I remember it so clearly. It's one of those bins on a pole. Blue. I used to drop Blackie's poo-bag in it.' She smiles, folding her arms across her chest. 'And today I noticed it was still leaning in an angle. It was definitely damaged.'

Ollie stirs in excitement, just managing to keep quiet. This piece of information was not in his notes. It's exactly why I find it useful to speak more than once with important witnesses.

'What sort of car was it?' I ask, merely to confirm what she told Ollie already.

'A small van. White, with a name on the side. In red.'

'What was the name?'

'I'm sorry, but I can't remember. It all happened so fast!'

I guess it would have been too good to be true. 'What else can you remember about the van? Did you by any chance see its number plate?'

'I'm afraid I didn't.' She is almost ashamed that she can't produce more specific information.

'What happened then, Mrs Taylor?'

She smiles as though unsure whether to share a secret. 'The van stopped at the far end of the car park. The driver got out and opened a sliding door on the side. Then they pulled out a big package. It looked like it was quite heavy.'

'They?'

She nods with a thoughtful frown. 'Two men. Yes. Unfortunately it was too dark to see what it was they were carrying and, to be honest, I didn't want to become involved in something illegal. Dumping is illegal, you see. And I may be brave, but I didn't feel up to going there and telling them off. After all, it was in the middle of the night and there was no one else about.' She produces a sad, apologetic smile. 'My neighbour Mrs Wheeler once told a ten year old not to throw a chocolate wrapper on the street and she got herself a nasty blow. So you can understand why I wasn't too keen to go after two men in the middle of the night.'

I nod. 'Sadly, you can't be too careful these days.'

'That's what I mean. Well, as I said, they dumped the package over the fence. First I thought it was meant to be tipped over the edge, but they didn't seem to be bothered. They got back in the van and drove off.'

'Can you describe the men?'

'I have been thinking about that, inspector. I don't think

they were very tall. Both were about the same height. Dressed in dark clothes. Hoodies, you know, those sweatshirts with a hood. You always see it on *Crimewatch*. People keep their face hidden when they have something to hide…'

She stops and pats her knees with both hands. 'Some story, isn't it? Of course I had no idea of the seriousness of the case, otherwise I would have called the police immediately.'

Afterthoughts of what one should or shouldn't have done are pointless, but they seem to reassure some people. 'Do you happen to know the make of the van, Mrs Taylor?'

She raises her index finger. 'I'm afraid I don't know much about cars but it was definitely a white van, same as my son's.'

I straighten, trying to keep my face blank. This is another snippet of information she failed to tell Ollie. 'Do you mean it was exactly the same van as your son's?'

'Well, yes.'

I open my mouth to ask her son's telephone number but she seems to have read my thoughts.

'No need, inspector!' She exclaims cheerfully, quickly getting up. On the buffet is a photo book with sunflowers on its cover. With a triumphant smile she picks it up along with a pair of reading glasses. 'I have some photographs, you see. Here it is. Look, these are my granddaughters. Aren't they lovely?'

'You must be a very proud.' Obediently I cast a quick glance at the girls, dressed in white cotton dresses, pink flowers in their blonde hair, a woman in a red dress behind them. All are smiling at the camera. More importantly, they are standing in front of a small white business van, which I recognise as a Citroen Berlingo. On its side a simplified image of a few tools and: *R.B. Taylor, your plumber*. A mobile phone number underneath.

Pressing a fingertip on the photo, she says dramatically, 'This is the van I saw that night, inspector!'

'You are very helpful, Mrs Taylor.'

Her shoulders drop. 'Well, yes, but I'm afraid that this is

all I can help you with, inspector. I didn't bring my glasses, you see. I was only out for a short walk.'

'What about when they drove out of the car park? Did you see their faces?'

'Not really, I'm afraid. They still had their hoods on and they switched on the headlights when they came near the road, so I was blinded.' She looks down at her hands. 'I wasn't sure what they would do if they saw me. That's why I was hiding in the shadows.'

'What about the driver's ethnicity?'

'If you mean the colour of his skin, inspector, he was white, I think, like you and me.'

'Anything else you remember?'

Shaking her head a white curl escapes from its position. She pushes it back with a hint of irritation. 'I am sorry, but no. I've thought about it since I've talked to Officer Ollie, but I can't think of anything else.'

I finish my tea and rise to my feet, gesturing to Ollie who quickly licks the crumbs of his second scone off his fingers. I take a small white card from my wallet. 'Thanks for the tea, Mrs Taylor, I appreciate your help. If there is anything else you remember, please don't hesitate to contact the police. Even the smallest detail can be important. Here's my card.'

She accepts with a smile, putting the card on the table without looking at it. 'I will do my best, inspector. This is a dreadful thing. I can't bear to think that I actually witnessed a murder. It's a horrible thought, don't you think?'

'If you wish, I can send someone from victim support. They are trained to help people deal with traumas.'

'I don't think I need someone like that, but thank you anyway, inspector.' She pauses, then adds with unconscious pleasure, 'I'm an important witness, am I?'

I'm sure there's a trace of a smile left on my face when Ollie and I leave the building and cross the street.

'She didn't tell me about the bin, Sir.' Ollie looks at me guiltily.

I nod. 'People tend to remember more details when they're questioned a second time. It forces them to dig deeper in their memory.'

'Yes, but... Sir.' He presses the button for the traffic light, a glow of embarrassment colouring his face. 'You just wait and people tell you... things.'

A bus from the local bus company stops with a jolt, its driver annoyed by the red light. Above his head fluorescent lights form its destination. *Padstow. By coast route*. The vehicle's sides, including most of the windows, are covered in mud the colour of clay. So much for the beautiful coastal view on the route to Padstow then.

'Not everyone has so much patience as you have, sir. ' Ollie continues. 'People talk because you listen.'

We cross the road in an awkward silence. I don't know how to reply and clearly Ollie feels he's already said too much. A group of a dozen young men dressed in yellow T-shirts appears from the railway station carrying rucksacks and trays with cans of beer. Another stag party that Newquay seems to have become infamous for of late.

Behind us, the engine of the bus roars. Black smoke and the mixed smell of diesel and burnt rubber. Ollie clears his throat. 'Shall I contact SOCO, sir?'

'Let's take a look at the bin first, Ollie.'

It is exactly as Mrs Taylor said. A dark blue metal litterbin is attached to a post that is slightly slanting to the right. The soil at the base is cracked, the bin itself is dented and bruised but it's not so obvious when it was damaged. Recently emptied, it contains a white plastic bag with some used beer cans and a folded newspaper with today's date. Wondering how many times the litterbins are emptied, I take out my mobile phone and dial the incident room. Looking at the white scratches on the bin, I ask Penrose to enquire whether someone from SOCO had a bright thought and has already examined the bin, but I remember clearly that the bin was outside the area secured by police, and her answer isn't a surprise to me.

11

APRIL

Returning from the appointment with my GP at Newquay Tolcarne Surgery, I find a new statement on my desk. A yellow post-it note is stuck on it. The words *Time, One, Two,* followed by a series of question marks are written across with a red marker: the most important issues in the statement are inconsistent with what Megan Taylor told us.

Thirty minutes later Marie Yates storms in with an obstinate blurt, saying, 'Why am I here?'

Her date of birth tells me she is twenty-one, but she looks more like a rebellious teenager. She is small and perhaps a stone too big. Her face round with chubby cheeks, she has a small nose and eyes set so deep that I can't see their colour. A black scarf with tiny silver threads is wound around the top of her head, almost covering hair that is dyed white blonde with marshmallow pink streaks.

'Miss Yates, please take a seat.' I stare at her. For some reason I expected a neatly dressed office worker, not this girl dressed in black with tattoos disappearing up her neck and studs lining her ears and brows.

'I've told everything I know to that other officer.' She's holding a big black handbag with at least a dozen zippers in solid steel.

'Please sit down, Miss Yates,' I repeat with a reassuring smile. 'The reason why you're here is because I have some more questions about the statement you gave us earlier.'

'OK.' Letting out a deep sigh, she lowers herself on to the chair, but she sits with a straight back and clutches the bag as though she needs a defensive barrier between us. Her protective behaviour almost tempts me to ask her to empty it on the table so that I can rummage through its contents.

'Thank you for your cooperation, Miss Yates. It's much appreciated.'

'I could hardly refuse, could I?' she replies sarcastically.

'You are free to go,' I say patiently. 'But I would prefer it if you could stay and elucidate some facts for me.'

Without replying, she studies the interview room. Dull grey walls, the odd poster stuck on it with blu-tack and yellowed tape. Two tables are placed in an L-shape, the longest end to the wall. A keyboard rests on one of them and a monitor is mounted on the wall. 'This isn't so different from what you see in a crime series on TV.'

I smile. 'It depends on the series. I doubt you'll ever come across a policeman like Frost or Morse in here.'

'I suppose.' Shrugging slightly, her black leather jacket falls open. Small breasts, nipples uncomfortably visible through a black sleeveless top that says: *I AM A LIMITED EDITION*. A tattoo that looks like an image of a rolled up snake is on her collarbone. I can't help but wonder if there are more tattoos hidden under her clothes.

When I look up and meet her smile I feel a light flush creeping over my face. Quickly I pick up her statement and hold it between thumb and index finger, not wanting to show that I'm finding it hard to concentrate on my job. She's not at all my type, yet she has an air of raw sensuality about her that appeals to me. I look at her statement. I've read it a couple of times and I can almost repeat it from memory. Although I don't need to, I pretend I am studying it closely. Penrose's name and signature are underneath. I can see from the way the statement is built up how she formed her questions, which she normally does beforehand. Penrose is strict, she works with the rules and she isn't likely to sidestep as the interview progresses. I have a different approach: I prefer not to ask too many questions. There's always one that isn't asked, that is forgotten or thought not to be relevant. I wouldn't like to come across a witness who accuses me afterwards of not doing my job properly because I have failed to ask the one important question.

'I'd like you to tell me what you did in the early hours of last Tuesday.'

She shifts with impatience, crossing one leg over the other, rearranging a wide black skirt that reaches down to her ankles. She wears short black boots with metal studs along the edges.

Instinctively I know that treating her with respect, rather than pumping her for formation, is the first step to building a relationship of mutual understanding. 'I'm sorry about this, miss Yates. I am aware that you have been very helpful, but if you don't mind, I'd like to hear everything again.'

'Why?' Her eyes are dark and piercing.

'There are some discrepancies.'

'I've told the truth.'

'I'm sorry.' As I force a smile, a sudden pang of pain makes me wince and I have to adjust my position.

'What discrepancies?'

I try to hide my irritation. As a teenager she must have been a real pain to her parents. 'I'm afraid I can't disclose the details of our inquiry at this point, Miss Yates. '

Her eyebrows move slightly upwards and there is something formed on her lips, but she says nothing. Instead she stares at me as if I am the one being questioned and repeats, '*What* discrepancies?'

My ideas of treating her with politeness and respect have almost faded. It feels as if she is stubbornly, purposefully obstructing my investigation. Or perhaps it is just me. The examination at the surgery hasn't improved my comfort. On the contrary. It certainly has increased the usually dull ache. Even more than embarrassing and disrespectful, it was painful. Worrying, also. I could read serious concern on Doctor Warren's face as I got dressed and he plotted his findings into his computer. Perhaps I am not in the right mood for an interview with as difficult a young woman as Marie Yates, but I know the alternative of being alone and facing more likely demons is even less an option.

'Just tell me in your own words what exactly happened that night, miss Yates. Please.' I have to try hard not to show her my annoyance; it will only act as a goad on a bull.

'All of it?' There is a mischievous light in her eyes. To Penrose she mentioned she met a man in a bar and went with him to a hotel. Sensibly, Penrose didn't take it any further.

'Perhaps you can spare me the details.'

She gives a stubborn shake of the head. 'Can I have a coffee?'

For a moment I close my eyes and breathe deeply through my nose. 'I offered you coffee or tea when you came in five minutes ago.'

'That was before I knew this would take longer than a few minutes.'

'Miss Yates, why are you being so difficult?'

'I'm not.'

'Yes you are. I don't know about you, but my time is precious. I have more important things to do than play games with a witness who makes everything so difficult that I am almost tempted to put her in a cell for an hour or so.'

'You can't do that!'

She's right, of course. I can't put her in a cell because she annoys me, not without risking a disciplinary. I wish I had brought Penrose in here, or Ollie, or anyone else, whose presence would temper my reactions to her.

'You'd better not try me, miss Yates.'

Our eyes meet in a battle that equals a medieval war between rivalling tribes. Sharpened bayonets or catapults firing buckets of boiling tarmac, spring to mind.

'OK, inspector.' Her sudden smile is a dazzle of sunshine.

It lights up her face and turns her eyes into diamonds. 'What do you want from me?'

'Tell me about Tuesday night.'

'I went out. Usually I go to the Central Bar.' She pauses for a moment, cocking her head to one side. 'Do you ever go to the Central Bar, inspector?'

'No.'

She corrects herself, 'No, of course not. Silly me. I would have known if you had.'

'Go on, miss Yates.'

The air in the Central Bar was heavy with voices and laughter. Alcohol spilled over glasses. There were young men dressed in T-shirts and shorts, perspiration stains under their armpits, and girls wearing tiny skirts with thin vests or just bikini tops. The music thumped, making the floor vibrate. Some girls danced with one another or just moved slowly to an inward rhythm. The guys mainly looked around, talked with raised voices and drank beer. A group of about a dozen friends arrived in Newquay for a stag night, wearing black T-shirts with 'bachelor' printed in pink on the chest.

'Hi, Gorgeous.' One of them spotted Marie standing alone, sipping red wine. He was in his mid-twenties, handsome and fit, with spiky blond hair and a tattooed rose on his upper arm.

'How do you know my name?' she shouted over the music.

'Just guessed.'

'What's yours?'

'Matt.'

Playfully she poked her index finger in his ribs. 'Are you the groom?'

'Good lord, no!'

She gestured toward his friends grouped together around a table in the corner. 'Which of you is the poor guy then?'

'Isn't it obvious?'

'I suppose.' One of his mates wore a cheap pink wig with

two long plaits. He gazed sheepishly around with eyes that betrayed how uncomfortable he felt. The print on his T-shirt said, *I am the luckiest man in the world.* Somehow he looked more like the opposite.

'Where are you from, gorgeous?' Matt asked in her ear, in an attempt to make himself heard through the noise.

'I live here. In Newquay.'

'I thought I noticed a Scouse accent.'

'Scouse? No mate, you've got that one wrong,' she laughed, tilting her head with a flirtatious smile. He grinned and she kissed him on his mouth, for a promising moment sucking his tongue.

His breath brushed her ear. 'It's a bit warm in here, isn't it?'

'Do you think so?'

'Yeah. Shall we go outside for a while?'

With a blank stare, she raised her glass to her lips and emptied it. 'Why not?'

Pretending not to see that he gestured something obscene towards his friends, she followed him outside. A handful of smokers grouped together under a striped canopy. Cigarette smoke lightly scented with cannabis curled up through shafts of light coming from the bar's windows. The streets were filled with barely dressed teenagers travelling from one pub to the other. Police were patrolling on every corner in an attempt to prevent excessive behaviour.

Matt's hand squeezed her bottom. 'My hotel is a bit further up.'

'OK.' She pulled him towards her and kissed him. Short and tempting. 'Which hotel?'

'The Victoria.'

'Wow! Posh.'

'My mate's paying.

'Perhaps I should go out with him.'

'He's marrying my sister. She won't marry him if she finds out.'

'Perhaps they shouldn't get married in the first place.'

He shrugged, indifferently. 'My sister's pregnant. She wants to do it properly.'

Marie grinned. 'More like she wants to keep him. Well, it'll have to be you then.'

He kissed her again, long and hard, pushing her back against a wall with his hips. 'Any objections?'

She giggled. 'From what I feel you have to offer? No, I don't think so.'

The hotel room was not as luxurious as she expected. Clothes were scattered on the floor and across the bed. A mobile phone on the windowsill, attached to a charger. Its display showed several missed calls. He switched it off with a dismissive wave of his hand.

She brushed her hands down his chest. 'Your wife?'

But he wasn't in the mood for a conversation. She thought that the short walk to the hotel had cooled him a little, but now she found it wasn't the case. Impatiently he lifted her, straddling her legs around his waist. His teeth pulled her vest over her head and he bit a nipple softly.

'Hey! Wait!' She pushed him off her.

Laughing curtly, his face expressed a mixture of surprise and disbelief. 'Hey babe, you seemed to be in as much of a hurry as I am.'

She looked around the room. 'Is there a mini bar in the room?'

He frowned uncertainly. 'Yeah. What would you like?'

'What do you have?'

Obediently he emptied a mini bottle of gin in a glass, added some ice cubes and brought it over to her. She sat on the bed, her pink-blonde head resting on pillows pulled up to the headboard, and picked up the remote for the TV. Coming to the other side of the bed he reached out and his hand disappeared under her top. This time she allowed him a step further. He slipped his fingers under the silver chain belt of her black miniskirt.

She smiled. 'Take it easy, mate, we've got plenty of time.'

Stripping off his T-shirt, he kissed her again, hard, deep, breathless. She could taste beer and Italian spices on his tongue. She teased him with small kisses, arousing him, and then pushed him away.

'Playing hard to get, eh?'

'Hmm. I like it long and good.' She reached out for her handbag. 'Wait a sec, will you?' Producing a little blue pill, she popped it on the tip of her tongue.

'What's that?'

'Something to make it even better.' Giggling, she pulled him closer, kissing him, the pill dancing from tongue to tongue. His hands explored her body. The little pill softened with mixed saliva until it disappeared in his throat.

'Hey!' He shouted in protest.

But she was already reaching down, struggling with his zipper. 'Don't worry, darling. You'll never forget this night!'

His breath was hot and overwhelming inside her lungs as he pushed himself into her. He was quick, too quick. Half sleeping he muttered an apology, a promise to make it up to her later. Quietly she turned away from him, pulling the bedclothes around her.

'Next time, babe, next time,' his voice slurred.

'There won't be a next time,' she told him softly.

Fully tiled in pale green with a motif of lilies of the valley the bathroom looked like it had recently been refurbished. She smiled. Neatly boxed in with frosted safety glass was Jacuzzi bathtub. The floor had built-in heating, warm under her feet. Emptying half a bottle of bath gel, Marie turned the brass taps and pulled a thick soft towel with a woven lily of the valley decoration from a heated bar.

It was close to three o'clock when someone knocked on the door. Marie emerged from the bathroom, the towel in a knot above her chest, another covering her hair. Wiping droplets of water from her shoulders, she waited and listened. Muffled giggles and stumbling footsteps disappeared. Picking up her scattered clothes, she dressed and picked up a wallet that has fallen out of Matt's jeans. There was a pile of twenty-pound notes, and about a dozen credit cards. Taking out five notes, she rolled up both damp towels and dumped them into her handbag. Then, without even looking at him, she left the room, closing the door firmly behind her.

A clear, almost full moon peered through a gap in the clouds. There were still people about. Uncontrolled laughter. Unsteady feet. Clutching her bag against her chest, Marie walked fast. She was tired suddenly and she longed for her bed, her own bed. Alone.

When Newquay Harbour was an important gateway for goods, the main terminus of the railway was at the Harbour. Wagons were lowered on a cable down in a tunnel dug out of the cliff. The line became disused and part of the track was now a footpath that ran from opposite the new railway station, along behind Victoria Hotel to the cliff tops above the beach. Halfway was a small stone bridge that went across the track leading into the town centre, other than that, the track with overgrown walls on either side was a route with no escape. No sensible girl would go there in the middle of the night. Marie didn't care. She was quick and fit, experienced in self-defence courses. Twice she met a group of half drunk young men. Her body language expressed no fear and they barely noticed her. Almost at the end of the track was a sudden gap in the wall on one side. A high, iron fence painted bright cobalt blue, was erected on the edge of the cliffs. A couple of benches offered a perfect view over the bay and beaches.

Marie slowed as she approached the benches. There was a yellow bin next to them. A plastic bag was hanging out, gently rustling in a wisp of wind. She halted for a moment, gazing at the sea several meters below her. She let her eyes follow the coastline that stretched out towards the north, buildings with dark windows dissolving in the countryside beyond the outskirts of Newquay. From the corner of her eye she noticed a movement. A flash of light on a cliff top. The brakes of a car yelling in protest.

There is a knock on the door. Marie stops abruptly. I have difficulty pulling myself back to the present after being so absorbed by her. She has a way of leading the listener into her story as if it is pure reality.

'Sir?' Penrose pokes her head around the door.

I lift my hand before she can say anything else. 'Five minutes, please, Jennette.'

She frowns in a quiet protest. Her gaze attaches to Marie, who is smiling back innocently. Penrose is not the least amused.

'Sir.' The door closes but the atmosphere has changed. All of a sudden Marie seems annoyed with the interruption.

'Go on, please, Miss Yates.'

'You know the rest already.'

'You told my colleagues, but you didn't tell me.'

'OK.' She continues but this time the story is not that compelling anymore, more a summed up list of rather boring facts. 'From where I stood I could see the far end of the supermarket car park. A white van was parked there and I saw a man chucking some big package over the fence. Obviously the body was meant to be dumped over the cliff edge.'

'How did you know it was a body?'

'I didn't. Not then. I realised what it was when I read about it in the paper. It sort of made sense.'

I pick up my pen and scribble something down. From between her black mascara lashes, she looks down at my paper, annoyed that she can't read it. I can't either. The scribble means nothing.

'OK. What happened then?'

'Like I said, I thought he would dump it down the cliffs.'

'Why didn't he?'

'How do I know? He was too far away for mind-reading.'

I ignore her sarcasm. 'Was he disturbed by something?'

'Yes. Well. I heard a scream and I suppose he heard it too.'

I glance at her statement. 'He?'

'The man from the van.'

'One man?'

'Yes.'

'Are you sure it was a man?'

'Yes.' She grins wickedly. 'I know what a man looks like, inspector.'

'OK.' I am well aware of the mockery in her eyes. 'Did you see anyone else?'

'No. Anyway, as soon as he'd dumped the body over the fence he jumped in the van and drove off. That's all.'

I am silent for a while. 'Miss Yates, I have a little bit of a problem here. I have a witness who says there were two men.'

She purses her lips. 'I saw only one.'

'It was dark. Could you…?'

'I'm not making this up!'

I lean back in my chair and study her face. 'I know the place and I know it's quite dark there at night. How could you see what happened from that distance?'

'It wasn't really so dark. And there were the car park street lamps.'

I cast a glance at my pretend notes. 'When the van drove off it had no headlights on. Is that right?'

'He switched them on when he drove away.'

'Was he driving or the other man?'

'There was no other man!'

'Right.' I lean back, thoughtfully unscrewing my pen, studying its insides.

She looks at me with a mixture of suspicion and anger. 'Are you calling me a liar, inspector?'

'I'm trying to find out whether it's you or the other witness telling the truth.'

'Look, inspector, whoever your other witness is, he or she needs to see an optician. I tell you there was only *one* man. Why would I lie to you anyway?'

'Why would Mrs Taylor lie to me?' Incautiously, I let the name slip from my lips. In this case it doesn't matter so much, but in other circumstances it would be a major mistake. I fumble with the papers, annoyed with myself, and hope she hasn't noticed.

'We have CCTV images from the van leaving the car park.' It's a lie, but she doesn't know that. She may have noticed the cameras but she can't know that they are turned off one hour after the shop closes and turned on again half an hour before opening in the morning.

'Well then,' she says after a long pause. 'What do you need me for then? If you have pictures of the van, no doubt you'll have the license plate and a picture of the driver.'

'Unfortunately those pictures are not always clear.'

'OK.' She fumbles with her bag. 'Is that all? Can I go home now?'

'Not yet. Can you describe the man?'

'Tall, I think. And big, square.'

'Clothes?'

Contemplating this, I can see her eyelids flutter in a suppressed giggle. 'He wasn't naked.'

I take a deep breath. 'What sort of clothes was he wearing?'

'I don't know. Dark, I suppose, but whether they were black or dark brown or dark blue, I couldn't tell.'

'Hair?'

She needs some time to think about this. 'He wore like a dark woollen hat, which he took off when he got in the van. He had blond hair. Longish.'

'You didn't tell us that before.'

'Maybe I wasn't asked.'

I'm sure Penrose asked her to give a detailed description. She's thorough and not likely to forget an issue as important as that.

Marie's eyes narrow and she tilts her head. 'You fancy her?'

'Fancy who?'

'That policewoman.'

'She's a colleague.'

She hears in my voice that I'm serious. 'OK, I forgot about his hair, OK?'

'Anything else you may have forgotten?'

'No. Can I go now?'

'Not yet.' I press on, sensing that her impatience triggers her memory. 'What time did you leave the hotel?'

'It was just past three.' There is no doubt in her voice.

'And at what time did you see the man with the white van?'

'I guess it must have been ten or fifteen minutes later.'

'So you're saying it was about twenty, half past three?'

She avoids eye contact, steady fingers opening and closing one of the zippers on her bag. It seems for the purpose of an ornament only. 'I suppose.'

'My other witness says it was later.'

'I didn't look at my watch all the time.' We both look at her bare arms. She's only wearing a small silver ring. No watch.

'In fact she claims it was half an hour later.'

She's not impressed. 'Then you'd better believe your other witness.'

I don't know why I go on with this conversation, which feels more like a cat-and-mouse game. 'I'm just trying to paint a picture of what happened.'

'OK. I'm sorry.'

'Apology accepted.' I nod and proceed with my sly lies, which I think are allowed in matters like this. 'CCTV shows the van driving towards the car park at ten to four. It left in the same direction five minutes later.'

'So what?'

'So what? It means it took you a long time to walk that trail. Maybe that's why I doubt the credibility of your witness statement.'

She pins her eyes towards the ceiling. 'Okay, you've got me there, inspector.'

'Explain yourself.'

'It was cold and my hair was still wet from my bath in the hotel. I had some vodka in my bag. I sat on one of the benches and I suppose I must have fallen asleep.'

'Why didn't you tell us about that before?'

'I was afraid you wouldn't believe me. Maybe I was a bit drunk, right? Can you trust a witness who is drunk?'

'I'm just gathering evidence, miss Yates.'

'Can I go now?'

'Yes.' I'm tired suddenly. I feel like I want to lay my head on the table and sleep.

She is surprised. 'You mean, I can go? Really? No more questions?'

'You can go, but I may need you later. Please let us know your contact details when you go travelling.'

Graciously she lifts her body from the chair, pulling her clothes as though they need adjusting. I follow, carefully placing the papers in the folder. As she moves towards the door, she manages somehow to brush her breast along my arm. A sudden, unexpected heat rushes through my veins. I feel myself blushing of which she becomes aware instantly. She laughs softly, triumphantly. 'Well, well, well, inspector!'

I bite my teeth and quickly step back to create some distance between us. 'Thanks for your help, miss Yates.'

'Marie.' She closes the zipper of her jacket up to her chin, as if trying to tell me something.

'Can I call you if I remember something else, inspector?'

'I'm sure my colleague gave you the number of the police station.'

'I mean you. Can I call you?'

'You can call the station.'

She smiles. 'I'll ask for you then.' She is challenging me as if there is a different conversation being spoken simultaneously.

I hesitate. 'One more question.'

'Yes?'

'Off the record.'

'Yes?'

I don't understand myself, but there is an urge in me, which I cannot ignore. 'Did you use a condom?'

If she's surprised, she doesn't show. 'Yes inspector, I'm not a fool. Of course I did.' She pauses and the expression on her face changes into an impenetrable mask. 'I don't like a man's… filth in me.' The outburst is sudden, short and bitingly sharp.

'Sorry, Marie, I didn't mean…'

'See you soon, inspector.' As she quickly turns on her heels, I see a glimpse of light in her eyes which tells me that she has noticed I called her with her first name.

12

APRIL

The meeting with Marie Yates has definitely distracted me, but it didn't help to calm my nerves. I feel restless and uneasy, my visit to Newquay Tolcarne Surgery still very vivid in my mind. Although Doctor Warren refused to speculate about my complaints and worries, I haven't imagined concern and caution in his eyes when we said goodbye. Perhaps pity too. I should have asked him when to expect the results of a blood test for blood counts which was carried out by a nurse immediately afterwards.

I find Jennette Penrose at her desk staring at a blank computer screen. Shaking her head as though waking up from hibernation, she delivers what she probably considers good news, 'forensics have finished with the house in Trispen.'

'Have they found anything?'

'Well, obviously everything still needs to be examined and with the Bank Holiday ahead…,' she frowns meaningfully but when she sees my face, she adds, 'but it seems pretty clear that Jane Croft was not murdered in her own home.'

'Oh.' It is a disappointment and a relief at the same time. Relief because I always find it a horrifying thought when someone is murdered in the supposed safety of his or her own home. Disappointment because knowing the scene of crime and being able to examine it millimetre by millimetre to consequently finding hard evidence gives the investigation an important head start. *'Wherever he steps, whatever he touches, whatever he leaves, even unconsciously, will serve as a silent witness against him,'* said Edmond Locard a hundred years ago. With his exchange principle he became the father of forensic science, which has developed so much further since he spoke his wise words.

'The Westons will be back today from their trip,' Penrose adds as an afterthought, referring to Jane Croft's next door neighbours. 'I'm planning to go and see them.'

The thought of being trapped in the building full of moments and opportunities to let my mind wander in the wrong direction is enough to make me find any excuse to get out. 'I'll come with you. I'd like to have a word with Mr Pengally too.'

For some reason mentioning Pengally's name triggers agitation. 'I've already interviewed him, sir. Why do you want to speak to Pengally too?' she snaps angrily, but before I can reply, her phone rings and she listens with concentration, scribbling down notes on a blank sheet of paper.

'Cheers, Sam. I owe you one.' She finishes the conversation with a deep frown, but she won't share her information with me. I know her moods and I know how she works. If it was important, she would overcome her irritation and tell me. Now it'll have to wait. I trust her opinion that it can.

Running a hand through her greasy hair she offers a vague smile that only half hides her obstinate feelings. 'Right. Off we go then, sir?'

Fifteen minutes later we leave Newquay behind us. The roads are already getting busier with tourists, expensive 4x4s and cars with surfboards on top. Penrose is tense, muttering under her breath, using obscene words addressed to arrogant drivers acting like they own the world they've just invaded. Otherwise we drive in silence. Somehow the atmosphere has changed. There is a tension, an antipathy in the air, which I have never noticed before. We've never been particularly best friends in that way, but we always get on well. Now it feels as though she is working against me rather than by my side. It must be something I said, or did. Or didn't. I am too worried about my own physical situation to enquire into what is bothering her.

Trispen is a small village situated on the A30 between Truro and Newquay. Its centre is small and old, spreading out to a much larger, more recent, suburban area. There are streets with sad looking council houses on either side as well as more spacious plots along the edges with semi-detached dormer bungalows and whitewashed houses that overlook hills with yellow fields of rapeseed. Further away I notice a hillside with blackthorn bushes, its small white flowers giving it a frosty look. It brings back a forgotten memory. I remember following my mother with a red bucket in my hand, bending, picking the blackthorn berries, dropping them in my bucket at a tenth of my mother's speed. My attention was easily drawn from my tasks as there were birds and butterflies everywhere, beetles and caterpillars crawling on the floor. A deep blue sky was above us, the sun warm on our unprotected faces. The berries would be used later to make sloe gin for my father. With a pang of guilt and regret I realise that I don't even know if my mother still makes it. Perhaps I should accept the on-going invitation to have a roast dinner with them this Sunday.

'Here it is, sir.' Jennette Penrose holds up a small bunch of papers pointing with them. 'Fifteen is... was Jane Croft's house.

I park in front of a semi-detached house with two floors and a pointed roof that is most probably an attic filled with half-forgotten stuff. One side has *Sunnyside* written in cheerful handwriting across the whitewashed wall. Flowerpots with early pansies sit on the doorstep, yellow primroses are lined along the path leading to a front door with frosted glass panels. For a moment, I stare at the yellow and black police tape rustling in the gentle breeze. It makes me feel sad that Jane Croft will never set foot again in her beloved home.

Penrose sums up, 'The Westons live next door, on 16. Gary and Gail. They use only the ground floor. Arthur Pengally rents their top flat.'

I nod. 'We'll speak with them later. First I'd like a look in Jane's home.'

'Forensics are already done here.' Clearly she thinks that it'll be a waste of time.

'All the same.'

As we get out of the car, she purses her lips, agitated. Just as I try to find words to relieve some of the friction between us, my phone starts ringing. A cheerful ringtone quietens the small birds rustling in the hedges, and fills the quietness of the afternoon in a rather inappropriate way. I downloaded the tune in a fit of madness, and have since then failed to delete and change it for one less outrageous. Snatching it from my pocket with the intention to switch it off, I look at the display. No name, just a number, which I recognise with a jolt of panic.

'Mr Tregunna?'

'Speaking.'

'This is Newquay Tolcarne Surgery.'

For a moment the world has come to a sudden halt. Penrose is already ducking under the tape, her figure obscured in a mist. An ice-cold chill touches my spine.

'You saw Dr Warren today, Mr Tregunna?'

'That's right.'

'He has the result of the blood count and he would like to discuss that with you.'

'I see.' I say, but I don't. Normally results of blood tests take days, don't they?

I look at Penrose, who is tapping a toe on the edge of the slate doorstep, impatience drooping from her hunched shoulders.

The surgery's receptionist is not finished. 'Dr Warren asks if you can come in at ten past five?'

'Today?' I feel stunned. Shocked. Numbed. This can only mean bad news. Very bad news. Never before have I been called by the surgery for an appointment; it has always been the other way round.

'Yes. Would that be okay, Mr Tregunna?'

I try to joke. 'Is it that urgent?'

Her hesitation is a tell-tale sign that it is, yet her reply is firm and neutral. 'I don't know, Mr Tregunna. This is what Dr Warren has asked me to do.' There is an edge of cautiousness in her voice. Obviously she can't afford to tell me anything that goes beyond the now so strict rules of privacy.

'I see.' I stare at Penrose as if I am unsure whether I am in the real world or stuck in a nightmare. 'Yes. OK.'

A car drives by, slowing, passengers looking in my direction, gaping at the house of a murdered woman with a mixture of horror and excitement.

'We will see you at ten past five then, Mr Tregunna.'

'Yes. Thank you.' I slip my phone back in my pocket with numb fingers.

'Something wrong?' Penrose has come back to me a few paces, scrutinising my face as if sensing something is amiss.

'It was my GP.' I can feel droplets of sweat around my hairline. 'I'll have to see him again. Today. Urgently.'

'Oh.' I hadn't told her about the earlier appointment but it doesn't seem as though it comes as a surprise. I sometimes think that police stations are the worst for private secrets. Perhaps failing to involve her in some way caused her frustration, which is now a mixture of disbelief and concern.

'What's wrong, sir? If you don't mind me asking?'

'It's nothing,' I say, briskly cutting her off. Suddenly I can't bear the thought of going into Jane Croft's home and rummage through her stuff while her body is still in the mortuary. 'Shall we go? It looks like the Westons are home. Best to see them before we visit Mr Pengally.'

'Yes, but… Andy…' She rarely uses my first name. 'You're not ill are you?'

I try a wide grin, but fail. 'I hope not.'

13

MAY

I float comfortably on a warm cloud that keeps the nasty real world far away from me. I doze, wake, sleep, I deny being awake.

A bright and happy laugh from a child makes me open my eyes. There is a chair next to my bed. Empty. The black nurse with the large golden earrings has left. Amongst her daily duties she found a couple of minutes to sit with me, listen to my worries, trying to ease my depressive thoughts. Filling me with optimism instead. It only works for as long as she stays.

Squeezing my eyes shut, I try to imagine that Lauren is with me, having replaced the nurse, sitting quietly at my bedside. It is nice to create an imaginary world in which everything is rosy and happy. No lurking tumours growing quietly and unnoticed deep inside the body, no shadows on the horizon of my future. Instead, there is Lauren Gardiner with her red hair and pale blue eyes, and freckles that make her vulnerable and all the more desirable.

I hear a distant regular bleeping. It sounds like someone is playing a computer game with little figures jumping up and down with every press of a button, avoiding traps and enemies lurking behind bricks. In the other bed Roy Wood is breathing loudly, on the edge of snoring. His endless pleas to be allowed to go to the toilet have stopped as he realises that he has come through the operation. I'm not the only one in here whose lifestyle has changed forever.

The sky is a pale grey, light enough for a promise of some sunshine later, but for the moment it seems to be raining. I can vaguely remember a thunderstorm rumbling across the hospital grounds throughout the night. Veins of lightning threaded the sky and the windows shuddered with each thunderclap and gust of heavy rain. Simultaneously, the temperature has dropped at least ten degrees. The window overlooks the road that links the several hospital buildings. Two nurses in cardigans over blue uniforms hurry towards the bus stop, struggling to control an umbrella that the wind snaps inside out with every gusty blow. On the other side of the road is a man in a long light mackintosh. As a car steers through a puddle at the kerbside, dirty water sprays up, targeting his shoes and trousers. He halts, lifting an arm and gives an angry, obscene gesture with his hand.

'Are you feeling better today, Mr Tregunna?'

I haven't heard her approaching, the soles of her shoes make no sound on the lino. It's a tall and skinny woman in her late forties with brown hair and a pointy chin. She pushes forward a trolley, on which are mugs with tea and coffee. 'Cup of tea? Breakfast?' Her cheerfulness is almost offending. I don't want to think of anything that comes near food.

'Yes please.' It comes from Mr Wood's bed. He is not allowed any food. There's a tube in his nose through which he is being fed with a pale creamy substance. Yet he seizes every opportunity to try and get someone to bring him something to eat. A big burger and fat fries being his absolute preference.

'Are you Mr Tregunna?' The woman replies flippantly.

'No, but he doesn't want anything anyway. I can have his portion, otherwise we're wasting taxpayers money, aren't we?'

'I wouldn't worry about that now, Mr Wood.'

His words, implying that I will deny the offered meal, have an opposite effect on me. Oddly, I suddenly feel hungry. 'I'll have a cup of tea, please.'

The woman nods encouragingly. 'And some toast, perhaps?'

'I don't know.' I hesitate, trying to find words to explain that I'm not sure whether my body is working in the same way as it did before the operation, but even here I find it difficult to talk about it.

'You'll have to eat, Mr Tregunna. You don't want to faint, when you get out of bed.'

'Get out of bed?' I wonder briefly if I have been sleeping for days. Was it only yesterday that I lay on the table in the theatre, glancing at the masked faces of the surgeon and assistants before I was knocked out by the anaesthetist?

Tucking a strand of hair behind her ear, she cocks her face to one side and looks at me with a mixture of apprehension and expectancy. 'We'll try to get you into a chair for a while, then maybe you can get yourself to the bathroom later today.' She pours milky tea from a metal flask and adds cheerfully, 'After last night's thunder and lightning, it will be a beautiful day.'

As if on cue the sun breaks through from behind a thick bank of clouds, casting highlights on the shiny lino floor that hurt my eyes.

'You see?' She gestures with her head and places a mug on my bedside table alongside a plate with a buttered slice of granary toast.

'Thank you.' I try to read her name from her nametag, but it makes me uncomfortable, as if I'm getting caught staring at her almost absent bosom.

As she adjusts my pillows behind my back, a shadow emerges from behind her.

An Asian man halts next to my bed, thrusting his hands deep into the pockets of his corduroy trousers, as though he's visiting some acquaintance and doesn't know whether to shake their hand or not. His black hair is combed back from his forehead in straight lines and kept there with hair gel that smells like an antiseptic.

'How are you, Mr Tregunna?'

Doctor Masood Rakesh. My heart is suddenly racing with a mixture of anger and frustration. If I was still attached to a machine measuring my blood pressure, it would be in the highest state of alert right now. I want him to go, it is as simple as that. I will never forgive him for the rudeness with which he so bluntly approached me on the day I had the first examination in the hospital.

'I am very well, thank you.'

Clearly he decides to ignore my irony. 'Better today than yesterday?'

I don't answer. For support, I glance at the woman with the tea trolley. She envelops both Rakesh and me in her wide smile, which now feels more like an offence.

'I understand you suffered gas pain.' His tone of voice means to give friendly understanding, as if he knows exactly how I feel. He doesn't even come near.

'It was better once I was given morphine.'

He nods. Behind his dark rimmed glasses his eyes drift off towards the window, following a young blonde woman with more attention than he can manage to pay me. He's not really interested in me. He has probably heard it all before.

'We've taken out the tumour,' he says bluntly. 'Doctor Cole will tell you the details as soon as the report comes in from the lab.'

'Thank you.'

He runs his hand through his hair, checking the gel still keeps it in place. 'Mr Cole is away for a couple of days... if there is anything you'd like to ask, then you can ask me.'

Ask him? Never. 'Thank you.' Hiding my hands under the blanket, I clench them into fists. I can suddenly understand why someone could kill someone in cold blood. No matter the witnesses, I feel like killing him with my bare hands.

I become aware that Rakesh has not finished. He is telling me about the possibilities of chemotherapy. Chances of survival, relapse. I'll have to bear that in mind. Even when an operation seems to be successful, it doesn't always mean that the whole tumour is removed. He is brusque, blunt. He doesn't seem to care about the effect his words have on me.

'Thank you,' I say, interrupting him in an equally disrespectful manner.

'All right.' With a slow smile on his lips and melancholy in his dark eyes, I can feel he pities me. He is already expecting me to die within the next year.

'Don't hesitate to contact me if there's anything I can do for you, Mr Tregunna. I'm always happy to help.' I'm sure he doesn't believe a word of it himself.

He disappears, leaving me frustrated and undoubtedly still with raised blood pressure. I turn my face to the window, wanting to forget the reason why I'm in hospital. I want to wipe Rakesh's words from memory. I need to find something to distract me and sadly, the only thing I can think of is my job: the murder of Jane Croft.

Penrose is still working on the case. If I can get hold of the latest statements and reports of the investigation, if I can look at the case from a different angle, from the point of view of the murderer, maybe I can find out something.

Without thinking it through properly, I reach for the bell.

'Do you need assistance, Mr Tregunna?' It's a different nurse. She is young, blonde and with long skinny legs. Brenda. Her name doesn't match her appearance. Her frown is deep, her lips, with a trace of lipstick, are tightly pursed.

'No. I just wonder… where my clothes are.'

'In the cupboard.' She gestures with her head, annoyed. She has better things to do than tell me the obvious. 'The one in the corner is yours.'

'And my mobile phone?'

She frowns even deeper, flashing me a look of pity. Have I not understood that I am in a hospital, that no mobile phones are allowed? Then, from somewhere, she finds a twitch of a smile. 'You will need a pay card for the phone in the hall, Mr Tregunna. If you haven't got one, I can get it for you.'

'I see.' I gaze at two small cupboard doors in the corner of the room. Next to it is a small kitchen unit that holds towels, disposable paper mattresses and carton bowls for vomiting patients. I realise I'll have to get up myself and take my mobile phone from one of the zipped pockets of my bag.

Perhaps the earlier suggestion to get out of bed is not that bad an idea. The sooner I talk to Penrose the better. I want to know how the investigation is going. Consequently, I'd like to know, and fear at the same time, if my successor has found the murderer already and closed the case. For the sake of my self-respect, I hope he hasn't achieved in a couple of days what I couldn't in a few weeks.

14

APRIL

Both in their early sixties, Gary and Gail Weston have lived in Trispen all their married life. At first, they had an old cottage in the heart of the village with low ceilings and moulded walls that caused so many breathing problems with their eldest son that they had no option but to move to a newer house. When their two sons flew out twenty years ago, they converted the first floor into a little flat to rent out to holidaymakers in the summer. Now the flat is let on a more permanent basis, with less hassle and a more regular income. According to Penrose's notes, Arthur Pengally came to live with them about two years ago.

Gail Weston has seen us coming, half hidden by net curtains, making it no secret that she is curious. Yet it takes a while before she opens the door, and she almost manages to be convincingly surprised.

Her hair is dark brown streaked with grey. She has a rather pale face with bright red blushes on her cheeks as if someone put a round stamp on them. She is wearing black trousers and a white blouse under a green cardigan. Glasses dangle on her chest by a red string.

'Police?' Her voice is a whisper of excitement.

'DC Penrose and DI Tregunna.' Penrose produces her warrant card. Putting the glasses on a nose too big and hawk-like to make her a beautiful woman, her watery green eyes glance over the rim like a mole in bright daylight. She takes her time to check Penrose's identity, but she doesn't bother to see mine.

'Is this about poor Jane?' Her voice trembles as if on the brink of crying.

'We are investigating the death of Mrs Jane Croft, Mrs Weston,' replies Penrose in a formal tone. 'Your next door neighbour, as we understand. We would like to ask you a couple of questions.'

Gail Weston hasn't moved an inch. Her hand is clutching the collar of her white blouse as if it is a cold winter day and her body language makes it clear that she wants to shut the door in front of us.

'Mrs Weston, do you mind if we come in?'

She hesitates, as if debating whether police officers are to be trusted. Perhaps it would have been a different matter if we'd been wearing uniforms.

'We know nothing about it,' she says finally, her eyes two watery pools of misery.

Noticing Penrose stirring impatiently, on the brink of using her authority, I produce a reassuring smile. 'Your rhododendron has a most beautiful colour,' I say, trying not to wince as Penrose stares at me. 'This is just a routine visit, Mrs Weston.'

'But we weren't at home!' She folds her arms tightly across her chest. But with mentioning the dark red rhododendron in the garden, I have touched a soft spot.

'When exactly do you mean, Mrs Weston?' I ask, my voice gentler in response to her obvious distress.

Her blush stretches out, disappearing under her collar. Nervously she rubs the side of her nose with the knuckle of her thumb.

'Well, all the time, I guess.' She's still unsure, unmoving. 'When it… happened.'

I've come across people like her before. Innocent people, having nothing to hide, yet in the sudden presence of police, they start acting as if they seriously believe they've committed a crime.

'It's just to eliminate you from our investigation, Mrs Weston.'

'Like I said, we know nothing about it. We've just come back home.'

'In that case… ' I stop, and let the silence speak for me.

'Actually, we would like to speak to Mr Pengally.' As if we have rehearsed our roles, Penrose picks up my thread at exactly the right moment.

'Oh! I see! Well, Mr Pengally is not at home. He left about an hour ago.' Smiling with relief, she believes our focus has been safely directed to her tenant. She relaxes, her brain working rapidly, realising that she can turn our visit into an opportunity to learn more about the death of her neighbour. 'Well, perhaps I can help you while you wait until Arthur comes back? He won't be long now, I think.'

'We hope so.'

'Well then.' Excitement crosses her face as she steps back to open the door wider and let us in. 'Perhaps I can make you a cuppa?'

'That would be lovely, Mrs Weston.'

'I always think things are much easier with a cuppa.' Now that she has made up her mind, she's more than willing to please us. She gestures us into a small living room cramped with furniture in a supposedly modern style. Cream faux leather and chrome legs. It has neither warmth nor identity. 'Sit down, please, officers. My husband has gone out to collect his paper, but he'll be back shortly.'

Penrose walks to the window, pulling aside a slip of the net curtains as if expecting Mr Pengally and Mr Weston to be hiding behind the bushes.

Mrs Weston whisks a big ginger cat away from the headrest and I sit on the end of a sofa that looks comfortable, but is not. My bottom is aching again and I can't help thinking about my second appointment with Doctor Warren.

'Tea won't be long!' she sings, before hurrying to the kitchen, leaving us to study a series of photographs in different frames, different sizes, different ages. There's a long row of children and grandchildren, covering years at school, graduation and marriage. It seems impossible to make out whether she only has one child or many more. Meanwhile we hear her busying herself with a kettle, teapot, cups and saucers. Slightly amused, I think of how she reminds me of my late grandmother. At the same time I can't help wondering whether Penrose was right after all and that the Westons aren't worth our visit. Gail would have told us instantly if she knew anything that could shine a light on the mystery of Jane Croft's death. It would have been better maybe to send Ollie Reed. He would have been loved and cherished by Gail Weston.

'I guess you won't say no to a homemade bake, officers?'

She is back with a green plate of freshly baked cookies, each topped with a cherry, which she places on the coffee table along with a pile of matching smaller plates. I am beginning to understand why Ollie Reed is so keen on door-to-door enquiries, which is maybe a little unfair to him. He clearly gets results from these home visits.

'Did you know Mrs Croft well, Mrs Weston?'

'Of course I did! We've both lived here for years.'

She moves the cookies in our direction. The smell is mouth-watering. I haven't had breakfast this morning, having been too nervous for my visit to the surgery. All of a sudden my eyes are glued to the cherries. My stomach rumbles like the foreboding of an eruption.

'Did you know her husband and daughter?' The question is merely a wild guess, spoken without thinking first.

I can hear the kettle boil in the kitchen. Gail Weston hesitates in the doorway. She frowns at Penrose who is still standing at the window. 'Not her husband, no. In fact, to tell you the truth, I never knew she even had a husband.'

'She had a daughter, so it's likely she had a husband too,' Penrose chips in.

'Well, yes, but I mean, really, at first I thought he was dead.'

'Did she tell you that?'

'Well, no, I just assumed. I guess it was because of the way she talked about him.'

Fumbling with her hands, she seems uncertain suddenly. 'How do you take your tea, officers?'

'One sugar, please, Mrs Weston.'

'And three for me, please.'

She rushes to the kettle. I try to find a more comfortable position and Penrose peers out of the window as if she is expecting visitors. It is quiet. Nothing else moves but a magnified lone goldfish in its glass bowl on the windowsill. It reminds me of a TV show long ago and for a moment I have to suppress a childish giggle. The presenter had replaced the fish with a piece of carrot cut in the shape of a goldfish, took it out and ate it in front of his terrified audience, all the while talking cheerfully to his guest. Whether his guest was involved in the plan or not, he remained as stone-faced as the presenter, while the audience was stunned to silence.

Gail Weston is back carrying a tray with green mugs. She hobbles across to the chair facing the door and settles herself down, squishing her shoulders against the back until she is comfortable. She appears more relaxed when Penrose finally chooses a seat.

'You had a holiday, Mrs Weston?' I say casually.

'That's right, inspector. Mr Weston and me went up to Bournemouth. His sister lives there. Her seventieth birthday.' She smiles as though reliving the party. 'We were invited to stay in the hotel. All paid for by my sister-in-law's children. It was lovely.'

'When exactly was that?'

A sad expression crosses over her face. 'I've been thinking about that, inspector. I mean, really, perhaps poor Jane would still be alive if we hadn't been out?'

'That isn't likely, Mrs Weston.'

'Yeah, well, that's what Mr Weston tells me, but all the same... Anyway, we arrived in Bournemouth on Friday. The party was on Saturday, but we didn't want to do it in a hurry. My husband doesn't like driving so far and as I have no licence... Anyway, it was a lovely party and we spent a quiet Sunday with Mr Weston's other sisters and brothers, two of each, and we left on Monday morning, just after rush hour.'

'So you came back home on Monday? Late afternoon?'

'No. We went to see my sister as well, in Torquay. We thought, as we were almost passing, and Mr Weston not keen on driving for so long, I mean, it wasn't very busy on the roads, being Monday and all that, but we thought we'd stay the night in Torquay. My sister insisted that we stay another night so that we could see her daughter's family as well, so we came home at about midday today.'

'How did you find out that Mrs Croft had died?'

'Her daughter came to see us. In fact, she left about an hour ago, before you arrived.' She pauses, turning her wedding ring round her finger. 'She was with her... partner. I invited her in, but she wouldn't. Like I said, she was with her partner and as Jane would never accept her... anyway, poor Stella was shocked to find that she couldn't even enter her mother's house. There were still people all over the place and there was a policeman on the doorstep to keep everyone away.

'That's right.'

'Stella was quite upset about it, to be honest. She hadn't realised she wasn't allowed in, you see, with her being the daughter and all that.'

Trying to recall my conversation with Stella Croft, I fail to remember whether I warned her that her mother's house had yet to be examined. Making a mental note to call her and apologise, I change the subject.

'Mr Pengally... '

'What about him?' She interrupts quickly, as though I have asked her to betray her tenant and enlighten us with his secrets.

'As you and your husband were out, I hope that Mr

Pengally can shine a light on Mrs Croft's last whereabouts,' I say slowly.

She rolls her eyes. 'I bet he can!'

I straighten my back with the indication that things are getting more interesting. 'What do you mean, Mrs Weston?'

'Well,' she says, slightly embarrassed. 'He had a crush on her, had Arthur.'

'A crush?'

'Yes, you know, he wanted to date her and all that, but she wasn't really interested.' She pauses. 'Well, she didn't tell me as much, nor did he. But he asked her out once, that much I know. He took her to a quiz night in the pub.' She chuckles. 'I mean, what gentleman would do that on a first date?'

'Perhaps he thought she was bright enough?'

'Oh, I don't doubt that! In fact I seem to remember they actually won that night - a bottle of red wine. She let him have it, but he gave it to Mr Weston. Very kind of him.' She frowns. 'He's an AA, you see, is Arthur.'

'I see.' I can't remember anything about a drinking problem in Penrose's notes and I make a mental note to follow this up. From the corner of my eyes I notice Penrose has also picked up on this, annoyed with herself, presumably.

Gail Weston raises her brows. 'Anyway, there was no meeting after that.' The intonation doesn't invite further questions, but I press on.

'Do you know why not?'

'Well, no, I don't know for sure, but I presume she refused. He was rather disappointed, he said, because he liked her a lot. And she seemed well educated. For further pub quizzes, I guess.'

'Hmm. Was there another man in her life?'

'You mean lovers, like?'

'Or a good friend?'

She shakes her head vigorously. 'No lovers. I'm sure of that. I mean, I've never noticed a man staying the night with her.'

'Any other friends, regular visitors?' Penrose points at the window. 'You can see her drive and front door from here. You might have noticed something.'

Mrs Weston purses her lips. 'I wasn't spying on her!'

'I'm sure you didn't, Mrs Weston,' I say soothingly, 'but maybe you saw something coincidentally?'

'Coincidentally? Well, yes, maybe I did.' She seems to make up her mind. 'Like last week, there was an old lady visiting her. Skinny, she was, tiny.'

'But you don't know her?'

'Never seen her before. But she came in a couple of times that week. First time was last Monday, I think, and I saw her again on Wednesday. But of course, since we went to Bournemouth on Friday morning…' She smiles sadly.' 'Other than that, I can't help you, officers. I'm sorry.'

'When did you last see Mrs Croft, Mrs Weston?'

'That must have been last Thursday.' She looks up to the ceiling as if finding inspiration in the cracks of the plasterwork. 'It must have been before twelve. I had an appointment at the doctors, you see. She came out and we said hello, but that was all. Well, to be honest, I was afraid I'd be late for my appointment, so I was in a bit of a hurry. They're a little bit fussy about that at the doctors.' She frowns. 'No excuses whatsoever when the doctor is running late, but when us patients aren't there in time, our appointment might be cancelled. I don't think that's fair, do you?'

'Hmm. Did Mrs Croft say anything else? Like did she have plans to go out? To meet someone?'

'Well, yes, of course. She was seeing Stella that evening. Like on most Thursdays. I think she said something about going out together. I can't remember. Something to do with music, I believe.'

'Was there anything about Mrs Croft that struck you as odd?'

'Well, no, I don't think so.' She hesitates and I see a shadow of a doubt crossing her face as she remembers something else.

'Now I come to think about it, inspector, perhaps there was something. Maybe she was dressed like she was going out, but when I saw her, she was carrying a bin bag to her bin. But she looked rather smart. Well, she usually does but that day… it was different. I remember wondering why she was dressed like that just to be doing work in the kitchen, emptying her bin, and all that.'

'What exactly was it that she was wearing?'

'A grey skirt and a white blouse. Her pearl earrings. Tights and black shoes.' She pauses, thoughtfully. 'As I said, she looked very smart.'

'Did you say something, maybe mention her clothes?' I ask.

Her eyes widen in surprise. 'How do you know that? I forgot all about it!' She is silent for a moment. 'I asked her if she was going out. Not for any particular reason, inspector. I hope you don't think of me as nosy.'

'Curiosity is one of people's natural virtues.'

She looks at me uncertainly for a few seconds. 'I suppose. Anyway, she said she was meeting one of her former foster children. She'd never told me anything about that! Having had foster children, I mean.'

This is news to me, but I try not to show it. 'Did she mention a name?'

Penrose is suddenly alert too, leaning forward like a dog straining at a leash. She fumbles with her notebook, scribbling down the details, aware that this may be useful information after all.

'Oh, no, nothing like that, I'm sorry, inspector. As I said, I was in a hurry and I thought I would catch up on that with her later.'

'Did she say anything else?'

'Well, I kind of said that it was amazing that we didn't know, about the foster children I mean. I'm sure Mr Pengally didn't know either, and she said something like they'd had a few, foster children, I presume she meant.' She looks guilty, as though she feels she's been caught lying. 'I'm very sorry, inspector. I can't imagine I forgot about that!'

'Not to worry, Mrs Weston.' I try to sound casual, but inwardly I'm feeling hopeful. This is an unexpected development. Penrose feels the same. Her pen has stopped for a moment.

'I couldn't believe it, inspector, about her having had foster children. I mean, I don't think she'd ever been visited by one.' She blushes as she speaks, and adds quickly, 'Not that I am a nosy person, inspector.'

I suppress a smile. 'Of course not.'

In my peripheral vision, I catch a glimpse of a car parking behind mine. Mrs Weston follows my gaze, the relief on her face is almost physical. 'That'll be Arthur's car.'

15

APRIL

Arthur Pengally is in his mid fifties, but he looks at least ten years older. Short and bulky, he has a broad flat face. The corners of his mouth droop along with his fleshy cheeks, which gives him a grumpy expression that is enhanced by thick brows that overshadow his eyes.

He doesn't seem happy with our visit at all. Patting his greying hair as though checking the dimensions of his balding skull, he looks at Penrose with a mixture of disgust and accusation. Clearly he wasn't impressed when she spoke to him earlier.

'Haven't I told you enough?' he says grumpily, lifting a shopping bag from the boot of his car.

'We're working hard to find Mrs Croft's killer.'

'All right.' His expression doesn't change, but he points towards the house. 'You'd better come forward. I'd rather not have this conversation on the street.'

His flat is tidy, everything in its place. It has one bedroom and a living room, which is simply furbished with two different armchairs, a small TV on a set of drawers, a dozen framed watercolours scattered on the walls. The ceiling light has captured dead flies in the bowl of pink frosted glass and there's a faint smell of dirty socks.

Ignoring Penrose totally, he gestures towards a small round table, aluminium legs with a red Formica top, and four matching chairs. 'Take a seat, please, inspector. Can I offer you something?'

Penrose lowers herself onto one of the chairs, taking out her notebook. I prefer to remain standing.

'We've just had a cup of tea with Mrs Weston, but thank you.'

'I see.' He inclines his head with a hint of cynicism in his eyes.

'I'm aware that we have spoken with you already, Mr Pengally, but some more questions have come up.'

Pulling a cigarette from a crumpled packet, he studies it as though negotiating whether he's already passed his daily dose of nicotine. 'Doesn't matter. We're all in this together, inspector. All we want is Jane's killer behind bars for the rest of his life.'

'Exactly.'

Penrose has been quiet and standoffish since we met Mr Pengally outside the house. Now his words coax a harsh light in her eyes. Even if I hadn't read between the lines of her statement of Mr Pengally, I would understand immediately that for some reason she despises him. From the way he ignores her presence, I gather Arthur Pengally feels likewise.

Fiddling with his cigarette between his fingertips, he perches on the edge of a chair, which looks as though it can barely carry his weight.

'What would you like to know, inspector?' His voice has the rasp of an inveterate smoker. As if to underline my assumption, he retrieves a disposable lighter from a kitchen drawer and lights his cigarette in cupped hands.

'Mrs Weston tells me you're AA.'

My tactless words throw him off balance. His eyes flicker nervously and his mouth twists. 'Right. In my humble opinion, finding the killer of poor Jane is more important than my reputation.' He hesitates, scanning the room for inspiration, and blows out a cloud of smoke. 'I hope you'll understand that I'm certainly not a weirdo or a stalker, inspector.'

'A stalker?'

'You know, someone who keeps following someone...'

'I know what a stalker is, Mr Pengally, but what makes you say that?'

His broad face flushes with embarrassment. I can see regret in his eyes and the wish that he hasn't said anything beyond answering my questions.

He looks at Penrose suspiciously as though debating to refuse to say anything in her presence. 'Whatever people may say, I am definitely not a stalker!'

'OK.' This road is leading nowhere. 'How well did you know Jane Croft, Mr Pengally?.'

His mouth twists in a wry smile. 'Not as well as I wished, I have to admit.' He lowers his eyes to a point between his feet on the floor. 'We had been out once or twice, but that was as far as it went. One time we went to a quiz night in the local pub. I was pleased that we ended second. She insisted I took the prize as I was the one who took her there in the first place.'

'What was the prize?'

'A bottle of red wine. The quiz night is just for fun, inspector, nothing of a competition in it. First prize is normally a hamper from the local farm shop and the second prize a bottle of some sort donated by the pub itself.'

'I understand you don't drink anymore?'

'That's right, sir.'

'Yet you accepted the wine?'

'What else could I do? It was the first time Jane and me went out. I didn't want to spoil things by telling her I'm an AA. People can be funny about it, you know?' He pauses. 'Anyway, Mr Weston was pleased with the wine.'

I smile. 'How long ago was that?'

'About six months ago. I asked her out for dinner once and as far as I was concerned, we had a pleasant evening, but after that she refused my invitations.'

'Did she explain herself?'

'She said she didn't want to encourage me because she

wasn't allowing herself to get involved in a relationship. Nothing personal, she said, she just didn't want trouble.'

'Trouble?'

He raises his eyebrows. 'Her former husband seemed to have been a bit of a nuisance.'

'In what way?' I ask neutrally.

'She didn't say. She didn't want to talk about him because he was history, those were her words.'

'Meaning he was dead?'

'No, I don't think so. Meaning that he wasn't part of her life anymore.'

'OK. Did she talk about her daughter?'

'Not a lot. She wasn't very happy with her daughter's choice of partner.'

'Do you know why?'

'She kept quiet about that too. I never saw him when her daughter visited her mother, though. I presume he was a real disappointment to her.'

'He?'

'Her daughter's partner.'

I look at Penrose, to prevent her from announcing that Stella Croft has a female partner. Apparently, Jane really kept very quiet about that. 'OK. When did you last see Mrs Croft?'

'You mean see as in notice, or see as in talk?'

'Both.'

'I last talked to her about ten days ago. We met briefly in the library, I offered to wait for her and carry her books, but she said she was meeting a friend somewhere. Which was not true, because she came home about twenty minutes after me.' His eyes move slightly to focus on something behind me. 'I was disappointed, but I accepted her reasons.'

'Did she mention anything else about seeing someone?'

'You mean other than her little lie that she was about to meet someone? I don't know. The way she talked about it, I gathered it was a man, but I truly believed her when she said she didn't want a relationship. Not with anyone.'

'You didn't see any of her visitors?'

'I'm no stalker, inspector!'

I pause. I can sense his anger, which must be based deeper than I presumed. 'Is that how Mrs Croft thought about you?'

'Not Jane, not her, inspector, but that damned woman from below here.'

I wander to the window to check his view. It overlooks the road and a part of Jane Croft's drive. Fuchsia bushes are lined up between the bungalows. A few sparrows sit on branches that gently rock in the breeze.

'Did you notice if Mrs Croft had any visitors lately?'

He nods. 'Well, only an older woman. I mean old. Like in her eighties. Visited her a couple of times last week. Before you ask, inspector, no I don't know the woman, nor do I know her name.'

'Why are you so angry, Mr Pengally?'

He glances at Penrose with a world of accusation in his eyes. 'Because mistakes from the past never leave you, inspector. They always come up one day, whether they're relevant or not.'

'Anything you'd like to tell us, Mr Pengally?'

He gets up, drowning his cigarette in the sink. 'No doubt you'll find my details in one of your files, inspector.'

16

MAY

It is visiting hour again. I lie on my back and stare at the ceiling. The fly is still there. It is either a dead fly forever stuck there until it disintegrates or my eyesight is playing tricks with me. Someone has pulled the curtains around my bed.

A throat is cleared. My father is standing at the foot end of my bed, his fists clenched around the footboard as though he is waiting for a sign to trolley my bed away from this hospital room. I can barely see the expression on his face. A sudden beam of sunshine hits the top half of his body, setting his white fluffy head in a mysterious halo.

He is tall and stiff and towers over my tiny mother both physically and emotionally. Perhaps without realising it, he has always been someone who effortlessly tried to persuade us of his opinions. I think, perhaps he's always been close to being a bully. It wasn't until I finished a short course in psychology that I came to understand his drives. As a boy he'd love to ponder and chew over a sheet of paper. His short-lived dream was to become one of the greatest poets of modern times. This was until he was talked, and beaten, out of it by a father who had been a coal miner until he was made redundant after the closures of the mines. Poetry was for shy and girly boys. Meeting my mother renewed his hopes and ambitions. He wrote piles of poems in an urgent need to express his love and longing for her. Perhaps being encouraged by her enthusiasm and admiration, he had a period of hope that, against all odds, he would add his name to the list of the most famous poets of the nation. Instead, my mother got pregnant and his dreams went quickly up in wisps of smoke with the realisation that he now had a responsibility to carry on his shoulders and that perhaps his father had been right after all. He never spoke about it, however. I grew up with an instinctive feeling that his misfortune was my fault. In general, he was a quiet, pensive man with sudden outbursts of frustration and anger. I suspected in his mind he could never stop juggling with words, trying to find a way to express himself on paper rather than spoken. Sometimes he addressed me as 'her little bastard of a son' by whom he was trapped in a world of ordinary people of which he liked to think was alien to him.

By the time I understood the meaning of the word bastard, I didn't feel hurt or embarrassed. Instead I went through a period of silly hopes that one day it would transpire that I was the son of a rich man who would appear on our doorstep and take me with him. Yet, looking in the mirror, seeing his smoky grey eyes in my own, his straight nose and pronounced jaw, my hopes and dreams seemed to be based on shifting sands. As a teenager, I sort of prayed, although I didn't believe in God, that my hair wouldn't turn grey at twenty-two, as his had, which fortunately didn't happen: genes blessed me with my mother's thick black hair.

In an obstinate way of distancing myself from him, I joined the local football team. He despised physical activity. But because there was much more of him in me than I wished, I wasn't athletic enough to run around the field without getting out of breath. I was then transferred to be a goalkeeper, an unloved position for most players, and I soon found making a dive for a ball wasn't for me. When I broke my wrist in an unfortunate landing, I was given the opportunity of withdrawing from the team without losing my dignity.

At fourteen, I fell deeply in love with the new music teacher. She was young and blonde, with perfect legs and breasts. Because I wasn't by far the only boy in school admiring her, I searched for a way to stand out from the other boys. In the school library I penned down a translation of a foreign poet, unknown to me then, a poem of love and despair. I sent it to her after altering a couple of key words to make the poem more up to date, more physical and erotic. As a result, my parents were summoned to school. Although the school director was not very pleased with my literary efforts, I cherished the moment because I finally found myself able to please my father, to make him proud of me. His feelings shattered when he learned where the origins of my poem came from: the library book along with a copy of a tattered Playboy.

'Roger, please, he's just waking up.' My mother's eyes flash between our faces. She loves us both and finds it hard to take a side, but remaining safely in the middle has never been an option for her.

He ignores her and erupts, 'Why haven't you told us?'

Noticing the accusation and hurt on his face, I don't know what to say. I feel guilty.

Dressed in a black, white and pink striped jumper, black trousers and loafers, my mother sits quietly at my bedside. Unaware of my gaze, she looks down at her hands, folding and unfolding them around the handbag in her lap as though she's been told her fingers need the constant exercise otherwise her joints will lock. As usual, her shoulder length hair, black speckled with grey, is pulled back in a thick ponytail, a fringe half hiding a frown above her gold-rimmed glasses. They are slightly coloured, which makes her brown eyes seem hollow and dark. As she sees me awake, she takes my hand and squeezes it tightly. Her eyes are red, her face drawn with concern. She has been crying. For me.

She asks whether I'm in pain. I tell her that the nurses bring me so many differently coloured and shaped pills that at least one of them must keep the pain bearable. She doesn't ask how I feel.

My father starts pacing alongside my bed, his jaw set, facial muscles flexing. His mouth opens and closes, but my mother shakes her head as vehemently as she can. 'Roger, please, sit down. You're making me nervous.'

He stops and stares at her incredulously, astounded for a moment, shifting his weight from one foot to the other, then he sits down on a chair, which is turned slightly away from us. A sudden gust of wind, then a heavy shower beats the window. He purses his lips. His anger is an aura enveloping his body.

In an attempt to regain control, he lifts a polystyrene cup of tea and blows violently across the surface to cool it, yet he's too upset to take any sips. My mother sits motionlessly, watching him carefully, ready to interfere as soon as he resumes his rants. I suspect her façade of quietness allows her to keep control over him. Yet I know her well enough to recognise the shattered emotions inside her.

Finally, having reconciled himself to the topic again, he places the cup on the windowsill and turns to confront me. 'Why?'

'Roger, please, not now...'

He ignores her. 'Andrew, why didn't you tell us?' He has never called me Andy.

Lost for the right words, I feel like shaking my head, but I'm afraid the movement will cause me pain.

'I don't know.'

It isn't an answer he can deal with, for it steals away his storm and thunder. 'Why did you have to be so bloody... stubborn... to keep it all to yourself?'

'Roger, please. Can't you see he's not feeling well?' My mother's voice is soft and soothing, her hand touches his forearm. Shaking it off, he presses on.

'Why? Tell me why, Andrew.'

'I couldn't.'

'We are your parents!'

'That's why I couldn't,' I admit lamely, instinctively

knowing that at least my mother will understand.

His shoulders drop. Resting his arms on his knees, his hands dangle between his legs as he blinks. For a moment he stares at me angrily, then his eyes lower to some point on my bed, avoiding mine. I suspect by the movements along his neck that he is attempting to swallow back his emotions.

'Roger.' For the first time I see the strength of my mother's character, which allows her to remain calm in the face of all that has happened to me. I swallow with guilt, unable to comprehend how mothers somehow deal with the most horrendous circumstances.

'Don't you think we have a right to know?' His voice is devoid of anger now, as if finally the reality of things is kicking in.

I'm not sure how I feel about their rights to know everything about my life, my body, but it is not the time to provoke him. 'I'm sorry.'

Nodding as if satisfied, he finishes his tea and instead of putting the cup back, he begins picking it apart, breaking off the edge of the polystyrene into tiny balls with unsteady fingers.

To my mother, this seems to be the sign she's been waiting for. Her train of thought appears to be more practical. 'What do the doctors say?'

I don't know how much to tell. 'Nothing much, so far. We'll have to wait.'

'Wait for what?'

I half shrug. 'The results, I guess. Examinations and scans.'

'So this isn't... the end?' Taking in a sharp breath, my father suddenly realises his choice of words. 'I mean, haven't they taken out the bad bits?'

'They hope they did, but it will take some time before they know for sure.'

He looks at the half crumbled cup in one hand, the other balling and releasing in a quiet rhythm only heard by himself. His chest is heaving with each breath, his jaw muscles flex as though he is chewing on something tough.

Someone once told me that one of the worst things that can happen to a parent is the loss of a child. It makes me think of Peter Prescott and his wife Trish. Did Jane Croft still have a mother or father? I begin to understand that my father's anger is not addressed to me because I tried to hide my health issues from them: it is his battle against fate.

'When will you come home?' My mother keeps her voice calm and soothing in an attempt to make her presence as unthreatening as possible. Yet the meaning of her words hangs in the air like the static before a lightning storm. She is expecting an instant and satisfying response from me.

'I don't know yet.' Pointing at my belly, I add miserably, 'First I have to deal with… this.'

'But… is the doctor… are they satisfied, so far?'

'I suppose.'

My mother nods quietly, exchanging a look across my bed with my father. 'We've read about it. When you come to find out about it, it seems quite… it's not so uncommon nowadays.'

'I don't think there's anything common about it,' I say rather bitterly.

'Yes, but…' Her voice withdraws to an undistinguished murmur, eyes pleading my father to correct what she is trying to say.

'Do we need to… learn something about it?' he asks awkwardly.

I laugh curtly and shocks of painful discomfort shoot through my body. 'It doesn't mean I'm disabled, Dad.'

'No, but…'

'Thousands of people seem to live with it,' I say, nodding my head to let him know that I follow his line of thoughts. 'Trained nurses will teach me. I'll be perfectly able to deal with it myself.'

I can almost believe it myself. The only problem is that I don't want to think about it. I just don't want to know…

There is a rush of clothes, quick footsteps of rubber shoes, soles squeaking on the polished lino. A dark hand emerges and half pushes away the curtain between my bed and that of the man next to me. Mr Bangura has had his operation early this morning. Roy Wood has been transferred to a room of his own. I hope it's because he asked for it himself, fed up with my snoring.

Two nurses appear. The pale blonde is new to me; Sarita is charcoal black, only her palms and gums are pink. Although nowadays we're probably not allowed to say things like that, I am still thinking in black and white. How else do I define them? One is short, the other tall? One is slim, the other fat? Isn't that discrimination as well?

'Ah, I see you're awake, Mr Tregunna! And visitors!' Standing beside my bed, her voluptuous bosom trapped in dark blue uniform, Sarita offers a welcoming smile that even seems to soften my father's expression. 'How are you feeling today?'

'I'm good.'

Sarita's expression is warm and compassionate. The white nurse has a face that doesn't know how to smile, let alone laugh. In contrast to Sarita's sparkle, she has dull grey eyes and her lips are pale and thin. She squeezes the belt of a blood tension monitor round my arm, waiting while staring into oblivion, not even acknowledging my presence, or that of my parents. I squint my eyes to read the name on the blonde's badge: Ella. I can recall a great-aunt Ella who was always dressed in black, a life without a smile. I only understood a little bit more about her after her death. Her husband died in the war and left her pregnant with twins who were always struggling with their health. What's in a name…

Ella picks up my hand and presses a finger on my pulse. Her eyes are fixed on her watch as she counts. Smiling, Sarita adds the results to my file, making it available for other nurses and doctors and whoever may be interested. She clips my file back to the foot end but before they both disappear my mother looks up, eyes almost begging.

'Is everything all right with my son?'

All of a sudden Ella knows how to smile after all, and along with it appears an attractive dimple on her left cheek. 'The blood pressure is a bit higher than normal. Otherwise he is doing very well.'

'What does that mean?'

'Nothing to worry about, Mum.'

I hope it's true. The awkward presence of my parents makes me tense and fidgety. Presumably my blood pressure will drop as soon as they're gone. The thought enhances my guilt. It is precisely why I haven't told them about the operation.

Another nurse appears. In his early thirties, with gelled blonde hair, Richard wears a uniform that is tight enough across his chest to show off his gym muscles. His short sleeves reveal impressively developed biceps and he looks like he can easily lift me above his head.

'Fancy getting out of bed, Mr Tregunna?' He places a little plastic beaker with two pills on my bedside cupboard.

'I don't know.' I do know there is nothing I would like more than to walk to the toilets on the other side of the corridor, or better, walk out of the door and leave the hospital behind me.

'He just had his operation yesterday,' my mother objects incredulously.

Richard gives an indifferent shrug. 'The sooner he's out of his bed, the sooner he can go home, ma'am.'

'Oh.'

I open my mouth, but I can't think of an adequate response. 'Maybe later,' I murmur finally. 'When visiting hour is over.'

Nodding that he understands, but that he won't forget, he retreats to my neighbour, closing the curtain again. We hear him asking Mr Bangura how he feels. We listen to the answer, his voice still drowsy by anaesthetics.

'Andy, about the... tumour. When you hear more... get the results... will you...?' My mother's voice is a trembling whisper. Perhaps shocked by her own words, she starts to sob, making her entire frame shake. Tears roll down her cheeks, but she makes no effort to wipe them.

In a rare attempt to comfort her, my father puts his arm around her shoulders and sits with her until she finishes. When she seems to have calmed, he stands up, placing his hand on her shoulder for a second, then turns without a word and leaves the room. In the instant before I see him disappear beyond the curtain, I notice his flushed face, his lips trembling.

'I'm so sorry, Mum.'

'I understand, Andy, I really do. And so does he. It's only... it hurts that you didn't trust us.'

She gets up, hands firmly clasped around her handbag. She's going to leave too, following my father. At this moment, he needs her more than I do. Yet it feels like they are both abandoning me and suddenly I feel so lonely that I have to suppress the urge to cry.

17

APRIL

My decision to drive to Bristol is merely based on a need to leave everything behind me for a while. Escape reality. For it is no longer the murder of Jane Croft that is keeping me awake.

When I visited Doctor Warren again, the expression in his eyes was serious enough to tell me that I hadn't come to waste his time. He made it clear that he believes that there is definitely something wrong with me. The results of a blood count, one of the tests that he's had done in the morning, has confirmed his suspicions. He explained that more tests were needed but I could see his eyes speaking volumes. He wouldn't speculate about what it is or how bad it might be, as he couldn't be certain at this point. But he was worried enough to pick up the phone himself to refer me to a specialist in Royal Cornwall Hospital in Truro. An emergency examination will be carried some time next week. I will receive a phone call with the exact date and time.

After a long and sleepless night of tossing and turning, switching on the bed lamp and the TV on and off again several times, I have concluded that I can't face my colleagues this morning. Everything about my life, my world, my future has just fallen apart. I can tell no one, yet I feel that everyone will be able to read the truth in my eyes. Penrose knew about the appointment; assumptions and speculations are easily made.

The last thing I want is pity.

I'm not at all sure whether Simon Croft, Jane's ex husband, can shine a light on her death, but I managed to let Penrose believe that it's vital that I speak with him, ask him about the foster children. Perhaps I find out who Jane was still in contact with. It's an excuse to justify my drive to Bristol.

Simon and Shirley Croft live in a detached council house on the outskirts of Bristol. I find the front door ajar and when I knock, a hoarse voice invites me in. A short and narrow hallway brings me into a kitchen that smells of food and cigarettes. Perched on a faded green plastic chair, a woman is gazing at me suspiciously through a pair of glasses and a bluish cloud of cigarette smoke. Her elbows rest on either side of a full ashtray. Wisps of ash swirl briefly when she moves her hand.

'Who are you?' she says bluntly.

'I'm sorry. I knocked. The door was open and…'

'I was expecting someone else.'

'I'm sorry.' I hesitate, finding it hard to believe that this is a woman Simon Croft left his first wife for. 'Mrs Croft?' I say, waiting politely on the doorstep.

'Who wants to know?'

'My name is Andy Tregunna from Newquay. I'd like to ask you some questions.'

'Are you the police?'

'Yes. I would like to…'

'I ain't done nothing wrong.'

'This isn't about you.'

She doesn't answer straightaway but raises her hand to inhale, blowing out as much smoke to cloud the room. 'What's he done this time?'

'Mrs Croft, perhaps I should explain…'

Shaking her head, she smothers the cigarette with a gesture of disgust, pressing it slowly on the edge of the ashtray. The remains of the cigarette are carefully put down on a package. Then she leans heavily on the table and lifts her body to stand. I can smell sweat and the mustiness of clothes dried in an unventilated room.

Her greyish brown hair droops untidily by her neck, white and blue plastic earrings dangle off her earlobes. She is wearing a black vest that releases two bare meaty arms with swollen hands. On her middle finger glitters what looks like a cluster of fake diamonds. Cellulite on her legs shows through the thin cotton of a smudgy pair of sports trousers. Her feet and ankles are swollen, toenails painted a bright red in yellow plastic flip-flops, a sunflower on only one of them.

I become suddenly aware that she has not risen because of me. An electric kettle has come to the boil on a counter filled with dirty cups and plates. It switches itself off with a sharp click.

'I'm having a cuppa.' It sounds like an invitation rather than a statement.

With a wry smile she follows my gaze as I scrutinise the dirty cups, wondering about the health and safety rules that seem to have more grip on British society nowadays than the law itself.

'Thank you.'

With her head she gestures towards a choice of three other chairs round the table. All four are different, however one seems to have been part of a set with the kitchen table.

'He's not here,' she says by way of explaining, sounding rather triumphant, and filling a white china teapot.

'This is about…' I stop, wondering suddenly how careful I need to be in bringing the news of Jane Croft's death. I don't know what their relationship was like, if any.

She has turned her head though, and from the corner of my eyes I sense rather than see a movement through the window. Someone is approaching the house: a skinny young man, dark jeans hanging dangerously low on his hips, face hidden in the shade of the hood of a faded black sweater. The uniform of today's youth. Shirley Croft swiftly runs the side of her hand across her neck, a gesture apparently well known to the young man, who disappears quickly from sight.

I smile inwardly. 'Your son?' From the looks of her he could well be her grandson, but I dare not ask. 'It's not because of him that I'm here.'

Lifting her shoulders, as though all of this is of minor importance, she finds a gold-rimmed Wedgwood cup and saucer stored at the back of a cupboard.

'Sugar?'

'One please.'

Her abrupt manner somehow seems to settle nicely between us. She dumps a bottle of milk on the table in front of me, the teapot, the china, obviously used only for guests, and a mug saying I LOVE MUM for herself.

'If it's not for my Danny, then... what?' She pauses to point at the window. 'Why are you here, officer?'

I wait until she has sat herself down again. 'I'm currently based in Newquay, Cornwall, investigating a suspicious death.'

Relief spreads over her puffy face. 'And whose death might that be, inspector?'

'Mrs Jane Croft.'

'Mrs... Jane? Simon's ex?'

'I'm afraid so.'

Her lower lip has dropped shut and we fall into a conspiracy of collective silence. In the background I can hear the sound of children's laughter and running water: the walls seem to be thin.

Finally, she mutters, 'Well, well, well.'

'Did you know Jane at all, Mrs Croft?'

'Not very. I met Simon after they divorced. I had no dealings with her.' Suddenly her eyes widen. 'How did she die?'

'We are treating her death as suspicious.'

'We ain't done nothing wrong.' Once more her eyes drift towards the window. 'It ain't got nothing to do with us.'

'I'm just after some background information. Ideally, I'd

like to talk to your husband.'

'Ah! Then you've got yourself a real problem, son!' She chuckles nervously, yet I can see the tension releasing from her muscles. Whatever she expected, or feared from my visit, it has nothing to do with Jane Croft's death.

'When will he be home? I have a few other appointments in Bristol, I can come back later.'

'He's not living here anymore.'

For some unknown reason it doesn't surprise me. 'Do you know his address, Mrs Croft?'

She half stifles a nervous giggle. 'He always joked about it, you know? That's why we went up to Clifton Suspension Bridge. To chuck his ashes.' She is quiet for a moment. 'It were a lot of ashes. More than we ever expected.'

I sit a moment, perplexed. The clock on the fridge ticks insistently, counting away the seconds.

'Are you saying your husband is dead?'

'Every bit of him.'

'Simon Croft?'

'The one and only.' Her irony is incredulous, but in a way I can understand it.

'When did he die?'

'It were two days before Christmas.'

Four months ago. 'I am very sorry.'

She lights the cigarette she smothered earlier, inhales and watches the smoke curl up to the ceiling with squinted eyes. 'He went out to get the turkey and buy me a Christmas present. At least that's what he said. And he never came back.' She stops to inhale. 'I had to chuck the turkey.'

'A heart attack?' I guess, wondering suddenly if Jane had known and if she had, why she hadn't told her daughter. Whatever the state of a relationship, Stella has a right to know. It would be less embarrassing for me if someone had told me. Penrose... no, I can't blame her. The decision to visit Simon Croft today came out of the blue. I don't think any of the team has come as far as inquiring about him.

Shirley Croft shakes her head. 'Stabbed and robbed. They found him in a dark alley.'

'Stabbed?' I straighten up, alert all of the sudden.

'Yep.' There is a hint of sadness in her eyes. I sense she has cried a lot of tears over her husband. It is only four months ago that he died, yet she manages to maintain an appearance of being untouched.

Lifting her mug of tea she blows off the heat, sending a faint smell of garlic in the air. 'He was stabbed. I'll never know he bought the jewels he promised me. His killer must have taken it along with what was left of his money. Only the turkey was there. But I had to chuck that away because rats had eaten half of it already.'

'I'm so sorry.'

Shaking her head, she tightens her lips. 'What's happening to the world, officer? Why can't a man like my Simon walk on the street in the dark anymore?'

Cynically, the youth she chased away earlier, springs to my mind. 'Did they find the killer?'

'Of course not! They say he was just unlucky. In the wrong place at the wrong time, that sort of bullshit.' For a moment anger flares in her eyes, but then she realises that it is pointless. 'He must have went to the pub, after shopping. Had a couple of pints and was heading home when those Blackies ripped him off.'

'Blackies?' I raise my hand slightly, wanting to advise her that it is against the law to discriminate anyone against her or his colour. 'Mrs Croft, you can't say…'

She gives a stubborn shake of the head. 'I know what you want to say, inspector, but it is exactly how I feel. Anyway, they stabbed him and left him to die. Cowards. Police say it was probably a gang, but they're too scared themselves to do something about it. They should clear the streets from those thugs, inspector, not handing us leaflets with warnings to stay indoors at night.'

'I'm sure the police here do their best.'

'Yeah?' The single word comes out with grinding slowness.

'They can't be everywhere.'

'They know about this gang, inspector, they're all living on the estate, half of them illegal immigrants. No jobs, just living on benefits. They get twice as much as I get. They rob and steal and make it unsafe for us normal Britons to live in peace.'

I hesitate, then dismiss the idea of correcting her. There is no point. I pick up my cup, the tea is surprisingly good. Droplets of her angry outburst still hang in the air. Her fingers fumble with the cigarette pack, clearly debating whether to light a new cigarette. Then I see a single tear running down her cheek.

'I am lucky to have my children.'

'I am so sorry,' I say again, clumsily and feeling ashamed somehow. 'Do you have a photo of your husband?'

'In the other room.' Without moving she gestures towards the door.

I feel like an intruder in her life and I half wish I hadn't come at all. At the back of the house, the living room is neat and tidy and cold, dominated by a big flat TV screen that is attached to the wall. The furniture is mainly in light oak, polished to a shine and obviously rarely used. Shirley Croft spends her life in the kitchen, with a small TV above the sink. I never understand people who have a nice living room and yet don't spend a minute in it, other than cleaning it. Or have a Christmas dinner with relatives they rarely see. It's such a waste of space.

On the mantelpiece above a gas heater I find a framed photo of a man sitting on a park bench, a white dog on his lap. As I pick it up, I look out of the large window that overlooks a long and narrow garden. On one side is a green stained fence, to which bamboo sticks are aligned, allowing a route for bean plants to grow later in the season. In the middle are neat rows of young plants with labels on sticks along a small path of weathered flagstones. A small glasshouse at the end is filled with trays of seedlings. Shirley Croft has given up her patio for a backyard full of homegrown fruits and vegetables.

The youth, his sweater over the open glass house door, is digging a trench. Sweat makes his forehead shine and there are dark stains on his black vest. He is not aware of my presence.

I look at the photo. Simon Croft reminds me of his daughter Stella. The same high forehead, the same smile, yet there is something of a coldness in his eyes that makes me suspect he has been a difficult man to live with. This might explain the fact that Stella had no contact with him and also the divorce. Somehow, I know that he and Jane must have been worlds apart. I put the photo back and return to the kitchen.

'You've got a lovely plot back there, Mrs Croft. Who's doing the gardening?' I ask matter-of-factly. Shirley Croft has found a tin, which is now open on the table. Absent-mindedly she nibbles a chocolate biscuit and sips her tea.

'Me. It helps me to relax. My son is there sometimes, for the heavy jobs.'

'Do you grow your own vegetables?'

'Grows quicker than I can eat it.'

I remember her bitter remark about her pension. 'Do you sell it to your neighbours?'

She lets out a grunt. 'Sell it? Inspector, we are all in the same boat. Pensioners living on a tip the government allow us in this so-called welfare state. Money we worked for all our lives and now we have to be grateful for it. A couple of quid every week.' She picks up the fabric of her trousers, holding it between two fingertips. 'We buy our clothes in charity shops. We grow our own food in our back gardens. No inspector, I don't sell my veg to neighbours who have as little as me.' Her head is lifted with a gesture of pride and dignity that makes me very small suddenly. 'We share, inspector, we share and we help.' Once more she plucks her trousers. 'I'm not always dressed like this, you know. We were just about to plant potatoes for the next season.'

'Your son?'

'He does the digging. I try to keep him busy in his spare time, keep him away from bad influences.'

'Has he got a job?'

'Still at school. I don't want him to get a job. I want him to have a proper education, to have a good job later in life.'

I stare at my teacup, aware that my first impression of her was terribly wrong. Without realising it, my eyes stare at the cigarette pack. Due to new taxes, they have become almost unaffordable nowadays. I've heard colleagues complaining about it.

She picks up the package, smiling, knowing my thoughts. 'This is a real treat, inspector. I used to smoke, we both used to, Simon and me. Had to give it up, sadly. Now every so often the son of a neighbour travels to Europe and he brings us stuff. Cheap cigarettes and all.' *Share and help*, I think to myself.

She smiles suddenly. 'You're all right, for a policeman.'

When I shut the front door behind me, I realise that I haven't asked her about the foster children. And she hasn't asked me about Jane Croft, how she died. Shirley Croft has enough problems of her own.

18

APRIL

Based in Bristol, DI Ashley Grey is everything his name suggests. He has thick grey hair that curls to his neck and around his ears, thick grey brows and pale eyes. Even his skin has an unhealthy greyish shine. He's wearing a light grey suit and a white shirt. His dark red tie with embroidered yellow 'smilies' suggests a slice of humour, but I cannot find it anywhere.

As we shake hands, our eyes meet and we weigh each other up like boxers from opposite corners of a boxing ring, wondering who will lash out and hit first. To him, I'm a rival rather than a colleague. It is an uneasy start and it makes me almost regret that I didn't bring Penrose.

Grey is regarding me with cold assessing eyes. 'What can I do for you, detective inspector?' He makes it sound as if his boss has instructed him to be polite and helpful and is obliging only with his future career move in mind.

I decide to start carefully, waiting for which way the wind blows. 'I'd like to talk to you about Simon Croft.'

'So you said on the phone. What about him?'

We sit down in his office, a square cubicle with a small square window that looks out at a brick wall. The top of his ink and nicotine stained desk suggests that it is old enough to have already been in use in the period smoking was still allowed in the office. It is overloaded with files, which tells me he is very busy, or just untidy. There is something reserved and watching about him, as though he is asking himself whether to treat me as an ally or enemy. I see the tension rising in his muscles.

'I'd like to offer you coffee, but…'

'That would be lovely. It's been a long drive.'

His grey eyebrows rise, making it clear to me that I misunderstood: it wasn't an offer.

'Perhaps it would have been easier and quicker to deal with this on the phone,' he says wryly.

'I happened to be in the area,' I lie.

'Nothing to do with Simon Croft's case, I presume?'

'Not if our cases aren't connected.'

He is not at all amused. 'Simon Croft's file's closed. I told you that. It was a plain robbery, which happens unfortunately.'

I nod patiently. 'Did you find who did it?'

He presses the teeth of his lower jaw into his upper lip. He looks like a grinning llama, ready to sneeze into my face.

'Listen, detective inspector, Bristol is nothing like Newquay. We have to deal with serious crime here, areas with gangs fighting each other for whichever reason.'

'You suspect one of those gangs killed Simon Croft?'

'That's what's in my report.'

'But what if it's not?'

I wonder if he has a button under his desk he can press and order coffee quietly. If not, I guess I won't have any at all.

'Were you the investigating officer in charge?'

'Still am. Officially.'

I lean back in my chair and stretch my legs as though expecting I'll be here for quite a while. His lips suddenly curl in a tiny smile and I imagine a flicker of humour in his grey eyes. Then, with a frown, he gets up, opens the door and chooses the first officer that comes into view to order two coffees. His voice is harsh, with a hint of rudeness, and as I look past him, I see a woman's brows rise, red lips tighten and chin lift. I half expect her to object to being used like a waitress, but after a moment of hesitation she nods. I can't see Penrose reacting like that, but then again, I can't see myself ordering my officers to get coffees either. Perhaps that's what Grey meant when he said that Bristol and Newquay are very different.

Just before he closes the door, I see a row of desks, most of which are covered with papers, piles and folders, and empty polystyrene coffee cups. Vacated desks have chairs pulled back as though they have been left in haste. Along with the young female officer are three men looking at computer screens and tapping buttons on keyboards with both index fingers.

Once more Grey presses the teeth of his lower jaw into his upper lip to make him look, intentionally or not, like a mischievously grinning llama.

'Coffee will take a while, I'm afraid, Mr Tregunna. The machine's gone by its use-by date.'

I nod. Silently I think the coffee-machine is probably not the only piece of furniture that is out-dated. The walls are painted greenish yellow, covered with sad still-life watercolours. The frames are a dark wood with brass edges, the mounts are browned. On the windowsill is a young palm tree in a terracotta pot on a white saucer, soil dried out long ago, fighting a losing battle.

'We're waiting for approval for a refurbishment,' Grey says with an ironic smile.

'I guess we all have to try to keep our head above the surface.' I try to sound sympathetic to win his trust.

He inclines his head by way of nod. 'We're supposed to have a new police station built, but there are issues with planning permission.' His face twists into a sad grin. 'Something to do with a rare kind of beetle, I believe. Endangered species.'

Our coffees arrive sooner than expected. Two plastic cups half filled with something very dark. A third cup holds sachets of sugar and powdered milk. The young officer pushes open the door with her hip and looks at me with a mixture of curiosity and caution. She has an open round face with short brown hair and blushed cheeks that would suggest underlying heart problems had she not been so young.

'Thank you,' I say, as Grey just nods his appreciation.

I see her walk back to her desk with a slightly positive jump to her paces. Whatever Grey's moods, they haven't influenced the young officer. Yet.

'Well, detective inspector Tregunna.' For some reason, his mood, and his attitude, has changed.

'Andy,' I offer amicably.

His eyebrows lift imperceptibly. 'They call me Grey.' There is a hint of regret in his voice and I understand he's telling the truth. Sitting down behind his desk, his hands grip the armrests as if he's visiting his dentist.

I pick up my coffee and empty one sachets of sugar and two of the powdered milk into it. It floats on the surface. I use a pen from the inside pocket of my jacket to stir it.

'Now, about Simon Crofts death.'

He leans back to give the impression that he is relaxing. A tiny vein throbbing at the side of his temple tells the opposite. Rubbing the side of his nose with the tip of his thumb, he smiles ruefully.

'You will find the details in this folder.' He picks up an orange carton folder with *Croft, S.J.* written on it in black marker pen and drops it in the same movement.

I take a deep breath and let it out slowly through my teeth before I reply. 'Look... eh... Grey, I'm not here to undermine your investigation. I'm sure you've done all you can to find his killer.'

'You don't have to patronise me.'

'I'm sorry if you feel that way.' I pause. He plays hard to get. It's feels like climbing a crumbling rock. 'I just want to know whether his death and the death of his ex-wife are related.'

'I've had Beth copy everything I thought might be useful for you.' Leaning sideways he retrieves a thin pink folder from his top drawer. 'There was no need for you to come all the way to fetch it. I could have sent it to you.'

'I'd like to hear it in your own words.'

He gets up and stares out of the window for a few moments, his body language telling me he's still not convinced that I'm not here to trick him. I imagine he is a difficult man to work for and to work with. I begin to regret that I didn't bring Penrose or any of the other officers working on the investigation. Perhaps thoughtful DC Reed would have been a better choice.

'We received a phone call that there had been an accident. When police arrived, they found Mr Croft in a dark alley a couple of hundred yards from his home. By then he was already dead.'

'Evidence?'

'The alley was in fact some sort of ditch between two rows of council houses. Rubbish, fly tipping, rats and needles. We found DNA of half the population of Bristol.'

I can feel his frustration. He doesn't seem to be a bad policeman after all.

'Who phoned the police?'

'A woman with a dog. The dog wouldn't leave the alley, so she called her son to bring a torch.'

'Any suspects?'

He smiles ruefully. 'More than you would dream of. The day before he was seen in his local pub. Had arguments with the landlord about not having paid his bill, with a mate who claimed Croft owed him money and with a guy who believed Croft had something going with his wife.'

'Was he in financial difficulties?'

'He lived on benefits, but he had a job with a local building company. Apparently, he was a hell of a bricklayer. His only problem was that every so often he just didn't show up. Spent the day in a pub or went out fishing.'

'Why didn't he pay his bill in the pub?'

'According to the landlord and regulars in that pub, Croft was very tight. He thought he had to pay too much, so he decided not to pay at all as long as the landlord stuck to his guns.'

'What do you think could have been the motive for his death?'

'There isn't any. Alibis are all watertight. That's why we believe it had something to do with a gang. He just happened to be in the wrong place at the wrong time.' He pauses, repeating his llama act, only this time I don't think he will sneeze. 'Wife was in pieces. Had an alibi, anyway. She has three daughters and one son from a previous marriage. The daughters were at home, the son was playing football for some local team. Twenty-two witnesses plus the coach etcetera to confirm his whereabouts.'

'Relatives?' I wonder about Stella.

He inclines his head. 'A sister. She had an address for his daughter, who, by the way, didn't attend the funeral.'

'What about his ex-wife? Did she come to the funeral?'

His eyebrows lift in surprise. 'I didn't even know he had an ex-wife. Anyway, she wasn't there either.' He opens the orange file on his desk and shifts through the papers, finding a printed list that covers half the page. 'We made a list of those who attended the funeral.'

'Very thorough.'

'No big deal.' He shrugs. 'More or less a dozen were present. His sister and brother-in-law wouldn't speak to the wife, or any of her family for that matter. The wife brought her son and daughters, three I believe. Two neighbours, for whom he looked after their dog when they were on holiday, attended. I suspected that they felt sorrier about having to find someone else for their dogs. The landlord was there. Came only, I presume, to remind his wife of the debts at the pub. And finally, a drinking pal and the builder he sometimes worked for.' He pauses. 'I had the impression he wasn't liked much.'

'But no motives to kill him.'

'No.'

I let the information sink in. There is nothing obvious that proves the death of Simon Croft is in any way related to his ex-wife's, still I have that nagging feeling that both DI Grey and I have overlooked something.

'What was the actual cause of death?'

'Stab wounds. No knife was found.'

'How many?'

'How many what?'

'Wounds.'

'Several. Hang on, I'll get the post mortem report.' His fingertips leaf through the papers until he finds what he is looking for. There are printed copies of photographs from the body. They show a broad, large man, bold headed with a ring of dark hair that starts above his ears. His eyes are open in an expression of shock and disbelief. His red checked shirt is pulled out from under the waist belt of his baggy jeans. Several dark stains where the fabric has been ripped open by the knife. Another photo shows his body on a stainless steel table in the mortuary. There are five wounds, scattered across his belly and stomach.

Grey decides that he has answered enough questions and that it is his turn to ask some now. 'Any similarity with your body?' he asks casually, putting the photos back into the folder.

'None I can think of.' I hesitate. On second thought, he has been cooperative. 'She was stabbed in the neck, dumped at the edge of a car park.'

'Any suspects?'

'No. A neighbour by her windowsill watering plants was the last person who saw her. That we know of, that is. Mrs Croft was picked up by an old lady with a small car. Blue Renault Clio. She must have returned home, because in the evening other neighbours saw lights in her house. She used to go to bed after the ten o'clock news. Nothing seemed out of the ordinary.'

'The old lady?' He chuckles.

'Eighties, rather frail. The neighbour remembered her because he was a bit suspicious about the old lady's driving abilities. He thought he should have warned Mrs Croft about it.' I pause for a moment. 'We haven't found the old lady yet, but I doubt if it is significant. Besides, Mrs Croft's body was found on the other side of a fence. Witnesses have seen someone dropping the body there.'

'CCTV?'

'Newquay is full of cameras but when you need the images, most of the time they turn out to be useless. It was a white van, probably a Peugeot Partner or a Citroen Berlingo. It was seen on camera driving along the road, coming and going. No useful images of the driver. Number plates were fake. Different in the front from the back. The van was caught on other cameras, but it drove out of town. That's where we lost it.'

'Motive?'

'None whatsoever. Originally she owned the bungalow she lived in, but she made a financial arrangement with her daughter about it. The daughter owns the house and rented it out to her mother.'

He studies his nails, then picks up a letter opener from his drawer and pokes its point under the nail of his index finger. 'We found Mr Croft's wallet in the back pocket of his trousers with ten pounds and a receipt from Tesco, where he bought a turkey. Anything stolen from his ex-wife?'

'Her handbag is still missing, along with her purse, but according to her daughter, she rarely had more than twenty pounds on her.'

Grey leans back and folds his hands behind his neck. 'So we both have nothing.'

'Apart from the fact that they were both killed within a time frame of six months.'

'Which is why you're here.'

'Which is why I wanted to see you.' I hesitate. 'You didn't mention anything about his foster children.'

'I'm not aware he had any.' The expression on his face shows his surprise.

'Not recently, but he had some with his first wife.' I stop, noticing that suddenly he is on alert. 'There may be a motive to kill them both.'

He places his elbows on his desk, laces his fingers and

rests his chin on them, 'Tell you what, Tregunna, I think you may have a point here.'

19

APRIL

Eventually DI Grey turns out to be helpful after all. I suspect it's because he shares my feeling that there might be a link between the two deaths. With a comic lifting of one eyebrow, as if warning me not to say a word, he calls in the same female officer who brought us our coffees. Introducing her as DS Fiona Libby, Grey's face is stony, not even moving his eyes and he says by way of explanation, 'Libby can turn any stone, once she suspects there's something beneath it.'

A second cup of coffee and twelve minutes later, she hands me a strip of paper with a name and contact details of Helen Tilley of South West Foster Care. By that time Grey has gone to a meeting with a committee that keeps the renovation plans for the station within focus. He would've liked to have been of more help, but being the chair of the committee he finds he can't afford to pull out on such short notice. I promise to keep him informed and he produces his rare ironic smile, releasing the same promise with much less reluctance than when we met.

Unfortunately Helen Tilley is out; the South West Foster Care's receptionist is unable to make an appointment. Ms Tilley is available from Tuesday till Thursday between nine and ten. The rules, she adds without further explanation, are strict. Making a mental note to call again the next morning, I drive away from the car park and soon find the outskirts of

Bristol, heading for the M5 southbound. There is a business park with several dull grey buildings. Some have a 'For Sale' on them. Following a lorry whose driver takes advantage of the superiority of his vehicle and enters the roundabout just in front of me, a sign flashes by. I brake and at the last minute decide to turn left towards A. B. Allan, Construction Company.

It is the company Peter Prescott works for. Although I have no reason to suspect that he is in any way linked to Jane Croft's death, his visit to the station, and the way he spoke about his wife, is still clinging to the insides of my skull. I can't put my finger on it, but it feels like there is something amiss. So unexpectedly seeing the company seems an opportunity too good to miss.

Allan's office is a converted container block in the middle of a dusty yard scattered with building materials. It is painted bright yellow with a board on its front side with the company name and an undecipherable logo. Net curtains behind the windows and three geraniums on the inside windowsill, give evidence of a female touch.

Allan is tall and lean, red-faced with huge thick glasses that magnify his hazel eyes, and bald except for a few long, ginger hairs which are glued over his skull with bluish gel. Wisps of fluffy hair grow out of his jug-ears. His face looks like it wears constant sunburn, with little pieces of skin coming off his nose. A slow smile shows a row of big, yellowed teeth.

The sleeves of his candy-coloured shirt are rolled up as he handles a delivery of pallets full of roof tiles. Listening to the drone of the offloading machine, I wait patiently from a safe distance. As the truck finally folds its hoisting arm, shoulders are tapped, papers signed and grins exchanged.

I step forward into the dusty aftermath of the disappearing truck. Allan enters his office, but emerges in the doorway as I approach it.

'Can I help you?' It must be pretty obvious to him that I am not a regular customer.

'I need some information.' I show him my warrant card.

He doesn't flinch. Either he has nothing to hide for the police or he is self-assured enough to believe that he'll keep his secrets safely away from me.

'Do come in, inspector.'

Two desks are placed opposite each other in front of the window. One is neat and almost empty, the other is scattered with bills and folded building plans. Following my gaze, he grins wryly. 'My secretary has the day off. Well, the nursery called. The little boy is ill.'

He lifts a few sheets and replaces them on top of another pile, seemingly with no other relevance that they're papers.

'I don't dare use her desk.' He grins boyishly. 'She hates the way I work. Every Friday she expects me to clear my desk, sort the papers so that we start with a clean slate on Monday.'

'And do you?'

'I come back most Saturday mornings.' He scratches the top of his head with a sheepish grin. 'My wife says I do that to avoid the weekend shopping.'

I suspect he abides more by the rules of his secretary than of his wife's.

Without asking, he puts a mug in a coffee machine on top of a metal filing cabinet in the corner and places it on his secretary's desk. 'Sit down, please, inspector. I'm sure she won't mind as long as you don't leave behind dust or sand.'

'Thank you.' The smell of coffee quickly fills the office.

Outside I hear the engine of the forklift truck roaring, men attempting to make themselves heard through the noise. A wave of dust drifts in. I wonder what the secretary will say about keeping the door open.

'What can I do for you, inspector?' He places his own mug on top of a small pile, not at all bothered that it leaves a wet, brown stained circle on it. Sitting down he stretches his legs, rocking his chair on two legs, stirring his coffee absentmindedly.

'Sorry. Do you take sugar?'

'One, thank you.' Presenting me a box half filled with

sugar cubes, he sits down again.

I clear my throat. 'I believe you have a Peter Prescott working for you.'

'That's right.' He hesitates, a flicker of concern in his eyes. 'I hope nothing is wrong with him?'

'I just need some background information for an investigation.'

'And what is it that you are investigating, inspector?' he asks dryly. 'It must be rather serious, otherwise you would have sent some of the local constables.'

'A murder investigation.'

His pale eyebrows rise. 'I hope Peter isn't in some kind of trouble?' He doesn't say so, but I sense he means to ask whether his employee has been murdered.

'I don't believe so.' Suddenly I feel a bit absurd having come here. I don't know what brought me here. Peter Prescott has no link with Jane Croft. He just happened to report his wife missing while we were waiting for the official announcement of the identity of the woman's body. As I learned afterwards, his wife turned up the same day, end of story. Yet I am here enquiring after him. Why? Would I have come if I hadn't noticed the construction company coincidentally? Would I have come at all if I had been able to talk with the woman from South West Foster Care?

Even that is a bit farfetched. I'm here to put the dots on the i's, so to speak, to make sure the death of Jane Croft is in no way related to that of her husband. Both died an unnatural death. Miles apart. A Coincidence. I was just keen to get away from Newquay, to distract me from thinking about what's wrong with my body.

'I understand Mr Prescott works for you as your manager.'

'That's right. He's the overall production manager for the Southwest. He deals with materials and our subcontractors. He makes sure everything arrives at the sites on time, not too early or too late. He makes sure the plumber arrives in time to do his job before the electrician shows up. Or the other way round. Depends. You get the picture.'

It is a world I don't know much about. 'How many building projects are running at the same time?'

'That depends. Sometimes we do a rebuilding, restructure, an annex, sometimes a whole new estate.' There is a significant tone of pride in his voice.

'And Mr Prescott comes here… regularly?'

'Once a month. Sometimes more often. Depends. To sort out papers.'

'With the secretary.'

'You get the picture.' He pauses with a look full of irony. 'And we talk about future plans, how to schedule things, quotes for new projects, or what have you.'

'Where does he normally stay?'

'Stay?'

'If he needs to be in the area for longer than a day.'

'Ah, I see what you mean. Yes, sometimes there are appointments with architects, supervisors, you name it. Discuss changes, mainly, extra costs. I don't worry about that. Peter is handling it all very well.' He is silent for a while. 'Sorry, you asked where he stays? Well, to be honest, I don't really know. Sometimes we have a drink together in a pub after work. The missus offered him a spare room in our home a few times, but he declined. Didn't want to interfere in our privacy. Needs to get up early. Doesn't want to disturb us.' He chuckles with a private joke. 'Anyway, I guess Peter just wants to keep his privacy. Which is fine with me.'

'So you don't know in which hotel he stays?'

'Don't need to. I can always contact him on his mobile.' He stops, suddenly a bit uneasy. 'I guess my secretary can tell you. She deals with the receipts.'

'There's no diary with his appointments?'

He pauses. Wariness appears in his eyes and face, like a child realising that eating the biscuits from the tin hasn't gone unnoticed.

There's something he is not telling me. But is it relevant

to my investigation? I am not sure why am I here, why I'm following the whereabouts of Peter Prescott. But there's definitely something about him that makes me feel uneasy.

'I presume you'd better ask Peter,' Allan replies finally, sipping his coffee, peering at me over the rim of his mug. He seems to make up his mind. 'I guess, he doesn't really need to stay the night in Bristol. I mean, it's just a couple of hours drive home, isn't it?'

'About three hours.'

'Well, it's just that sometimes I wondered about it, but my secretary doesn't seem to be bothered about his expenses, so, I thought, why would I?'

'Are you saying that Peter Prescott sometimes deliberately stays in Bristol?'

Allan is clearly uncomfortable now. 'Look inspector, I don't want Peter to get in trouble. I wouldn't know what to do without him. To be honest, he's a hell of a good worker. He's been with me for the last ten, twelve years and I'm sure at one point we would have gone bust without him.'

'It's just some background information,' I say, intrigued as to why he's holding back suddenly.

'So, you're not after an alibi?'

I feel almost embarrassed, realising that it hasn't occurred to me to check Peter Prescott's alibi at all. I could have asked him myself, instead of bothering him behind his back.

'Well, I'm sure he's got nothing to hide.' Allan gets up, leans towards the filing cabinet and pulls open the top drawer. 'Did you say you're investigating a murder, inspector?'

'I did.'

'Who?'

'The victim? A woman. Late fifties. Jane Croft. You may have read about it in the papers.'

He seems relieved in a way. 'The name doesn't ring a bell. I'm sure Peter has nothing to do with it.'

His tone makes me smile. 'To be honest, Mr Allan, I'm almost convinced that he has nothing to do with it. I happen to believe that it was purely coincidental that he came to the station to see me when we found the body.'

He shrugs, pulling out a big black book, which he pushes under his arm. 'I hope everything is all right with his missus?'

'What makes you say that?'

'Dunno. He doesn't talk about her a lot. I just got the impression that she's not well.' Wearily he shakes his head. 'Nothing to do with your murder, inspector. She's had a few miscarriages and ever since she's been a bit...'

His voice drools off into an awkward silence, regretting his words already.

'Unstable?' I offer gently.

'Hormones, I presume. Postnatal depression or something like that.' He pulls a wry face. 'I'm sure my secretary could tell you more about that.'

It seems to me that the secretary is a brilliant source of knowledge and wisdom.

'How well do they know each other?'

'I don't know. She's a beautiful young woman. I guess they ...' He stops, the guilt on his face making me understand where and why Peter stays in Bristol every month.

He places the black book in front of me on the secretary's desk. 'This is where she keeps track of appointments.'

'Nothing in a computer?' Suddenly I realise what is missing in his office. Computers. A printer. It makes me wonder suddenly about his secretary's age. My first inkling was that she's a sixty-odd year old former teacher of a boys school, but his mention of a young child contradicts that. Yet she doesn't seem to work with a computer.

'We use laptops,' Allan replies, following my train of thoughts. 'Mine is in my car. My secretary has taken hers home.' He chuckles boyishly. 'No printer. We've got enough paperwork already. She makes a backup every day, stores everything in a computer with some specialist back-up company. It's never let us down so far.' He points his index finger towards the diary. 'But we keep this diary up to date.

Just to allow us a quick glance when someone phones. Or in case of a power cut. Quicker than finding it in a computer system. For me, anyway.' He finds it amusing to show his ignorance with computer systems, but I bet he'd be able to find his way. 'Peter's appointments are only in it when it also involves me. Anyway, which date are you after? His last visit?' Flicking through the pages, he quickly finds last week's dates. It tells me that Allan had a dentist appointment on Monday at ten past nine, the secretary had half a day off in the afternoon, and on Tuesday Peter Prescott saw an architect of a company called M & P, which Allan translates as Miller & Parker.

'I hope that whatever you're investigating, inspector, this'll put Peter in the clear.'

I get up. 'Thank you for your time, Mr Allan.'

'Glad to have helped.'

Shaking my hand, he picks up both empty mugs and follows me outside. Pointing towards the end of the yard, grins and explains, 'Kitchen's in the canteen.'

Four cars are parked in front of an old wooden building with a rusty corrugated roof. A dusty man emerges in the doorway, a wide grin on his face as he notices Allan with the empty mugs in his hand. There is a feeling of camaraderie between the two men, which I envy suddenly. It makes me want to invite Allan for a drink in the pub, or lunch maybe. I dread the moment of getting into my car and being alone again. I don't want to have time to think about the examination or the dubious reassurance from the hospital's nurse that I will receive a phone call if it transpires that an immediate reaction is required.

I don't think I have ever felt so lonely when I drive off Allan's premises.

20

APRIL

There are small teddy bears, single and bunched flowers, most of them dried and weathered, safe for the odd fresh one, faded cards propped against the fence, buds and petals scattered on the rocky soil beyond. Someone has made an effort to arrange the bouquets into a nice display. I wonder briefly who it was. It may as well have been a complete stranger with a strong sense of organisation or passion. It can't have been Stella; I know she hasn't found the courage yet to visit the place where her mother was found. Much to the relief of Mrs Weston, who declared dramatically that it would definitely have been a reason to move elsewhere, Jane didn't die in her home. That's one of the reasons the investigation isn't progressing as fast as I wish.

I don't know why I have come here. Maybe I hoped to be able to relax. Instead I feel the tension from the investigation is all the more pressing. As I stare towards the horizon I feel the calm of the sea. My fists are clenched on the top rail of the fence, but now I release my muscles. On the beach below are a few dog walkers leaving long trails of footsteps in wet sand. Late surfers are trying to catch a wave, but the sea is too calm. One of the fishing boats is leaving the harbour. Even from this distance I can hear the plopping sound of the engine.

The air is soft and salty. I am hungry. I ought to go home and make myself something to eat, yet I feel like I can't face my empty home. Situated on the other side of the hill on which most of Newquay is built, it overlooks the lake and part of the tidal estuary of the Gannel River. According to legend, the river is known for an unusual noise referred to by superstitious natives as the cry of a troubled spirit that forever haunts the scene. I would like to be able to say that I've heard it, but that would be a lie.

As I turn to walk back to my car, my eye catches a face. A photograph of Jane Croft amongst the flowers has been slotted into a plastic sleeve, dotted with droplets of condensation. It is as though the air has cried for her. I read *We will miss you. Ruth and Anne*. Jane's sisters. There are cards with other names, or some just with a single *X* or *RIP*. Nowadays these expressions of sympathy have become more and more common. It began with flowers from family and close friends, but these days complete strangers mourn a life they only know from the papers. Perhaps I am being cynical, believing that some do it merely to tap themselves on the back.

I have to stop myself from scrutinising the notes and cards that are attached to the flowers. I have a weird feeling about a display like this. It's as if I expect to find a note from the killer amongst them. *I'm sorry, but you had to die*. Or just: *I'm sorry*. Like an arsonist coming back to watch his own fire. Spectators are sometimes filmed for that reason.

'Inspector!'

Marie Yates is dressed in a thin black coat that almost reaches the floor. It hangs open in the front, revealing legs in thick black tights and a grey dress that is too short and too tight, showing off the outlines of her bra and knickers. On her head is a purple scarf with tiny mirrors sewn on it. The light breeze lifts her white blonde fringe. Today her hair has a lilac gloss. Her eyes drift past me and see the flowers. Her lips tighten and there's a flicker of sadness in her eyes. 'This is where it happened.'

I correct her. 'This is where the body was found.'

She's clutching a plastic supermarket bag in her hands.

'That's what I mean. I know Jane wasn't murdered here because I saw that man dumping her body like a piece of garbage, remember?' The way she uses Jane Croft's name makes it sound like she was a close relative.

This time I don't correct her. None of the statements I have read mention a third witness to confirm either Marie's one man or Mrs Taylor's two. I'm still not sure which of them lied, deliberate or not. It was dark. Megan Taylor's eyes may not be that good anymore; Marie was further away.

'Are you all right, inspector?'

'It's been a long day.' I'm half debating telling her about my scheduled appointment in hospital tomorrow, but she tilts her head and says, 'You look awful.'

I smooth my chin as though preparing for a reply. I can't find any. She may be right. I feel awful, so I may as well look like it too.

'Sorry, inspector, I didn't mean to say that.'

'It's all right.'

As if on cue, we start walking along the fence and soon find ourselves on the corner of Newquay's busiest main road through town.

'You were out today.' It sounds almost like an accusation.

'I was.' Brake lights glare and passers-by hurry across the zebra crossing as the alarm bleeps.

'I thought you might be ill.'

Looking sideways at her, I ignore her last words. 'Did you phone the station? Have you remembered something?'

Her smile is secretive and hesitant at the same time. It's as though she can't make up her mind whether to stick with me for a while or run off to somewhere safe.

'No. I just wondered if the other witness has changed her statement.'

'Why would she do that?'

'I kind of started to doubt myself. She could have too.'

'Have you?'

'I don't think so. I mean, you can't imagine seeing one

man when there were two.'

'Unless you're anti-cross-eyed.'

She giggles, picking up my casual tone. 'I've never heard of that.'

I smile. 'Nor have I.'

She cocks her head to one side and looks at me with a mixture of pity and irony. 'You haven't answered my question.'

'I wasn't aware of one.'

'Did the other witness change her statement? Did she confirm that there was one man?'

'I haven't been at the police station since this morning.'

She purses her lips like a prude teacher who has never been kissed in her life and criticizes everyone who has. Her shopping bag is changed from one hand to the other.

'Fancy a drink?' With her head she points towards a café across the road.

I hesitate. I shouldn't, really. I'd better go home, get something to eat, have a bath, prepare myself for the examination in the hospital tomorrow.

'I can do with one,' she says by way of encouragement, as though she is admitting the need of a daily dose to survive.

I hear myself say, 'Why not?'

I can't recall afterwards how or when or why, but somehow we end up in my flat. I feel light headed. Stupid. I shouldn't have drunk so much, I should have eaten something. But tomorrow's hospital appointment hangs above my head like Damocles's sword. Clearly I have been trying too hard to erase that from my head. Or perhaps I've just come under Marie's spell, her dark eyes darting on me, her movements suggesting a promise for a passionate, physical encounter. It must be the mixture of alcohol in my veins and a sense of dread, or just fear that from tomorrow my life will change drastically. Squeezing my legs between her thighs, she picks at an aluminium condom packet. As she flicks the foil on the floor, I smell a mixture of strawberries and latex. She's quick and experienced at putting it on me. Then, with a groan, she rides me like I'm a wild horse that needs to be tamed. Hands guide mine to her nipples and as instructed I squeeze them hard between thumb and index finger. She's wild and unrestrained, urging me to go on and on, ignoring me when I breathlessly have to tell her that I can't. She wants more, but I have to disappoint her. With a growl she rolls off me and finishes her climax herself, not bothering about me watching her. I've never seen a woman masturbate in my presence and I find it exciting and disgusting at the same time.

21

APRIL

A people carrier passes me and stops under the glass roof that shields the entrance of St Austell Hospital from weather conditions. A frail old man, sucked into a wheelchair is lowered on an electric platform. His hands shake while he tries to keep control over a walking stick that sits between his legs. His wife, just as small and as frail, is waiting for the driver to push the wheelchair into the hospital. She casts me a shy and apologetic smile because I let them go first.

With something that comes near to a shock, I wonder who, when the time comes, will push my wheelchair. When… if it'll ever come to that. I almost envy the old man for having lived as long as he has, with a wife who still cares for him.

The woman at the desk is in her late twenties, with chestnut brown hair that has a significant red shine. Long black lashes surround blue-green eyes that seem too big for her pale face. On her lapel is a small badge explaining that her name is Ellen and that she's the receptionist. Pressing the phone against her chest, she ticks my name on a list and tells me to wait in the hall.

I choose a seat that has its back to a wide pillar with posters from several charities. I know no other country with so many different charities. Cynically, I wonder what will happen to its manager's income when they will all be combined into one big national charity. So much money wasted before it gets to the poor that need it most.

There are two rows of chairs opposite each other, two small square tables between them, each piled up with magazines that seem to have been here longer than the receptionist. On a wall is a whiteboard. Written with a green marker pen it says that that Dr Cole is delayed forty minutes, Dr Mackenzie is on time and Dr Emery is out, please inquire at the receptionist's desk.

The old lady with her husband in the wheelchair has managed to park him opposite me. With a deep sigh she lowers her frail body on the seat next to him, holding her bag as though she's been asked to look after the queen's crown jewels. Her husband is dozing off, but every so often when someone enters the hall, he opens his eyes in shock, having difficulty remembering where he is. Every time he seems to need his wife's reassurance and with affection she taps his liver stained hand that rests motionlessly on the armrest.

Occasionally, the automatic doors open and someone comes in along with a wave of cool air, or leaves the hospital into the grey day. I pick up a magazine and browse through it until I notice it is almost three years old. As I put it back, a man comes in, carrying a leather case that seems heavy enough to contain rocks. His other arm is stretched out for balance. His whole appearance tells me his ancestors are Asian, perhaps one-eighth of him is European. His accent, emphasized by the way he moves his upper lip, confirms my assumption as he greets the receptionist who seems to be on the phone all the time.

The old man sniffs with an obvious hint of contempt. His wife mutters something under her breath to warn him not to speak out loud his opinion. With a nervous stare, she waits until the man with the case of rocks has disappeared in one of the corridors.

'We are not seeing him, love,' she says softly, stroking her husband's hand. 'We'll speak with Mr Cole today.'

Her husband is not convinced, moving his feet restlessly on the footrest of his wheelchair. I see a tear is escaping from one eye. He is old and frail indeed.

Five minutes later a dark blue uniformed nurse calls me. I have to follow her into the same corridor and after she has confirmed my name and date of birth and checked my weight, I am to be seated again. A couple emerges from one of the interview rooms, the man looks pale and the woman sobs into a ball of tissues. I can't work out which one of them is the patient. The nurse smiles as though she wants to tell me that I have nothing to fear.

'Mr Tregunna?' I am shown into a different interview room. It overlooks a neatly cut lawn that slopes gently down the hill. In the distance, I can see a small stretch of sea.

Massood Rakesh has no rocks in his case. Instead, there are files in carton folders. Some are new, some tattered and thick, containing lives full of misery and hospital appointments. Mine is amongst them, still spotless and thin, but I doubt it will keep that way.

With a casual smile he introduces himself and offers that I call him by his first name, like he is keen to become a friend of mine. His handshake is soft and I feel as though I am grabbing a hand of mashed potato fingers.

'I'm afraid Doctor Cole is running late today, Mr Tregunna,' he explains, 'I've been asked to take over some of his patients. If you insist on being seen by Doctor Cole, you can of course wait for him, but to be honest, I don't know what time you'll be seen.' He makes it sound as if I have no other option than to accept his offer. I contemplate telling him that I'd rather wait for Doctor Cole, but the idea of waiting for however long is even less appealing. I want this over and done with as soon as possible.

'Thanks. I'm all right.'

'Very well. Please take a seat, Mr Tregunna.' Obediently I sit down, trying not to wince as I do.

He frowns, opening my file, and studies the top page. 'Hmm. Have you come alone, Mr Tregunna? Or is there someone, your wife perhaps, waiting for you in the corridor? We can call her in, if you like?'

'I'm alone.' I hope it doesn't sound as sad as it feels.

His bushy black brows rise from behind dark rimmed glasses. 'Perhaps it would have been better if you'd brought someone. For support.'

I shake my head and say curtly, 'I'm all right.' I feel no desire to explain to him that there is nobody I could have brought.

Shaking his head disapprovingly, he scrutinizes the computer screen, looking over his glasses like a short-sighted mole in broad daylight, tapping the keyboard with the tips of two index fingers.

'Right,' he says finally, leaning back, lacing his hands across his belly. 'Well, I have the results of the colonoscopy.'

I nod. The embarrassing examination after Marie spent the night with me. A thin, flexible tube with a camera went in my body. I am here to hear what the camera found.

'Yes. No good news, I'm afraid, Mr Tregunna. We were hoping to find polyps, but that wasn't the case, sadly. You've got cancer.'

I stare at him, appalled, shocked; but most of all in disbelief about the inhuman, cruel way he announced the message. My blood throbs in my ears and a droning sound overwhelms his voice telling me the worst news one can imagine, explaining in medical terms that are more confusing than informing.

'I have made an appointment for you,' he concludes, eyes hooked on the computer screen, oblivious to my feelings. 'Dr Cole will want to see you. He will probably want to take some extra samples. Biopsies. After that, he will discuss the next step with you.'

'Thank you.' My voice is hoarse. It rasps like a sharp knife on a steel cutting board. I feel like sinking on my knees and weeping until my mother comes to pick me up.

'I'm sorry, Mr Tregunna,' he adds as though someone invisible has reminded him of his manners. It's a phrase to him, words without a true meaning.

I understand suddenly why the old man in the wheelchair

got nervous by the sight of this man alone, his wife's instant understanding of what made him feel on edge. I wish that I had insisted on seeing Dr Cole, even if it would have taken the rest of the day. I'm in no doubt that Cole would have shown more compassion than this man could ever fathom.

'You will receive a letter with the details, Mr Tregunna. And an appointment.'

I must have missed something. 'An appointment? For what?'

'Yes.' He presses his lips hard together for a moment, making it no secret that I am wasting his time. 'Would you like me to explain it again?'

'No. No, I have understood you very well.'

He nods, having expected this. Offering a smile that leaves his brown eyes ice cold, he says, 'Meanwhile, go home and have a drink.'

He is massaging his fingers before reaching out for his mashed potato handshake. I choose not to notice. How can I accept the handshake of a man who has just cruelly shattered the fragile glass of my hopes for the future?

Unsteadily, head held high, tears of hatred and contempt burning behind my eyes, I walk out of his consultation room. The nurse stops her conversation with the old couple. She smiles at me, oblivious that I am not in the mood to exchange anything. To me, she is the personification of anything that stretches out towards evil Mr Rakesh.

Clutching a form for a further appointment in my hand, I stand still for a moment. The nurse seems to think her sympathy is lost on me. With a smile, she gestures the old couple into the room I have just left. A horror almost explodes on the old man's face. There is no way for him to escape Mr Rakesh, because the nurse has taken over the hands of his wheelchair and is pushing it forward.

The difference is that I hadn't seen this coming. Obviously the old man has dealt with Mr Rakesh before, probably having had the same cruel experience as I just did.

The receptionist, Ellen, explores a diary and writes a date and time on the blue appointment card. I nod. I'm still too shocked, too numb to take in whether that particular date and the time are convenient for me. This time I'll have to go to Treliske, the hospital in Truro. I don't really care. It seems like the world has come to a complete stop.

Ellen hands me the appointment card with a knowing look. It knots my stomach so tightly that I feel physically sick suddenly. I hurry to the doors, which open too slowly for my comfort. Outside I breathe in deep and slow. A gust of wind in my face, I feel the first spots of rain before I notice that the sky has blackened above me, yet in the west it is still almost clear blue.

My knees wobbly, my pulse racing, I walk towards the overflow car park. On the corner, a woman has just come out of her car. Fumbling with her keys, the wind suddenly lifts her shirt. Turning to look round quickly, she frowns as our eyes meet. Then she opens a deep red umbrella and hides her damaged dignity underneath. I can hear raindrops thudding on to the fabric. Her high-heeled shoes click on the tarmac. I hope she is not the next patient who has come to see Dr Cole but will be whisked off to Mr Rakesh to relieve Dr Cole of his workload. It's better if she's come for an appointment with Dr Mackenzie or even with the absent Dr Emery.

The rain changes into big drops that fall down with the force of hailstones. I have to run the last metres to my car.

I sit behind the steering wheel and stare as the rain makes a secretive pattern on the window, blurring my view. I can't make myself put the key in the ignition and start the car. I feel like crying and shouting, calling Mr Rakesh names. Somehow it is easier to blame him. Deep inside I know that it wouldn't have made much difference if he had been more careful and not let the words tumble out. I feel like a sailing yacht breaking through the waves and heading for shallow waters, rock pinnacles hidden under the surface. Any minute, any second, the sharp edges will tear open the keel, water will leek in and I will drown. My life is like a paper napkin, torn into tiny shreds that are picked up by the wind and blown in several directions, as if I have never even existed.

A bus rounds the corner and comes to a jerking stop just yards away. Its windows are steamed up on the inside and the passengers are blurred visions. A cloud of black smoke blurts from the exhaust, obscuring a woman waiting under the shelter of the bus stop, for a moment. The door opens and people tumble out, running too fast towards the hospital entrance to bother about opening umbrellas.

It is not the world that has changed. It is me. Everything around me remains unchanged. It is the diagnosis that leeks into my consciousness, telling me that I can no longer close my eyes for the fact that something inside me is wrong. Perhaps, after all, Mr Rakesh has done me a favour by telling me the truth so bluntly. Still, I will never forgive him.

22

APRIL

Helen Tilley is in her mid-thirties, wears dark trousers and one of those long and wide blouses that some women believe hides obesity. Her brown hair is pulled back from her face and twisted into a knot on the top of her head. Displaying a cold efficiency, she makes me feel sorry for the foster children she deals with. For their sake I hope she's just pulling strings on administrational and supervisory levels.

'How can I help you, Detective Inspector?' She cast a quick glance at her watch.

The office is officially closed for visitors but as it transpires, Helen Tilley dutifully agrees to make an exception for me. In more than one way I am grateful. After I left all my hopes and expectations for the future with Mr Rakesh in the hospital, I sat in my car for about an hour, staring out of the window, not seeing anything. Scared, confused, angry and worried sick. I didn't know what to do, as there is nothing I can do. Only wait. Or work.

'Thanks for seeing me at such short notice, Mrs Tilley, ' I say politely.

She lifts shoulders dusted with dandruff. 'We are stretched to the limit,' she says rather accusingly. 'We are buried with paperwork.'

'Tell me about it.'

'And certain... events in the media recently, however

rare, put more and more pressure on us.'

I nod in agreement. 'I appreciate your help, Ms Tilley.'

'Hmm. I'm not so sure that I can be of help, Detective Inspector, but nevertheless... go on.'

She's abrupt and to the point, barely giving me time to explain the situation and what I've come for. With regular intervals her painted eyebrows rise and her forehead creases, expressing a variety of mixed feelings and thoughts. When I pause, she shakes her head as though she's already made up her mind that she can't help me.

Simon and Jane Croft may have fostered children, but that was before her time. She doesn't remember their names. They are not in the computer system, which she obediently checks by rapidly tapping on a keyboard and a split-second look at the screen. She explains that they started working with a computer system a couple of years ago. Perhaps her predecessor once had the intention to store the older files, but there was no budget to hire someone to scan thousands of documents.

I don't attempt to hide my disappointment. 'So there is no information whatsoever about foster parents and children, say, from the last twenty years?'

'Not in our current system. Even if we still had the files to hand, I would have kept them from you for reasons of confidentiality and privacy, inspector. Unless you produce a search warrant.'

'I can get one,' I say, bluffing, and she knows it. There is no way I can persuade Guthrie to make an effort in that direction. He'll probably say I lost my mind.

'But I do have some good news for you, inspector. It's our policy to keep the files for so many years.'

I light up. 'So there is a file on Mr and Mrs Croft?'

There is a hint in her blue-green eyes that tells me she's not deprived of all humour, albeit, it transpires, very dark and cynical. 'They're stored in a self storage warehouse on an industrial estate just outside Bristol.'

'Can I see them?'

Pressing her hands on her desk, fingers wide apart, she gives me a pitying look. 'It would be a needle in a haystack. From what I've been told I understand that the files are more or less dumped into carton boxes. No one seemed to have had a system, or even the presence of mind to write anything on the boxes.' She stares at her fingers and then looks at her watch meaningfully. Her time is limited. Mine is too.

She produces the faintest of smiles. 'If you are that insistent, inspector, and I have the feeling you are, then I suggest you try Mrs Turton. She held sway here for years. Maybe she can help you. Not with the files, obviously, but she seems to have had quite a memory.' She taps the keyboard again and somewhere in the office a printer comes to life, producing an A4 sheet with a single line on the top displaying a name and an address in Tavistock.

Small and rather frail, Eileen Turton wears on her face the expression that life has become a huge disappointment. She has short dark blonde hair with an inch of grey roots and so thin that I can see her skull beneath it. Her eyebrows are little more than a thin line painted on with maroon pencil. Her face is unhealthily pale and almost transparent, with cracked jowls hanging loose. Beside her mouth is a dark mole with three long black hairs. She studies my face rather than my warrant card. I can almost hear her brain click. She's suspicious and reluctant, and I can understand why she isn't willing to let me in. After all, I'm a complete stranger to her. Yet, she seems to be curious.

'How can I help you, inspector?' Her tone implies that she can't imagine she can be of any help. Or maybe she just doesn't want to.

'I'm investigating a murder,' I explain quietly, deciding to win her trust first.

She raises the brow lines and her forehead changes into a spider web of creases. 'What makes you think that I can help you?' Her tone is sceptical with a hint of sarcasm.

'A woman was killed last week. Her ex-husband was killed six months ago. I believe that they were foster parents years ago.'

'And does that mean something?'

'I don't know. That's what I'm trying to find out.'

'And how did you get my name and address?'

'Mrs Tilley from South West Foster Care said you might remember.'

'Did she?' She takes a moment to make up her mind. 'Well, you'd better come in.'

The living room has furniture in the style of the sixties. A bookcase is filled with old looking books and a complete edition of Encyclopaedia Britannica, spines with faded colours and titles in gold. The brown carpet is worn out in places where chairs are moved frequently, and the folds in the gold and maroon curtains have faded, but it still creates an ambience of wealth. Oranges and yellows dominate and seem to add a warm glow to her life.

As I sit down, she remains in the doorway for a few moments, lost in long memories. Then she shakes her head, tugging at the white cuffs that pop out from under the sleeves of her orange cardigan as if a sudden chill reaches her.

'Who is this about, inspector?'

'Jane and Simon Croft. The fact that they both died of unnatural causes makes me rather suspicious.'

'I see.'

'They were divorced years ago. Mr Croft re-married. They had no contact, yet they were killed within six months of each other. So far there's no clear evidence that their deaths are linked, but the option is still open. As far as I know, the only link between them is the fact that they used to foster children. I believe that Jane Croft was seeing, or about to see, one of her former foster children before her death.'

She frowns, rubbing the bridge of her nose with her thumb. 'So you're after the foster children.'

I nod, sensing her dismay. 'I'm currently following

several lines of inquiry, Mrs Turton.'

'What exactly is it that you want from me, inspector?'

'I was hoping you can help me with the names of the Croft's foster children.'

'I'm sure you understand that the information is confidential.'

'All I want is a chat with Mr and Mrs Croft's foster children. Hopefully to eliminate them from the investigation.'

She comes forward and sits down on the edge of a chair, her back as straight as an arrow. 'I seem to remember there was a daughter.'

I nod. 'That's correct. But at the moment she's in pieces about her mother's death. At this point, I don't want to trouble her too much.' For some reason, I don't tell her that Stella Croft isn't yet aware that her father died too.

Looking thoughtful, her eyes a watery blue, she lifts her chin. Her loose jowls vibrate. 'What if I refuse to help you?'

I decide to tell her the truth. 'Then I'll have to get a warrant and go through boxes of files that South West Foster Care has stored in a warehouse. It will take time. And money.'

I make it sound as if it annoys me that the official rules are delaying the inquiry. In truth, I am pretty certain that DCI Guthrie will believe it's all nonsense, and will refuse to get me a search warrant. I must admit the whole issue is maybe farfetched, but there are no other clues

Instinctively she knows. 'I'm afraid you'll have to get your warrant, inspector. I can't help you.'

'I understand.' I try to remain calm and reasonable. 'I have to deal with a daughter who's just lost her mother in a brutal killing. The only thing I can do for her at this stage, is bringing the killer to justice.'

'That's not my responsibility.'

Her abrupt words make me realise putting up a fight will be a waste of time. I am getting nowhere with this woman. At some point in her career she must have had a bad experience with police. She doesn't trust me and somehow I have become an easy target for revenge.

'It is mine.'

Leaning back in her chair, she smiles with a coldness that makes her look more like Helen Tilley than she would like. Placing her hands on the armrests, she appears to want to get up, to end the conversation, which, in my opinion, hasn't even started yet.

Suddenly I feel jetlagged, exhausted, as though I haven't slept for days. From nowhere, unannounced, a pounding headache comes on. Trying not to make it look like she has defeated me, I rub my eyebrows with the knuckle of my index finger.

'If that's all, inspector, I'd suggest… '

My phone rings, its increasing sound erupts from my pocket. Annoyance crosses her face as though she's personally offended by the interruption. For revenge rather than anything else, I retrieve my phone from my pocket and check the caller's name on the display. It is anonymous.

'I'm sorry, I really must take this call,' I lie.

It is the hospital. Mr Rakesh is apologising curtly for disturbing me, not meaning it. Instantly I wish I wasn't so keen on answering this call.

I have difficulty concentrating on him. He's telling me my case has been discussed with Dr Cole and the team. He is aware that I already have an appointment in a month's time, but I am expected to come to the hospital within the next couple of days. I will then see Doctor Cole and hear what they've planned for further treatment.

His words fall like pebbles in a pond. Dull plops and rings of waves grow bigger until they rustle into the reeds.

'So there is no doubt that it is cancer?' I interrupt him abruptly, one tiny part of me believing that this is all down to Mr Rakesh, making a huge mistake.

'I'm afraid so.' I remember his shocking boldness when he suggested going home and having a drink. Since then I despise the man. I have already worked out several ways of killing him without getting caught. But there's too much of a risk to even consider my chances of getting away with it. Spending my last days in prison can't be worth it.

Eileen Turton is fidgeting in her chair, clearing her throat, moving her hands to rise from the chair, clearly with the intention to politely get rid of me. I am wrong. Although I can almost feel her hesitation, she rests her head on the backrest and looks at me with more emotion and compassion. Even if I wanted to, I can't move; I seem to be paralysed in the chair.

'What about an operation? Treatment?' The mobile shakes against my ear.

'Well,' Mr Rakesh replies slowly. 'That'll be discussed with you, Mr Tregunna. Sooner rather than later. Luckily, we've caught it rather early. We now have a relatively fair chance.' He stops as if in mid-sentence. 'I thought I'd rather let you know before the secretary calls you.'

How considerate, I think, not saying anything. Without thanking him for his effort I switch off my mobile and put it back in my pocket. As the significance of Mr Rakesh's words sink in, I have the strange swimming sensation of a man whose senses are moving into overdrive. The speed of my life increases so fast I can barely keep up with it. It is as though I will reach my destination without being able to stop myself. I am on a rollercoaster with no control over the brakes.

Eileen Turton is folding and unfolding her fingers, looking down at them as though trying to find inspiration. 'Mr Tregunna, I'm very sorry.' She's avoiding my eyes.

Her pity feels like an insult. I have to struggle to keep my self-control. I'd like to hit her in the face and at the same time I want to put my head against her chest and cry. Yet I don't want this cold, emotionless woman to witness my despair. I feel like crawling into a dark hole in the ground, licking away the salt Mr Rakesh has rubbed into my wounds. I had a sinking feeling that it would come to this, but it feels completely different when it is confirmed with a strong sense of urgency. I guess hope is what keeps us all going.

'Would you like a cup of tea or coffee?' She offers a

comforting drink and her sympathy at the same time.

I blink at her, astounded by the gentleness that has suddenly crossed over her face. I didn't think she had it in her. She's reading my thoughts with a hint of sadness. Without waiting for a reply, she gets up and disappears into the kitchen. The phone call from Mr Rakesh has changed everything. Suddenly I am not a policeman anymore, but a human being and Eileen Turton is a social worker.

I can smell fresh coffee before I hear her come back. She brings in a tray with two cups and saucers and a matching sugar and milk bowl. They are delicate gold-rimmed China with pink roses on. Her eyes move across my face with sympathy before she leaves to fetch the teapot.

'Well now, Mr Tregunna.' She has deliberately stopped referring to me as inspector. 'To be truthful, I don't know what to say.' She tries to soften the atmosphere with a swift twisting of her upper lips.

'It's all right.'

'Would you like to talk about it?'

I take a deep breath and exhale through my nose. 'About what?'

Her smile is genuinely warm and full of sympathy. It changes her face completely. 'I understand, you know. My husband had bowel cancer.'

Her last words drop another silence between us, but this time it is rather an understanding intermezzo. She's offering me something without any form of demanding.

'Did he die?'

'Yes.' Memories, long consigned to the dark corners of her mind, begin to surface. Etched images and conversations, nuance for nuance, word for word; scenes like ones from horror movies, emotional drama's and light comedies pass her face and for a moment she's stepped into a completely different world.

Then she smiles and shakes her shoulders. 'Ironically, he was declared free of everything five years after his treatment.

A week later he crossed a street and was hit by a lorry.'

Suddenly the dull grey shades in her eyes have disappeared. I feel like a schoolboy sharing a secret with a friend who's just sneaked a kiss from a girl behind a shed. Eileen Turton's eyes are twinkling now and she looks as though she is about to giggle. Our eyes meet and I can't stop the words tumbling out.

23

APRIL

I have very little recollection of the drive back to Newquay. Eileen Turton offered me homemade vegetable soup and crispy French bread. She seemed adamant that I eat something, yet understood that I had lost my appetite. Shortly after Mr Rakesh's phone call, I received a call from a receptionist, telling me that I am expected to see Doctor Cole on Monday, followed by a pre-op assessment, and the actual operation being scheduled for the end of the week. I feel like time is not going simultaneously with my life. It is as if I am constantly catching up with events that have taken control of my life, my future. Or rather, what's left of it.

Tears run down my face. My throat hurts, my heart is pounding in my head, yet I'm not crying. I wish I could. It will relieve my headache, the tension in my chest. What's the point in crying anyway? It won't change the situation I'm in.

The investigation has almost dissolved in a thick grey mist. Since Jane Croft's body was discovered, she has hardly left my thoughts. Now there are more important issues to think about. I'll have to abandon my first murder investigation and leave it in the hands of a colleague. I will have to tell DCI Guthrie. Who will take over from me? Will he allow Penrose the chance, bearing in mind that she's been part of the investigation from the beginning? I worry about the investigation, but at the same time I don't care. This is all about my body, my health, my chances of having a future as bright and carefree as you expect when you're young.

I cross the Tamar River, Cornwall's county border, with a sense of relief that I am close to home now. I'm not Cornish born and bred, but I do understand their feeling of being at a loss beyond the Tamar. My phone rings as if it has been waiting for me to enter the county. It shatters the silence like the collapse of a pyramid of glasses that is filled from the top with champagne in an attempt to break some silly record. I haven't put my mobile in the cradle or connected it to the speaker system. It is illegal to use a phone whilst driving, but I just can't ignore the idea that it might be something important. Like the murderer of Jane Croft has come forward. Then, for a split-second, I have a crazy idea that they've discovered that Rakesh has been mixed up my file with that of someone else.

Penrose. I wish I hadn't answered. 'Yes Jennette?'

'We've had a phone call, sir.'

Without realising I have slowed down. A car passes me, pulling a caravan - holiday makers or just coming for a weekend. A woman sitting in the passenger seat gestures that I shouldn't be on the phone. She's right. I have to focus my attention on the road.

'Listen Jennette, I'm driving.'

'But sir?' There is hesitation in her voice, replacing the earlier tone of excitement.

'Is it important?'

'I presume so, sir.' She pulls back, not understanding my reaction.

'I'll find somewhere to park and I'll call you back.'

'OK. I'm at the station.'

I disengage and drop the phone on the passenger seat. Her words hang in the silence of my car. In a few days I will know more about the plans Doctor Cole and his team have scheduled for me. Meanwhile I seem to be trapped in a huge soap bubble waiting for it to burst. I can't deal with the waiting. I need something to keep myself busy, otherwise I'll drive myself mad. The case is all that I have left.

Fifteen minutes later I pull into the motorway services with a petrol station, a 24-hour supermarket and a Little Chef restaurant. I go to the toilets and buy a can of Coke and a packet of five Mars Bars. Five for the price of four. The fifth is free.

Back in my car, I connect my mobile to the car system. The display lights up with a list of missed calls. Leaning my head on to the headrest I stare out of the window. A single drop forebodes a shower. I sip my Coke and eat two Mars Bars. I smile softly, remembering a silly family joke: the one that is free tastes so much better than the other ones.

The windows have steamed up. I feel hot, feverish suddenly. I press the button to open the window and feel cool and wet air on my face.

The cry of a child drifts in, making me turn my head unconsciously, redirecting my attention for a few moments. A young mother hurries on the pavement towards a little boy, escaped from her reach. He stumbles and lands on hands and knees. The mother bends forward to examine a red spot on the palm of his hand. A tissue is taken from her trouser pocket, a lick of her tongue to stop red tears from running down his leg.

With a sudden jolt, a memory jumps up. A fall. Not my mother, but my father hurrying towards me, leaning over, and uttering words of comfort. The streams of blood running down my leg rather than the pain made me panic and for a long moment I feared for my life. I must have been about the same age as the little boy. At that age I had years, decades of the future to look forward to. The thought makes me regret suddenly that those years have gone by almost unnoticed.

Buttons are pressed and Penrose answers almost immediately.

'Sir?'

'Yes, Jennette. I'm sorry.'

'Where are you, sir?'

I don't want her to know where I am, as her next question will be what I'm doing and when I'll be back at the station.

'Sorry, Jennette. What's the news?'

'We've had a phone call from Mrs Gardiner, sir. The mother of the twins.' Sarcasm marks her tone. 'She says she needs to speak to you as soon as possible.'

Lauren. I take a sharp breath. 'Why?'

'She says she has some important news.'

I let out a long silent whistle. Maybe this is the snippet of good news I've been waiting for, yet I cannot feel as much excitement as I would before the discovery of a tumour. I feel disconnected, as if someone has erected a wall of milky glass between the investigation and me. The voices beyond are muffled. 'That sounds like good news, Jennette. When are you going to see her?'

'Well, that's a bit of a problem, sir. I've been trying to call you.'

'Sorry. Why, what's the problem?'

'She insists on speaking with you, sir.'

Any other time I would have been delighted to have an excuse to see Lauren Gardiner again. Now I feel like I'm standing in front of a brick wall. What's the point of dreaming about a chance of a future that involves Lauren? I am a dying man, hardly worth offering to a woman.

'OK, thanks, I'll contact her.'

'When? Tonight?' Her voice is curt, let down. Clearly she feels offended that Lauren didn't want to talk to her and I have only made things worse by not suggesting to pick her up before I see Lauren.

'I'm on my way back from Devon, Jennette. I'm not sure what time I'll be back in Newquay. If it's not too late, I'll pop in Mrs Gardiner's tonight. Otherwise it'll have to wait till tomorrow.

The young mother and the little boy are walking back towards their car. She has lifted him in her arms, holding him safely. Whatever she said to him, his pain seems to have gone and he smiles through his tears. I wish I were young again, I wish I could turn to my parents for warmth and comfort.

My parents. I need to tell them. The question is, how do you tell a father, a mother that their child is dying?

24

APRIL

Dressed in grey jogging bottoms and a matching jacket over a pink vest, Lauren Gardiner opens the door, bracing one arm on the frame as if waiting to hear me try and sell her double glazing or solar panels. With her hair tucked up in a curly mess on top of her head she looks gorgeous.

'Inspector.' She sounds warm and sleepy.

'Mrs Gardiner, I received your message.'

'Yes. Right.' She frowns as though suddenly remembering an appointment with the dentist.

'Isn't ten o'clock a bit late, inspector?'

'I'm sorry. I thought it was urgent.'

'It was kind of urgent hours ago.'

Her sarcasm hits me like an insult. Self-pity comes to the surface as I think of all the tears I shed in the last couple of hours. It suddenly feels like there are many more to come.

'I was on my way back from Tavistock when I was told about your call.' I almost stammer. It hurts to feel like I am an unwanted intruder. The smell of the sea is strong on the wind. Raindrops are leaking down my neck, soaking my shoulders, sending a chill along my spine.

'They said you were off.' She makes it sound like an accusation.

'I'm sorry.' She produces a faint smile. Less offensive. 'You'd better come in. But I'm not waking the boys up.' Her last words hang between us.

She steps back to let me pass. I can smell her shampoo, something sweet that reminds me of ripe fruit. Apples and cinnamon.

'You're wet. Can I make you a cup of tea? Coffee?'

I hesitate. 'Anything stronger?'

She closes the door behind me. The lock clicks. I can sense her doubt rising. This is not supposed to be a social call. Maybe she regrets already letting me in.

'I'm afraid there's only white wine.'

'If you don't mind?'

She bites off a smile. 'All right then.'

The TV is on, the sound turned down. Ten o'clock. A newsreader is reporting on a peaceful protest march that got out of hand. There are bricks thrown, policemen with shields and dogs. It is like a film, the protesters are the actors, the policemen somehow on the wrong side of sympathy.

On the coffee table and mantelpiece are little bowls of coloured glass, a candle burning in each one. A faint smell of vanilla hangs in the air, warm, homely. I sit in the same armchair I sat in when I visited her with Penrose and stretch my legs. It is surprising how easy it is to relax. Tiredness kicks in. My eyelids are heavy and it's difficult suddenly to stay awake. Coffee would have been a better idea than white wine. It feels like I'll never want to leave this place.

Lauren disappears to fetch wine and glasses. On the armrest of the other chair is an open book, its title something with *Africa*, and its cover upright, showing a couple silhouetted against a pink and orange sunset.

She fills two wine glasses on high stems. A plate with cheese biscuits sits between them. It looks like I am seen as a friend, rather than a policeman to be wary of.

'Are you all right, inspector?' She frowns, examining me as if my skin is covered with rashes and she's trying to determine my allergy. 'You look tired.'

'It's been a long day.'

'I'm sorry. I didn't realise.' She blushes with embarrassment. 'I guess it could have waited until tomorrow morning.'

The wine is sweet and very cold. It is tempting to drain my glass and ask for more.

She is nervous suddenly. 'It was about five when I called you.' This time it sounds more like a statement than an accusation. She laces her hands together, wrapping them around her knees. A pose of relaxation and at the same time she is hardening herself for what is to come. 'I can't tell you how sorry I am, inspector. I honestly didn't know. If I'd known what they were capable of…' she gestures uncontrollably, eyes misting with tears.

'Your boys?'

She doesn't reply, lost in thoughts that make her frown.

'How are they coping?' I offer a smile loaded with sympathy. I want her to feel safe with me. Trusting.

'It's good that they have each other, that they can share the… experience.'

'Do they talk about it?'

'Not to me. I guess… I hope they talk to each other.' Her eyes drift away. She's somewhere else. A smile has reached her lips and for some unfathomable reason I feel a pang of jealousy.

'They're identical twins. Two boys with one mind, so to speak. Sometimes I feel like I am an intruder in their world, a complete stranger.' There is sadness in her eyes. 'They share a world of their own and I am not always part of it.'

Her bottom lip trembles and I want to kiss her. As if she can read my mind, she looks up suddenly and an awkward silence settles between us. We look at each other and look away at the same time. We are desperately seeking words, but there are none.

My stomach flutters. Authors of romances would maybe call it a somersault. But it is nothing romantic like that. It is my mobile vibrating in my pocket. I hold my hand against my side, wishing I'd switched it off, hesitating to take the call with a chance of spoiling something. But then... it's past ten. Who would call me at this time of night? My mother? I don't want to talk to her. I'll have to see my parents soon enough. Tell them. I will. Soon, but not now.

'Aren't you going to answer? It may be important.'

'Of course. I'm sorry.' I retrieve the mobile from my pocket and stare at the display. No caller ID.

'Yes?' I say curtly.

'Andy?'

'Yes.'

'Where are you?' The voice is high pitched and so loud Lauren must hear her too.

I sigh. 'What do you want, Marie?'

'I asked: where are you?'

I glance at Lauren. 'I'm with a friend.'

'A woman?'

The bold question embarrasses Lauren. Her eyes flash and she starts checking the candles in their glass holders, cheeks coloured pink. An odd silence stretches out, filling the air, clinging like strands of a cobweb.

'That's none of your business,' I tell Marie.

'So you *are* with a woman.' It sounds like a statement spoken with a voice that expresses a world of female disappointment. Like a woman hurt, neglected.

'Yes, but I don't...'

'I wanted to see you tonight.'

I can feel Lauren stiffen, the smile frozen on her face, her complexion a little paler, or maybe that is just my imagination. I want to disconnect, but I can't. There is something in Marie's voice that makes me feel like I'm missing the point.

'I wasn't aware we had an appointment, Marie.'

'Is she pretty?'

'Who? What? Marie, I don't think...'

'Answer me! Is she pretty?'

I stare at Lauren, whose expression is now vacant. Her face doesn't even begin to hint at what's on her mind. 'Yes,' I say slowly. 'Yes, Marie, she is very pretty.'

There's a yell like an animal caught in surprise by its predator. Then the connection is ended abruptly.

'I'm sorry,' I say awkwardly, not really knowing what I'm apologizing for.

Lauren's pale blue eyes are cool, disconnecting. 'Your girlfriend?'

'I don't have a girlfriend. Or a wife. Or anyone else.'

'Oh.' She looks down, sips her wine. 'She sounds like one.'

'She's a witness in the murder investigation.' My reply can't have been more stupid. Lauren raises an eyebrow, her face full with resentment. 'My apologies, inspector. It's not my business.'

I wish it were.

She stands up abruptly, mumbling something about more cheese biscuits. I too feel like running away, like hiding my head under the bedclothes and pretending that nothing bad has happened.

She comes back with the rest of a packet of cheese biscuits, taking her time to arrange them on the plate. Neither of us has eaten any.

'Listen, inspector.' Her tone is cold, distant. 'It may be better if you come back in the morning.'

'You haven't told me what this is all about,' I say gently.

She looks down, leaning forward and examining the biscuits as if they are all different and she's allowed to choose only one.

'You'll have to talk to them yourself, inspector. They lied. I am so ashamed. They sto… they took something. From that dead woman.'

Before I can say something, ask for an explanation, she gets up and takes a rolled up plastic bag from the cupboard under the TV. Her hand disappears in it and when it comes out, she drops something on the table as if it is burning her skin.

25

APRIL

Joe and Stuart sit closely next to each other, hair wet from an earlier shower, school uniform perfectly in place. They are quiet, ashamed and looking down at their hands. The TV is off. No music comes from upstairs this time. A smell of toast hangs in the air as if to remind me that soon the boys have to go to school.

'Tell the inspector how sorry you are,' Lauren instructs, her voice still heavy with anger.

'Sorry sir,' echoes from two similar mouths.

I sit down and Lauren perches on the armrest of the couch. There is no offer for coffee or tea.

'And now I want you to tell the inspector everything. And I mean everything!'

A glance of identical pairs of eyes is exchanged. Their faces are pale, knowing that this time their mother isn't going to forget so easily what they've done.

'Joe found it.' It sounds like a statement rather than an accusation or a betrayal. Stuart, the most sensitive of the two, pokes his elbow into his brother's side. 'Tell him, man!'

'It was me, sir.' Joe looks up shyly. I can see a mixture of defeat and shame, yet there is also a hint of provocation. He is sorry for what happened, but a tiny bit of him is even more sorry that their secret is discovered.

'Tell me what happened, Joe.'

'It all happened so quickly. I didn't think. I saw… what I saw on the other side of the fence. I was curious to find out what it was. So I climbed over. Well, you know that already.' His voice is thin, weighed down by guilt and his mother's anger and disappointment.

'Go on,' I say.

'The plastic was open on one side and I lifted it to look inside.'

'You climbed over because we heard it,' Stuart intervenes suddenly.

Joe nods reluctantly, encouraged by his brother's loyal assistance. 'I saw her hand first. The mobile phone was sort of wrapped in a hankie. But as it rang I could see it light up through the fabric.'

I lean forward. I know already about the phone, but this new information is all the more significant. 'So you're saying that Jane Croft, the dead woman, had in her hand a handkerchief and in it was a mobile phone that was ringing?'

'Yes sir.

'And you took it.'

'I didn't mean to take it, sir. I just thought…' Joe stammers, his face red and on the brink of crying. 'I sort of wondered… why she wasn't answering.'

'And then you thought to answer it for her.'

'Well, yes, maybe. I don't know.'

'OK. So you took the phone from her hand, and then, what? Did you answer? Did you speak to someone?'

'No sir. It stopped ringing before I found the right button.'

'Did you take a look at the display? Was there a name, or a number?'

'I didn't really see, sir. It all happened so quickly. I realised then that there was a body in the plastic and… I don't know sir. I just had the mobile in my hand and I switched it off when I saw Mum come out of the supermarket.'

'And you kept it hidden.'

His face is now a deep red with shame, a tear rolling down

his cheek, which he wipes away with anger and frustration. 'The woman wouldn't use it anymore, would she?' Through a layer of his shyness the provocation emerges all of the sudden.

'Joe!' Lauren snaps incredulously.

His eyes are filling with tears. I look away. Up to a point, I can understand why Joe did what he did. Nowadays a mobile phone is a must-have for everyone, even for young children. Like Gollum knew he ought to get rid of the Ring but couldn't, the possession of the mobile phone was as precious for Joe. Perhaps at his age, I would have done the same. However, I can't dismiss the fact that he kept a significant clue hidden from the murder investigation. If he hadn't taken the phone home with him, forensics might have been able to find out why Jane held her phone in her hand, or why her murderer didn't take it off her. Perhaps we'd now been steps closer to finding the murderer.

Joe must have kept it in his hand or his pocket all the time, even when they were at the police station. Maybe they were too young to be aware of its significance. Perhaps we'd have been steps closer to finding the murderer by now.

'Joe, when you came home, did you switch it on again?'

'Yes.'

'Did you use it at all?'

'Eh, we called a few friends.'

It's so easy to imagine them sitting on the edge of the bed, hunched over their treasure, the fact that they obtained it illegally shoved to the back of their minds.

'Has there been anyone who phoned you? Other than your friends?'

There is a quick exchange of nervous realisation that all their little secrets are going to be revealed. They have already faced their mother's fury, now they know that they have to endure mine as well.

Noticing their distress, I offer a little smile, to reassure them that I'd rather listen to the truth than more lies.

'It rang several times, sir.' Stuart said slowly.

'And did you answer?'

'Yes we did.'

'Who was it?'

'I don't know. She was really angry. She asked where I was.'

'A woman? Did she say her name?'

He shakes his head, casting a quick look at his brother. 'We thought, well, Stuart thought that she wanted the phone back.'

Taking a deep breath, I feel my heart quicken. It suddenly dawns on me that the phone may not have been Jane's at all. If she somehow managed to get hold of the phone of her murderer, then this phone can turn out vital for the investigation. 'Did she actually say that it was her phone?'

'No, she just asked where I was, but Stuart thought it was because she wanted to come to our home and collect it.'

'What did you say?'

'Nothing, sir. I was just… scared.'

Stuart nods vigorously. 'We didn't want mum to find out.'

'I'm so sorry, inspector.' Lauren is almost in tears, deeply disappointed by her sons' behaviour, embarrassed with the realisation of its importance.

'I'll have it examined,' I say matter-of-factly. 'Hopefully we can still retrieve some information off it. And I hope it will lead us to catching the murderer of that poor woman.' When I look at the boys, I keep my voice and expression serious. 'If there is anything you two haven't told me yet, you'd better do that now. We will find out anyway.'

Two identical bottom lips tremble. 'Mum said we could get in serious trouble.'

I suppress a smile. I hardly ever see the point in getting angry about something that can't be undone, yet the boys need to know that what they did was unacceptable. 'Like obstructing an officer of police in doing his duty? Stealing something that wasn't yours? Taking an item of evidence away from a crime scene?'

I don't know enough about kids their age to have an idea what they do or don't understand, but the horror on Lauren's face tells me enough. She gets up, her head down, and tells her sons that it is time to go to school. I think we are all, in a way, relieved that the conversation is over. For them, is it out of their hands. It is in mine now and for some reason I hesitate doing what I know I should do: handing Jane Croft's mobile to forensics. Yet deep down I have already come to a different decision, one that could well finish my police career prematurely.

'Stuart, where are your shoes?' With Lauren's voice the world comes back to its normal pace and the usual little dilemmas of life to deal with.

As I rise to my feet, Stuart ducks to find his shoes under the sofa, but Joe stands beside me, pulling my sleeve. 'There's something else, sir,' he says timidly. Now that the secret is out in the open, they seem more than willing to be helpful.

'I kept the phone hidden under my pillow at night,' he explains, casting a shy look at his mother. 'That first night, I must have pressed the phone because suddenly I heard a voice.'

'The same woman?'

'No, it was a man.'

'What did he say exactly?'

'He said, when are you coming home?'

26

APRIL

DCI Guthrie barely looks up when I enter his office. His desk is placed at a sidewall, so that when he turns in his leather chair, he can look out of the window and enjoy a stunning view across the bay. On the opposite wall is a painting of a golden sunset, the cliffs in darkness and sparkles of light on the waves entering a Cornish cove. An old tin mine on the cliffs to the right and on the left is the lone figure of a man balancing on the edge. I don't know why the painting has always appealed to me. Or perhaps it's just that I can't fathom how a man like Guthrie can feel the hidden emotion of the whole piece of art, the loneliness and desolation of the portrayed figure in particular. I've often toyed with the idea asking him if he bought the painting himself or was given it as a present. Probably the latter.

'DI Tregunna. I'll be with you in a sec.' Waving a hand towards two chairs at the other side of his desk he keeps his eyes on an open file in front of him.

His face is smooth, presumably after numerous appointments to inject Botox. Dyed brown hair falls just half an inch longer than is the fashion, some of the curly ends escaping to brush against his collar and his cheekbones. His complexion wears the unhealthy shine from a bottle at a beauty salon. From an old picture I know his teeth used to be slightly crooked, now they have been transformed into two even, dazzlingly white rows.

As always, his desk is clean and tidy, a wooden tray with two pens and a small glass jar for paperclips. On the corner edge are two trays, IN and OUT. The out-tray is empty most of the time, the in-tray half filled with manila folders in various colours. In front of him lies a blue one, open. He has either just started reading it, or he has randomly grabbed one from the tray in order to give the impression of a working man.

He leans back and his eyes stare over a half rimmed pair of reading glasses. 'How's the investigation going?'

I hesitate. He attended the daily briefing this morning, standing nearest to the doorway with his arms folded across his chest as though hoping to be called out by someone he finds more interesting. The good part about him is that he rarely opens his mouth. He seems to trust those who work on the cases he supervises, but aims his humiliation afterwards, when he catches you in the corridor, or worse, in the canteen. His voice will generally be cold and loud, drumming through open and closed doors, even through walls, until all conversations and fingers tapping on keyboards have stopped.

Peering over his fashionable reading glasses on his perfectly shaped nose, he repeats the question.

'The investigation is on-going, sir. Everyone is working very hard.'

'No news then?' His eyes dart back to the file on his desk for which he seems to have more attention than for me.

'No sir.' I clear my throat. 'Actually, sir, that's not what I'd like to have a word with you about.'

He doesn't appear to have heard me. 'You've got a whole team of CID and uniforms working on this case, Tregunna.' Closing the file thoughtfully, he puts his elbows on either side, lacing his fingers and resting his perfect chin on them. His voice is smooth, with only a steel tone for the more experienced listener. 'And you haven't found the murderer.' He casts me an insulting look, an accusation about all my failings in the way he lifts his upper lip. 'Do you have any idea how it makes me feel when I have to attend a press conference? When they ask questions I have no answers for?'

Press meetings are the least of my worries. All I know right now is that I feel like I am on the set of a police series. I always thought that facing a ridiculed superior was for the benefit of the story. Until I met Guthrie I would never have believed that such people really existed.

'We're doing our best, sir.' I bow my head, not because I feel like I have to apologise, but because from experience I know it is the best way to deal with him.

Only half satisfied, he rises from his chair, pulling his snow-white cuffs as if he has rolled his sleeves earlier to appear to be working hard. He stands near a filing cabinet. According to the cynics, it's only there for the purpose of the very expensive looking coffee machine. Pressing a button, the air fills with a mouth-watering smell. He fills a single white mug, which he puts carefully on his desk. The coffee machine already forgotten, he turns his full attention to me. His screenplay written, there is no line whatsoever that says to offer me coffee. Just as well. The less time I spend in his office the better. The feeling must be mutual.

'I hope you haven't come here to ask me for more men,' he sneers.

Sitting down he opens a drawer and finds in it a small bottle with sweeteners, making a show of dropping two little white pills in the otherwise black coffee.

'No sir, in fact, this is rather personal.'

His perfectly plucked brows rise and for the briefest of moments I imagine I see a flash of interest. 'No problems I hope?'

I can hear his brain click as he tries to remember anything that he might have picked up about me from previous conversations. Clearly, he draws a blank, looking at me quizzically. Other than Penrose, I haven't told anyone about my appointments with my GP and consultants at the hospital. I know she wouldn't tell a soul, let alone Guthrie.

My appointments have been sneaked in within my working hours, or a couple of hours off when I had an examination.

I keep my voice down, emotionless. 'I have to undergo an operation next week, sir. I am scheduled for Friday. Come in the day before. A pre-op assessment is on Wednesday.

'I see.' He purses his lips. 'Any idea how long this will take?' As expected, he shows no personal interest whatsoever.

'I don't know exactly how long for, sir.'

'Serious?' he asks, but his expression says that he doesn't want to know the answer.

'Keyhole operation.'

'Ah!' He leans back, feeling on safer ground. A keyhole operation means a one-inch incision, a surgeon peering into your body with a mini camera. It gives the general impression that it is of minor importance and in Guthrie's opinion, not worth talking about.

He laces his fingers behind his neck. 'Do I need to put someone else on the case, Tregunna?'

'The team is good, sir. I'm sure they can manage without me for a couple of days.' I stop for a moment. 'With you supervising of course, sir.'

'A couple of days? What does that mean? Two days?'

'I'm not sure. I presume it'll take at least the rest of the week.' I don't believe it myself but the last thing I want at this moment is that he'll decide to bring in someone to replace me. My intention is to come back to work as soon as I can.

His lips form an O as if to attempt a whistle. He hesitates with an expression of dread in his eyes. The idea of having to handle the case himself hangs like a sword above his head.

'The press is still very much onto it.' He is quick with his excuse. Sometimes I think he should have chosen a career in politics, as he is very good in avoiding questions and answering unasked ones to his own benefit. 'I can't agree with you, Tregunna. This is all too delicate. Since you don't know how long you'll be away, I'm afraid I'll have to replace you.'

'Yes sir.' I knew it would be his reaction, but I still feel disappointed.

'Right.' He glances at his golden watch. As far as he is concerned the conversation has finished. 'I'll see into that, Tregunna. Just make sure that you take the time to brief someone. I'll let you now ASAP.'

I put my hands on the armrests, ready to get up. The smell of coffee has now filled the whole office and I promise myself that whatever happens next, I will go to the nearest café to get a decent coffee. Even if he were to offer me one now, I would decline.

'Thank you, sir.'

'Anything else, Tregunna?'

'No sir.' I don't even hesitate. Perhaps I should tell him about my ideas and speculations about the murder investigation, but they are all too vague to explain, let alone unverified to spend police time on. Even to me, at this moment in time, my thoughts seem more like shots in the dark than issues to be followed up thoroughly by the investigating officers. I wonder briefly what Guthrie's reaction will be when I sum up newly discovered facts about the suspicious death of Jane Croft's ex-husband, their former foster children and the possibility that the clue to her death might be there. Or tell him about Peter Prescott who was almost too keen to report his wife missing, but didn't say a word about his secret lover. I can't explain why I haven't mentioned the discovery of Jane Croft's mobile phone. I tell myself that it is because I want to protect her and her sons from further dealings with the police force. But deep down I know that I have kept this to myself out of some sort of strange childish need of persistence to remain in charge.

It is only when I open the door of his office, one foot already on the doorstep, that his voice catches me. 'Ehem… are you all right, Andy?'

Calling me with my first name is so rare for him that I am taken a little off-balance. 'Yes sir.'

'Sure? Nothing you'd like to talk about?' he asks, but his eyes are drifting away from me and nothing has altered in his face, which has all the emotion and depth of an empty plate.

I would rather tell the window cleaner, who has more empathy in his sponge than DCI Guthrie has in his whole body. If he knew the truth about my future, about the tumour and all its implications, he would smirk over it with his mates. If he has any. 'There's nothing, sir.'

27

LAST DAY OF MAY

It has been raining almost all day, the sky clearing towards late afternoon. Now a lovely sunset with bright pinks, oranges and purples colours the sky. It will be June tomorrow. In the morning I will go to the station and find out the latest reports on the murder investigation. I'll have to hand over the investigation to my successor, DI Maloney. I haven't told anyone about my condition and I expect I'll have to deal with curious, suspicious and speculating stares. Then at lunchtime I'll have to go to the hospital in Truro to prepare for the operation.

My bag is packed. Two brand new pyjamas, T-shirts and boxer shorts, toiletries, a book, unread on my bedside table since Christmas. My phone is charged. Written and signed instructions to my solicitor are in an envelope, sealed and stamped, on my kitchen table. Ready to be mailed tomorrow. Just in case. All memorabilia from our marriage are for Lucie. A small sum is for her son who I've never seen, yet somehow I feel responsible for. Technically he's not mine, I know that, but he was conceived while she was still married to me.

I still haven't called my parents. I know I have to tell them what's going to happen to me. It's pathetic, but I just can't. I can't face my mother. She will cry and wail. I also can't bear to see my father, whose silence will be just as devastating. They'll need to know, but I don't know how to tell them. A letter? That too will devastate them. Cruel. I'm their only child.

It's half seven. I have emptied and cleaned the fridge. There's enough milk for a cup of tea in the morning. Cornflakes, though stale, have already made a feast for the birds on the balcony. The last slices of bread have provided a meal of sandwiches with an overripe tomato. As far as I know, there's nothing left to be done.

I can't relax. The TV, ironically, has a program about a family torn to pieces because three sisters have been diagnosed with breast cancer within a period of six months. They inherited their disease from their mother and grandmother. All three have a family. Sons. Daughters. I dread to think of what will go through their heads.

The book of my life is falling apart. Page after page is torn out, lying loose, as though preparing for a premature take off. Suddenly I feel there's no future for me. I feel like crying, but there are no tears.

My mobile rings. It vibrates on the coffee table, moving across its smooth surface as though the caller is using a remote to control it. I don't move. I don't want to talk. Not to anyone. I want to be left alone.

The ringing dies and the silence settles in. I once saw a TV programme about a family living in a small rural village. When the parents died, three sisters and two brothers were still living in the house. One of the sisters married, but returned within a year. Although the siblings were living together, the rhythm of their lives had different solo parts. Every Thursday morning at eight one of the women went out to do the shopping in the local convenience shop. She was always the first customer of the day, waiting outside for the shop to be opened. The eldest brother worked for the council. He cut grass and straightened hedges. Regardless of the weather, he ate his lunch on a bench under a chestnut tree on the village green. He never spoke to anyone, nor did he look anyone in the eyes. He was always in his own little world. At the weekends, he spent most of his time in a cage with fifty pigeons. He held them gently, talked to them, stroking their feathers, feeling the rapid heartbeats on his fingertips. The younger brother was even more introverted. He had no job, but wandered about the village, occasionally picking up litter to drop it in a bin. Every day he walked the same route, vacant eyes staring in front of him on the ground, mumbling stories that no one could hear. He was often followed by cruel children who yelled and threw chestnuts at him. He didn't appear to notice. Like his siblings he too preferred to be left alone. He liked toddlers, however. They could make him smile, showing an uneven set of yellowed half-broken teeth. It never occurred to him that children were frightened of him. On his daily trip, he passed the local grocery and collected five boiled sweets in a paper bag. One for him, one for each of his siblings. He'd eaten them all by the time he came home, rattling them against his teeth like the rusty chain of an old bike. One evening, he went to his room in the attic earlier than usual. He said that he was tired and that he wished to be left alone. So his brother and sisters did. The villagers wondered why they never saw him anymore. The grocer had to cancel his next delivery of boiled sweets. When someone had the guts to ask about him, the siblings shrugged, replying he may still be in his room. Two years later they had a leak in the roof that had to be repaired. When the local handyman declared the only way he could get access to the roof was through the attic window, the siblings said it was impossible. Their brother was in his room and wanted to be left alone. A few months later, the electricity had to be rewired. Refusing the electrician access to the attic was no longer an option. After all that time the brother was still in his room: a dried out mummy of a man who wanted nothing else than to be left alone. His siblings had done exactly what he asked.

A story so weird is one you can't forget. Now, the thought of dying prematurely in my own bed, without anyone knowing, makes me feel even more depressed. Briefly, I consider phoning Lucie. There are no hard feelings between us. The grudge and bitterness have gone, faded away after the divorce, which, I have to admit, was the best thing we ever agreed on. I know she is happy now with her new husband, their son and a new baby on its way. I could never have given her that happiness.

I pick up the phone, thoughtfully. We were married for eight years. She knows me like nobody else. She knows how I feel and perhaps she's the only one who can find the words to comfort me in these moments of pathetic solitude. Thinking about her pregnancy however – she must be in the sixth month by now - I dismiss the idea of calling her. Somehow my cancer and her pregnancy don't go together. It will upset her, and for what reason? There's nothing she can do about it.

I feel uneasy and uncomfortable. Now that I know there is something malicious growing inside me, it's almost as though I can physically feel the lump.

One part of me is glad the surgeon will cut it out; the other part is still not sure about the operation and its aftermath. Cutting the tumour also means cutting a part of my colon. The growth is too big to only cut out the damaged area, stretch the colon and stitch both ends together. A specialist nurse tried to explain to me what it means and how it will affect me for the rest of my life but when she mentioned the word stoma I stopped listening. I know it's foolish, but that was how I felt. I have signed the consent form however, stating I agree with what they will do to me.

The phone rings, this time it's the landline, which I rarely use. Curiously I look at the display. Anonymous. Hesitating, I stare at the screen, wondering who it might be. My mother, having an unusual fit of telepathy, knowing, feeling, that something's amiss? Inquiring about my health, whether I've eaten my fruit and veg? Have I been drinking too much?

'Are you still cross with me?' The voice is soft and a bit hoarse. Sexy. It's tempting to respond to it in these hours of loneliness. I don't recognise it immediately. For the briefest of moments I think it's Lauren. The wish is the mother to the thought. My heart jumps, flutters in my chest like a butterfly trapped in a glass jar.

I take a deep breath. 'No Marie, I'm not cross with you.'

'You didn't want to talk to me.' I ignored her calls on my mobile. Somehow she's found the number of my landline. 'So you must still be angry.'

'I'm not.'

She's quiet for a few moments. 'I'm sorry I interrupted your romance.'

'She's just a friend.'

'So you didn't sleep with her?'

'No.'

'You came home?'

'Yes. Listen, Marie, what do you want?'

'You said I could always call you.'

'I did.' I wish I hadn't.

'Is it OK then?'

'How can I help you, Marie?'

'I don't know. I kind of thought… if I could talk about what I saw at the car park that night, maybe some memories will come back to me.'

'I'm off duty. In fact, I'm on… sick leave.'

'I'm sorry.'

'Perhaps it's best you call the station.'

She chuckles. 'Shall I ask for the girl who was with you when you interviewed me? The one who's in love with you?'

'Penrose? In love with me? I don't think so.'

'That's the one. No thanks. I'd rather talk to you. You can… listen.'

I sigh. 'Marie, there's no point. I'm going into hospital tomorrow. I won't be at the station for the next couple of days, maybe weeks. Talk to Penrose or to DI Maloney. He's on the case now.'

There is a short silence. 'Hospital?'

'Hmm.' I wish I'd kept my mouth shut. Somehow it feels like every snippet of information I give her will turn against me at some point.

'Hospital. As in doctors and beds?'

'Yep.'

'Wow! Are you dying, or what?'

'Sort of.'

'You're not being serious?'

'I hope I'm not.'

She's slightly taken aback, realising hopefully that she should really call the station. 'So that's why you sound so... sad.'

'I'm not sad,' I reply, though suddenly there is a lump in my throat and my eyes are becoming misty.

'Listen. Do you know The Sailor's Bar?'

'Of course.'

'I'll meet you there in half an hour.'

'Marie, I don't think that's wise.'

A short silence. 'Half an hour,' she repeats, and abruptly cuts off the connection.

I stare at the blank screen. Of course I can call her back. There's no need at all to go and meet her. Penrose can handle her. My successor Maloney can. Even Ollie Reed can. If Marie has remembered something, she'd better talk to someone at the station. Not to me. Nor should I talk to her.

She's sitting at the bar, dressed in black jeans and a thin black blouse over a purple vest that barely covers her torso. A stud shines in her belly button. On her white blonde hair sits a black fedora and large earrings dance on her shoulders. She is chatting to a middle aged man who looks like he thinks he's already talked her into bed. He leans towards her, looking down her cleavage, licking his lips after every sip of his pint and blocks her view for a moment, allowing me to hesitate once more.

'Andy! Darling!'

It's too late to turn away. Gracefully, she lowers herself from the bar stool, pushing the man aside to hug me as if to demonstrate to him that there's no point in chatting her up. Her breasts are against my ribs and her breath is warm on my face.

'What can I get you?' She gestures vaguely at the bar. The man is wondering whether I'm worth killing.

'A Coke.'

'A Coke? Why… I see. Of course. Ice?'

'No ice.'

'Let's move into that corner.' Her dark mascara painted eyes are grinning as she glances at the man beside her. 'More privacy.'

Before I can object she brushes me towards an empty table and goes to order our drinks at the bar. I sit obediently, wondering why I came, knowing that she will end up in my bed and that like the other time, I will regret it in the morning. Yet the thought of spending my last night alone, attempting to do normal things, is too much for me to bear.

PART TWO

JUNE

28

JUNE

My father collects me from hospital and drives me home. My mother makes tea and coffee and arranges biscuits and cakes on a plate. Nervously wriggling her hands, she tells me that she cleaned my fridge and bathroom, but I sense she's been everywhere. Good old, caring mum. I find fresh orange juice, milk and butter, fruits and vegetables, eggs and cheese stocked in the fridge. Healthy. She has folded and piled towels in the bathroom cabinet that have never undergone such care before.

Exchanging looks every so often, they do their utmost to enlighten me with tales of people who lived with a stoma for years and they didn't even know, or people they've heard of being cured from cancer. It's heart-warming and depressing at the same time.

It's a relief when they leave once the dishes are done and everything in my kitchen is spick-and-span, but as the sound of their voices and footsteps fade, the silence screams through the emptiness of my flat. In hospital I counted the days, the hours, minutes. Now, the loneliness is even more devastating. The silence is a new threatening disease. Every time I look at the walls they seem to have moved closer to me, closing in as if I'm outgrowing my shell. I almost wish I were still in hospital with nurses working around my bed, the occasional laugh, a chat about nothing in particular with the patient in the other bed.

My flat is on the first floor of a small apartment block that overlooks a large pond, which has a stretch of park alongside it, a café on the water's edge and rowing boats for hire. I have never noticed before how busy the park is. There are fitness freaks running the path around the lake with dancing ponytails and sweat between shoulder blades, occasionally stopping to stretch muscles or find breath. There are grandparents and young mothers with small children feeding the ducks, and, consequently, there are the ever-scavenging seagulls. There are people with dogs who come three times a day, gathering at benches for a chat. I notice a man and a woman several times every day, with two dogs each, and I become suspicious that they may be having a secret affair, but I haven't even seen them holding hands.

I don't seem to be able to turn the tides of depression. I neglect myself, eat and sleep at irregular times, not bothered with washing or showers. Instead I become hooked to the daily soaps of which I even watch the repeats. I giggle with *Loose Women* at lunchtime, develop an eye for antiques and curiosa and I become more knowledgeable with the countless quiz programmes.

On the kitchen table, three piles of paper are mounting up, one with envelopes with bank statements, bills and seemingly undeniable offers. It is amazing that in this day and age of computerised systems, we still receive so much paperwork. You can stop receiving paper bills, find them online instead, but the same companies keep sending useless information by paper. Another pile contains circulars: a repeated reminder that a conservatory will increase both my quality of living and the value of my property. I briefly contemplate contacting them and telling them not to bother me unless they know how to fit a conservatory on my small balcony. Hang it in the air? I brush the brochure aside, knowing full-well another is on its way.

The third pile is bulkier and contains newspapers waiting to be read. I'm not particularly bothered with the news, but I want to keep them in case I want to find out anything about the progress, or lack of it, with the murder investigation.

Eventually it's my mother who sends me a wake up call. I have declined the suggestion to stay with my parents for a while. I had to fight my mother's plan to come to mine every day. I'm sure she means well, but the thought alone of having to endure their care is claustrophobic. Now, we have settled into a routine of short visits every other morning. Surprisingly my father seems to understand my need for privacy and whilst my mother busies herself in my bathroom and kitchen, he goes out for walks or errands. Annoyed with the growing pile of newspapers, she declares firmly that she will take them home and use them to protect the table when she polishes her brass and silver.

With more energy than I have displayed for the last couple of days, I protest and start sorting the papers before she can implement her threats. One paper seems to be missing. It is nagging me so much that when my parents have left I call the newspaper office and ask them to send me a copy. I need those papers to fill me in on the days when I was in hospital.

I feel like a criminal obsessed with his own work when I cut the photos and articles about Jane Croft and the dissolving investigation. I read every article thoroughly and glue them on A4 sheets. With reluctance I admit that Gerald Hill isn't a bad reporter at all. He is sharp and to the point and he keeps to the facts, rather than Kim Naylor who adds so much of her own thoughts that the whole story seems to move in a completely ludicrous direction. I realise I'll have to watch what I tell her in the future.

After five days of soap stars, antiques hunters and Jeremy Kyle for company, along with staring at a blurred photo of Jane Croft and examining the newspaper articles, I go out for a walk. A cool breeze comes from the Gannel Estuary, filling the air with hints of salt and mud. Bright white clouds drift in from high above the Atlantic. Shafts of light peer through the gaps. After all those days in hospital and at home, I find I have much less energy than I thought. Perspiration crawls over my skin, making me shiver. My knees tremble, my heart races and to make things worse, I feel insecure about the small bag that is attached to my belly with adhesive tape. I'm scared that it may fall off suddenly and, although it is well hidden under my clothes, I imagine that everyone is looking at it.

Stumbling back to the safety of my home I see a figure entering the café on the water's edge. It is a woman with red hair. My eyes are wet, blurred. I want the woman to be Lauren Gardiner, at the same time I hope she isn't. She is often in my mind. Too often for my own good. When I come close enough to see her face through the windows, I am relieved that it's not Lauren, for the woman is now in the company of a man who's holding her hands and staring deep into her eyes. When I come home I'm so exhausted that I go straight to bed and wake up twenty hours later.

The next day I drive to the town centre. I didn't really intend to, but I end up at the car park on the cliffs. I'm bitter that my first murder investigation started here and has come to an abrupt halt. I realise all of a sudden that I'm still angry and frustrated that Guthrie chose to replace me. From what I've read in the papers, DI Maloney, the man Guthrie appointed to replace me, has so far failed to successfully end the investigation

The car park is almost vacated. The only cars there, are parked as close to the supermarket entrance as possible. At the base of the fence are still the items that remind you of a life ended too soon. Faded and weather-beaten cards and ribbons, a single cuddly bear.

It is a cold and wet day, sky and sea equally grey, the horizon invisible in low clouds. Hands clasped around the fence, numbed by the icy cold steel, I stare at the spot where Jane Croft's body was dumped with an indignity that no-one deserves. A hundred feet below are dog walkers on the beach and surfers waiting for a good clean wave. The beach stretches out towards Newquay Harbour. With incoming tides, some of the coves will fill with seawater, cutting of the odd tourist who underestimates the force of the sea, resulting in a shameful rescue by the RNLI.

Seagulls fly low over my head, as always, searching for easy food. They've taken over the car parks and bins, scavenging for leftover pasties and chips. The lampposts have long spikes on top to keep them away, but the white birds still manage to sit on them with their orange flip-flop feet, eyes searching for food and relieving their bowels.

A dirty blue car parks next to me. A middle-aged woman gets out, holding a tattered shopping bag. The husband remains seated, unfolding a paper.

Suddenly I feel uneasy, as if I'm being watched. The man in the blue car is hiding behind his newspaper. Three boys in school uniforms use the tarmac as a skate park. White shirts spill from cheap black trousers and ties hang loose around their necks, probably only tightened in a rush before lessons. They have no coats or jackets. Rucksacks are hanging low on their hips. One chucks his bag on the pavement and swirls round on his skateboard, using the edge of the pavement for his stunts. He barely misses an oncoming car, which makes his mates laugh with a mixture of relief and shock. One of them makes an obscene gesture when he sees me watching. The other two laugh and the three circle the car park as though they own the world.

A young couple in love come walking towards me. Perhaps they suspect that I am weighing up my options, whether jumping will solve all my current problems or only add to the problems of others. The tide is coming in. Below, the sea crashes onto the rocks. It would be so easy. Quick maybe. Or not.

'Sir?'

I half expect them to ask me whether I am all right. If I need any help. Clearly they don't want to get involved in something as horrific as seeing a suicidal man wondering whether the time has come.

Can I take a photo of the pair of them, standing at that fence? It would be lovely if I can manage to capture Newquay in the background. I smile as I am instructed in how the camera works. Unaware of what happened here a few weeks ago, they pose together, laughing and hugging in front of the spot where two innocent young boys discovered the body of a murdered woman.

The woman from the blue car next to mine returns with a trolley. There are packs of beer cans, bags of crisps and at least three bottles of wine. I don't know if she's organising a party or just shopping for her husband's daily intake. As she unloads the trolley, her husband folds his paper, not bothering to give her a hand. As she pushes the trolley back to the bay, putting the coin in the pocket of her coat, he waits for her return drumming his fingers on the steering wheel. It makes me briefly think of Stella, calling her father 'a waste of space'. I don't know what Jane would have said about him, but Shirley seemed to have thought the world of him.

The loving couple has walked further on, taking pictures of each other and trying 'selfies' with stretched arms. Their careless laughter makes me think of my own days of hope and love without a care in the world. I feel like an old man.

Retrieving my phone from my pocket, I switch it on and listen to a lady accusing me of ignoring the seven new messages that are waiting for me. Impatiently I save them for the time being, then I press buttons to choose a name from my contacts list.

29

JUNE

Jennette Penrose answers her phone as if she's expecting a call from a lover. Her voice is husky and for some reason sounds hopeful. I can't work out whether she is disappointed that it's just me. Once the how-are-yous are answered to satisfaction, I tell her in all honesty that spending long days on my own and doing nothing is driving me mad. I'd like an update from her on the murder inquiry.

She is reluctant to give information. 'There's not much news, sir.'

'I read in the papers that someone's been arrested.'

'Yeah.' She hesitates.

It occurs to me that she is at the station and isn't free to talk. 'Listen, Jennette, can we meet somewhere?'

I can almost feel her reluctance. 'Like where?'

'The café at the Boating Lake?' The venue seems too innocent to object to and she agrees meeting me there at the end of the day.

I do my shopping in the supermarket. Having put a few ready-meals in my trolley, I change my mind and buy chicken fillets and fresh vegetables instead. A stir fry is just as quick to prepare and more healthy. Walking slowly towards the till, I suddenly find the manager in my path. He's carrying a box of items to stack on the shelf, looking at me as if trying to remember where he has seen me before. I have lost some weight recently and I'm sure he doesn't connect my pale tired face with the policeman he spoke so many angry words to.

I am knackered when I come home, yet I feel better than I've felt in days. It'll take a couple of weeks before I'm allowed to go back to work. If ever. Meanwhile Penrose can fill me in about the investigation and I'll have plenty of time to do a little more digging behind the scenes.

As she approaches the café at the Boating Lake, Penrose's face has an expression that tells me she already regrets agreeing to meet me. I guess she couldn't refuse me because she understood my need to remain involved somehow in what was once my investigation. Now she's no longer certain.

'Are you all right, sir?' She asks, as she emerges in the doorway, blinking in the sudden shadows. She scrutinises my face before carefully choosing a chair.

'I'm good, thank you.'

'How's the pain?'

'All right.'

She senses my reluctance to talk freely. I know it annoys her that she doesn't know exactly what I was in hospital for. Feeling her dark eyes staring at me, I think I ought to tell her at least half of the story. If only to secure her as my accomplice. But I can't. The bag stuck under my clothes is embarrassing enough for myself, let alone for a colleague. I suspect that she will no longer see me as a normal person, a normal man. I may have to cope with that in the future, but not at this moment. It's just too soon.

'Just some discomfort,' I reply, then quickly change the subject. 'Coffee?'

'I'd rather have tea, sir, if you don't mind.'

I smile at her, offering an olive branch. 'Don't call me sir, please, Jennette. I'm off duty now.'

A blush colours her face and her neck. 'All right, sir. Andy.'

My first name sounds too intimate from her lips. I remember Marie saying that Penrose has feelings for me. Maybe so. Maybe

I'm taking advantage. It's too late now to pull back.

A tray with a small pot of tea arrives to accompany my cappuccino. Before she pours, she nibbles a crusty almond biscuit that leaves crumbs on her lips.

'So how's the investigation going? The new DI all right?'

The case is now in the hands of DI Maloney. I worked with him a few years ago and I know him well enough to realise that he blames me for his career being side-tracked, albeit his relocation to Newquay only being temporary.

'I suppose.'

Her tone of voice reminds me of when I introduced Maloney to the team. Penrose disliked him from the very first moment. I could read her mind as he spoke his first words to her, trying to be amicable. 'Penrose? Tre-Pol-Pen. So you must be Cornish, hey?' He made it sound like an insult. She lifted her head proudly, but she was clearly taken aback by the unsubtle sneer to his grin.

Cornish born-and-breads consider anything beyond the Tamar River as abroad. DI Maloney feels the same, but in the opposite way. His move to Newquay was perhaps considered a considerable step up the career ladder, but from day one he aimed to move back from what he called 'Britain's back yard'.

'Any news on the case?'

'Well.' A wry smile crosses her round face as she stirs milk and sugar in her tea. 'I suppose you will want to know everything.' From the inside pocket of her jacket, she produces a brown rolled up envelope, held together by a blue elastic band.

'I've copied the most interesting statements,' she admits with an almost apologising smile.

'Has anyone been brought in yet? Any suspects? I read something in the paper.'

She hesitates, unconsciously looking over her shoulder. The café is quiet. The only customers are a couple in their early thirties, both so busy with their phones that they might as well have come alone, and a young family with three children.

One child is asleep in a pram, another is sitting on her father's knee, concentrating on a drawing with colouring pencils, and the mother breastfeeds a small baby while drinking coffee. Outside are the dog walkers, a young girl with her grandfather feeding the ducks and two rowing boats hired by four giggling teenagers.

'That'll be Arthur Pengally.'

I can't hide my surprise. 'On what grounds?'

'We're still investigating that, sir.'

I am curious. Arthur Pengally, the neighbour with a crush on Jane Croft. What did I miss? Why didn't I see any grounds to suspect him? 'Did he confess?'

'No.' It occurs to me that she doesn't say 'Not yet.' She doesn't believe Pengally is guilty.

'But,' she says, fidgeting in her chair. 'There has been a development.' I can see that she's debating whether to tell me or not. Obviously it is sensitive information and she doesn't want to get in trouble. 'Maloney is not pleased at all.' She finally goes on with a wicked smile.

'What happened?'

Lowering her voice, she leans towards me. Her large breasts are threateningly close to her cup of half-drunk tea. Tapping a flat hand on the envelope, she says, 'We've checked Arthur Pengally's background. We discovered that he was in police records. Sexual harassment. Two cases, both dropped by the victims.'

'There were no signs of that on Jane Croft's body.' I remember the white skin, no bruises that would indicate a sexual attack.

'Well, no.' She looks down, avoiding my eyes. 'The point is that we retrieved the information about Pengally just when Maloney took over from you. He jumped in instantly, apparently without checking all the details. He brought Pengally in for questioning on the grounds of the suspicion that he tried to seduce Jane Croft and that it went wrong when she objected. Hence her death.'

I remember her attitude towards Arthur Pengally, her instinctive feeling that there was something he kept hidden. Obviously he didn't tell us about the allegations, but Penrose dug deep enough to find them. Clearly her report resulted in Maloney being convinced that he had the murderer.

'But we've had to let Pengally go. We established a time frame in which Jane Croft disappeared and was found dead. Pengally had a solid alibi. He went to a pub quiz and it was confirmed that he hadn't left his team other than going to the loo for a minute or two.'

'So nobody's been arrested for Jane Croft's death?'

She shakes her head with a hint of triumph. 'Maloney doesn't like it at all. I think he thought the case was clear as glass. He intended to achieve in one day what you hadn't in the previous weeks.'

'I bet he did.'

She smiles sarcastically, encouraged by my reaction. 'He acts as if he's got stuck in some third world country.'

'Has there been any further contact with DI Grey from Bristol? About the death of Simon Croft? Any signs that both cases are linked?'

She nods seriously. 'DI Grey seems to think so. He has reopened the case, but Maloney is still sort of in denial. He knows that he can't swipe this case under the carpet.' She pauses to pour the rest of her tea in her cup. 'But basically, we're getting nowhere with the investigation, sir. Leads are running out and Maloney gets nastier by the day.' She stops, shocked by her own words. 'Surely you appreciate that this whole conversation was off the record, sir. Andy.'

'Of course.'

I can barely wait until I can look at the copies she printed for me. Seeing my eyes flicker in that direction, she smiles. 'When do you think you're coming back, sir? To relieve us from Shitbag Maloney?'

The irony of her choice of insult, unknown to her, stabs me as though I am the third victim of Simon and Jane Croft's killer. I am taken aback, shocked as it dawns on me that people might call me that behind my back. After all, I will fit the title better than Maloney.

'I'll see the consultant again in a few days, so hopefully I'll be declared fit for work soon enough.'

She nods with a thoughtful frown. 'I don't expect you'll be back on the case, though. Unfortunately Shitbag and Guthrie seem to be the best of mates.'

I smile. 'In which case it may be better for me to duck down for a little while.' With my head I gesture at the papers on the table. 'I have plenty of time to work under the surface.'

'That's what I hoped you'd say.' Her earlier reluctance disappears entirely as she produces a wide smile. 'As a matter of fact, Jane Croft's funeral will be held this week. Would you like me to text you the details?'

30

JUNE

In his forties, the barman in The Red Lion has a reddish ring of hair with one strand across his forehead, held in place with gel or hairspray. He's dressed in black trousers and a black short-sleeved shirt. Every now and then a red bow tie pops up from under his double chin. He cast me a stoic glance when I come in, eyeing me up as if predicting my choice of drink.

The place is empty except for a man flicking through a newspaper at a table near the window. The light behind him silhouettes his shape and it takes me a moment to recognise Peter Prescott.

'Good to see you, inspector.' Getting up quickly, he holds out his hand, a wry smile on his smooth face. Before I can say anything, he apologizes. 'I hope I'm not keeping you from something.'

'I was about to go out anyway.' A lie, but he doesn't need to know. I'm curious about his reasons to invite me for a drink all of a sudden, but I don't want to look too keen.

'Good.' He motions me towards his table. I cast a glance at his paper. It is yesterday's *Daily Mail*, opened at a sports page.

With a deep frown he looks at the glass in his hand as if only just noticing it is empty. 'What can I get you, inspector?' As he speaks, he glances at his watch. It's either a habitual gesture or a way to let me know that his time is limited.

'Only if you have another.'

The door opens and a flock of about twelve men enter the pub. From what they're barking about, I figure they've been playing bowls on the nearby pitch. Tapping shoulders, laughing that the winner will have to pay for the first round of drinks, they manage to confuse the barman. His stoic expression has disappeared. Despite his annoyance he remains polite to his noisy customers.

Peter lifts his glass. 'A pint, inspector?'

'Export, please.'

Negotiating his way through the noisy group, he pats his inside chest pocket and retrieves a large wallet, taking out a 20-pound note, and waving it to attract the barman's attention.

Peter places his order. He seems relaxed and at ease. Smiling at the barman, laughing briefly over his shoulder, he stands next to a woman who seems to have appeared from the powder room. Shoulder length blonde hair and features as pale as a porcelain doll, she is almost ageless. Crossing her legs absent-mindedly, she has a casual elegance. She's dressed in a tight black dress and a short, white, denim jacket. Classy, stylish, expensive.

Peter places two pints on our table and sits down opposite me. Unconsciously he looks at the bar. For the briefest of moments the blonde woman crosses eyes with him. A conversation unspoken.

'How's your wife?' I ask casually.

'Good. Fine.' He gulps down a quarter of his beer and licks his lips. 'To be honest, I guess I felt rather embarrassed by the whole thing. You were right all along.'

'That she came back?'

'She did, of course.' His face is vacant, his eyes shadowed by blond lashes.

Looking past his shoulder, I look at the blonde woman at the bar. There's something unsettling about her. The barman places a little bowl in front of her. Absentmindedly she scoops up a handful of peanuts and eats them one by one, picking the best ones with care. Her fingernails are long and painted bright red.

'I presume she's all right? Your wife?'

'Hmm.' For a few moments he seems lost in thoughts.

'Did you find out where she was?'

'Oh, yes.' Shrugging off his demons, he smiles. 'She went to see some relatives of hers. No close relatives to my knowledge. Nothing exciting.' I sense there's something he's not telling me.

'Without letting you know?' I ask sympathetically.

He nods, turning his glass in his hand as if checking it's still round. 'There seemed to have been some sort of emergency in the family. She left me a note, but apparently it fell on the floor. We found it afterwards.' He looks up, an uneasy expression crawls up between the lines of his smile. 'The funny thing is, I never knew about those relatives. She's always told me that she has no family at all.'

'The most Important thing is that she's back.'

Hooking a finger inside his collar, trying to make it stretch, he suddenly seems as uncomfortable as a cow in a sheep cot.

'Unharmed,' I add, making it sound as a question.

'Hmm. Yeah, of course. Unharmed. As far as I know.' A hint of irony touches the corners of his mouth. 'I mean, I can't read her mind, can I.'

'I guess not.'

He leans back, head tilted sideways as though one ear is better than the other. 'Anyway. Any luck with your investigation? I read in the paper that you have a suspect.'

'So it seems.' I feel a strange hesitation to tell him that I'm not currently working on the case.

He grins sheepishly. 'I understand that you can't talk about it.'

'That's right.'

'But I'm curious all the same.' He pauses briefly, thoughtfully. 'Maybe because I feel a bit… connected to your case.'

'In what way?'

'At the time, I was afraid that it could have been Trish. I

guess it was a bit silly, maybe, but at that moment, I was really worried.'

'You seemed worried she would do herself harm.'

His face tightens. 'She'd been though a difficult time.' He pauses to make up his mind, then admits almost reluctantly, 'She's had a couple of miscarriages. Huge disappointments. Then we had a stillborn. You can imagine what that's like, especially... well, she blames herself. She thinks it's all her fault.'

I nod, not really knowing how to respond. 'I'm sorry.'

'I keep telling her that it will all be all right, that things like this can take time, but she doesn't seem to listen.' He scrutinises his glass, as if searching for secret clues. 'I'm not as obsessed as she is, to be honest. I'm quite happy as we are. I don't need a child to make our marriage *complete*, as they say.'

'A woman feels differently.' I don't know where that wisdom comes from. I'm normally not one to understand women.

'I guess you're right. But sometimes it really annoys me. We keep going on in circles. Every month the same anxiety, the same disappointment. Distress. Hurt. Guilt. Tears. Lots of them.' He stops to smile sheepishly, almost embarrassed. 'I even went to see my GP. To check if my little soldiers are alive and kicking.'

I don't know what to say. His openness makes me feel a bit uneasy, as though I'm peering into a life without permission. 'Are they?'

'That's the point. I thought, if it's me, I can tell her, relieve her of her guilt. But there's nothing wrong with me. Only I can't tell her that, can I? It'll only make things worse for her.'

'Then don't tell her.'

He gives me a wry half smile. 'We've always had a good relationship.'

I don't ask him about his relationship with the secretary.

'All this hoping... I don't know why I'm telling you this, inspector. I've never told a soul.'

'They say I'm a good listener.'

'Yeah. Well, she's so… alone, you see. She didn't have many friends when we met, but somehow she managed to chase them all away. I don't think that helps. It's not good for her, for us, our marriage.'

'Parents?'

He hesitates for a moment, unsure if he's missed something. 'She lost her parents when she was she was eighteen. No relatives.'

'I thought you said…'

'I know. It surprised me too that she suddenly seemed to have found a relative. First I thought it was quite a good thing to happen. I was happy for her. But it was too late. Her aunt and uncle died in a tragic house fire. When I thought she was missing, she actually travelled to go to the funeral.' He pauses, uneasiness stretching the silence. 'I still find it odd that she didn't tell me. I mean, even if these relatives haven't been part of her life, not since we've been married anyway, I'd have been there for her, you know? Support her at the funeral. I mean, in my book, that's an elementary part of marriage.' He stops to tilt his glass, draining the remainder of his beer. 'Are you married, inspector?'

'Divorced.'

He seems not to hear me. 'She won't talk about them.' I can feel the hurt slipping through his words.

'Maybe she needs time. A sudden death, a house fire, can be very traumatic. Sometimes people try to imagine what it must have been like to be trapped, to know that there's no escape from hell and fury.'

'All true, inspector, but I want to help her.'

'Andy, please stop calling me inspector,' I interrupt, but he doesn't seem to hear.

'I just want to be there for her.'

'Knowing you'll be there for her when she needs you is already half of the support.'

'I hope so.' Once more he glances at his watch, tugging at

his shirt cuff as if his arm has suddenly grown longer. 'Anyway. Thanks for your time, inspector. I'd better go home.'

'Hmm.' I stare at our glasses. I've paid for a second round, this is our third. His glass is half empty, mine is almost full. As a true son of my parents I hate wasting food or drinks.

He rises hesitantly, as though unsure if our conversation has come to a satisfying end, searching for words that needn't be said. 'I'll finish this one, then I'll be off.' He stands, running one hand through his hair. 'Anyway, thank you, Andy.'

'No problem. Any time.'

'Thanks.'

He nods a goodbye and turns, shoulders drooping with relief. I'm not sure why he invited me for a drink. His rather abrupt goodbye makes me feel like I have been exploited somehow, but I can't see why. Something else is nagging me too. It takes only an few minutes to understand. We never spoke about my visit to his business partner. He must know about that, he must have gathered that Allan has told me about Peter's relationship with the secretary.

I follow him with my eyes. Leaving his empty glass on the bar top, he pauses briefly for a general goodbye. The barman's red bow tie pops up as he throws back his head to laugh. The blonde woman is still there. Her eyebrows rise. I can't hear what Peter says exactly, but she seems annoyed. Probably he's launched some anti-feminist remark. She looks like the kind of woman who's always on top of things like that, as though constantly personally offended, almost waiting for a cue to get angry.

The beer suddenly doesn't taste good to me anymore. I get up and follow Peter Prescott outside. He hasn't noticed me. He's heading towards the car park on Fore Street that overlooks the bowling pitch and Newquay harbour. Across the bay white foam crashes onto the rugged coast. The rocks are tinted with a warm evening glow. I can see the sandy beach of Constantine Bay in the distance, the whitewashed shape of Trevose Lighthouse waiting for the sun to set. It's an unmanned lighthouse now, but still an important beacon on this treacherous coast with its hidden dangers below the surface.

Peter Prescott halts near his car, turning towards the sea, holding his phone against his ear. I'm too far away to hear what he says. Instead I hear high heels click on the pavement behind me. Without turning my head, I know it is the woman from the pub.

Although my car is in the same car park, I start walking towards the town centre. There's a large grey and white seagull on a fence post. Its head turns slowly on its body, the shiny bird's eyes following me cautiously. I try not to look at Peter Prescott so obviously. My last sighting of him is when he turns to greet the blonde woman with a wide smile on his face. He doesn't seem in a hurry to go home to his lonely, depressed wife.

Peter Prescott is a man living with lies.

31

JUNE

The hearse is covered in similar wreaths as though everyone knew that Jane Croft loved pink roses. Shiny green and white ribbons have words of love printed in gold. Her daughter is holding hands with a young woman with short-cropped hair and a friendly open face. They sit shoulder-to-shoulder, one possessed by grief, the other sharing it. I wonder briefly what Jane would have said had she been able to see her daughter and the lover she so firmly denied. Tracy Webb never met Jane, yet she mourns along with her partner. Nobody can deny a love like that.

Surprisingly, Tracy's family are there, a mass of close-knit relatives. There's no doubt that Stella has found her own place among them. I am happy for her. Tracy's father is stocky built, like his daughter, a warm and proud shine in his eyes as they follow the rows of seats where his family are. Next to him sits a small thin woman. Only the wrinkles on her face tell her true age, otherwise she could pass for a teenager. She's dressed in jeans and a green zipped cardigan that gives her chestnut dyed hair an attractive shine. Four sisters, at least, with husbands and children, the youngest a few months old.

In comparison, Stella's half a dozen family members look bland; like individuals who have little in common. It is such a contrast that I could cry for Jane. There's her only brother Dave. Although he has recently married his third wife, she isn't here to accompany or support him. Ruth, widowed, Jane's older sister, sits stiff and tight-lipped, clutching a handbag that holds too many useless items. She's searching in it for the one thing she forgot. A packet of paper tissues is passed along the row, thrust into her unsteady hand. Smiling faintly at the man next to her, she clearly doesn't realise it's a member of Tracy's family that passed her the tissues. Out of solidarity with her sister, she would probably have refused it. Anne, a younger version of Jane, sits next to her. Staring blankly at nothing in particular, she seems untouched by her loss. Or maybe it's just an inability to show compassion in an unknown world.

Sometimes family instinctively divides itself into two parties on either side of the aisle. I'm glad that this isn't the case now. Stella's side of the room would be devastatingly, heartbreakingly, empty.

The service involves speeches from Stella herself, remembering her mother as a lovely woman, always in her thoughts, sadly missed. Tears run down her cheeks as she reads from a piece of paper held with trembling fingers, yet her voice is steady, trailing off only once as she mentions how her mother's life has come to such an abrupt ending. She regrets everything that she has wanted to say to her mother but didn't. It's one of the hardest parts of every sudden death.

There's a speech from Jane's former boss. He is a chubby man with a shiny red face and a brown wig that somehow doesn't match the colour of his face. He's either unmarried or he has a docile wife who doesn't dare to speak the truth. His voice is passionate and warm as he recalls some hilarious memories about Jane. He paints such a lovely warm woman that it makes me feel sad that I never knew her.

As he steps back, there's a bit of commotion when two speakers step forward at the same time. The funeral director looks confused, embarrassed and motions the woman forward. Ladies first. A policy embedded in British culture of politeness. The other speaker, a tall man in his forties, lowers himself onto an empty seat alongside the aisle, reading glasses and a folded piece of paper in his hand.

The woman is a representative of the local Women's Institute, of which Jane seems to have been an active member. She speaks of the deceased with sympathetic words, but seems short of a warm memory to share.

There's an odd silence when the woman's last words fade. Putting the piece of paper with the written speech on it in her handbag, she smiles as if she's a comedian who has been telling jokes that nobody laughs at.

The tall man introduces himself as Colin Fenchurch. Referring to Jane as 'Auntie', he has a fond but, sadly, short memory of the period he spent with the family. From where I sit, modestly on one of the back rows, I can see only the side of Stella's face. I notice her surprise as she listens to a man who's putting himself forward as a grateful and close friend of her mother's. I wonder why he seems to be the only one of Jane's foster children who bothered to come to her funeral.

The funeral is over, so is the tension. Now people can start dealing with the future again. A future without Jane. We gather in a room with brown walls, green carpet and chairs with purple seats. There are white plastic lilies in big vases in every corner, framed sepia photographs of woods and horizons on the walls. Soft music plays in the background as we sip coffees, eat carrot cake and lemon drizzle kindly supplied by a member of the WI.

Stella seems genuinely pleased to see me. 'So many kind words,' she sniffs. 'If only Mum could have heard.'

'I'm sure she did.'

She smiles sadly. 'I'm not a believer, inspector.'

'Do you know the last speaker?' I ask casually.

She shrugs, frowning. 'I spoke with him earlier, but I don't remember his name.'

'He seems to have been one of your mother's foster children.'

Her forehead suddenly creases as though she has forgotten something. 'She stopped doing it when my father left.'

'There must have been more foster children.' I make it sound like a question.

She looks over her shoulder as if seeking an excuse to get away. 'Maybe they had bad memories.'

'He seemed to have had a wonderful time with your parents.'

'Yes, well, they're usually softies, aren't they?' She smiles wryly, waving at no one in particular. 'Excuse me, there's someone I'd like to talk to.' Off she goes, apparently heading for the doorway. Perhaps she wants to catch up with someone who is about to leave. Or she needs a visit to the toilet. Or she just wanted to escape me.

A woman dressed in purple offers more coffee. A refill. As I accept a second slice of lemon drizzle too, I find Penrose next to me.

'I seem to have noticed you're having a second cake, sir.'

I look at her empty hands. 'I can recommend it. It's lovely.'

'So I understand.' She comes a little bit forward. 'I'm here with Maloney.' Her face is a shade of red, her eyes drifting nervously in the direction where the funeral director talks with her new boss.

'Eh, I'm not sure what he'll say about…' She starts, then pauses abruptly.

'He'll not be pleased with my presence?'

'I suppose.'

'It's not your fault,' I say, but we are both aware that I don't sound very convincing.

'Maybe I should… go.' She waves her hand vaguely, clearly short of an excuse not to be seen in my presence.

'I'll go,' I say gently. 'I'd like to have a word with the mystery guest.'

She's not sure where her loyalty lies. Perhaps it's with me, who she knows better than Maloney, but she seems uncertain that I'm the right horse to bet on. Or with Maloney who at least seems to follow her lines of thought, especially when he agreed with her on bringing Arthur Pengally to the station for questioning, or, as they say, helping with the inquiry.

I move towards the mystery speaker who seems to be in

an animated conversation with Jane Croft's brother. They're not unknown to one another.

'Inspector. I know this is maybe not the right time, but I'd like to ask you something.' Tracy is blocking my way.

'If this is about the investigation, I can't help you. I'm on sick leave.'

She frowns. 'Nothing serious I hope?'

'Nothing to speak of,' I lie.

She nods briefly. 'So you don't know if there's any progress?'

'I'm afraid you'll have to ask my colleague. The case was taken over by him.' I point in Maloney's direction. I know he has spotted me, but he tries his best to ignore me, which suits me well. 'DI Maloney is now the officer in charge.'

She smiles. 'I'd better leave it then. Stella's been speaking with him already.'

'The cake is lovely.'

'Hmm, yes. I heard someone inquire after the recipe.'

'Sensible idea.' I pause. 'Sorry, I'd like to have a word with the last speaker. Do you know him at all?'

Her face is blank. 'I'm afraid he's just left.'

32

JUNE

Employees are boxed in cubicles with computers on desks and plastic lunchboxes in top drawers. The walls are just high enough to cover them out of sight when seated. Every so often, one pops up like a meerkat on alert, stretching with a phone pressed to an ear or talking to a cubicle neighbour before ducking down again.

Colin Fenchurch is the meerkat's manager. The company, he explains, deals with bulk freight all over the world, from complete construction lines for factories to tiny plastic toys. Containers stacked up on ships as big as high storey buildings, traveling from China to South America, from Siberia to Tahiti.

His desk is situated at the far end of the room like a headmaster keeping en eye on his students while they're doing their exams. Waist high filing cabinets are lined up against the wall behind him. On top of them are trophies won by employee sport teams or individuals. Darts, pool, tennis, football. In a corner is a coffee machine that seems for personal use only. A bin lined with a blue plastic bag is spilling over with polystyrene cups. If I'm reading him right, he is a coffee addict.

I shake his hand and it's as though I'm sticking mine in a huge strawberry trifle. Trying not to flinch or wipe my hand on my hip, I sit on the chair opposite to him and run both hands over my knees as if to adjust my trousers.

'I'm sorry about this,' he says, gesturing vaguely at the meerkats who seem to be more on alert now. I presume Mr Fenchurch doesn't normally receive visitors.

'It's OK.'

He moves awkwardly in his chair. 'I'd rather meet you here than at home.'

'We could have met in a pub or café,' I say mildly.

'Sorry. No time.' He adjusts a couple of pens by laying them in a straight line in accordance with the veins of his wooden desktop. His desk is almost empty. There's no computer screen or keyboard, just a metal tray with a couple of pencils and two matching post trays. One empty, the other holding a bunch of paper held together with a red paper clip and an unreadable yellow post-it note. It makes me wonder what Mr Fenchurch actually does to earn his salary. He looks more like a pen pusher than someone who contributes his working hours to the company.

'My wife is... unwell.'

'I'm sorry.'

He nods gently. 'Why did you want to see me, inspector?'

'Actually I'm off duty. Sick leave. But I'm still working on the case.' I pause. 'The death of Jane Croft.'

It triggers his imagination. I can see questions flicker over his pale face, but he purses his lips as though he's on a diet and is adamant to stick to it, however enticing the treats displayed in front of him are. 'I see.'

'I saw you at the funeral.'

'Poor Aunt Jane.' He smiles sadly. 'I was their foster child for a while.'

'How long for?'

'About two years.' He seems to sink in memories. I'm not sure they are happy ones or sad ones.

'How old were you?'

He shrugs, relaxing as though he expected another subject. 'Let me see. I must have been about ten when I came to live with them.'

'Was it a happy time?'

'I was very fond of Auntie Jane.' He stops. I guess Colin Fenchurch is one of those people who answer a question without releasing any further information. He may be holding something back, or it is just a habit.

'And her husband?'

This time he frowns. 'What about him?'

'Were you fond of him too?'

'Not particularly.'

One of the meerkats approaches his desk, producing a pitiful smile for me. 'Sorry to interrupt,' he murmurs.

Colin Fenchurch shrugs off the apology, making him look more important than he is. 'What is it, Dean?'

A single sheet of paper lands on the empty desk. Colin stares at it as though he suffers from a phobia of items that could contaminate his life. Hands on the armrests of his chair, he doesn't intend at all to pick up the sheet. 'Yes?'

Dean doesn't seem to think there's anything odd in Fenchurch's behaviour. 'I just got a message that the containers for the flight from Buenos Aires haven't arrived at the airport.'

Colin Fenchurch drums his fingers. 'And?'

'Do we wait or not?'

Time is money. Empty spaces cost. A dilemma. Fenchurch's forehead becomes a horizontal blind that is pulled up and let down again. 'What do you think yourself?'

'Well.' Dean clears his throat. 'Rumour says that the company has gone bust. So I think there's no point in waiting for the container to arrive.'

'Is that your gut instinct, Dean?'

'I guess so. And besides, I may be able to shove the container on the flight the day after tomorrow.'

Colin Fenchurch leans back in his chair. 'What's your problem then?'

'Well.' The young man hesitates with a heavy sigh. 'The container is for B&M.'

This information seems well known enough to make

Colin Fenchurch flinch. His recovery is so quick that his brief hesitation is almost unnoticed. 'If B&M deals with companies that can't deliver their goods in time, then that's not our problem, Dean.'

'That's what I thought.' Smiling triumphantly, Dean picks up the sheet from the desk. 'Just to let you know, in case B&M gets in contact.'

I hide a smile. Knowing well enough to cover his own tracks, Dean has forwarded the problem to the responsibility of his superior.

'Sorry about that, inspector.'

'It's all right.'

'We're an international company. We send stuff all around the world,' he explains pompously. He sounds more enthusiastic about his job than about our conversation.

'Are you aware of the circumstances around Jane's death?' I ask carefully.

'Obviously I read the papers, inspector.' He's not spilling with words. He waits for my questions rather than telling me something of his own accord.

'When did you last see her?'

'The 10th of April.' Just over a week before she died.

'How can you be so sure?'

'Her birthday is on the 9th, mine the 11th. I take her out on the tenth for a meal every year.'

'How was she?'

'Same as usual.' A smile crosses his eyes as a memory pops up. 'She's always been good to me. She was in pieces when I had to leave.'

He doesn't mean their parting at the end of the yearly meal. 'And were you?'

His face crumples into vacancy again. 'You get used to being moved about. You make sure you don't get involved emotionally. Saves tears and hurt when you have to leave again. Start all over with another foster home.'

There's a world of hurt and loneliness behind his words.

So much that I don't know what to say.

'You said you were ten when you came to live with the Crofts. You were there for two years. You said you were happy. Jane loved you. Then why did you leave?'

He tries to keep his face emotionless, but I notice a little muscle movement twitching near his eye. 'Mostly trouble with her husband. I was thirteen. We couldn't get on. Social workers thought it best to send me somewhere else.'

'Were you happy about that?'

'I could deal with him.' There's a steely edge in his voice.

'Did it happen like that normally? Did you not stay with one family?'

'I don't know what's normal inspector. In my case it was like that.'

'OK. How did you get on with Stella?'

'We didn't have much in common.'

It seems an odd choice of words to me. 'Was she all right with having a foster brother?'

'I suppose.'

'You kept in touch with Jane. Did you ever meet Stella after you left? Or Simon Croft?'

'I only saw Auntie Jane occasionally. Like I said, we have a meal together on the 10th of April. We exchanged Christmas cards.'

He's well aware that he keeps too much below the surface for my liking. 'Are you married, Mr Fenchurch?'

'Fifteen years.'

'Children?'

A smile, a warm shine in his eyes. 'Two sons. Thirteen and ten.'

'Did you introduce Jane to your wife?'

The smile is gone all of a sudden. He's out of his comfort zone again. 'That's mainly the reason why I didn't want you to come to my home, inspector. My wife doesn't know anything about my childhood.'

'Why is that?'

He looks away, seeking an excuse to tell off one of the meerkats. There isn't one. They're hiding in their cubicles, having a secret bite of lunch or ducking to pick up a snippet of our conversation.

'I guess I was ashamed. There's still a stigma around foster children, inspector. And later, well, I don't know really. It never came up.' He pauses, frowning uncertainly. 'She'll feel betrayed if she finds out now.'

I understand what he means. Deep down, my mother hasn't forgiven me for not telling her about my illness. The accusation, the hurt, still hangs around her.

'What about Simon Croft?'

'What about him?' He is wary again.

'Did you know he's dead?'

He doesn't show surprise. 'I can't say I'm sorry.'

'How did you learn about his death?'

'You just told me.' Trying to hide my surprise about his reaction, I feel a flicker of irritation. He is smooth, too smooth.

'You said you two didn't get on.'

He hesitates. When he speaks again, his voice is lowered . Perhaps meerkats have a very good sense of hearing. 'I suppose you'll find out anyway, inspector, if you haven't already. Mr Croft didn't like boys.'

That is news to me. 'Meaning?'

He drops to a conspiratorial whisper. 'Meaning he didn't want boys in his house. He wanted girls.'

'Why?'

He produces a wry smile. 'For obvious reasons, I'd say. He couldn't tell the social workers, though, so he tried to get rid of the boys as soon as possible. The reason I stayed with them for almost two years was because Aunt Jane loved me. She didn't want me to go. Like the other boys.'

'Are you saying Mr Croft was abusing the girls?'

'That's what I understood.'

'Did Jane know?'

'In the end, yes. She felt so betrayed, so let down by

him. And deeply ashamed because she never had a clue what happened when she was at work. She worked full time at the local post office, you see. He just had odd jobs. He was more often at home than at work. In hindsight it all clicked of course, but at the time it didn't even occur to her what he did to those girls.' He pauses and offers a shy smile. 'That's why she left him.'

33

JUNE

Two eyes are staring at me. Dark with long black lashes and a faint green eye shadow. A little square of light is reflected in them. It's a strip of a face, like that of an Islamic woman wearing a burka. Except that it's not fabric that make the eyes look like they're peering at me, but paper sheets scattered on a kitchen table. It would be so easy to move a couple of sheets and cover those eyes. Yet I keep staring back as though they are hypnotising me.

Getting up, I stand at the window. The boating lake is grey and flat, the paths in the park deserted. A mizzle, a combination of mist and drizzle, has spread along the coast, crawling in from the sea. It brings the tourists into the towns as if they can't think of anything else to do than fill the shops and buy things they don't need.

I turn back to the table, sit down and stare in those eyes again, wondering suddenly where the picture comes from. Moving away other sheets of paper, the photo pops out of a small white envelope. Eyebrows are dark, un-plucked. Hair, a warm honey blonde, with a fringe half covering the faint creases on her forehead. The whole face emerges as I slide the photo out of the envelope. It's a snapshot of a woman in her early thirties, beach and sea in the background, two surfers riding a wave with more of them waiting for one to catch. I'm sure I've never met her, yet she looks familiar somehow.

The moment the photographer caught her in his lens, she was serious, thoughtful, sad even. But she has creases alongside her eyes and mouth that tell me an instant later she must have laughed, joked, teased, flirted. At the back I find small, neat handwriting: *Fistral Beach, June, Trish.*

There's a little note in the envelope: *This is a recent photo of my wife. Please find her. Peter Prescott.* Underneath, as an afterthought, is a mobile phone number.

All of a sudden I remember him thrusting the small white envelope in my hand. I recall his serious face, the worried look in his eyes when he said, 'I know something's happened to her, inspector. This isn't like my Trish at all.'

If I hadn't been so busy with the murder inquiry I'd have made sure to find out what Penrose did about it when I forwarded the envelope to her. I guess she did nothing, though, as it transpired that Trish Prescott returned to her home unharmed that same day. I should have returned the photo immediately. Perhaps I had too much on my mind, but that is no excuse. Peter Prescott deserved to be treated seriously and properly, but I'd done nothing to help find his then missing wife. Instead I shagged a possible witness in a murder inquiry. A shameful encounter that I'd like to forget altogether, but for some reason it's stuck in my mind like a record playing over and over again. I don't love Marie. I don't even like her. She was a stupid mistake. Weak is the man's flesh. A vulnerable moment in which I let myself go and I made love to her. Correction, I had sex with her. More infuriatingly, she was the last woman whose breasts I held, whose tongue was on mine, whose body opened to let me in. Perhaps it wasn't even having sex, but a pairing of beasts, following instincts rather than pleasure. She sat on me, bounced up and down on me. I remember the beastlike scream of her orgasm, the howl of a predator in the instant it catches its prey, a glimmer of what I thought was a wild passion in her eyes. As a man, I was delighted and arrogant that I had had that effect on her. As a normal human being, I was disgusted with her behaviour. A female scorpion killing the male after the deed. Job done. Useless. The memory is haunting me and with a sinking feeling I know instinctively that it will only stop when I hold a woman in my arms again.

Shaking off my thoughts, I dial Peter Prescott's mobile number. Wait. No reply. Redial. The second time it comes up with his answer machine. 'Hi, this is Peter Prescott. I can't answer your call at the moment. Please leave your name and number and I'll get back to you A.S.A.P.' He sounds curt and to the point.

As I disconnect, I change my mind. I dial again, and, with an odd feeling that I should at least apologise to him and return the photo of his wife, I tell him I'll be in the Vale of Lanherne from at half five tonight, inviting him for a pint. Perhaps it is time to ask him why he didn't tell me about his relationship with the company's secretary. And more importantly, why he didn't mention my visit to his boss, Allan, which must have at least struck him as odd.

I read and reread the papers Penrose gave me, but there's no clue hidden behind the words, nothing that reads between the lines of witness statements that she considered most significant and valuable for me to know. I make time charts and try to discover the smallest discrepancies in statements, but it leads nowhere.

At five, I wash and get dressed, change the bag on my belly with a lot more experience than when the nurses first showed me how to do it. I'm even growing to get used to it, checking it every so often already without really thinking about it. I shove the photo of Trish Prescott back into the envelope and put it in my pocket. A pint in the nearby pub might not be such a bad idea after all, even if it is with Peter Prescott, whom I hardly know. Perhaps I should join the police darts team. Make some friends, meet regularly for a drink. Have a laugh. Find something to look forward to, rather than spend the days in my apartment chasing Jane Croft's ghosts.

My trips to Bristol and Tavistock, visiting people like Colin Fenchurch and Eileen Turton, prove the point that I've become rather obsessed with the murder. Whatever I do to distract myself, look for other things to do, I just can't let go. It is even more nagging that I feel I have now reached the point that I have no leads left. Penrose keeps me updated on DI Maloney's progress, or the lack of it, as well. So far he hasn't managed to find the killer. Why am I so convinced that I can? Maloney has much more information than I. He has a team of detectives working for him. Why am I so bloody arrogant in thinking that I can achieve what he can't? Because I'm a better detective? Or because I still can't accept the fact that the case has been taken away from me? Do I want to triumph over Maloney or just over myself? Do I have to prove to myself, to anyone, that since the operation, I haven't become a dysfunctional, useless person after all?

The Vale of Lanherne is packed with football supporters. Sky Sports are broadcasting the Manchester derby. According to the voices, United have more supporters than City.

I find Peter Prescott at the end of the bar, tucked in a corner, furthest away from the noisy supporters. His smile wry, he lifts his glass in a silent toast when he sees me come in. The supporters roar. Excitement and protest as players appeal for a penalty, which is denied. More roaring and grunts.

'Nice to see you again, inspector.' There is a hint of sarcasm in his voice, which I prefer to ignore. Perhaps I half hoped that he wouldn't have received my message.

'I came across a note about your wife.'

He gulps down half his pint before answering. 'It's amazing that miracles do happen sometimes.'

I don't really follow his train of thoughts. 'Do you believe in miracles, Mr Prescott?'

He grins. 'Never did, but I'll have to change my mind about it.' He licks his lips, looking at his glass as though he regrets that he already drank so much. With a broad smile, he adds, 'You must hope that miracles happen sometimes, inspector?'

I'm not sure if he means this personally or professionally.

I hope he hasn't heard anything about my operation and condition. I don't want to talk about that, let alone about miracles that may or may not occur in life.

'What miracle has lightened your life, Mr Prescott?'

'My wife. Well, actually, the miracle happened to her, but it also matters to me of course.' I think of her miscarriages, the stillborn baby, her hopes and disappointments, her shattered dreams. It even made him believe once that she had committed suicide. Uncertain, I wait for him to go on. Perhaps he will tell me that she is pregnant.

'You remember I told you that she went to that funeral of her aunt and uncle? The ones that died when their house was on fire? Well, she got some contact details of other relatives. That's how she found out the whereabouts of her younger sister. They lost contact years ago and she thought she would never see her again. Now they have and Trish is over the moon.'

'I can imagine.'

'I've never seen her so happy, inspector, not for years.' He wipes his forehead as if it is covered in beads of perspiration. Not from hard labour, but from excitement.

'So everything is all right now between the two of you?' I try not to think of the secretary, or the blonde woman in The Red Lion.

'Yeah.' He looks into his glass as though hoping to find what to say next. Then, looking up, he changes the subject. 'Are you a football supporter, inspector?'

'Not really. Are you?'

'Likewise. Why meet me in here then?'

'I didn't even now the match was on TV.'

The guy next to me has overheard me. He looks at me incredulously.

'What can I get you, inspector?' Peter lifts his empty glass.

'Andy. I'm off duty.'

His brows rise. 'Are you? You strike me as a man who is always on duty. No matter the day or the time.'

I look away from him. 'Actually, I'm on sick leave.'

'Serious?'

'Not really.' It's not a lie. Fact is that there are many shades of seriousness.

'Well then, Andy, what can I get you?'

'A pint of lager.'

I look over my shoulder. The large flat screen TV on the wall is partly blocked by the supporters. Light blues amongst a majority of reds. There may be problems on the streets in Manchester after the match, but in here the atmosphere is just friendly and amicable.

'The barman tells me there's room in the back. Quieter. If you prefer?' Peter hands me a cold glass with condensation on the outside. 'Unless you want to stay here and watch?'

'No. Thanks.'

I follow him and we sit at a small round table with a menu in a metal stand and small white china bottles of pepper, salt and vinegar.

'I wasn't sure you would get my message.' Now that we are sitting together, I'm not sure how to start.

He picks up a beer coaster and studies it. 'Your message was redirected. I have a new phone. I've also got a new number.'

'Did you lose yours?'

'My phone? Not exactly. I had someone calling me all the time. Didn't say a word. Like stalking, but by phone.'

'Did you report it to the police?'

'What would be the point of that, inspector?' He shows a smile full of pity. 'The phone company advised that the easiest way to deal with that sort of thing is to buy a new phone. Get a new SIM card. New contract. New number.' He smiles ruefully. 'Come to think of it, it may well have been the phone company itself who was pestering me. To make me buy a new phone, a new contract.'

'You're very cynical.'

'No, I'm not, but it did cross my mind. It cost me a lot

of money and nuisance. Took me a while to transfer all my contacts, have new business cards printed.' As if it only occurs to him now, he shoves his hand in his pocket and produces a business card. 'My new number is on it.'

'No more unwanted calls?'

He shrugs by way of a reply. 'If I may say so, I was rather surprised by your message, Andy.'

'I didn't mean to disturb your day.'

'It's all right' He examines my face as though trying to read my thoughts. 'What made you call me?'

I dig in my jacket pocket. 'I found in my possession the photo of your wife.'

'Do you still have that one?' He laughs. 'It seems it's been weeks since I gave it to you.'

I nod. 'To be honest, I forgot all about it until today, when I was clearing some stuff. It was stuck between other papers. I thought you might like to have it back.' As I speak, I retrieve the envelope from my pocket and put it on the table between us.

'Thank you.' He doesn't make a move to pick it up.

'I'm sorry, Peter. I feel like I've let you down.'

'Why? She came back, that's what's most important. The same day.' He laughs with embarrassment. 'I truly don't know what I was thinking, Andy. Afterwards, I couldn't believe that for single moment I thought that she… might have had an accident.'

I push the envelope further in his direction. 'All the same, I don't need that photo anymore.'

Picking it up between thumb and middle finger, he looks at it thoughtfully. 'It was just a storm in a tea cup. It was a mistake on my behalf. I should never have had such… doubts about her. My apologies for any inconvenience I may have caused.'

One of the Manchester teams scores a goal. There are loud cheers and yells, disappointed grunts. Happy and sad, but at the end of the day the supporters just enjoy watching a good game.

Peter Prescott looks into his glass. 'You spoke to my boss.'

So Allen told him about my visit after all. 'I did.'

'Why?' He looks me straight in the eyes. I see only curiosity in his, no anger, no anxiety.

'I was in Bristol. Driving back to the M5, I happened to notice the company.' I hesitate. 'Look, Peter, I'll be completely honest with you. At that time it struck me as odd that you came to the police station to report your wife missing, thinking, believing, that she might be the dead woman you heard about in the news. There wasn't much information about the victim at that moment, but we did mention her age. Fifties.' I pause to examine his face, which is open and innocent. 'I wondered why you came to the police when you knew it couldn't be your wife.'

'That's exactly what occurred to me afterwards,' he says, leaning back and playing with a beer mat that tells us that Stella Artois is *Belgium's Original Beer*. 'At the time I must have been so worried about her absence that I didn't properly listen to the news.' He pauses. 'Is that why you went to see Allan? Did you think I had something to do with the death of that woman?'

'Stranger things happen.'

'I didn't even know her!'

'It just struck me as odd, that was all.' I offer a smile. 'Criminals can be very inventive, Peter. Scrupulous. You could have come to the station to find out what we knew.'

'Why would I do that?' His surprise is genuine. He may lie about seeing other women, but he has no criminal mind.

'As I said, things happen.' I smile softly and point at our almost empty glasses, asking by way of an olive branch, 'Another one?'

He checks his watch quickly. 'Why not?'

'Is your wife not expecting you home?'

'I don't think so.' A smile that comes near to a combination of sarcasm and pity crosses his face. 'She's watching a repeat of *EastEnders*.'

I don't tell him that I have almost become as sad and pathetic. 'My mother is the same,' I say casually. 'She watches every episode, yet insists on seeing the repeats. *EastEnders* and *Emmerdale*. For some reason she isn't a great fan of *Coronation Street*.'

I get up to buy us another round. When I come back the envelope with his wife's photo is still on the table, forgotten, and he's gazing at the TV screen of which he can only see the top quarter. There are some cheers and the men rush towards the bar and the toilets. Half time. Time to fill up and relieve.

'Mr Allan didn't seem to know where you stayed the night you went to Bristol.' I say casually.

'He doesn't need to know.'

'Do you have a secret girlfriend in Bristol?'

It was meant as a casual joke, but I've hit the bull's eye.

'Did Allan say that?'

'He seemed to think it was none of his business.'

'Then how do you know?'

I shrug, inwardly pleased about his slip of the tongue. His love life isn't my business. It's not up to me to judge him. Yet, I continue. 'It just struck me as odd that you seem to stay there one or two nights per fortnight. Bristol is only a couple of hours away.'

He picks up the envelope from the table and takes out the photo, staring at it silently. Then he nods, and says, not meeting my eyes, 'It is.'

34

JUNE

Penrose keeps me up to date about the murder inquiry. She dutifully copies files and hands them to me when we meet on a street corner, or in a pub, as though I am an undercover agent or a secret lover.

I know she hasn't informed DI Maloney about these meetings. Penrose makes her own decisions.

Most times we meet during her lunch break at the entrance of the railway station, a stone's throw away from the Police Station. Today she couldn't get away. Hearing her feeble excuse, I sense she suddenly has second thoughts about our meetings and she's trying to find the courage to tell me that we ought to stop meeting like this. In a desperate, not-wanting-to-let-go plea, I invite her to my flat. No matter what time it is. I know I'm not fair to her; I know her mind doesn't work quick enough to respond with a plausible excuse.

It's just short of teatime when she appears in the doorway, panting and complaining about not having found space in the private car park.

'Hi Jennette, good that you could come.'

'Well, yeah.' She lets out a long sigh, then her brows form a frown. 'Maybe I shouldn't be doing this,' she says, twisting her upper body to retrieve something from her trouser pocket. It's a piece of paper, torn from a notebook.

'Would you like to come in?

'All right then.' Stepping over the threshold, she puts the paper back in her pocket.

'Coffee?' She is one of those people who believes she can't survive without a regular caffeine intake. She only has tea when she feels she's had an overdose.

'Thanks.' She is still reluctant, uneasy, almost constantly avoiding my eyes, and keeping her jacket on her lap as though letting me know that she 's about to run away.

'Milk. No sugar?' I grin. A silly old joke between us from the time we were working as partners. For some reason I failed to remember how she drank her coffee, often presenting her with white coffee without sugar. She drinks it black with three sugar cubes.

Her small lips part in a crooked grin. The ice is broken.

'Thanks.'

Coming back from the kitchen, I find her sitting with her legs stretched as though she has decided to stay some more minutes. Lifting her eyebrows as I place a cafetiere on the table, she says appreciatively, 'That's what I call coffee.'

I push down the plunger, we watch together as the dark brown water gurgles its way up in a companionship which we never shared at work.

'Any news?' I ask, trying to find a tone that comes near matter-of-factly.

'Not really.'

'So, no progress at all?'

I open a package of chocolate biscuits. Nibbling one with tiny bites, she starts talking. Most of the leads have dried out. Witnesses have been questioned repeatedly. Forensic reports are scrutinised. The investigation has now more or less come to a dead-end. A couple of officers temporarily recruited from other areas are already back at their own base.

'Is Pengally still a suspect?'

Another biscuit. Crumbs tumble out and stick to her bottom lip. 'No evidence. None of the DNA matches his.'

'Anything else on the forensics? No DNA-matches at all?'

'None useful.'

She's toying with her fingers, running circles in the palm of her hands with her thumb.

'So Maloney is back to square one.'

A smile curls her lips. 'I suppose.'

'No other leads?'

The conversation is more difficult than an interview with a suspect who's been told by his lawyer to stick to 'No comment' .

'Not that I know off.' She leans forward as though she needs all her attention to toss three sugar cubes in her coffee, then starts stirring them in frantically.

'What about a connection with the death of Simon Croft, Jane's ex-husband?'

'One of the other officers has looked into that, but I don't think it got anywhere. I'm not sure it's been followed up.'

'Maloney unhappy?'

This time she produces a real smile. 'Don't tell me about it. He is a right pain.'

The uneasy path is left, it is now time to move on. She starts telling me the latest news about the team. Ollie Reed's date with the girl from the canteen. Nancy Hicks is pregnant and nobody at the station knows who the father is. Not even her, presumably. It's not what I want to hear, but I listen patiently, interrupting her at the right moments, waiting for an opportunity to change the subject. I almost miss my cue. All of a sudden she prepares to get up. 'I think it's time to go.'

The cafetiere is empty, so I suggest making a fresh pot and she smiles gratefully.

'I'll bring more biscuits too.'

When I come back from the kitchen, I find her studying the contents of my bookcase, reading the spines with her head tilted to one side.

'I'd never have thought you'd like Dick Francis.'

'Why not?'

'Don't know really. Somehow I can't see you connected

to the world of horse racing.'

I smile and sit down. 'It was a childhood dream. We had no money for riding lessons, which, I presume, made the desire even bigger. When I was eight, I got a few lessons for my birthday. I don't think I've ever felt happier in my life than when my parents took me to the local stables. I was a small boy, smaller than my age. I looked up at that big horse and saw the power of the muscles, the eyes, the teeth. He looked at me, sniffed, and I was helped onto his back. I don't know who was more scared, my mother or me. I started crying and they helped me off. My dreams were shattered.'

'So they finally found money for lessons and then you didn't like it.' It seems to please her that I too haven't lived without failures.

'Oh, it happens more often, I guess. My parents got their money back all right. Bought me shoes I needed more than anything.' I pause, caught in the memory. 'But the world of horses still appeals to me. Hence the complete Dick Francis collection.'

She sits down again, relaxing. 'Do you bet on horses?'

'I'm not a gambling person.'

'I'm not so sure about that.'

I'm surprised. 'What makes you say that?'

'I don't know. Maybe the way you go behind Maloney's back. And Guthrie's.' She pauses, looking at me thoughtfully for a moment. Then she gets up and finds in her pocket a crumpled piece of paper. Her face is expressionless as she stretches out her hand.

'There was a message from Mark Hinckley.' She hesitates, clearly uncomfortable. 'From forensics.'

'I see.' Now I am the one, suddenly, feeling embarrassed and blushing like a ripe tomato. Whether she notices or not, she doesn't react to it. A very short hesitation and she shoves the piece of paper across the coffee table in my direction. 'I don't know what it was about. Mark said something that made me think it was about the case.'

'Hmm.' I pick up the note that says nothing more than *Gardiner* and a mobile phone number.

Her eyes are accusing, suspicious. Clearly she's annoyed that this is something she doesn't know about. But it goes deeper than that. 'It was a good job that I intercepted Marks message before it got to Maloney.'

'I see.' I feel like a schoolboy, caught copying someone else's answers. 'Thank you Jennette.'

'Obviously Mark didn't know you were… not working.' Her chin is lifted stubbornly. 'When I explained about you, and Maloney, Mark wouldn't say what it was about. He insisted he'd only talk to you. I promised to ask you to get back to him.'

'I'll call him.'

She nods, but won't let go. 'Anything to do with the case?'

'Yes.' I hesitate only briefly. 'Let me call him, Jennette, then I'll explain.'

She sits on the edge of her seat, clearly still annoyed, but willing to give me the benefit of the doubt. Mark Hinckley is one of the forensic workers. Before I went to hospital, I asked him a personal favour and added that there was a good chance that it'll become an official request. Mark never asks questions and he keeps his mouth shut. I'm sure I'm not the only one who takes advantage of his talents.

'You got the message, hey?' He laughs in my ear. His voice is young, a bit high-pitched, not matching his appearance at all - he is in his mid-forties and weighs twice as much as he should.

'Yes, thank you, Mark.'

'Everything all right, Andy?' He's curious. 'I heard you're on the sickie.'

'I'm recovering from an operation.' I don't give him time to react to that. 'I'm here with Jennette Penrose. I'll get you on speaker.' I press the button so that Penrose can hear both ends of the conversation. 'What can you tell me about the phone, Mark?'

'Well, there's not much to tell, really.'

I try not to be disappointed. 'What do you mean?'

'The phone is a pretty new one. It's only been used for a few weeks. Three at the most.'

'Was it Jane Croft's?'

'It isn't registered. It's a pay-as-you-go. A ten-pound offer from a supermarket.'

'Any numbers in it?'

He pauses. I can hear a baby cry in the background. He is the youngest grandfather I know.

'Just one, unfortunately.' He pauses for effect. '

'Do you know whose number this is?'

'It's Jane Croft's landline. Which is not so strange, when you think about it. She must have dialled her own number. People do that to check if it is working, or just when they mislaid it.'

It isn't what I expected or hoped that he would find out from the mobile phone I retrieved from Joe and Stuart Gardiner.

'I can get you an anonymous list of calls to and from the phone, but it'll give you only the date, time and duration.'

'It's a start.'

'Anyway, Andy…' I can almost feel his weariness. 'Did you say the woman held it in her hand when she was found?'

I stare at Penrose. Her eyes are wide open and her lips form a silent swearword.

'Yes. Any fingerprints?'

'The hankie wiped most of it off.' He pauses. 'A lot of smaller prints, though. Kids.'

'Hmm.' I know exactly what he means. 'Any change of DNA through saliva or something?'

'We're still working on that, but I'm not very optimistic about it. We'll probably only find the DNA of those two boys, maybe their friends as well.'

'Hmm.' Inwardly I curse.

'She must have taken the phone out to dial 999. But she

didn't. No calls from that number registered as emergency calls.'

'Thank you, Mark, I owe you.'

'A dozen drinks by now.'

When I hang up, I meet Penrose's unforgiving eyes. 'Maybe you'd better tell me what that was all about,' she says coldly. 'Sir.'

35

JUNE

This time the front door is closed and I have to knock a few of times. Music drifts through the letterbox and I knock harder. If Shirley Croft is surprised to see me, it doesn't show on her face.

Dressed in a simple grey skirt and a cream jumper with a line of little gold coloured buttons on one shoulder, she steps back to let me in. Her hair is pulled back, tied in a thick ponytail that jumps cheerfully with every step.

The kitchen looks clean and tidy. Not a dirty cup or a teaspoon on the counter. There's even a faint smell of bleach that attempts to hide the cigarette smoke.

'I was just about to go out,' she says by way of explaining two shopping bags from different supermarkets on the table, a black purse next to it.

'I can come back.'

The sound of music drifts from upstairs. Someone upstairs flushes a toilet. Water rushes through pipes in thin walls as the cistern refills.

'No, I can go later,' she decides, already reaching for the electric kettle. 'It's just shopping. No hurry.'

'Thank you.'

With one eyebrow lifted, she points to the kettle. 'A brew?'

'Lovely.'

'I made some scones yesterday. To go with fresh strawberries.'

I lower myself on a seat, assuming the green plastic in which she sat at my previous visit is her favourite. 'Strawberries! From your own garden?'

'How else could I afford them?' she replies rhetorically, but her tone is joyful and her eyes, that were dull and brown at my previous visit, are now sparkling.

'I've been thinking about you, inspector.' Then, with a blush that makes her suddenly look two decades younger, she adds quickly, 'About what you said last time, I mean.'

'Maybe that's why I'm here.'

Opening a large cupboard door she produces a basket covered with a clean checked towel. 'They may not look like the ones from Tesco, but I can guarantee you that they're fresher and taste better. Danny and I got them out yesterday.'

With a grin, she lifts a carrot with fresh green leaves. The carrot itself looks like a deformed hand with three twisted fingers.

'Fresh and healthy,' she says, nodding, picking out three more and dumping them on the counter without worrying about the traces of mud.

'I'll put them in some paper for you, inspector.'

'I'm not sure...'

Like a magician with the inevitable hat, she produces some parsnips as well.

'I know you don't look after yourself well enough, inspector. You look like you've been ill. Fresh fruit and veg is good for you.'

My mother would love to meet her.

'Just wash and slice them, put them in a tray in the oven with an onion and some vegetable oil and there you go.'

It sounds easy enough. 'Thank you very much.'

'Or give them to some lady who will cook a proper meal for you.'

'My mother.'

She gives a mocking little laugh as she pours boiling water in a teapot.

'No lady in your life, inspector?'

'Not at the moment.'

'Then that is maybe why you look so sad.'

'Maybe.' I move on the chair, uneasy suddenly. 'Your husband and his former wife used to foster children.' I say, changing the subject abruptly.

She picks up the teapot, rocking it gently to help the tea brew.

'What about it?'

'Did you two also foster children when you were married?'

'Of course not. When I met Simon, Danny was only nine. My daughters were teenagers. A handful, all three of them. Sex and alcohol, police on my doorstep. All of it. Even if Simon had wanted to foster, I'd have refused.' She shrugs with an obvious indifference. 'It was his wife's idea, he said. I guess her only daughter wasn't enough for her. Couldn't have any more children, I believe.'

'Did Simon have contact with any of his former foster children?'

'I don't think so. If he did, he never told me about it. Didn't mention it particularly, but then I didn't really ask him, inspector. He knew people from before we met, just as I did. Sometimes those people belong to the past, if you get the picture. Sometimes we spoke about the past, most times we didn't.'

It makes sense. With a divorce, you lose about half of your friends and acquaintances. It's not always worth telling your other new half about them.

'He didn't say anything about his last foster child?'

She frowns. Her lips clamp together as if she's afraid that careless words will tumble out beyond control.

'What about her?'

I frown. Her. She obviously knows more about it. 'Did your husband talk about her at all?'

She doesn't answer immediately, passing me a mug of tea. No cup and saucer this time. I have been promoted to being a relative or a friend.

'I know she was the reason for his divorce.'

'What exactly was that reason, Mrs Croft?'

Her smile expresses pity as well as disappointment. 'Don't you know, inspector? Aren't you supposed to have investigated already if it is important enough to visit me?' She sounds bitter. 'Haven't you found the details in your files?'

'Are you saying there are police files?'

Her face grows dark with suppressed anger. 'That girl! Oh, Simon liked the girls more than the boys. He never kept that a secret, but he never touched them, inspector. Perhaps he had a quick glance in the bathroom, perhaps that was true, but I'm sure that was all. I have three daughters, inspector. I'm not stupid. I know what stepfathers, fathers even, are capable of. I've always been very careful. I've always kept my eyes wide open.' She pauses. 'It was one big lie, inspector, I can assure you. That girl… she came on to him, it was not the other way round. She seduced him. Oh, I agree that he shouldn't have let her, but she was… how shall I put it?… quite adamant. He just… one day, after a few drinks maybe, gave in.'

'So that part of the story is true.'

She nods with majestic arrogance. 'He told me himself. That was basically why I knew he was innocent, inspector. I didn't have to ask, he told me. That girl was evil, he said. Once he'd given in to her, it became clear that she had it all planned. Blackmail, that was all she was after. First it was clothes and shoes, later it was money. When in the end he refused, she burst out with her lies. Said he used to come to her bedroom in the night, force himself upon her. She showed the bruises. Mind you, she had waited a few days after it happened, that's what she said, so there was no other… physical proof of him on her. But she was examined and they found that she wasn't a virgin.'

'How old was she?'

She rolls her eyes. 'Thirteen, fourteen? Poor old Simon had no chance at all. Her tears meant more to his wife than his denials. She believed that girl and kicked him out of the house.'

'Was he charged for assaulting the girl? Under aged sex?'

'When it came to official charges, she pulled back. She said it may have been a mistake. But that was a few weeks later. By then, the damage was already done.' She pauses. 'If there's something in the records, inspector, it is lies anyway. I knew him, I knew when he was lying and when he was telling the truth.'

'Do you know the girl's name?'

'Oh yes! I'll never forget that! She phoned us, you see. He was quite upset about it. Raking up the past, sort of thing. Anyway, he told me about the call. Warned me not to let her in, if she came to our house. She's evil, he said, she comes from a family with blood on their hands.'

She's upset, two red spots form on her cheeks. She clicks her fingers. 'He said her real name was Rebecca Trewoon, but she was adopted. He didn't know her adopted name. He told me because he thought maybe she would use her other name to get to him through me. He said she might try to blackmail him again.'

'When did she call him?'

'Last summer.' The answer comes promptly.

'Did they meet, that you know off?'

'She phoned him, said she wanted to talk about the past, but I don't know whether he did, inspector.'

I'm not as sure as she is about trusting other people, but I let it rest.

'After some time she phoned again. Angry, she was, furious. I said he wasn't in, which was true, but she wouldn't believe me. Said I was lying. Accused me of keeping him away from her. She had to see him, she said, it was a matter of life and death. Well, as far as I was concerned, she could drop dead herself.'

'What was Simon's reaction?'

'He was not amused.' She smiles wryly. 'To tell you the truth, inspector, I don't know why you are here, but that girl... it sounds crazy, but it did cross my mind that she might have had something to do with his death.'

I squeeze my eyes half shut. 'What makes you think that, Mrs Croft?'

'I know I can't accuse people, not just like that.' She lifts a hand in the air and clicks her fingers. 'But it has crossed my mind that it was her who stabbed him.'

'When was the last time you or him had contact with that girl?'

'About six weeks before his death.'

'And you're sure they never met?'

'Well, to be honest, inspector, that's why I'm suspicious about what I've just told you. I mean, wasn't it rather odd that she never called back? Being so furious in the beginning, I thought she would never give up.' She takes a deep breath. 'But I never heard a word from her again.'

36

JUNE

There are messages waiting for me on the answer machine. The latest is new - my mother asking me if I need anything from the supermarket. I press the button to delete. I will call her later. First old message - Jennette, changing the time of our meeting tomorrow. As I listen I put my jacket on the coat hook and take off my shoes at the same time. Second old message - am I sure that I don't need double glazing? My bowels are loud, playing up as a result of a bad choice of meal last night. My stoma bag is filling. Whether it is only air I don't know.

I listen to the messages while I'm in the bathroom with the door open, changing my bag with quick and almost expert fingers.

Fourth old message - 'Andy, this is Eileen Turton. Listen, I had a look at some of the old files and something has struck me. Perhaps there's no connection at all, but I think it is... well, it's strange, at the least.' She pauses, as though waiting for my response. Then, realising her time is limited, she goes on quickly. 'You must find out about the Barrs. Patrick and Katherine Barr. They were also foster parents. The last time I saw them was at a funeral, some time ago. And I remembered that lovely little boy. He was there too and I spoke to him. He has a little boy himself, with the same blond curly hair and angel blue eyes. Of course, we spoke about the past and he mentioned his adopted sister. He said he'd seen...'

Her voice stops abruptly. There's only so much time for a message on an answer machine.

Fifth old message - I hope it's Eileen again, finishing her message, but it's my mother. As usual her words are carefully chosen. Jolyon Finn is coming to see them next week. Nothing special, but they would love it if I could join in for a game of bridge. Would I be the fourth player? Finn is an old school friend of my father's. Our families spent holidays on the coast together. They had two daughters, one a year older than me, the other a year younger. We built sandcastles and learnt to surf. We danced and we kissed. Holidays stopped abruptly after Finn's wife died and my parents moved on with coach trips to France and Holland. Fond memories. I smile. I will accept the invitation, happy to play bridge with them.

There's a message from someone hoping that I need a new life insurance policy. I laugh hollowly. Too late for that, mate. I doubt an application of mine will get through. Then there's a message from PS Moreton, still desperately trying to recruit me for a dart team in his local pub. He started his mission when he found out that I once was a champion in my days at the police academy. At some point I must have given in to his plea, because he wants to know if I will be fit to play next Wednesday. I've completely forgotten about it.

The eight and last old message is from Eileen Turton again. Unfortunately she doesn't continue where she was interrupted forty minutes earlier. Something must have happened since her first call, because she sounds more agitated. 'Andy, it's me again. Eileen. Listen, I left a message for you earlier. But this is really important. You need to see my files. If you can… if you feel well enough, that is. You'd better come and go through the files yourself. I'll be waiting for you. Doesn't matter what time. I'm not going anywhere. I think I have found something very interesting. Please come as soon as you can. Any time. I'll be here.'

There's a tone in her voice that makes me listen to both her messages again. Jotting down the names she mentioned in the first message, I press the button to call her.

She doesn't answer.

I try again and another time, worry making my legs weak. I am already debating whether to get in my car and drive to her home in Tavistock. The doorbell rings and with a sense of relief I pull it open, half expecting to find Eileen smiling on my doorstep.

But it's Marie, eyes black with kohl eyeliner and mascara, darker than ever under the white blonde fringe, this time with a purple streak. Lips a dazzling shiny red, she smiles widely.

'Marie.'

'They say you're still on the sickie.'

I ignore her. 'What do you want?'

'Am I not welcome anymore?'

'I didn't say that.' My mobile is still in my hands.

She looks past me. 'Is it inconvenient? Do you have company?'

'No. But I need to make some phone calls.'

Still sulking, she appears not to have heard, although I notice her red mouth tighten. 'Aren't you inviting me in?'

'I really have no time, Marie.'

'I won't stay long.'

Debating that it might be quicker to let her in and have her tell me the reason of her visit, I reluctantly step back, slowly closing the door behind her as she passes me and heads for the living room, led in by the sound of the TV. She peels off a purple, fake leather jacket, revealing a black vest that is too tight and provocative.

'It's new,' she says, following my gaze. 'Do you like it?'

I sigh. 'Marie, what are you doing here?'

'Visiting you.' To emphasize, she graciously lowers herself onto the chair I have been sitting in. A small movement of the corners of her mouth reveals that she has chosen the seat deliberately.

I can feel myself getting annoyed. I remain standing, trying to let her know that she isn't welcome. I don't want her here. Due to a curry takeaway last night, I'm suffering from cramps that nag me at irregular intervals. I have emptied my stoma bag three times in the last couple of hours. The door to the bathroom is ajar. I can smell the disinfectant I use, but it doesn't overpower the other, more human, aroma. And there is also my stoma bag. Although it has a small coal filter, I suspect it can't stop everything. From the bulge beneath the slips of my shirt I can tell it's filling as we speak. I feel embarrassed and humiliated and I want her to leave right now.

'I wouldn't mind a cup of tea.' Clearly she thinks otherwise.

'I'm not making one,' I say curtly.

'Coffee will do then.' Her eyes drift through my living room, scrutinising my life, my tastes, my habits, my character. Working as a detective has brought me to numerous homes. A home is like a soul, it tells more about its inhabitants than a thousand words can explain.

'No. I'm going out.'

Again she shrugs, letting me know she doesn't care. Gesturing around, she blurts out, 'You surprise me.'

In turn, her words surprise me. 'How come?'

'This… Spartan home.'

'It's how I like it.' This isn't entirely true. In my bedroom there is a pile of paintings bought at several exhibitions from local artists. Some are of a greater standard, some are from beginners, but they have in common something that appealed to me when I bought them. One is of a spectacular seascape of waves crashing on the north Cornwall coast. Another one is an abstract image with warm brownish colours, paints cleverly run over watercolour paper, creating an image in which the viewer can surround himself with imagination. That painting is facing me from the pile stacked against the wall next to my bed. Each time I look at it, it always seems to be different and I can lose myself in trying to find meanings and shapes in it. I don't know why I haven't hung the paintings on the still bare walls. Is it just laziness? Or maybe making decisions about where to hang which painting puts me off? Marie is right. It would make a huge difference to the Spartan impression of my home.

'I never expected you to have a... home like this.'

'You've seen it before.'

Her eyes widen for a moment, then her lips twist in a mischievous smile. 'You remember.'

Choosing to ignore this particular line of conversation, I say, 'I only moved in here a couple of months ago.'

'No wives, partners, girlfriends?'

I contemplate to point out that the particular question may be a little too late, but I keep quiet, not wanting to refer to the nights we spent together.

'No.' Unconsciously I fidget with the hem of my shirt. I should put it in the waist of my trousers but it comfortably hangs down covering the bag beneath. I'm not sure she is aware of it and I'd like to keep it that way.

'I'm very sorry, Marie, but... I'd like you to leave.'

'Why? I mean, I'm kindly visiting a patient. You can't just send me away.'

'I don't see why not.'

I'm being rude, but I'm also desperate. An awful smell makes my nostrils wince.

She doesn't move. 'It wasn't just sex, you know. Not for me.'

Wasn't it? I am not at all sure.

'I care for you also, Andy.'

'I appreciate that, Marie, I really do, but right now... I'm afraid I have to ask you to leave.'

'But... but I love you!' Her lips tremble and her eyes, wide and dark, express a desperation that takes me by surprise.

'Marie, I...' I don't know what to say. I want to laugh, but I know how inappropriate that would be. I don't want to hurt her feelings anymore than I already have.

'OK. I understand.' Her voice is low in her throat.

'I'm sorry Marie. There really is something I need to do,

so for now I will have to ask you to leave.' I hesitate. 'But... you can come back. If you like.'

She casts me a look that is a mixture of surprise and hesitation. Then she nods and picks up her jacket. The door clicks behind her in its lock and I know it is too late to respond to her exclamation about loving me.

37

JUNE

Eileen Turton's house is strangely dark. Quiet. Deserted. The curtains are open. I stand on the doorstep, uncertain. Worried also. Snippets of her last message pop up, the echo of her agitated voice still bounces in my head. 'Andy, it's me again - this is really important - you need to see my files – I'll be waiting – not going anywhere – come as soon as you can.'

'I'll be here,' she said. Only she isn't.

I hesitate, debating what to do next. I didn't expect this, not after hearing the urgent tone in her voice. I don't know her well enough to have a logical answer for her absence, but I do know that she wouldn't have gone to bed. And she certainly wouldn't want me to drive all the way from Newquay - for nothing.

I look over my shoulder. The street is empty, the houses are dark. Disappointment kicks in and all of a sudden I feel exhausted. I'm not as physically fit as I used to be and I dread having to drive home again without having seen her. Putting my foot carefully between the flowering plants under the bay window, I peer into her dark sitting room. Pot plants and memorabilia on the windowsill partially block my view. A small L.E.D. light on her TV says it's on stand-by; somehow the red glow is enough to notice her shoes, her feet in them. It's almost midnight. She must have fallen asleep with the TV on before it switched itself off.

She was waiting for me.

With a mixture of guilt and shame I knock on the window, carefully first, then harder. She doesn't move. She doesn't even stir. I take a deep breath. My heart throbbing in my ear, I push away horrific thoughts I don't even wish to contemplate. I press the doorbell. Once. Twice. Again. It echoes in the hallway. I'm vaguely worried that it's loud enough to wake the neighbours, but Eileen's feet still don't move. Unless she's really deep asleep, something is very, very wrong.

I swallow a few times but the lump in my throat won't move. The coward in me is trying to reason that I'd better go. Home or find a cheap hotel in town. I am tired, knackered and the thought of a comfortable bed in a hotel is extremely inviting. Tomorrow is another day. I can come back and see Eileen in the morning. Everything will be all right.

Only I know it isn't.

There is a blue ceramic pot on either side of the front door, both filled with trailing petunias. Eileen Turton strikes me as too careful to leave her spare key in such an obvious hiding place. Yet I check. As I lift one of the flowerpots, my hand scrapes over the rough surface. Dust, old leaves, the cold metal of a single key under the second pot.

Weighing the key in my hand I hesitate. My heart knows what to do but my mind tells me to be careful, be sensible. Even with a key it is out of the question to enter the home of a woman I hardly know. I can't justify the action as a policeman following a lead of the investigation.

Making up my mind, I try one more knock on the window, one ring of the doorbell, one call with my mobile. But every sound I make bounces back, telling me to act rather than wait for something I know instinctively won't happen anyway.

I shrug, shaking off the doubts. She asked me to come. It was important. She would wait for me. That's exactly what's still on my answerphone. At least I have one way to prove my innocence.

I slide the key into the lock and the door opens with a

single turn. My footsteps sound like staccato gunshots on the black and white tiled floor. The house has an empty feel, as if it has already lost its soul. The smell of roses and lavender is fading into something else, sweet and dark. There's also a bitter aroma, rotten, like a kitchen bin left open.

'Eileen?' I keep my voice low, yet it echoes in the cold silence. I am frightened to disturb her, imagining her shock when she finds me in her house so unexpectedly. 'Eileen?'

Her head is laid back on to the backrest of the couch, a cushion under her neck for comfort. Another one is held onto her chest, as if she is cuddling a small child. Her eyes are closed, her glasses slightly pulled askew. Picking up her hand, touching it gently with my fingertips, her skin feels so cold that I drop it instantly. It falls beside her on the couch with a dull thud.

The silence is almost overwhelming. She is not breathing. Neither am I.

My fingers are unsteady as I find the switch of the lamp on the table beside her. The light doesn't wake her. Of course it doesn't. Even in the warm light of a pink lampshade, her lips are an unhealthy blue, her face equally pale, ashen. I feel for a pulse, put my ear close to her mouth. Nothing. No heartbeat. Not a wisp of shallow breath. She must have been dead for a couple of hours.

I sit down and look at her, swallowing away dry lumps and tears that gather in my eyes. Poor Eileen. Another life lost. She told me she had no relatives, none that she knew of anyway. Who will mourn for her? Any of the foster children she cared for so much?

Somewhere in a nearby house a dog barks and I almost jump. All of a sudden the policeman in me is on the alert. I know I shouldn't touch anything, let alone change things from the original crime scene but the open curtains make me feel exposed to prying eyes from outside. I rise to my feet and close them before I kneel beside her and do some quick checks without touching her. My first inkling was that she had a heart attack but when I notice fresh scratches from her fingernails on the wooden part of the armrest I change my mind. Thinking about the messages she left on my answerphone and remembering the urgency in her voice when she asked me to come as quick as possible, I don't need a pathologist to confirm that she has been murdered. From what I gather, someone has pressed the pillow on her face. She was hardly aware of the danger, she didn't put up a serious fight until her last moments. Or maybe she was just paralysed by the shock, the horror of the knowledge that someone she trusted would do her harm. I freeze, shocked by my own thoughts, realising I'm already bypassing the idea that this happened by some intruder or burglar.

Horrified suddenly, I wonder whether I am responsible for her death. Perhaps if I'd come immediately after her first message… If I had jumped in my car straight away, and not sat with a microwave meal and watch a repeated episode of *Eggheads*. Somehow I can't ignore the nagging feeling that I could have saved her.

'I'm so sorry, Eileen,' I say softly, looking at her as if hoping to get her reassurance that it had nothing to do with me at all.

Only I know it would be a lie.

The cushion has slid down from her chest to her lap and I notice now that her white blouse is torn open at the front, one small button missing. A decent, flesh coloured bra is half pulled up. One side a normal cup, the other is filled with foam. One side of her chest lays half bare. A crumpled piece of skin with a dark mark where once there must have been a nipple. I feel like crying when I think of her kindness and understanding. Even when I told her about Mr Rakesh's message, she didn't tell me that she'd had a mastectomy.

Staring at her chest, I know how undignified she would feel knowing that everyone would be staring at her. I can't possibly leave her like this. Pictures of what's left of her breast will be stored in police files for years to come. When shown in court, everyone will know. As a policeman I know that photographs and videos of the crime scene are important, crucial and I simply can't wipe that out. As a compromise I take out my phone and make photographs of her, each from a different angle. I shoot a short video film for as long as the memory allows it. Then I lift the rim of her bra and pull it up, so that it covers her breast decently. It is the least I can do for her.

To definitely rule out that she may have surprised a burglar, I go from room to room, closing curtains before I switch on the lights. I check the kitchen, looking for evidence of a forced entry. The front door was locked before I entered, so is the backdoor in the little annex behind the kitchen. The key is in the lock, another one is dangling on the key ring. A light above the door of the neighbour's shed is just bright enough to see a path of flagstones, which leads through a narrow back garden towards a small wrought iron gate. Shoulder high wooden fences on either side, lined with mixed plants and shrubs, form friendly borders with both of next doors gardens.

On the kitchen counter is a dish rack with a single plate, a glass bowl, a handful of cutlery. Half filled with water is an electric kettle, next to a red Celebrations tin where the chocolates have been eaten and is now half filled with digestives. In the sink is a mug with a teaspoon in it, a ring of milky tea at the bottom. A small saucepan is left on the hob containing a couple of cold boiled potatoes and carrots, probably meant for a roast dinner the following day.

The stair boards creak as I go upstairs. I feel like an intruder. Her bedroom door is half open. The curtains are closed and the bedclothes are made up. On top of her pillow lays an oversized white T-shirt with a Mickey Mouse print on the front. I can't help a sad smile. Who would have thought of Eileen wearing things like that?

Her bed is light oak with a matching wardrobe and dressing table. Cheap necklaces with coloured beads are drawn over the top of the mirror. A jewellery box sits undisturbed next to a silver hairbrush set. Whatever the killer has come for, it wasn't to steal her jewels.

The spare bedroom door is closed. I cast a quick glance inside. An ironing board stands between two single beds, made up as though guests are expected to arrive at any time. The bathroom is too small to be really comfortable. Over the frosted glass door of a shower cubicle hangs a faded green towel, a plastic shower cap is draped over the tap. The toilet is perched next to it, its seat down.

It's all that remains of the private life of Eileen Turton.

Somewhere in the house a clock chimes. It disturbs the silence and I stand for a moment, holding my breath, listening, counting. Twelve. Suddenly I panic. Taking the stairs two at a time, I land on my hands and knees on the floor, leaving fingerprints, and a dark scratch from my shoe on a white tile. More traces to prove I was at a crime scene, where a woman is murdered. Sooner or later there will be police and forensic specialist crawling over the place, running in and out like busy ants. They will scrutinise every square inch of the house, take minuscule samples of every bit that comes anywhere near look suspicious. What they will find is a mountain of evidence that I was here: a policeman on sick leave who stupidly thought he could solve a complicated murder case in his spare time.

I have been in every room. Not only have I touched the body, but also light switches, doors and door handles, the banister, even the wooden part of the armrest where Eileen sits. Basically I have touched nearly everything that could possibly be touched. Prints of my hands and fingers will be up for grabs. Forensic specialists like Andrea Burke will have a feast here, proving how right Edmond Locard was when he launched his exchange principle on physical evidence: everyone who has been at a crime scene not only leaves something behind, but at the same time takes something with him. I may have lost a hair, an eyelash, even a speck of dandruff, threads of clothing, a tear, a drop of saliva. Particles of sand from the beach may have slipped from my soles. Perhaps some nitwit from forensics can prove that the sand comes from one particular beach in Newquay, a beach I walk on regularly.

There are traces of me all over the house, invisible for the eye. For reasons of elimination, my DNA is stored in the police database. Soon enough it will pop up on someone's computer screen. A perfect match. As a policeman working on a crime scene, there is a logical explanation for the DNA. But I'm on sick leave. How can I explain why I was here? I let myself in with the key hidden on the doorstep. In the middle of the night, for God's sake! Who will believe me?

Quickly looking round, I dismiss the idea of finding a towel and remove my traces from every surface I may have touched with bleach and water. I don't want to wipe those of the murderer. Eileen deserves better than that.

I become aware of a sinking feeling that I have to do something, but I don't know what. I can't stay here much longer, I can't risk being caught. The best thing would be to call the police. But what possible reason can I come up with about my presence? Why I can't explain why I didn't phone the police straight away? It will put me on top of the list of suspects. As a policeman, I wouldn't blame them.

Obviously the police in Newquay, in the person of Maloney, won't be in charge of this case, but I don't doubt that he will inform his colleagues and make me a suspect. Nobody will believe my conspiracy theory about the foster children, which is, I must admit, too far-fetched to take seriously. Eileen's death will perhaps change the police's point of view, but I doubt it will cause a complete change of mind. Until now, Maloney has been more than keen on catching the killer of Jane Croft. He will be very pleased having me as a scapegoat.

Suddenly I am very calm. I can't go without doing what I initially came for. Eileen called because she had important information for me. She had found something in her old files, something I needed to know.

Patrick and Katherine Barr.

I turn towards a small Ikea style desk in the corner. There

is a computer screen on its top, the computer itself and a printer copier are in an open space on the left, below a small drawer that contains stationary and a ream of print paper. On the other side is a drawer with suspension files. I quickly read the labels: electricity, insurance companies, bank statements, savings accounts, general correspondence. I take out the latter and find Christmas cards, some of which seem decades old.

There are no copied files from her work.

I turn round. Try to think. Where would Eileen have kept files that were valuable to her? I can't remember having seen anything upstairs, but I go back to check. There are wardrobes and drawers containing clothes, socks and tights. I get frustrated. I know the files have to be somewhere, but the shock of her death, the presence of the dead body, the feeling that I ought to get out of here as quickly as I can, blocks my mind. I can't think. I'm too tired. I want to go, find a bed, sleep. Waking up tomorrow to find out that this is all a terrifying dream. But Eileen found something that was important enough for someone to kill her. If I want to find Eileen's murderer, I will need those files, I owe it to Eileen and to Jane.

Back in the living room I stand still again, scrutinising every piece of furniture as if I can look inside of them. Think. The best hiding place is the most obvious place. You don't hide a diamond ring in its original case in a drawer with socks or underwear, you keep it amongst other, cheaper jewellery in an old soapbox. You don't keep a painting of an old master in a safe in the bank, you hang it on your wall, visible for everyone or stuck behind another. You hide papers amongst other papers. Visible for everyone, but invisible for someone who is looking for them. Paper. Books.

I stare at the bookcase. The encyclopaedia. Obviously the books are in alphabetical order. Like you would keep your files. Thoughtfully, I touch the old spines. The bookcase is deep enough to allow space behind the books. With a strange feeling that Eileen is laughing behind my back, I pull one of the books out. Nothing. Unconsciously I weigh it in my hand.

Open it.

Eileen must either have been paranoid or gifted with a wicked sense of humour. She has cut the middle of the pages out, creating enough room for a decent size brown envelope with a white sticker: Hickmott. In the envelope are folded A4 copies of the original files, paper cuttings and photos. The first volume of the encyclopaedia contains three envelopes: Abbott, Atherington, Black, but the Barr file is missing.

If the deaths of Eileen Turton and Jane Croft are linked, than the missing file is a true indication that the murderer took the Barr file. Which means his or her name would be in it, or at least there would be an indication about the murderer's identity. Eileen found it. She had do be eliminated.

I'm about to leave when something else dawns on me. Eileen said she found something important, she would make copies for me. Copies. I spin round. The computer is turned off, but not the printer. Every so often a green light shines as a reminder that it's waiting for a command. It's a three-in-one, printer, copier and scanner. True to her word, Eileen made copies for me. The last page is still on the glass panel under the lid. The copies are in a tray underneath. I press the button and a red flashes as a sign that it needs paper which is probably why the murderer didn't notice it. As I refill it, it starts printing one more page.

Yet more fingerprints. Forensics will have a feast here. Pulling my sleeve, I wipe every bit of the printer that I may have touched. The drawers and cupboard door too.

In the stationary drawer I find an elastic band. Without looking at them, I roll the copies tight, bind them with the elastic and put it in my inside coat pocket.

After some thought, I leave the original paper in the scanner. Perhaps the police will find significance in that.

I check my watch. Half past one. Putting the backdoor key in my trouser pocket, I go back to the living room. For the last time I look at Eileen's cold face. I hate to leave her like this, but I know she will understand.

'I am sorry, Eileen,' I say softly, my voice sounding like a bomb explosion in the stillness. 'I won't let you down. I promise.'

One minute later I leave the house like a thief in the night, having left the front door key where I found it.

38

JUNE

Having sorted the papers in chronological order, the history of the Barr family is displayed on my kitchen table, starting with their assessment papers when they applied to become foster parents. Patrick and Katherine Barr had three boys of their own, the youngest was six at the time of their application. According to comments from social workers, with each foster child the Barrs made a real effort to give it a loving and warm home.

There was a minor issue with the oldest son who was caught with a young girl, but it was considered a one-off incident. A stroppy teenager, difficult to handle, Archie's behaviour made Eileen and her colleagues a bit suspicious about Patrick and Kate's ability to be good foster parents, but nothing was done.

I make a list of their foster children, Esmeralda Cooke (previously Jane Smith), Jeremy Lawson, Jilly Fisher, Becky Eve, Laura Keane and Mickey Rowse, and all kinds of social care workers, heads of nurseries and schools they got involved with.

When nothing obvious springs to mind, I go through the papers again, adding all the dates mentioned. Then I make a chart, putting the names of the Barr family in the middle, the foster children in a circle around them, attached by each social care worker that was dealing with the child at the time. It transpires that most of the care workers didn't seem to stay much longer than two years.

Three photos are copied together on a single A4 sheet. I stare at a blurred black and white photo of a happy family, laughing, with arms on shoulders. There is a woman with dark hair and pearl earrings, one hand resting on the head of a sleepy Labrador. A young boy leans on to her shoulders, his fair hair cut so short on the sides that his ears seem too large. He grins widely between them. The father stands back a little bit, three other boys with the same dark hair as the mother, stand side by side in front of him. Underneath a single note: *With Jeremy*. Jeremy Lawson. According to the dates he was their second foster child. He stayed with them for only four months.

The second photo shows the same woman, older, hair longer, wearing glasses that express the fashion of the time. The same dog sits beside her. On the other side is a young girl with very dark hair. Her face has a serious expression, as if she isn't used to being photographed and doesn't know how to look. There's no note explaining who the girl is or when the photo was made.

The third photo on the bottom is of the whole family again although later in time. Somewhere along the line the dog must have died. Two boys are skinny and have the uncertainty of young teenagers not knowing what to do with their arms and legs. The oldest boy appears rather cocky, his lopsided grin so charming that it already shows his later attractiveness to women. The third boy, the youngest, is lying in front of the family, his head held up by his elbow. The father sits on a chair, balancing a young girl on his knee. There is a date written vertically next to the photo: *Christmas Day, from left to right are: Dad and Laura, Lenny, Archie, Mum, Georgie (lying in front).*

Checking the names and dates again I discover that Esmeralda Cooke (previously Jane Smith) was their first child and for a short period they also had Anthony Ball living with them. Jeremy Lawson, from the first photo, followed. Becky Eve arrived shortly after Jilly Fisher left the family. Becky stayed about eighteen months and was replaced by. Laura

Keane. If the photo's are in chronological order and Laura was the girl on the third, than Becky or Jilly must have been in the second photo. Mickey Rowse was the last of the foster children.

I study the photos again, but they are just snapshots and not very clear. I turn on the TV for possible news on the death of Eileen Turton. From the corner of my eye I see the newsreader appear on the screen. Breaking news is in red at the bottom: a suicide bomb in the Middle East, Five people killed, two of which were children under the age of four. What a waste of lives. Other news. As if this is less important, a car has crashed into someone's house, in fact, into someone's bedroom. The driver is found dizzy and still half drunk in the wreck, the woman whose bedroom he drove into is still missing. Workers are made redundant in a small local pasty factory. They're standing at the gate with tears in their eyes. Having dedicated half of their lives to the company, they just can't believe it's all over. The weather forecast predicts sunny spells and showers. That must be the easiest way for a forecast: they'll always get it right.

Nothing on Eileen.

I lean over my balcony. The boating lake is a mirror, with the sun shining bright on it like a strobe light in a football stadium. The postman arrives in his red mini van. Letterboxes rattle.

I go back inside, stare at my chart that looks like a toddler's drawing. My eyes are so fixed on the names and dates that my mind goes blank. Distracted by what the postman may have dropped in my letterbox, I walk down the staircase to collect it. Amongst the usual collection of bills and circulars is a postcard from Italy. Regards from Naples. On the back it says: *Get well soon. Chris.* Nice. A colleague. He was going on holiday when I went to hospital. The card is dated eight days ago. He'll probably be back to work by now. Maybe I should give him a ring and thank him for his card.

My eyes are drawn to the chart again. The names are

highlighted in the middle. Patrick and Kate Barr. Archie. Len. George.

This is madness. I'm looking for the proverbial needle in the haystack. I don't even know if there is a needle.

I put my laptop on top of the papers and Google the names on the list, half hoping that one of them pops up in a newspaper article, framed as a suspect in a murder case somewhere in the country. As I say, it's madness.

Just as I lean back for the umpteenth time, realising that frustration is surging up inside me, my phone rings. My voice must sound happy and cheerful about the interruption, because I hear my mother ask, 'You feeling better?'

'Yes.'

My reply catches her by surprise. 'I'm just calling to find out if there's anything you need.'

'I don't think so, Mum, but thanks all the same.'

She doesn't appear to have heard. 'Your dad and I are going to Morrisons in a minute. Do you need anything? We can come over and bring it on our way back.'

'I'm okay, Mum, really.'

'Oh.' She almost sounds disappointed. Maybe she feels better knowing that I need her caring.

'I thought you were phoning to invite me for tea tonight,' I joke.

'Well!' I feel ashamed when I hear the joy and happiness in that single word. 'Of course you're welcome, darling! As I said, we're going to do our weekly shopping. What would you like to eat?'

I already regret having invited myself. Eileen Turton's dead body pops up in my mind with irregular intervals, stopping me from concentrating on anything else. I know already I won't be enjoyable company, certainly not in the way my mother expects. And besides I want to get on with this file. The answer to all my questions is somewhere in it. I know it. It will take time, but I will find it. I owe it to Eileen

'It doesn't matter, mum. Anything will do. Eh, no broccoli,

please.' I think of my diet instructions. 'Or any other cabbage. And not too many onions.'

She chuckles. 'Of course, love. Are you sure you don't need anything else?'

'I'm sure.'

Reluctantly she disconnects, unsure if I told her the truth. I make a cup of black coffee and eat the remainder of a packet of chocolate biscuits, munching away over the Barr file. Archie, the eldest, has gone through his A-levels effortlessly, apparently after his father threatened to find him a job in a local butcher. By then the boy had an outspoken opinion about being a vegetarian. Leonard was quite the opposite. Never missed a day at school, eager to become a lawyer or a judge. Wanted to study law, but failed somewhere along the way and ended up as a road worker at sixteen, much to the disappointment of his parents. George, the youngest, became a soldier and died in the Middle east.

Something is nagging me about Archie and Len. Once more I go through Eileen's notes. I remember an issue with Archie and a foster girl, but she isn't named. Becky Eve has been with the Barr family at about the same time as the incident happened, from June till October the following year. Twelve at the time, she seemed to have been extremely difficult to deal with. Archie who was then sixteen and the two years younger Leonard, both fell in love with the girl, who, obviously, was too young. Yet I gather from carefully chosen words from the care worker involved, that something happened between the eldest boy and the girl. It isn't specifically mentioned, but between the lines I read that a physical relationship was the reason that the girl was sent elsewhere shortly after.

Perhaps it means nothing, but I make a note on a yellow post-it and stick it to the computer screen.

I need to talk to Patrick and Katherine Barr. There's nothing in their file that links them with the death of Jane and Simon Croft, but I have a gut feeling that there must be something. If there isn't, then why did someone kill Eileen

Turton? And why is the family's file missing?

I pick up the phone and dial the number with an area code I don't immediately recognise.

'Hello?'

'Is this Barr?'

'No. I'm Richards.'

'I'm sorry.'

An odd silence echoes on the line. There is something in it that makes me wait, rather than apologise again and disconnect.

'Were you looking for Patrick Barr?'

'Yes, I am.' Sometimes instincts prove to be right. 'Is he there?'

'Sadly, he died.' There is more in her voice that tells me that she's hurting.

'I'm sorry to hear that.' I hesitate. 'Long ago?'

'Last year.' Her voice grows slightly higher, with a hint of disgust. 'A road accident. Some drunk hit him and left him for dead. He died in the ambulance.'

'That's terrible.'

'It was.' She hesitates. 'He lived with my mother. They had only been together for a couple of months.'

I hesitate. It sounds too far-fetched to try. 'Did you know his first wife at all? Katherine?'

'No.' The reply is curt, like a snap.

'Do you know where I can find her?'

'I'm sorry. I can't help you.'

Before I can inquire after the sons, Archie and Len, she repeats how sorry she is and disconnects abruptly.

Most of the news is repeated. The item about the car that was driven into someone's bedroom is shortened. The woman has been found in what's left of her bed. The husband had a lucky escape because he had just got up for an early shift. The government has made plans to kill all badgers in Devon and Cornwall's countryside because they are believed to spread diseases among cattle. Farmers are happy, animal rights protesters disgusted.

No news on Eileen yet. I imagine her sitting in her cold house. It feels so wrong that her body hasn't been discovered yet. What can I do? Call the police anonymously, with the chance that they'll trace my phone number? Call from a phone box, with the chance that I'll be caught on CCTV? I feel so guilty that it's almost as if I have killed her myself.

The news finishes with the weather forecast. With a shock I realise that it's past five o' clock. My parents are expecting me.

I get up and change into a clean shirt that covers the stoma bag on my belly. I should do some shopping and buy a few more shirts. Some I own are tighter than others, making the bag stand out too much for my comfort.

When I close my laptop, one corner of the yellow post-it note peeps out. Making a mental note that I need to speak with Katherine Barr and find out what happened to the foster girl, presumably Becky Eve, and why she was removed from the Barr home, I leave my flat and head for my car to drive to my parents.

Two women bring the traffic to a sudden halt when they decide to cross the road on a zebra crossing. Although they can't be much older than forty, one of them reminds me of Eileen somehow. As I wait patiently in the queue I become aware of a single tear in my eye. Thinking of Eileen I feel a burst of anger rising. Her death was unfair, leaving her alone in her own cold home like that is even more unfair, and inhuman.

It's when I drive onto the roundabout at the Gannel, that I make up my mind to return to her house immediately after the meal with my parents.

39

JUNE

It is past ten o'clock when I get in my car. My mother ushers me in, carrying a saucepan with the remainder of her homemade tomato soup. 'Have this for tomorrow, love. Nice to have for lunch with some toast.'

She wraps the pan in a plastic carrier bag from Asda and places it on the floor below the passenger seat. 'Drive carefully, dear. Don't let it spill on the carpet.'

I promise and drive off with no intention whatsoever to go home. I have made up my mind. I have watched the ten o'clock news in companionship with my father. However Eileen's death may not necessarily become a news item, which presumably depends on what other news there is, I can't be certain that her body has not been discovered. Each day, each hour, it becomes more likely that a friend or a neighbour gets suspicious about the closed curtains in her living room, her kitchen. At one point someone will call the landlord or the police and some poor soul will be faced with the discovery of her decaying body. I can't let that happen.

As important to me, it also means that from that moment, I can't enter her house anymore to pick up the other files. My gut feeling tells me that I will need those files. All of them. I may be wrong, but something tells me that they may turn out to be crucial in finding Eileen's murderer. And Jane's, Simon's. This is my last and only chance. If I don't find her files tonight, I will never find them.

My mother has given me a couple of plastic carrier bags. She obviously wondered what I needed them for, but she was tactful enough not to ask. She seemed delighted that she can help me, although she can't possibly know my true reason for needing them.

It is almost midnight when I drive past Eileen's house. It is dark. No police tape, no uniforms on guard. After the warmth of the day, the night is cold, with an edge that chills my bones. The sky is the colour of tarnished silverware, an almost full moon sets the world in a secretive shine.

I have studied the area on Google Earth and know how to gain access to the alley behind the terraced houses. I park the car in a street two blocks away, leaving it unlocked as I don't want its orange lights flash when I lock and unlock it with the button on my key. I have to take that risk. Although I can never be certain nowadays, I'm pretty sure there are no CCTV cameras. Yet I have changed into dark trousers and trainers, and a hooded sweater with DKNY printed in white on my chest. My face is shadowed by a baseball cap and I have put on a pair of glasses that once belonged to my father. I don't even remember how and why they got left in a box in my car, but now they prove to be useful. The glasses blur my vision, but it'll do when I'm outside Eileen's house, within reach of possible CCTV or curious eyes from neighbours suffering with insomnia.

The key is still under the flowerpot. The house seems the same, but the smell is different. Someone's perfume, after shave? Or is it just the decaying body? Nevertheless, I feel nervous and uncomfortable, half expecting Maloney and the whole police force to emerge from a dark corner.

It is almost impossible not to look at Eileen. The smell is bitter and sweet at the same time, penetrating into my clothes, my pores. Pressing a towel against my face, and inwardly uttering a curse, I promise her silently that I will call the police from a phone box on the way home as soon as I'm finished here. I've seen enough CCTV footage to know that I can make myself unrecognisable.

Nothing has changed in the sitting room. I sigh with relief to find the bookcase still intact, and not emptied on the floor, the envelopes with the files gone.

Pulling on latex gloves I start methodically taking out the volumes of the encyclopaedia, finding envelopes in almost every one of them. Some are thin and barely touched, some are thick, the paper worn, torn at corners. Carefully piling the envelopes in my mother's plastic carrier bags, I place the books back in the original order.

The envelopes are not particularly heavy, but I am afraid that the carrier bags will tear and collapse on the way to my car. I can't afford to drop them, having to kneel on the street and gather them back. It will attract too much attention, raise too much suspicion, especially afterwards, if and when the incident links to Eileen's body. As a result I carry two at the same time, clutching them to my chest rather than dangling off my hands.

My heart is pounding in my chest by the time I walk back to the house to collect the last of the bags. The next steps will be crucial. I thought about this, weighed the options and chances, and I've decided to leave Eileen's house as I found it myself the previous night. Therefore I must open the curtains and leave the backdoor key in the door, which means I have to leave the house for the last time through the front door.

I need not worry. Everything in the street is calm and quiet. No dog barks, no cat gives me a fright by appearing suddenly from one of the hedges. The cars parked in the street all seem deserted, yet I feel as if hidden eyes are watching me secretly. It must be guilt. I am a policeman, I'm supposed to live by the rules and stick to the law.

Getting into my car, I become suddenly aware of the smell of sweat. It's on my chest, between the shoulder blades, under my armpits, on my forehead and under my nose. My hair is damp. I have been dead calm during the process of bringing the files over to my car, yet suddenly I become scared. I feel hot and cold at the same time. I am shaking so much that my sweaty hands slip off the steering wheel. I take off my father's glasses and throw them on the passenger seat beside me. They are steamed up from my face.

Putting the key in the ignition I quickly go through my movements and I think of the mistakes I may have made. None that I can think of, but I know I'm not really concentrating. There is a sudden urge to get on the road back to Newquay. Disappear in the night. Away from Eileen, from Tavistock, from dark and sinister Dartmoor .

There is something behind me. A smell. Perfumed soap. Dismissing it, I start the engine and I lean a bit forward to turn on the radio. Easy listening music floods into the car. It will help me relax once I'm on the motorway amongst other innocent drivers. There won't be much traffic at this time of night. Surprised, I noticed that nearly half an hour has gone past since I left my car and headed for Eileen's house for the first time.

Something moves behind me. Too late I realise I haven't imagined the sweet smell after all. With a sinking feeling I become aware that something slides around my neck, tightens until I can feel the rough material of nylon rope on my skin. Instinctively I let go of the gas pedal, ready to brake.

Breath wisps over my hot face. A low voice says in my ear, 'Drive!'

40

JUNE

Shock makes it impossible to move a single muscle in my body. My foot slips from the pedal, causing the car to slow down immediately. 'Drive! Do as I tell you. I warn you, no funny jokes. All this needs is a firm pull.' To emphasize that she won't hesitate to use it, she pulls the rope so that my head is forced against the headrest.

'OK,' my voice rasps.

For an instant, I allow myself to believe that my colleagues are playing candid camera with me. Led by Maloney, no doubt.

'Drive!'

I look in the mirror. She doesn't hide her face from my view. White teeth shine in the light as the headlights of a car finds them.

'I'm so sorry,' she says, obviously not meaning it. 'You have become a threat, Andy. You know too much.'

I wish I did. At least I'd know why she's holding the rope around my neck and why she's killed Eileen Turton and Jane Croft.

Something clicks in my head. First old message. Second old message. I should have realised it when I listened to my answering machine. Old messages are those that have already been listened to. I hadn't, but someone else had. Someone who had access to my house. Someone who had somehow obtained a key. Someone who heard Eileen saying that she found something important about Patrick and Katherine Barr.

'Your name is somewhere in one of those files,' I say slowly.

She chuckles. 'As I said, you know too much.'

'Why did you do it?'

'You don't understand.'

'Then explain it to me. Maybe I can help you.'

She chuckles again, but doesn't reply. Offering to become an accomplice may indeed be a bit far-fetched. She's too clever to walk into that trap.

'Why did you have to kill those poor women?'

The music on the radio is replaced by someone who receives phone calls from listeners. Subjects are unlimited. Strange to broadcast a programme like that when most of the population are asleep.

'Turn off the radio.'

'I find it quite interesting.'

'I don't. Turn it off and shut up!'

Aware of the rope around my neck, I find it hard to concentrate on driving. I think of the road ahead, the long drive across dark and deserted Dartmoor, then onto the A30 westbound.

'Where are we going?'

'Shut up and drive.'

'Which way? I need you to tell me where you want to ...'

'Go to the A30 to Bodmin.'

Bodmin. It means that I have an hour to go. By the time we arrive at our destination I hope to have worked out a way to escape. Survive, if I can. She has killed before, at least two times, and she won't hesitate to do it again. The only advantage I have is that I am not as innocent and oblivious like Jane and Eileen were. I am stronger, and I will fight.

Approaching service stations, I try to persuade her to use a toilet, but she keeps quiet, only making it clear to me that she knows what I'm trying to do by pulling the rope tighter.

Finally we leave the A30 when we pass Bodmin. The

sky is clouded, the moon disappeared. The local road winds through the night, narrowing at places and even becoming a single track every so often. I know this road. We're still heading for Newquay, but we're on the coastal road where, in summer, busses and four-wheel drives get stuck in the narrow bends, causing queues behind them, whereas in winter, and in nights like this, these roads are deserted.

'Where are we going?' I try again. My throat is dry, my eyes gritty. This is the second sleepless night, presumably my last ever. Perhaps it would have been better to die in the theatre, Cole and Rakesh by my side. At least I wouldn't have known.

'You'll see.'

'I need to know where I'm going or else...'

'Shut up. I'm trying to think. We should be there soon.'

I press on. 'Do you mind if I switch on the radio?'

A sharp pull of the rope is enough to quieten me for a while and we drive in silence again. Once more I have enough time to think. She won't pull the rope and strangle me while I'm driving. Too much hassle for her. I just have to wait until a chance comes up.

'Slow down.'

'I can't stop on this road.'

'I said slow, not stop.' She takes a deep breath. 'Now in a moment we'll come to a junction. There's a narrow lane straight across. Get in there and keep going.'

We pass a sign. *Crugmeer. Hawker's Cove*. At least I know where I am. Crugmeer is a tiny hamlet with a farm and holiday cottages, Hawker's Cove is on the edge of the Camel Estuary, where the old Life Boat Station used to be. There is a handful of former pilot cottages. I can already smell the sea and for some reason I find it comforting.,

She seems very well prepared. Halfway the hill we turn into an even more narrow lane overgrown with grass and brambles. We stop next to an old cottage. Walls crumbled, the window frames looking so frail that a touch would turn them to dust, the house seems to have been abandoned decades ago. In the backyard I catch a glimpse of a small caravan, but even that seems old and unused.

'Now, get out of the car.'

I rest my hands on the steering wheel for a moment and stare through the window. 'What if I don't?'

'You'll regret it.' Her tone is an arctic wind. She means it.

Obediently I get out of the car. She really thought this through. The rope is long enough to allow her to adjust it without coming too close to me. Under normal circumstances, I would have won a fight with her, but I've just had an operation. Due to anaesthetics and the damage the tumour did to my body, my energy is worn down. She is young and healthy, I feel weak and vulnerable and I'm scared that she'll hurt my stoma.

All my hopes for an escape come to an abrupt end when I see what she is holding in her hand. The small black object faintly shines in the moonlight.

'You can't shoot me.'

Her voice blank, she replies, 'Only you can decide if it's worth a try.'

Never in my career have I found myself facing the wrong end of a gun. Small and light, easily fitting into a ladies handbag, it is one of those fancy guns that women carry with them to give a feeling of confidence. Self defence. It probably won't be very reliable, yet I can't take the risk. Not at a few meters distance.

'Put your hands up so that I can see them. Walk slowly to the back of the house.' Keeping the two ends of the rope in one hand, the gun in the other, she has too much advantage to consider a surprise attack. There's no point in finding out which of the two weapons she will use. Perhaps both.

'What are you going to do with me?'

'Quiet.'

'What if I scream?'

'Nobody will hear you. If anyone does, they will think it's a fox or an owl.'

'Don't be silly. If I cry help, nobody will believe I'm a fox.'

'This isn't a game.' To underline the seriousness of the situation, she lifts her hand and points the gun towards my chest. Even from that small gun, the bullet would do a lot of damage, let alone what it would do to my stoma. Doctor Cole will have a hell of a job stitching together what's left of my bowels. If any.

'OK.' I walk in front of her, hands up beside my head to make sure that I'm not taking a weapon out of my pockets, or trying something foolish.

I reach an old, tattered backdoor through knee-high weeds. Nobody has been here for ages. Even in the dim light I can see that there is hardly a stroke of paint left on the weathered wood.

'There's an upturned flowerpot at your left. You will find a torch and a key.'

She has well prepared our little expedition, thought of everything.

'Switch on the torch and point it to the door. Unlock.'

The lock is remarkably smooth, recently oiled. At this stage, it doesn't surprise me anymore.

'Go inside.'

I feel like a character in a computer game, constantly waiting for instructions by a press of a button on a console or a keyboard, obeying without a thought. When she says jump, I jump. When she says run into that tunnel full of hidden dangers, I'll have to.

The torchlight is bright. She's behind me in the shade. Perhaps I can shine it into her eyes, which will maybe give me a second of surprise, a second to find her arm and kick the gun away, pulling the rope out of her other hand at the same time. Or, a second to pull me off balance and shoot me. It isn't worth the risk. The only hopeful thought is that if she's intended to kill me, she would have done it by now.

Someone has made an effort to modernise the kitchen, but was interrupted half way. Kitchen units have no fronts and the walls are half tiled, boxes of them are piled against the wall where there's room for an Aga. Electricity cables are waiting for someone to install the sockets and to connect to the mains. There's a counter with protective cardboard taped on it, a stylish modern tap, mirroring the light of the torch.

'Go on.'

A door leads to the hallway. Everything is dark. Stairs lead up to even more darkness.

'Open the door to your left.'

I move my hand holding the torchlight. The room must once have been a drawing room. The two small square windows are boarded up at the outside with chip wood, some of the glass panels broken. An old desk is almost in the middle of the room, on top there's a metal flask with an empty cup. A fireplace is full with ashes and feathers from a rook family nesting in the chimney. Against one wall is a cabinet, its doors removed, a few pieces of abandoned crockery scattered in the dust.

There are two chairs, one a wooden kitchen chair, the other a comfortable looking reclining chair. It has an electric control unit to adjust it to an old or disabled person's needs and wishes. Useless. No electricity. Behind the door is a single bed with a bare mattress, its head and foot ends are brass bars.

'Go to the bed. Slowly. No tricks.'

The mattress creaks under my weight. I'm half expecting her to undress herself. Perhaps this is all show. A perverted sex game. Tie me to the bed. Keep control over me, make me beg. She must be mad.

'Hold the torch in both hands and point it to the floor between your feet.'

Sensing her rather than seeing her at the other side of the bed, she is absorbed by the darkness, the only light a small circle on the floor between my feet. I half turn, expecting her to start touching me, but she only mutters, 'Sorry.'

Then there is a splitting pain at the back of my head and the world explodes, shattering the remaining pieces of my life.

41

JUNE

My head feels like it has been stuck between two concrete blocks for a while. I have a splitting headache and a feeling of nausea sits in the pit of my stomach. I am disoriented. I don't know where I am or how much time has gone by since I lost consciousness. I half drift away in something that may have been a bad dream, a nightmare. Against all odds, I hope that I'm still in hospital, but there's nothing white here, no smell of antiseptics. The door to the hallway is open and I can see the glow of the rising sun in the east.

As things slowly come into focus I realise that I'm not in a hospital. Neither am I in my own bedroom. I try to get up, but something is holding back my hands and feet. There is a thudding spot on the back of my head and I sense something warm and sticky in my hair. I lift my head to examine the room, but I feel that splitting pain at the back of my head again, and before the world explodes, I quickly close my eyes.

Opening them again a few minutes later, my memory comes back. I remember an evening meal at my parents' house, a cup of tea, a TV programme about gardening, a comedy, the news which my father never misses. Some small talk with my mother. A pan with tomato soup. I wonder if it is still in my car. Probably.

I remember the drive from Tavistock through the night, the narrow lane across the fields, heading for the coast, being guided to this house. She must have hit me, knocked me unconscious.

Trying to get up, I find that my hands and feet are bound to a single bed. Swallowing with a sudden pang of fear, I try hard to relax. Don't panic. Wriggling my hands, I thrash around on the bed, hoping that miraculously I can get loose, but the only thing I achieve is causing the bedsprings to creak.

The noise has alerted her. She comes in, her mouth tight, dark eyes serious. Her white-blonde hair stands out against her usual black clothes. 'You'd better save your energy, you won't come free. Tie-ropes. I'm sure you know how trustworthy they are.' I do. Nowadays they're used by police instead of handcuffs.

'Let me go, Marie, please untie me.'

'No.' It doesn't sound like there is any doubt or hesitation in her mind.

'*You* lied about that night, not Megan Taylor.'

I see her teeth light up as she smiles. 'Of course people would believe me rather than an old woman who wanders on the streets at night.'

She seems very confident. No doubt she knows what she's doing.

In books and films killers are sometimes distracted by their victim, persuaded to talk self-consciously about their crimes, about their plans for the nearest future. Although, at this moment, I'm not really interested in the reasons for why she killed Jane Croft and Eileen Turton, and undoubtedly me, I ask her, 'Why?'

But she shakes her head. 'Take it easy, Andy. No tricks. Just do as you're told.'

'Or else?'

'You'll regret it.'

'Are you going to kill me too?' I ask, my voice hoarse and bitter. 'Why? What have I done to you?'

'You shouldn't have come back for the files. You weren't supposed to see them.' She sits down at the foot end of the bed, confident that I can't take her by surprise. Unfortunatel she's right. My hands and feet are tied, there's no way I can fight her.

'How did you know about the files anyway?'

She laughs, curt and triumphantly. 'You left the papers on your table.'

As simple as that. She must have found a spare key from my house somewhere, probably when we spent that night together. Got easy access. Went through the files, read my notes, probably laughed about the charts I made. I shouldn't have been so careless.

'What did Eileen and Jane do to you that made you hate them enough to kill them?'

She shakes her head with eyes full of pity. 'I thought you were a clever policeman, Andy. But you don't understand it, do you?'

'Tell me then.'

'I have no time for chitchat.'

'You killed them. You killed Jane Croft. And poor old Eileen.'

'You're wrong there, Andy.' Annoyed, she starts pacing the room, hands clasped around her shoulders, arms folded across her chest.

I press on. 'Why did you have to kill them, Marie?'

I see her eyes drift away, as though she is trying to grasp a far memory. 'I can't talk to you, Andy. Not now. I have to go.'

'Are you leaving me here?'

Panic is rising in me. I think of Eileen, sitting on her own favourite chair. Dead for two days already. How long before someone will discover her body? How long before someone will find me? The building is derelict, maybe there is a fence erected around it, warning people not to go in. I can't remember.

'You're insane,' I say, trying to keep my voice calm.

'Insane? I don't think so.' She leans on the armrest of a chair. 'As I said, you don't understand.'

'Then explain it to me. Why did Eileen have to die?

Because of what's in her files?'

'She called you. She found out.'

No surprise there. Marie must have been in and out of my house several times when I wasn't there. Listened to the messages, knew that Eileen had found something.

'I really have to go now, Andy.'

'When are you coming back? I'm thirsty. Hungry.' Strangely, I think of the tomato soup.

She stands in the doorway, looking at me with that same absent-minded smile that I saw on her face earlier.

'Don't worry. I'll be back and I'll bring you some water. Anything else? A pizza? A burger?'

'Anything will do.'

'You're not a vegetarian, I hope?'

'No.' What a bizarre conversation this is.

'Marie, why don't you just let me go? I promise I won't say anything.'

She gives me a sad smile. 'I wish it were true, Andy, I wish it were as easy as that.'

'It is! I won't say a word. Just let me go. Please.'

She shakes her head. 'I can't do that. You may not understand now, but you will. I know you. You just won't let go before you've figured it all out. I can't let you walk around with that knowledge.'

I hesitate. She knows what she's doing. She may feel sorry for me in a way, but she will kill me anyway. The first kill is the most difficult, afterwards it becomes easier. I will be her third victim at least. Maybe her fourth, if she had a hand in Simon Croft's death as well.

'Did you also kill Simon Croft?'

She shakes her head stubbornly. 'Stop it now, Andy! I really have to go now. It's for your own good, you see.' A hint of a strange smile tugs at the corners of her lips before she turns. She leaves the door open behind her. She is confident that I won't be able to escape. When I hear her outside opening and closing a car door, it is too late to ask for my blue travel bag with items to change my stoma bag.

42

JUNE

As the hours go by, I have to admit my defeat. I've lost track of the time. Marie must have removed my watch, just to confuse me. Sunlight comes through a crack in the board covering one of the windows, it falls across the floor behind the door Marie left open.

I can hear the engine of a tractor roaring in the fields, the dull stamping sound of a fishing vessel or maybe it is an early trip of the Jubilee Queen, taking tourists out to the sea for a glance at the odd seal or dolphin. But there are no footsteps, no voices coming close enough to start screaming for help.

I pull and twist the plastic tie ropes that keep me tied to the corner posts of the bed. Vaguely remembering that a bed like this arrives in parts when delivered, I try to tip it over in order to find a way to demolish it. It doesn't work.

I stare at the cracks in the plasterwork on the ceiling; I try to decipher the titles of nine books left in a corner on the floor. Inevitably my mind wanders off to dangerous places. My stoma bag is filling. I don't know what will happen once it is full. Will the bag burst? Or just come lose from my body? Marie will come back. She will. There is a stoma care bag in my car, with stuff to change it. I'd rather not think about what might happen if she comes too late.

If I were a character in a book or a film, I would easily have escaped. Sadly, those fortunes only live in the imagination of the writers. Giving up, trying not to think about my physical condition, about the disease or my stoma bag filling, I concentrate on unanswered questions. Marie. Something doesn't add up. Obviously she lied about what she saw the night Jane Croft's body was dumped over the fence. Megan Taylor saw two people, Marie insisted there was one. She put me on the wrong track. Deliberately. But if Megan Taylor was right, and one was Marie, then who was the second person?

I saw signs that Marie could be very cold and emotionless, but for some reason I can't see her as a brutal murderer. Perhaps my opinion is somewhat clouded because of the history we share. I don't dare think about that now. My career will be in real trouble when Guthrie finds out that I have slept with a witness who now turns out to be a suspect, a murderer. A clever lawyer will axe my testimony into pieces. If it ever comes to that.

Suddenly I become aware of a change in smell. Fumes. Diesel. I recognise the sound of my own car, the little ticks when the engine cools down. Footsteps hesitate, then come closer. A key turns in the lock. There's a light and flowery perfume in the air.

'I brought you a bottle of water and something to eat,' says Marie. She seems cheerful as if she's come for a social visit.

'I need to use the toilet.'

She frowns. 'Not now.'

'I have to, Marie, I can't...' I stop abruptly. I've almost begged her. There are limits.

'I said not now!' she snaps, eyes pointed at the ceiling in concentration.

Something in her behaviour frightens me. 'What's the matter? Did you hear anyone?'

'Shut up!'

'I can shout.'

She shakes her head, angrily. 'You still don't understand.'

Tossing a two-litre bottle of still water on the bed she

starts unpacking a brown paper bag. The smell of food drifts through the room and I get to understand exactly the meaning of mouth-watering. Lowering herself on to the reclining chair, she stretches out her legs in front of her. She is wearing a short denim miniskirt, thick black tights and her usual purple fake leather jacket.

'By the way, the tomato soup was lovely.'

I try not to flinch. 'My mother makes the best soup in the world.'

'You're very lucky with that mother of yours.' For a few long moments she drifts off in thought. Not happy ones. Her mouth tightens. She must have been a lonely, lost foster child, cut off from family ties, bounced between children's homes and foster families. No parents to anchor to. Bizarrely, I feel pity for her.

'I've brought you a cheeseburger. With everything on it.' She leans forward, stretching out two yellow polystyrene boxes.

'I can't eat with my hands tied.'

She studies my wrists with serious eyes, contemplating, unsure. 'OK, I guess it can't harm to free one hand.' From her handbag she produces little pliers. 'Are you right or left handed?'

'Right handed.'

'OK.' She cuts the tie rope on my left hand. I should have lied, but I didn't expect this.

'Eat.' Taking off the lid she passes me two polystyrene boxes. One has a burger spilling with sauces, the other is filled with chips. 'How long are you planning to keep me here?'

'As long as poss.'

She opens a sachet of tomato ketchup with her teeth. A dollop of ketchup squeezes out and lands on her chest. She mutters a curse that would chill my mother to the bone.

'What are you going to do with me?' I try to sound casual, dreading to show her how uncomfortable and scared I am.

'Don't be so impatient, Andy love, everything will be all right. I promise.'

'Don't you think I have a right to know?'

She frowns, munching her fries thoughtfully. 'Know what exactly?'

'For example, why did you bring me here? Why tie me up? Why not kill me if you're going to anyway?'

'I'm not a killer.'

I almost choke on a chip. 'Of course not,' I say cynically. 'You don't kill. You just help people go to heaven.'

'Don't...'

'How else do you explain your actions?'

She stands upright suddenly, chin up, face contorted, eyes piercing with an expression I fail to understand. 'I said, I am not a killer.'

'OK.' I shrug, licking ketchup from my finger. Better not annoy her. I don't fancy being knocked unconscious again. 'I don't mean to offend you.'

'It's OK.' Like an inflatable doll from which air is released, she sits down.

I try again, more careful this time. 'Why are we here, Marie?'

'I have to protect you.'

'Against what? Against who?'

She shakes her head. Her long black earrings shake as if from an earthquake. 'I can't tell you. You just have to trust me.'

Silently I chew. The cheeseburger is getting cold and the chips are soggy, but I am too hungry to be picky.

Suddenly she stands up again, tossing the remaining half of her burger in the paper bag, shoving her box of chips to the side with her foot. Her face is white, eyes wide open. She's worried.

Her ears are better than mine. She has already heard the sound of an engine coming closer slowly, stopping nearby. Stationary. Switched off.

'Not a word!' With the gun back in her hand, she lifts her head to listen.

Perhaps teenagers know about this place, use the bed for a secret rendezvous. If I scream, Marie will shoot me. Or them. I can't risk it.

43

JUNE

Footsteps are coming closer. Marie is hiding behind the door, the hand with the gun lifted up to her chest, ready to use. Someone must have noticed my car. As Marie curses softly, the footsteps come to an abrupt halt. I can almost hear someone breathing.

Then there is a voice, high-pitched and clear. A woman. 'Where are you, darling? Becca? I know you're in here somewhere!' I let out a sigh of relief. It is a woman, presumably looking for a daughter, expecting to find her here with some boyfriend she doesn't approve of.

Marie stands frozen, eyes wide in panic. The footsteps are in the house now, on the floor in the hallway. The door to the drawing room, where we are, is the only one left open. I hesitate. I can scream for help, but that'll put the woman in danger. Marie is pointing the gun at the doorway. She can kill me, but I don't want anymore innocent victims. The woman is only looking for her daughter, she's got nothing to do with this. But I can't let her go either. She may be the only visitor to this derelict house for days. I open my mouth.

'Sh,' hisses Marie, moving her hand to point the gun at me now. That's better. She can only shoot one person at the same time.

A silhouette fills the doorway. Light spills from behind her. She is small and almost skeletal, with blonde hair and dark roots pinned back with black clips and tucked behind her ears. She's wearing a black velvety dress, a single string of pearls glow against the black material, matching earrings in her earlobes. With black pumps and pale tights she is dressed for work, an appointment. A funeral.

I can instantly see that she is no match for Marie. I almost wish she hadn't come in. With a bit of luck she'll think that she has caught us in some kinky love game and will run off in embarrassment.

I can't be more wrong.

Staring at me for what feels like a long time, the woman turns towards Marie, not even flinching when she sees the gun.

'I knew you'd be here.'

Marie looks uncertainly, not replying, dropping the hand with the gun.

'I just knew it!' The woman comes in, shaking the strap of her handbag from her shoulder. I feel like I am reading a book of which all the pages are from a different story.

'I only wanted to help,' Marie says, shoulders slumping, her dark eyes suddenly full of misery.

The woman smiles. 'Oh, but you did, my love, you did! It's just perfect that you brought him in here.' There's an edge in her voice that makes her sound false. Marie also heard. Clearly she understands the situation better than I do.

'I didn't mean to…'

'You lied to me, Becca!' The woman's voice rises all of a sudden and to my horror I recognise the signs of some sort of mental illness. This woman isn't going to release me. On the contrary. As if I can see with Megan Taylor's eyes, I realise that it was these two women she saw in the car park that night.

'Who are you?' Presuming I have nothing to lose, I jump in. 'Who are you, Marie? Or do I call you Becca?'

She holds her breath. For a moment she is astonished because it's her I look at. Then she shakes her head like an obstinate teenager, but doesn't respond. Her courage seems to fail and she coughs as though she's inhaled something toxic.

'She hasn't told you?' Chuckling almost happily, the other woman rearranges the pearls around her neck, and checks her hair with her fingertips. 'You haven't worked it out yet, inspector?'

But I keep looking at Marie. The name has found a place in my mind. 'You are Becky Eve.' I say slowly.

The woman picks up the kitchen chair and places it in the doorway. Crossing her legs carefully, she sees me staring at them. 'I'm really disappointed in you, Becca. I thought I could trust you,'

'I just wanted to help.'

For a moment I think she's missed the point, but she knows exactly what's going on. 'Help? By kidnapping a policeman?'

'He knows too much,' replies Marie, defiantly.

The woman grins, humour missing her eyes. 'You don't have to tell me that, love. But I was already working something out.'

'I don't want you to kill him too.'

'I'm afraid I have to now, love.' Her eyes are empty in a face that could be pretty if not for the frown and the pursed lips, its corners slightly up in a mad grin. There is something familiar about her, but I am too scared to get my brain in working order.

'I don't want you to kill him, Dot. I… I love him.'

Becca. Dot.

'Could anyone please explain why we're here? And what will happen next?' I say in a failing attempt to sound cheerfully, as though we are all playing a role in a bad comedy.

Marie doesn't seem to listen. She's pointing the gun at the woman now. 'I don't want you to kill him,' she repeats almost pleading.

The woman chuckles. 'I won't, my love, but you will!'

'What?' Marie gasps and I get that sinking feeling that the woman has already drawn up her plans so carefully that they can barely fail.

'Yes. You will have to kill him, my love. You brought him here. He is your responsibility now.'

'But I can't kill anyone. I'm not like you.' Marie's voice is that of a young child, pleading against all odds.

'Oh yes you are, my darling. You are exactly like me. He is a threat to us, don't you understand?'

They seem to think I do understand. Other than I know now that Marie isn't her real name, suspecting that Marie once was Becca, and became a foster child with Patrick and Katherine called Becky Eve, I don't understand what's going on between the two women. Except that Marie doesn't seem to be the killer of Jane and Eileen after all.

I look at the woman again. She has taken the clasp from her hair and it cascades on her shoulders, curls dangling alongside her cheeks. My brain clicks like the end of a pen. I'm sure we've never met, but I have seen her before. On a photo.

Marie has come forward. 'We can run, Dottie. Together. We can build a new life where nobody knows us. We'll be happy, together at last.' She pleads, hands clasped, the gun forgotten.

'What about him then? Don't you understand that he will come after us?'

'We can leave him here.'

'Leave him to die, you mean?' Dot chuckles. High. Mad. 'Oh, you are cruel, Becca love, cruel and evil you are! Like me!'

'No! I'm not like you!' Marie stamps her foot angrily. Something has turned the tide between them. A bond has snapped. 'You killed all those people. And for what? What have they ever done to you?'

'I had to protect you, my darling.'

'You could have done that years ago! But you went away and you never came back for me.' Marie's anger is opening floodgates, breaking dykes. I sense that her last words are an important underlying issue. Only I haven't a clue what this is all about. My presence seems to be forgotten. I try not to move, not to breathe, not to draw their attention. I only listen.

This isn't the time for questions.

My brain clicks and all of a sudden I see the resemblance. Not the mouth, nose or shape of the head, but the eyes, the high forehead, and the ears. They are related, but Dottie, or whatever her name is, seems too young to be Marie's mother.

'Are you two sisters?' I ask, despite my intention not to draw attention.

The silence is like a microphone switched off in mid speech.

'Yes,' Marie replies after a long silence.

Dot interrupts with a jolt of fury, 'No, we're not!'

'Why don't you…'

Dot looks at me, ignoring Marie as if she's not there at all. 'She is my daughter.' Proud. Possessive.

'Dottie, I…you don't…' Marie stops, face ashen.

Seemingly unaware of the impact of her bombshell Dot continues, 'you seem to have chosen him over me.' The accusation hangs in the air like a death sentence.

'I didn't say I chose him over you.'

'Yes you did. You brought him here. You were hiding him from me.'

'Because I knew you were going to kill him!'

Dottie lets out a deep long sigh. 'Well, yes, of course, my dear, he knows too much.'

I know I should keep quiet, but I can't. 'So it was you, Dottie, who killed Jane Croft? And Eileen Turton?'

'Of course it was me.' Her voice is emotionless. No pity, no apology, no triumph either. Just a cold fact.

'I know who you are,' I say slowly. 'I recognise you now. You are Peter Prescott's' wife.'

Her laugh is as hollow as her eyes, deprived of all humour. 'Of course I am! I am pretty, lovely, Trish Prescott, a prisoner in her lovely, lonely, house.' She sounds bitter, rancorous. 'A house is a shell, do you know that inspector? A house is nothing but walls and a roof. A shelter against rain and storm. But it is nothing else.'

'You are Trish Prescott who disappeared for two days. Peter was worried about you. He came to the station to report you missing. He said there was a possibility that you were... depressed.'

Her face is vacant. 'That's right. But I am not suicidal. The pregnancies and miscarriages, even the dead little boy, inspector, it is all part of my punishment. I knew that somewhere in this country my daughter was still alive. I was forced to abandon her, but I was certain I would find her. And I did.' She glances at Marie, who sits, still frozen, eyes wide open in shock and disbelief. 'I was too young, Becca. I was only thirteen! Too young to be a mother. I didn't even know what was happening to me.'

'But... you are my sister!'

Dot lowers her eyes to the floor, her voice a more normal tone. 'I wasn't lying to you, love. I am your sister. And your mother. I'm both.'

I can see the knowledge register in Marie's mind, matching up with details she already knew. Leaning on the dusty desk, her legs seem to have collapsed under her. 'My mother?' She lets out a long breath that sounds more like a sob. There is an expression of disgust on her face, which makes Dot reach out for her. There's so much resemblance between them that I can't believe that I haven't noticed it before. Why didn't I see it when Peter Prescott gave me the photograph of his wife?

Marie is crying like a lion cub caught by a predator, looking for her mother in despair. 'If you are really my mother... then why did you go away? Why did you leave me with... him?' Stepping away, towards me, she shakes off Dottie's hands as if she feels dirty by their touch.

Dot is frozen in action, dropping her arms as if they have suddenly become too heavy to lift, eyes flying back to a memory almost wiped out, like a deleted file on a computer being retrieved by an expert. 'They made me, Becca. I had no choice.'

'But you knew what he was like!'

'Please, love…'

'And yet you left me! And what happened to my father… Why hasn't he…' Marie's voices trails off as the horrible truth finally dawns on her. 'Was it… him?'

'I am so, so sorry, darling.'

Once more Dot tries to catch Marie in an embrace, but she steps back.

The information is buzzing in my head. I try to work it out, but everything is blurred. I see from the expression on Marie's face that it's even more difficult for her.

'I came back for you, Becca, I really did! I had a room and I had a job. Don't you remember? I came for you, but they wouldn't let me take you.'

Marie's eyes are wide, blank, blocked in a horrible memory. 'I remember,' she says slowly, as if in a trance by hypnosis. 'I remember everything now.'

'Becca…'

'You killed them. You killed my parents. And you left me with them.'

'They didn't want to let you go.'

'You killed our parents!'

'He was a monster, Debbie, you know that.'

'You knew… but left me with him.'

'I already said I'm sorry about that. He was a monster. She deserved no better. Neither of them! She never believed me when I told her what he did to me. How bad can a mother be? She just denied everything.'

Marie nods quietly, looking down at her hands, tears dripping on them. I'm getting a picture that becomes clearer with every next word. A girl, Dottie, abused by her father. The mother closing her eyes and ears from the truth. Dot must have ran away after giving birth to a child she couldn't love. When finally she came back her parents refused to let the girl go. How old was Marie, Becca, at that time?

Marie is sobbing quietly, her worlds, her hopes and beliefs, shattered. Yet her mind is working overtime. Between two deep breaths she says, 'That day I thought you were my sister, I thought you came back to save me. You said to go to my room and pack a bag. But when I came down, you were gone. It was just them and… and so much blood.' She pauses to wipe her nose with the back of her hand, not worrying about the snot left on it. 'You promised, but you never came back for me.'

'I had no life, darling. Honest. I lived on the street. I had no roof over my head, no money, nothing.'

'You said you had a job. A room.'

'That was true! But it all went wrong. Social Services took you. They said I couldn't look after you. They said they would look after you.'

'How can a mother abandon her own child?' Marie says rhetorically.

Both women are crying now, tears dripping on chests, shared pain, regret and guilt, yet they are miles apart.

'I'm so sorry, Becca, my love.'

Once more she reaches out, and this time, for a few moments, Marie lets her, stoically. It is not a loving, forgiving embrace. For a few long moments Marie stares at her mother, then shakes her off, steps back and looks at the gun still in her hands. Slowly she brings it up.

'Becca! What are you doing? Put that gun away, love, someone might get hurt.'

'Yeah,' says Marie, absentmindedly. Then Dot moves so quickly that I only realise afterwards what happened. The gun is pointing at me suddenly and I stare in Dot's cold dark eyes.

'No, Dot, please, don't hurt him! We can run away. We can be together, Dottie. He won't say anything.'

'Don't be silly. He's a policeman. He will never stop trying to find us. We will never be free.'

She is right. It's in my character never to give up, which is probably the reason why I'm in this situation now.

'You can't do this to me, Dot. I love him! He is the first man I can trust. He is…'

'You think you love him, but it'll pass.'

'No!'

'You know it can never be. Not when you want to be with me.'

'But I...'

'You lied to the police. You helped me with the body. You're my accomplice. You're a criminal now, love.'

Marie's brain is too full with information. It seems to have stopped working. Narrowing her eyes, her mouth opens but no sound emerges. She is focused on something miles away that seems to be coming closer, getting larger, like a speeding freight train. She's on the platform, contemplating the right moment to jump.

Dot sees it too. Horror mirrors in her eyes. She changes tone, pleading softly, desperately. 'We have found each other now, we'll not part. I promise. I'll get divorced from Peter, the bastard – he can live with that mistress of his, have her children. I don't care anymore. He'll have to pay though and we'll have enough money to build up a new life together.'

Marie is only focused on one thing, the gun in Dot's hand. 'Please don't kill him, Dot.'

But her sister, her mother, shakes her head. 'Men are all the same, you know that, love. They love you in the beginning, they rape you and in the end you are left with nothing.'

'Andy is different.'

'You know it's inevitable, darling.'

'No!'

PART THREE

JULY

44

JULY

I am still on sick leave, waiting for the results of the latest scan, which will have a direct impact on my future. Annoyingly, my consultant hasn't yet officially declared me fit for work. I believe I am, but he won't listen to me. The sad truth is that I'm bored doing little else than worry and scare myself with dark thoughts about my future or stare at the ceiling and watch all kinds of to soaps, quiz shows and repeated episodes of decades-old comedies. When I swallowed my pride and more or less begged Guthrie, he gave me the task to prepare the case against Dorothy Patricia Trewoon.

That is why Eileen Turton's files are in my flat. So are piles of other papers retrieved from police forces around the country. It has been a painstaking task to go through them meticulously but it has at least been worth it in the sense that I didn't have the time to worry. I now have a pretty clear picture of what happened, what led to all the killings that involved not only the death of Jane Croft and Eileen Turton, but also that of Simon Croft, Patrick and Kate Barr and several others. Everything is linked to the original file of a five-year old girl who found her parents butchered to death in a farmhouse in Hawker's Cove, near Padstow, the same building Marie brought me to that night. The story that commenced with John Trewoon and his abnormal affection for young girls is a sad and heart-breaking one and I know it will shock the media and the entire population of the country. An abusive father, an ignorant mother, a scrupulous denial, damaged childhoods. Two sisters, one a mother and sister at the same time, the other abandoned and lost, separated by do-gooders like Eileen Turton who mean so well, but never understand the bond of blood.

Of course I don't know the exact details and I have to fill in the blanks with my own imagination, but I am convinced that what I believe happened comes close to the truth.

Trewoon must have started abusing his daughter Dorothy from an early age. I doubt that it could have been a complete secret for his wife, but she kept quiet, she closed her ears and eyes, and let her child down.

Dorothy's pregnancy at twelve was kept well hidden from the neighbourhood. If there were any questions about her growing belly or if there were suspicions about the birth of Rebecca Evelyn, Trewoon quickly wiped any gossip off the surface by bullying everyone who dared suggest anything dark.

Dorothy was fifteen when she ran away from home, hopeful with the expectation of a better life. She made a solemn promise that she would come back for her daughter once she got herself settled. It was a long road, but two years later, when she thought she would be able to give Becca a proper roof over her head, she set off to the farmhouse in Cornwall for the last time. A visit that started with hope and love but ended with a bloodbath. And with a promise to the then five year old Becca, a promise she wouldn't keep.

Dorothy married and became Patricia James. Despite her plans to reunite with Becca, she realised that the revelation that she had a daughter with her own father would be devastating news for her husband, and that it would be a threat to her new life and the safety of her future. So she kept her secret to herself, stocking up anger upon frustration, fear upon hope and uncertainty, ignoring her guilt and conscious of the promise she made to her daughter. Inevitably her first marriage didn't last long. When she met Peter Prescott, he gave her his love and affection, as well as an outlook on a family of their own. Patricia, then Trish, focused on her new future and it wasn't so difficult anymore to push her dubious background to the very back of her mind, including the existence of her daughter. Everything changed with her first miscarriage.

Meanwhile Becca's life had been difficult and troublesome. Although her first foster home was loving and warm, she just couldn't believe she had a better future ahead of her. Deep down she was hurting and vulnerable, but she failed to show that to the do-gooders who weren't looking below the surface. A string of disappointments consequently resulting in anger and uncertainty made her difficult to deal with. She was moved from one foster family to the other and the only thing she could do to protect herself from more hurt was to harden herself. To the outside world she became a girl without feelings, without emotions and it wasn't difficult to understand that she wasn't loved.

Patricia endured miscarriage after miscarriage, one disappointment after the other and she was convinced that not being able to produce a child was her fault. She became nervous and unreliable as guilt planted in her head the idea that she was a bad person who didn't deserve to have a child after she so cruelly abandoned her first. Perhaps she could have dealt with her inability to conceive one more time, perhaps she would have accepted it in the end, but everything got worse when she discovered that her husband had an affair with his company's secretary. It blew her hopes and expectations into thin air. In a primitive need for defence, she started focusing on a desperate search for her lost daughter, who seemed to have disappeared in a system of overprotective social care workers and too many foster families. Trish found herself lost in a labyrinth of paperwork and unwilling carers. Along with her shattered dreams, her failure in finding her daughter triggered the beginning of madness, albeit well hidden. Instead of finding strength and comfort in the safety and security of her home and with her husband, even if he was cheating, she developed a frantic surge for revenge and punishment for all those who prevented her from being with her daughter. Which, in her twisted perspective, was nearly everyone who had been involved with Becca's life.

The first murder was merely by accident. A furious blow and the woman who appeared to have been responsible for taking Becca away after their parents were found dead, had an unfortunate fall down the stairs. As it was treated as an accident, there was never an investigation and she got away with it. However, inspired by this first death, the second murder was well considered and planned in detail. Trish was not stupid. She read books and articles about serial killers. She discovered that changing her actions increased her chances of not being caught. She also learned about Locard's exchange theory and, although she realised she wouldn't be able to win the battle against hard evidence, she did her utmost to work beyond that by using disguises and wigs. She also wore a plastic suit under her clothes, scrupulously disposing of everything afterwards. She welcomed Peter's regular trips to Bristol, even his secret nights with the secretary as it gave her plenty of time and freedom. When he was away, she hired cars and vans and she drove for miles to find her victims and carefully developed master plans for her next killings.

Becca finally found some peace and happiness when she came to live with Rob and Suzanne Yates, by whom she was adopted. However, all those years she'd harboured the vague memory of a young woman making her a promise to come back for her, had made her go back to Cornwall, the county where she was born. She found the farmhouse near Padstow deserted and derelict as, due to its horrific history, it had never been sold.

The two Trewoon girls met purely by accident when Becca visited Jane Croft who she spent a reasonably happy time with and Trish was observing the woman in preparation of working out a way to kill her.

It should have been a happy ending there, but it wasn't.

Becca, or rather Marie Yates, still felt let down by her new-found sister and couldn't easily forget and forgive. And Patricia had developed such a habit of hatred and revenge, finding so much satisfaction in the power of deciding about life and death that she wasn't to be persuaded to stop her killing spree. When Marie refused to live with her long lost sister, Trish knew only one way to respond: make Marie an accomplice to her next murder. She killed Jane after taking her out for a meeting with a so called mutual acquaintance and she forced Marie to help her dispose of the body. They did this during the night when Megan Taylor saw two dark figures who were actually the two women dressed as men.

I am pretty sure that we would never have found the murderer of Jane Croft, and consequently of all the others, if Marie hadn't felt the need to come forward, to get to know me and more or less keep up to date with the developments of the investigation. But it was Patricia's jealousy when she found out that Marie had fallen in love with me, that caused her downfall.

I have spoken with Dorothy Patricia Trewoon a few times. Even more skinny and frail than she was when I first met her, she is only a shadow of herself. When I look at her, I find it difficult to imagine that she was capable of so many brutal, carefully planned murders. There are times that I feel sorry for her. I guess you could say that she was the first victim, but when I see the vacant look in her eyes, I doubt if she fully realises the impact of what she has done and how many innocent lives she destroyed.

She doesn't even show regret about having shot her own daughter. Ironically, she never enquired after her and I'm not at all sure if she knows that Marie is still alive, albeit comatose and unresponsive. Peter has recently moved out of Cornwall after he filed for a divorce. He's refusing to see his wife and I don't have the impression that she cares. Yet sometimes I see a glimmer in her eyes that tells me that her self-inflicted isolation is only a shell of protection.

As I put one of Eileen Turton's files on top of the pile on my kitchen table, I suddenly notice the edges of a photo sticking out. Without looking at it, I know it's a blurred photo of a pale face with a dark spot where once was a stud in her left brow. Rebecca Evelyn Trewoon; I can still only think of her as Marie Yates.

The memories of those last minutes with the two women are etched in my brain and I am sure that I will never forget them. Poor Marie. Although it wasn't me that pulled the trigger, in a way I know I am responsible for what happened to her. I feel guilty and ashamed when I think that I may have encouraged her. She must really have believed that she loved me and that I loved her. I can't see why else she threw herself on top of me when I was tied to the bed. The first bullet went into her shoulder, which was right on top of my chest, my heart. It would have killed me immediately. The second one worked its way into her brain. Marie was unconscious, but still breathing, just. I managed to retrieve my mobile phone from my pocket and dialled 999.

Perhaps it would have been better if Marie had died in the air ambulance somewhere between Newquay and the hospital in Truro, but her body was young and strong. Poor, poor Marie. She has always been a victim and if nothing changes with her situation, if she remains in her comatose cocoon of oblivion, she always will be.

With sadness, I rise from my chair and look out the window on which gusty winds splash large raindrops. The sky is leaden, a dark and dull pewter. The clouds are thick and low, no cracks for a single shaft of sunlight between them today. Grey and sad, it attempts to pull me into a pool of depression. Thinking of Marie, I know that life is too precious to let it happen. I need to get away from this world of sadness, hurt and death. I need to get some fresh air. And I know where I want to find it.

I grab my coat, dismiss an umbrella, and pick up a plastic carrier bag with two identical boxes wrapped in gift paper. The

flowers drip when I retrieve them from a bucket in the sink where they have been waiting for two days full of hesitation and doubt.

Lauren opens the door so quickly that I allow myself to believe that she has been looking out for me, yet she sizes me up in the doorway, as if not quite sure whether to let me in. Then she turns and I follow her down the hall, watching her hips move in her jeans. Secrets never die. Hopes don't either.

She is pleased, albeit a bit embarrassed with the flowers. Her boys are excited when they unwrap their presents. The identical faces red and grinning, they shake my hand and quickly disappear upstairs to explore their new mobile phones, pay as you go cards with a small amount on each of them. Lauren's blush becomes redder and more attractive as she mumbles that I should not have done that. The boys should be punished for stealing the phone from Jane Croft's dead body, instead they now seem to be rewarded for the act. I don't tell her that it was the fact that her sons were playing with the phone that made Peter Prescott come to the police and trigger my suspicions. It transpired that it wasn't Jane's phone, but his wife's and I am pretty sure Jane managed to retrieve it, hoping she would be able to call for help.

Lauren makes tea, offers homemade chocolate pecan plaits, the boys' favourite home baking. I look out of her window at the small yard. The surfboards are upright against the wall; two wetsuits hang on a washing line, dripping in the rain.

I sit down, leaning a bit forward, hoping that my sweater covers the bulge on my belly. I don't know if anyone told her that I am wearing a stoma bag. It's not something I can easily ask her.

'How is Marie?' Lauren asks, lowering herself on the edge of a chair.

'No change.'

'The case?' Sensing that I rather not talk about Marie, she changes the subject, unaware that this makes me even more uncomfortable.

'It will be difficult. I guess it all depends on the capabilities of the defence lawyer.'

Patricia, Trish or Dorothy, was very clever. There is hardly any hard evidence against her. She had planned everything so well and despite the fact that I consider her a serial killer, I doubt that she will get a life sentence.

'More tea?' Lauren says tactfully.

'Thanks.' I clear my throat. I have come to tell her the truth about the death of Jane Croft because I believe that Lauren deserves to know. Or rather, it is an excuse to see her again. Depending on our conversation and her reactions, I might consider asking her out for dinner, if I can find the courage.

I start telling her about Jane Croft and Eileen Turton, about Marie and Dorothy, but soon enough I find myself changing the subject. As if everything is somehow connected, I tell her about the cancer, the operation and the stoma, I explain the impact that it already has on my professional and personal life. There is pity in her eyes, and shock, an awareness of the gravity on my life and future, but it is not as bad as I feared.

'What will happen now?' Her tone is rather neutral and, briefly, I wonder if she's already creating a distance between us.

I hesitate. 'I don't know. The consultant said that chemotherapy afterwards, may be a possibility. Or radiotherapy. Both, I don't know yet. Depends on whether he managed to cut out the whole tumour. The scans will tell me more.'

She nods quietly, hands folded together, fingers laced as if in prayer. 'When will you hear?'

'The appointment is tomorrow.'

She looks down at her hands for a few moments. Then chin up, eyes steady, she offers a lifeline. 'If you like, come for a coffee afterwards. If you feel up to it, that is.'